XAN BROOKS is a writer and broadcaster specialising in film. He was an associate editor at the *Guardian* and, before that, a writer and editor at the *Big Issue* magazine. This is his first novel.

D0057843

CALGARY PUBLIC LIBRARY

MAY   2018

XAN BROOKS

THE CLOCKS IN THIS HOUSE ALL TELL DIFFERENT TIMES

SALT

LONDON

PUBLISHED BY SALT PUBLISHING 2017

2 4 6 8 10 9 7 5 3 1

Copyright © Xan Brooks 2017

Xan Brooks has asserted his right under the Copyright, Designs and
Patents Act 1988 to be identified as the author of this work.

*This book is sold subject to the condition that it shall not, by way of
trade or otherwise, be lent, resold, hired out, or otherwise circulated
without the publisher's prior consent in any form of binding or cover
other than that in which it is published and without a similar condition
including this condition being imposed on the subsequent publisher.*

This book is a work of fiction. Any references to historical events, real
people or real places are used fictitiously. Other names, characters, places
and events are products of the author's imagination, and any resemblance to
actual events or places or persons, living or dead, is entirely coincidental.

First published in Great Britain in 2017 by
Salt Publishing Ltd
International House, 24 Holborn Viaduct, London EC1A 2BN United Kingdom

www.saltpublishing.com

Salt Publishing Limited Reg. No. 5293401

A CIP catalogue record for this book is available from the British Library

ISBN 978 1 78463 093 5 (Paperback edition)
ISBN 978 1 78463 094 2 (Electronic edition)

Typeset in Neacademia by Salt Publishing

Printed and bound in Great Britain by Clays Ltd, St Ives plc

MIX
Paper from
responsible sources
FSC® C018072

Salt Publishing Limited is committed to responsible forest management.
This book is made from Forest Stewardship Council™ certified paper.

THE CLOCKS IN THIS HOUSE ALL TELL DIFFERENT TIMES

THE FOREST

I

SUNDAY EVENING, AFTER tea, she travels out of town and through the woods to visit with the funny men. According to Nan, the trip has only just been arranged, which means there is not a moment to waste. Chop-chop, shake a leg and save your questions for later. Her grandparents are like that, they can rarely be doing with questions. Whether it's a treat or a chore, they want everything done right away. At least Nan can be nice. Grandad is the worst. When Grandad says jump, you only ask him how high.

It's obviously an honour, being invited to the woods. That much is plain even when nothing else is. She can tell by the painstaking way that Nan plaits her hair and by the sight of the floral-print dress from the camphor-wood chest.

"There now, you'll suffice. I dare say I've seen worse."

"You've seen worse every Friday night in the taproom."

The old woman laughs shortly. "Indeed I have," she says. "Some of those who come in, we ought to be putting straw down."

At first Lucy had hoped she might go to the woods in a painted charabanc, like the one they took up to Frinton-on-Sea, with parents and offspring lined up on wooden benches, everyone singing and passing around sandwiches. Instead the journeys are made inside Coach's rusting, decommissioned old Maudslay, which she quickly decides is just as good. She grows to love the retired army truck – its pitch and its rattle;

its constant clanging vibrations. She can sit in the back and watch the streets scooting by, or lie full-length to observe summer clouds overhead. The truck bed contains grit, soil and straw. But if her grandmother worries about the floral-print dress getting dirty, it seems she's much too kind to complain.

On the landing, in the dark. Hours beyond her regular bedtime. "Oh look, here she is, just when I was starting to worry. Did you behave yourself?"

"Yes thanks, Nan. They were all very nice."

"Well then, there we are." Nan's head bobs in relief. "What a nice thing to happen. What a stroke of good fortune." Behind the door at their backs, her grandfather is snoring.

The first visit is apparently deemed to have been a success because Lucy is invited again on the following Sunday – then again and again on the Sundays after that, through June and July and deep into August. After a spell she takes her inclusion for granted and clambers up eagerly to join Winifred, Edith and John. As befits her junior status, she is always the last to be gathered and the first to be dropped, but once on the road the children become equals. The girl feels happy, exalted; one of a band of unsecured bodies in the back of the truck.

The skies are clear and the air is warm. They ride out in daylight and are brought home after dark. She sees the squirt and spatter of stars, which the city keeps hidden. She can make out the Plough and Orion's Belt, too, but the rest of the spread is a mystery to her, like hieroglyphics from the time before Christ, or the Russian alphabet with its upside-down letters. Each star is a sun and each sun, Lucy thinks, must therefore be surrounded by invisible planets in perpetual rotation. Exactly how many stars can she see from her berth in Coach's truck? Why, surely hundreds and hundreds and then a few hundred more. Looking at the stars, she feels impossibly small.

Winifred stirs, half-asleep at her side. "What were you saying again?"

"The stars. Up there. There are too many stars."

"What rubbish. You say silly things, Luce. It's not us that are small, it's the stars. I could reach out my hand and pick a thousand like daisies."

"Do it," says Edith. "Reach out and pick Lucy a big bunch of stars."

Galaxies joggle and reel above their heads. They only begin to fade out when the truck rolls under the street lamps of the city.

"My mum and dad might be there on one of those stars."

Winifred cackles. "Your old man's in the ground, don't get fancy ideas. Probably right next to mine. Probably right next to Edith's and John's, come to that."

"Her mum might be though," Edith allows, sleepily.

More often than not she is home by midnight. She carries a key in her sock and lets herself in to find the public bar empty and the cigarette haze hanging and the Labrador dozing on the floor. Her grandmother has retired for the night, although she keeps half an ear open to ensure all is well. The girl brushes her teeth and climbs the stairs. She douses the landing light and gropes to locate her bed in the eaves. Sleep steals quickly upon her and it is a good sleep, deep and replenishing, the kind that only innocent children are permitted to have. All the same, these late nights take a toll. No matter how deeply she sleeps, she falls into Monday feeling utterly spent.

On her first trip to the forest, Lucy had imagined the funny men as something like a circus troupe, or a band of wild gypsies, given to dancing and tricks. But that isn't it; they are not that way at all. What they remind her of more than anything are her cousin Jo's dolls, which had been picked up second-hand or passed down from her mother. The dolls were delightful but each one had seen better days. You could play with them quite roughly because they'd all been broken before.

Coach heaves his truck off the main road and rides it up Turpentine Lane. Then he turns off the lane onto a lane that's smaller still, almost a track, with a long line of grass sprouting up its middle. Finally, after a jolting, bone-shaking five minutes of this, the vehicle veers to its left and completes the journey on a narrow bridleway, its steel sides scratched by brambles, its belly scraping the uneven ground. Lucy barks her knee and bites down on her tongue. When she clings on to the side, twigs stab at her hands.

The truck lurches to a halt. The birds are all singing. They have come to rest in a wide woodland clearing, roughly the size of a football pitch, which ends abruptly against a hard line of trees. "Here we are, bang on time. Here's my lorry-load of little helpers." For an instant, still getting her bearings, she assumes Coach is shouting behind him to the passengers in the bed. Then she realises that he is calling out to the funny men.

The funny men are a curious bunch. Nothing could have prepared her. She wants to stare but she doesn't mean to be rude, except that maybe staring is expected because what else can you do? The world is home to outlandish creatures. But she has never seen men as outlandish as these.

Coach steps out of the cab to help her climb down. Then he gives the girl's shoulder a squeeze and tips her a wink so swift and conspiratorial it all but passes her by. "Tonight we're extra blessed because we have ourselves a brand new helper. Her name's Lucy Marsh and I can vouch for her manners. So please be sure to mind your Ps and Qs. We'll have us no blue talk tonight."

She turns to face them but it is all too much. They are too fabulous; she cannot hold her gaze steady. Is that a red-checked tablecloth laid out on the grass? A forest picnic has been run up in readiness. They have brought biscuits and cake and what appears to be a trifle inside a glass bowl. The girl had not reckoned on food but now she's seen it her stomach is growling. Still staring at the trifle, she says, "Hello, pleased to meet you. My name's Lucy Marsh. Pleased to meet you. Glad to make your acquaintance."

"Charmed and delighted," replies the man in the copper mask.

The funny men have each been named for Dorothy's companions in *The Wonderful Wizard of Oz*. Either that or Dorothy's companions have been named after them. When they emerge from the shade, she can study them more closely. She sees the bedraggled Scarecrow, who possesses a tanned, tangled head, and the hearty Tin Woodman with his immobile copper face. She catches sight of the handsome Cowardly Lion, who fears human contact and appears to trust only Fred. And sat bright-eyed among them is Toto the dwarf, who is not truly a dwarf but is simply missing both legs. Toto has enthroned himself in a wheeled wicker chair. He is the king of the group, the gathering's grandstanding leader. Even Coach, it seems, is prepared to bend at the knee when the dwarf requires attention.

"Wotcha, cocks," Toto says.

7

Edith isn't shy, she has been out here before. "Is that trifle in the bowl?"

The Tin Woodman says, "It is indeed. Made specially for you."

"I was going to eat it," says Toto. "You're very lucky I didn't."

Seen on a map, Epping Forest is not very large and quite close at hand. And yet each of these bouncing, clanging trips is like a journey back to the distant past. The truck pulls out from the kerb and trundles for a spell through the modern world of Edmonton, with its surging traffic of motorbikes and automobiles and horses and trams. These are the streets that the girl has lived on for years. They pass the twin-gabled school she will be departing soon. Over there is the park where she fell and chipped a tooth.

But with every passing mile, the world regresses, grows younger. Coach's truck runs out of her neighbourhood and into an industrial fringe of corroded factories, railway sidings and enormous brick warehouses. This is the landscape from a future that has already been and gone.

London slides away beneath the Maudslay's tyres. It protests its departure with a ringing percussion and is suddenly behind them: the children sit up in the bed and watch the city recede. Then here come the suburbs, which are still under construction, so that the buildings sit rude and raw on strips of freshly-laid turf. The suburbs are new but they have been designed to look old; the houses whitewashed and timbered in antique Tudor style. The suburbs annoy her. They make no sense at all.

Go faster. Coach stamps the pedal, defying the speed limit

because who's going to stop him? Out here the traffic turns lighter; the land is practically rural. At intervals Coach honks his horn and swerves to overtake a horse-and-cart, and when this occurs, the horse flinches and the farmer braces his shoulders as though anticipating a blow. The children wave merrily as the truck thunders by. But only once in all of their visits does a farmer wave back, at which point they are so astounded they don't know how to respond. Their hands drop in unison and they gawp at him like idiots.

The people out here lead primitive lives. Coach ploughs past tumbledown cottages, Norman churches blotchy with lichen, and overgrown cemeteries filled with drunken headstones. Now faster, still faster. The engine is screaming, the day draws to an end and the towering trees come crowding in all around. Then finally, with a grind of gears and a left-turn so violent it feels more akin to a leap, they leave civilisation and enter the fantastical forest, where anything can happen.

And maybe this, beyond obedience and politeness, is the real reason she goes. Maybe this, were she ever called upon to explain her actions, would be her chief line of defence. Your honour, she would say, I went back because the forest is fantastic, which is another way of saying that anything can happen. This is why she climbs into the truck every Sunday. And this is why, as long as she lives, she will never completely regret her trips to the forest, in spite of the trouble they cause and the horrors that follow. Try as she might, she will never forget the thrill that she feels on turning off Turpentine Lane and into the trees.

The forest is ancient. It exists outside time. It sprang up when the planet was freshly cooked and still cooling. It remains, even today, a place of possibilities. Under the trees it

9

is easy to believe that the deer might talk and that owls might fly backwards and that an ordinary fourteen-year-old girl – the kind of girl people rarely pay much attention to – could sit down on the grass and picnic among beasts. She might shake hands with a ghost or dance alongside a lion or spoon trifle into the mouth of a storybook dwarf.

Toto is as uncoordinated as a baby. His hands have a palsy. The condensed milk and tinned fruit have got all over his front and it doesn't help that he is laughing so hard. Coach claims that if John eats any more trifle he'll wind up looking like trifle and this has reminded Toto of a little tree up the path that is the spitting-image of Edith; how none of them could believe it the first time they saw it. The Tin Man says Toto wants his eyes tested, the tree looks like a tree, same as all the rest. But the dwarf is adamant. He insists that it's Edith in profile, the resemblance is uncanny. The new girl, he adds, will vouch for him as an expert witness. "What did you say your name was again?"

"Lucy Marsh, sir."

"Lucy Marsh, so it is. One way to settle this. Come and have a look for yourself."

"Toto, for God's sake, give it a rest."

Edith rolls her eyes. "Lucy, I've seen it. It's really doesn't look a bit like me." And now everybody appears to be at least laughing a little.

"Nothing else for it, I'm going to show you this tree." The glass bowl has been emptied but the dwarf does not mind. He peers at the girl and his smile is lovely, like the last ray of daylight. It shows how his face would have looked before it was scarred, before anything happened. He says, "Miss Marsh, come along, our adventure together starts here."

G IVE HIM HALF a chance and Grandad will tell his favourite story again – about the mighty old Griffin that first flourished then failed on the western side of Ermine Street. What a sight it once was and just look at it now: its cream trim all blistered and its net curtains gone yellow. Then again the whole street is failing, so there's nobody to see it, aside from the other stragglers who are all failing too. Grandad says it's the council's fault: the council picked up a pen and caused all of this ruin. They should have brought in the caterpillars and put us out of our misery. Why not flatten the buildings while you're about it? No point starting a job if you're going to leave it half-done.

The tragedy is that it was a decent business, the Griffin, or he would never have said yes to the lease in the first place. The pub was well placed on a thoroughfare, providing for merchants, travellers and local tradesmen. There was a long stone trough where a man could water his horses, and a cobbled yard with stalls to board them. Upstairs were arranged six good guest rooms, and guess how many were occupied on a Friday night before market and then have a guess at the number filled on a Friday night now. The saloon bar used to take restaurant orders but there's no call for that anymore; he laid the cook off last year and has the girl work the taps for whoever drops in. The passing trade has gone trading elsewhere. Were it not for the drunks he would have no custom at all.

A curse on the council and its so-called arterial road. Because what would you call Ermine Street if not an arterial road? It earned itself the title before the title existed. You can't invent a new classification and say this one but not that. You don't pin a map on a board and start redrawing London. These are the arguments she hears again and again. Sat at the table, he plays pat-a-cake with his hands, constructing a tower that never extends beyond two floors. He blames the council. He blames the brewery. He blames the licensing hours. He blames the war and the Spanish flu and never you mind that the war and the flu are now several years in the past. He says that when so many have died it rips the heart from a country. "If it weren't for the drunks we'd have no custom at all."

When she first arrived, clutching her brother's hand, their worldly goods crushed inside two packing cases, the place had struck her as splendid. It no longer strikes her as anything much. The Griffin is too massive to manage on a skeleton staff. The cornices fill with cobwebs that cannot be reached without fetching the ladder. The linoleum is so greasy that the squares attach to the sole of a shoe. A plane of glass that was shattered has been replaced with plywood. The public toilets are so bad even the drunks will not use them.

The thought comes eventually that Ermine Street has been dammed. Not damned like a sinner but dammed like a stream. In diverting the traffic, the council dropped the gate and cut off the supply. See how swiftly the riverbed dries. Observe the mounting panic of its stranded inhabitants: the shoppers that hop here and there in a frantic search for cool puddles; the businesses gulping and flapping on either side of the road.

The small tradesmen might just endure if they can keep their overheads low. However hard the times, people still need bread and milk, or cheap cuts from the butcher, or even a second-hand dining set from Mick's Bric-a-Brac. But the Griffin, that colossus, is too big to survive. It is smothered by rental demands and the recent hikes in excise duty. It requires a deep, steady flow to account for its bulk and its costs. It will be the first to go down. The butcher knows it and old Mick knows it and Grandad knows that they know, which makes his temper worse.

Poor Ermine Street. It does not feel very splendid. The place has grown sad. Weekday mornings at eight, a bent old man leads his blind shire horse past the pub, headed out of town. Late afternoons, the pair pass by the opposite way. Every morning she spies them, Lucy fears that the man is taking his horse to be slaughtered and rendered for glue and her breath hitches with relief when she sees it brought back.

It turns out her grandfather has also noticed this ritual. He says, "One day, mark my words, Dobbin's not coming home."

But listen. That sound outside the window is the world going by. It moves at speed, with a rattle and rumble. It spatters the hem of the pedestrian's skirt. Away in the world it's 1923, very nearly midsummer. At her scratched and stained school desk, the girl hears that the British Empire has never been greater. It grows by the day, it covers half the globe, and this is undeniably good news: it only goes to show that all things are possible. At large in the saloon bar, she thrills to newspaper reports of dance crazes and labour disputes and Bolshevik revolution and fabulous discoveries inside the tomb of a pharaoh. She reads about the angry, unwashed rabble that threw tomatoes at King George. His Majesty was not used to such treatment. He did not know where to turn, he looked completely aghast. She reads of a pilot who flew across the

Irish Sea and of another, more incredibly still, who flew clear over the United States and did not put his wheels down until he could see the Pacific. And she concludes that her grandfather is wrong, that it is not true what he says; that the world is expanding. Everywhere you look, people are being asked to go further, to delve deeper and to plant British flags in far-flung fields. More than anything, she longs for adventures of her own. She hopes that one day she might visit the sky in a plane.

Outside it's bright, it's modern times. The war and the flu are several years in the past and good riddance to both, because the world has moved on. It is a time of fresh starts and clean slates and unblemished sheets of paper. Pin them on a wall and set about redrawing the nation. A man can map out the future using Indian ink.

The saloon door is heavy. The youth has to lean hard with his shoulder until it abruptly swings out and spills him unceremoniously inside.

"We're not open yet and I can't serve you anyway. So it doesn't even matter that we're not open."

"Why not?"

"You know very well why not," Lucy says. "Unless you've had a few extra birthdays you haven't told me about."

She knows Brinley Roberts from her classroom at St Stephen's and allows that he ranks among the least objectionable boys there. He's as lean as a greyhound, with an oversized Adam's apple and a preternaturally deep voice which seems to startle him more than anyone. Ostensibly he visits the Griffin in the hope of obtaining ale and cigarettes, although Lucy has started to wonder whether this is merely a ruse. More likely, Brinley comes in search of human company. Specifically, she thinks, he wants to see her.

The boy arranges himself at a table and proceeds to excavate his fingernails. "Why weren't you in school today?"

"Working, wasn't I?"

He says, "Doesn't look like much work. Staring out of the window."

"Well, did I miss anything special? At school, I mean."

"No," Brinley sighs. "I can't say you did."

In a moment she will relent and let him purchase a stout or a Porter, and then this pale, gawky youth will feel impossibly accomplished and manly. But for the time being she remains at the window, vaguely engaged with wiping out ashtrays yet with her eyes constantly trained on the bright street beyond. She saw the shire horse set out, but it is late getting back from wherever it goes.

"The Magna Carta."

"How's that?"

"The Magna Carta," says Brinley. "That's what you've been missing when you steer clear of school."

She stands at the glass and watches Ermine Street. She fears for the horse and she hopes it still lives. She knows she won't settle until she sees it go by.

3

THE SPIRITUALIST CRISS-CROSSES the country with his assistant, the imp. The spiritualist is elderly and imposing and must once have been handsome. He sits high aboard his two-wheel trap, like a garish figurehead at the prow of a ship or a primitive rendering of St Nicholas, before the illustrators were called in to add the fur-trimmed hat and bulging sack of presents. Hand-rolled cigarettes have stained his beard and teeth. His embroidered robe has worn through at the elbows. Around his neck is strung an oversized scarab amulet, which he refers to, in sonorous tones, as the Eye of Thoth-Amon. The amulet, he boasts, allows him to commune with the dead.

The spiritualist's name is Uriah Smith. And as he rides forth, his liver-spotted paws on the reins, he cranes his neck to loudly school the imp in the particulars of his trade. He has not known the imp long and suspects the boy may be slow-witted. He is explaining that spiritualism is a noble vocation and not so different from detective work. This is why Sir Arthur Conan Doyle, the famous author of the Sherlock Holmes stories, has become so drawn to the craft. Spiritualism, like sleuthing, depends on conducting solid research and on making enquiries, because the more you know about a client in advance, the better the service you are able to provide. So it pays to familiarise yourself with a person's history and to ferret out their deepest, secret desires.

Spiritualism works best when it is a collective endeavour. Do your homework properly and a little miracle takes place. The client steps forward and meets the spiritualist halfway. In this way you spin the tale that they wish to have spun. Every good story, he says, is about halfway factual. The real magic blooms in the space between the performer and his client, between the truth and the lie.

The imp asks, "Is there much money in it?"

"Pots of money. Buckets of money. Heed my words, boy, this time next year we will be living like kings."

Mollified, the imp beams out at the retreating country lane. His soft heavy belly sits on his soft heavy lap. His short legs swing excitedly from the end of the trap. At intervals he will rub the pads of his fingers against his right thumb to produce guttering blue flames that generate feeble warmth. This is his one great gift, which he has picked up overseas – a war wound of sorts, although not as bad as some others. The spiritualist, of course, is a preposterous fraud. But his fat imp assistant may be possessed of true magic.

"Are you still back there, my boy?"

"Of course I am. Why wouldn't I be?"

"No reason; just checking. You are a most curious creature."

"I'm still here, Uriah."

"Good news. Sit tight. What with my amulet and your tinderbox fingers we are extremely well met. This time next year we will be performing at concert halls."

"At what?"

"Concert halls! Concert halls!"

"Yes," says the imp. "I should like that, I think."

There are no concert halls in this part of Kent. Instead the road winds past hop gardens and oast houses, fording and re-fording a chocolate-brown river. Periodically they catch a glimpse of grand homes, either set back behind walls or proudly perched on the hillside. It is said that during the war a man could stand on these slopes and hear the thump of big guns from the other side of the Channel. Each thump made a widow and the widows now live in these homes. Uriah likes widows; he stalks them like game. The trick, he explains, is to approach with great caution. Kent is a rich region and that brings its own dangers. The downside with rich people is that they hate and fear poor people. They're liable to recoil or turn violent if you run at them too freely. That's why he is at pains to remain patient, discreet, altogether unthreatening. Tread lightly; research thoroughly. Sooner or later the money will follow.

"Softly softly, catch a monkey. You know the expression."

"What expression?"

"The monkey," sighs Uriah. "Ah well. Never mind."

The imp is formally known as Arthur Elms, although this name was provided by his adoptive parents, so it follows that once, long ago, he was known as something else. He was a fat, ignored child and a fat, ignored soldier and now he lives rough and remains fat, no matter how little he eats. And yet Uriah is wrong; the boy is not slow-witted at all. His brain, if anything, is an engine on the verge of overheating. Faint, swarming voices crowd the bore of his skull. Sparks fly from his fingers when he rubs them together. Few people like him but he is minded not to care, for he is at heart a bright and merry fellow, forever in flight from some mischief or other. Sometimes this is a mischief he has seen others create. Sometimes it is a mischief he has put a hand in and stirred.

He says, "If we sold that horse and trap we might have lots

of money. We could book into an inn and order up a roast dinner."

Uriah, though, is having none of it. "Sell Queenie?" he says. "Oh dearie me, no."

"How much do you reckon we'd get for her, though?"

"For Queenie?" He laughs and then coughs. "Our Queenie is priceless."

"And what about the amulet. How much is that worth?"

"More than priceless," he says flatly. "It is worth a price beyond rubies."

The way Uriah tells it, he and the imp are a double-act, rather like a pair of vaudevillians. One day, he says, they will see their name up in lights. Arthur Elms can hardly wait; the very thought gives him goosebumps. But for the time being he is content to learn the ropes of the spiritualist trade and perform his role as best he can. So he takes a seat in the corner of over-furnished front rooms and watches as Uriah circles his prey and slowly reels them in. The old man runs his black stare across the pictures on the wall and the items on the mantelpiece, mining them all for whatever information they hold. His questions are perfectly calibrated, immaculately arranged. They are inviting empty vessels to be filled as directed.

Uriah's clients, Elms has observed, are usually brittle, well-spoken women who carry the faint whiff of ill-health. These women have mislaid their husbands or their sons – or occasionally their daughters – and desire nothing more than to locate them again. So Uriah takes each woman by the hand and, lowering his voice, explains that the amulet he wears is nothing less than the fabled Eye of Thoth-Amon, plucked from the ruins of an Egyptian tomb and possessed of a power to bring comfort to the lonely. Then he scrunches his face and sends out the Eye and it seems that the Eye is able to find these lost souls every time. The Eye reports back that they are happy and whole and that all send their love and at this news, more often than not, the brittle women start weeping. Sat in his corner, the imp is entranced. Obviously he knows that the Eye is a fake. But it looks so impressive and Uriah handles it like a master.

"Oh Madame, he loves you," Uriah is saying and by this point the spiritualist, too, appears to have worked himself to the brink of tears. "I'm getting that very strongly. The Eye of Thoth-Amon is most insistent. It tells me that true love never dies. It is an eternal flame."

The widow nods her head and swabs at her face.

"But I am sensing doubt, Madame. I sense that you do not believe what the Eye has told us today."

And now the widow is alarmed. She has spent the past few minutes weeping and moaning and calling out her husband's name. What would make the spiritualist think that she remained somehow a sceptic? "No!" she says. "That's not true at all."

Uriah appears still to have his doubts. He scratches hard at his yellowing beard. Almost rhetorically he asks, "What further proof can we offer? What further marvels can the Eye perform? Good heavens, I suppose Madame requires some physical manifestation of what we have been discussing. This idea that love outlives death and that true love that never dies."

"No! No, not at all."

"The love that is an eternal flame," Uriah says – and this is the imp's cue to bring his thumb and fingertips together – to produce the brief friction that causes the flames to jump out. Time and again he obliges and time and again the result is the same. His final act brings the house down. The widows go to pieces.

"I do wonder, however, whether you ought not to act shocked by the thing," Uriah tells him when they are back out on the road. "It seems to me that you would be very shocked. You might elect to cry out or rise up from the chair. You might say, 'Goodness gracious, my fingers are alight'."

Legs swinging from the back of the trap, the imp makes a Herculean effort to take Uriah's advice on board. "I could start screaming and crying, like an infant that's been burned."

"You could," says Uriah.

"I could shout, 'Oh fucking hell. My fucking hands are aflame'."

"All I am requesting," Uriah says sharply. "All I am requesting is some outward acknowledgment of what a remarkable thing is taking place. Because when all's said and done, that is what it is. There's no denying it's a remarkable thing."

"I could fall over, perhaps. I could . . ."

"How do you do it?" Uriah asks, interrupting the imp's flow. "Out with it, boy. Tell me how it is done." But he might as well ask a salmon to explain its reasons for swimming upstream or a hummingbird to demonstrate how it is able to suspend itself in thin air, because Elms's skill is a mystery and he is minded not to question it. Fate singled him out, it was as simple as that. One moment he was minding his own business – standing by the sea out at Cape Helles, the flies buzzing against the sandy walls all around. The next, hey presto, along came his gift. The voices. The flames. They startled him as much as anyone.

"It happened, that's all," he mutters. "Some things just happen."

"And does it hurt very much? It must sting dreadfully."

"Not very much. It only feels a bit warm."

"Fabulous, fabulous. What a stroke of good fortune." A moment later, he adds, "This time next year we shall be living like kings."

In the meantime, however, they are living like tramps. Pickings are scarce. The nation's in the doldrums. Nights, the pair bed down in hay barns, or between the ivied colonnades of a cemetery tomb, or under a sheet of tarpaulin in the back of the trap, where Uriah keeps the imp awake, first with his talk of the spiritualist trade and then later with his snoring. Daytimes they feast on the animals that the motor vehicles have left them. Some of these animals have been smeared beyond all recognition. Others are perfectly preserved, as though lulled to slumber. But you need to get to them fast; once the flies have begun settling it is already too late. With a skill borne out of long years of experience, Uriah finesses his penknife to fillet squirrel and grouse. He strips the skin off a rabbit as though peeling a banana; uses the point of the blade to hook out the intestines and kidneys. One evening they find themselves a sleek piebald faun, its body still steaming, only a few minutes dead.

Uriah eyes his friend fondly across the campfire. "Now tell me the last time you ate as heartily as this."

"Me?" says the imp, his teeth working at a piece of gristle. "I don't know, can't remember. Long time, probably."

"Poor soul, it must be quite a trial. Big boy likes you needs constant replenishing."

"If we sold Queenie, we could eat like this every day."

"Queenie," shouts Uriah. "Queenie, cover your ears."

Onward they travel, the spiritualist and his imp. Can this

even be counted as Kent anymore? They turn the trap onto a lane that diminishes by degrees until it becomes no more than a rutted woodland track and press on through a light drizzle until they arrive at an open-sided shed that is used to store timber. The two men clear out the logs and wait out the rain. Then Elms departs for a spell in search of kindling and when he returns the old man peers out with inexplicable shyness and says, "Do it again, my dear boy. Show me how it's done."

"Do what?"

"You know perfectly well."

Under heavy cloud cover the flames are brighter than before. When the fat tramp rubs his fingers they curl and dance like the corona around a Christmas pudding. They catch at the kindling and turn from blue to orange. Then Uriah leans in and takes Elms' hand, marvelling at the warmth that still clings to his skin. And the intimacy of the gesture knocks out Elms' defences; it makes him loud and sentimental. Choking back tears, he says that he loves old Uriah who has become like a father to him. He wants to make the spiritualist proud. He says that nobody has been as good to him as Uriah has been.

"God's little imp," the old spiritualist says.

"I don't even know what that means."

"God's little imp. That's what you are. The very last vestige of the irrational world." He licks his stained teeth and grins shark-like through his beard. He tells the fat tramp that he should not be afraid; that he has been built for great things and that they will do those great things together. Uriah will teach him. He has taken him under his wing. One year from now they will be living like kings.

"Did the amulet tell you all of that?"

"The amulet." Uriah laughs. "The amulet is nothing, it's worthless. Or rather, it's two worthless trinkets. Look closely and you can see where I glued it."

Warily he puts out his pale fingers in order to study the thing. But the firelight is fitful and it throws spastic shadows – and perhaps Uriah's handiwork is better than he claims. And perhaps, for whatever reason, Uriah is not telling the truth.

"I don't believe it," he says. "It seems to me it must be worth pots of money."

The rain has stopped but the woodland is dripping. Elms parks himself by the campfire, sitting on his heels. And at his back, the old man keeps talking. His talk is torrential, he is swept up in the moment. He says he has spent his life among tinkers and thieves, beggars and frauds. He has been struck by policemen and wintered at a prison. He has bedded too many women and sat with too many widows and has called out the dead enough times to know that what's dead is dead and that there is no real magic beyond the cheap magic of talk, until one day on the road he spies this fat, unwashed fellow who might have been belched out of nowhere.

Elms pokes a stick at the flames. "Maybe I should say, 'My hands have caught fire. Fetch me a bucket of water!'. . ."

Uriah ignores him; he is building to a crescendo. He booms, "Fifty-eight years I have wandered this earth. And I have never encountered anybody remotely like you."

Morning draws in. The track winds on through the trees and presently drops down to parallel a glistening black river, shallow and swift. Uriah uncouples Queenie from the trap and coaxes her across to the water to drink. Elms trots at their heels, his teeth chattering, his round belly swinging. He takes a stone from the beach and attempts to skip it, but the river is rocky and he misjudges the angle. He picks up another and slides it out underarm.

"My dear, silly boy. You need to find something flatter, with more weight. Slate would be perfect but you keep picking up pebbles."

So Elms stoops to collect an oblong stone, the size and shape of a primitive house-brick. This he hoists in his grip, gauging the distance and gathering his strength.

Staring out over the lacquered surface, Uriah says, "Slate's what you're wanting. Not piddling pebbles."

This time Elms swings the stone sidearm, very quick, so that it strikes the old man at the point where the skull joins the neck. The impact jars his arm clean up to the shoulder and makes Queenie shake her withers.

Uriah lands on his side in the shallows. His left leg is kicking.

Elms stands over him. After a short, shocked moment, he says, "Are you alright, Uriah?"

"Na-gug," says Uriah. He toils to get his arms under him and his head from the water. Dark blood is now blotting his upturned coat collar.

The imp leans in, bends his knees and brings the stone down again. This time the blow is experimental, almost tender, as if by tapping the old man he might somehow revive him. "Gug," says Uriah.

Elms discards the stone, rubs his palm on his coat. He says, "I'll go get some help. I'll be back very soon."

He hastens off the low bank and over to the trail where he finds a tree stump to sit on. There he forces himself to count to fifty in French. As he does so, he kneads his white fingers into the joint of his shoulders and studies the dispute of three squirrels in the boughs overhead. Round and round the tree they go. It makes him dizzy just to watch.

Back on the shoreline, he turns the spiritualist over and slips the Eye of Thoth-Amon from around his neck. Next he unbuttons the coat pockets and locates a penknife, some coins and a ten shilling note. His gut is joggling. His arm is in uproar. Breathing hard, he drags Uriah out into the rushing water and then turns him loose. The current carries the body about twenty yards downstream before it fetches up against one of those protruding black rocks. He believes he can make out the man's head and knees amid the egg-white of the foam.

His shoulder is hurting; his trouser legs are soaked through. He can barely lift the reins to guide Queenie to the track, let alone raise the trap to manoeuvre her back into harness. "Dear old Queenie," he murmurs. "Poor old horse," and high above his head the squirrels embark on some fresh altercation.

When they come back onto the track, the animal finds its rhythm. Elms' shoulder is sore but he knows the soreness will pass. He has been hurt in the past and the pain never lasts very long. The joint will heal and the trouser legs will dry and everything will be well because great things are forecast. He keeps his good hand on the reins and watches as the path turns away from the rush and roar of the river. It straightens and widens and turns to tarmac again. Half a mile out, he sees a sign for the town.

4

U P AHEAD, THE deep dark woods. On the drive out, bouncing in the bed of Coach's truck, the children discuss the individual merits of the strange, funny men. Winifred admits that while she feels a particular bond with the Cowardly Lion, one struggles to find much to say to him because frankly he doesn't have much to say in return. As such, she would probably have to claim the Tin Woodman as her favourite, except don't tell the Lion, because that would hurt his feelings. Edith says that she likes the Tin Man as well, but her preference is Toto. John leaves off sucking his thumb long enough to venture that he quite likes them all, he can't rightly pick one. Maybe Toto or the Scarecrow, although he concedes that the Lion's nice too.

Fred says, "What about you, Lucy? Who's your best funny man?"

"I've only met them once. I don't know yet."

"Come on, pick a name. You can always change your mind later."

On her previous visit she had spent the most time with Toto. "They all seem very nice," she says hesitantly. "So far, I think the Tin Man might be best."

"Ah, Tinny," says Fred. "He'd be loving this conversation. His ears must be burning."

She is still familiarising herself with her travelling companions: with solemn Edith and spirited Fred and the ungainly

John, who is surely too old to be sucking his thumb yet continues to do so with a constant grim application. Overall, she likes them and thinks they like her back, which is just as well, it would be awful if they didn't. It would make these journeys awkward; they're so snugly packed. Each time Coach brakes and accelerates, he either throws Lucy against the others or the others against her.

"Ouch!" says John.

"Sorry."

"Do us a favour, Lucy," Edith says. "The next time you come, leave your knees and elbows at home."

One curious thing about the children in the truck: in terms of their backgrounds, they might be peas in a pod. Like Lucy, it turns out that Winifred lives with her grandparents. Like Lucy, these grandparents manage a public house in north London. And Edith's situation is only a little different: she is being raised by an uncle and aunt near Alexandra Palace. Her uncle used to own and run his own restaurant until the business went bad and he was forced to close down. Then John explains that he lives with his mother and his mother's new husband, who is called Mr Parnell. John says that although the house is a decent size, he has to share his bedroom with three other boys, Mr Parnell's noisy sons, which he does not like, although he supposes it could be worse. It could be four other boys. It could be five. Eventually, after a period of deep thought, he says, "It could be six other boys."

It mostly falls to Fred to keep these journeys diverting. Fred pulls faces, sings songs and does voices. Her conversation moves so fast that Lucy has a job keeping pace. One moment Fred is mimicking an Italian gentleman named Mr Falconio, who is apparently engaged in some ornate and ongoing feud with her family. The next she is breathlessly recounting an exchange she had with Coach, or Tinny, or making laughing reference to something she describes as "the Terrible Unmentionables". Lucy has no idea what this means although she eventually grasps that "the Terrible Unmentionables" is Fred's convenient, cover-all label for any awkward topic of conversation; for anything that people would prefer to avoid. She supposes it may conceivably refer to the funny men too.

Fred says, "Nobody likes to talk about the Terrible Unmentionables. John doesn't like to talk about the Terrible Unmentionables, but then John doesn't like to talk about anything, do you, John? Poor little bastard, the cat ate his tongue. But I don't mind, it's not so bad. Oh, Falconio! Falconio! Don't bring up the Terrible Unmentionables! Who did you say your favourite funny man was again?"

Lucy looks up, startled. "Who, me?"

"No, not you, I'm talking to Falconio. Oh Falconio! Yes, of course you. I'm asking you."

"The Tin Man, I think."

"Oh yeah, that's right. Old Tinny. You've got good taste, Lucy, I'll give you that. But then everybody likes the Tin Man the best. He's the most dashing. He's the most romantic out of all the funny men. The ladies like Tinny and he likes them right back."

Edith says, "The Tin Man likes whatever he can get his hands on."

"Hooks," corrects Fred. "But Lucy, what would I do if he decided that he liked you most of all? More than Edith and me? Wouldn't that be awful? What would we do?"

"Kill ourselves," suggests Edith, deadpan. "Kill Lucy. Kill Tinny."

"Kill John," cries Winifred.

"Oh come on, Fred, that's your answer to everything."

"Kill John. Do it now, why hang about? Kill John."

John grins uncertainly. "Shut up you."

Fred turns back towards Lucy. "I mean it, what if he decides he likes you the best? He might do, you know. You're dead pretty, Luce."

"Oh no," she says. "I'm really not, it's just the dress."

"No, you are, don't make me out as a liar. How dare you accuse me of lying, Falconio. Look at you. And now look at me." She contorts her face; crosses her eyes. "Look at me, I'm hideous."

"No. No."

Exasperated, Edith says, "Stop going on. You both look about the same, if that settles the matter. You both look the same. You're both hideous."

Beneath the trees, the funny men. They are brought to the woods in a truck identical to the one that Coach drives, aside from the fact that the bed is covered by canvas, and it is driven by a man named Crisis, who is all but identical too. Coach and Crisis must be siblings, the resemblance is so close; possibly cousins at a push. Both men appear to work together, somewhere close to the forest. She cannot tell whether Coach and Crisis work for the funny men or if it's the other way around.

Coach pulls the truck broadside and wrenches the handbrake. "Funny men, meet the helpers. Helpers, meet the funny men."

"Delighted and charmed," says the Tin Woodman, stepping forward.

Is he truly her favourite? She allows that this might be the case, although who can say, it's only her second trip out. Fred says that he is dashing, but what does being dashing entail? The Tin Woodman wears a mask made from galvanised copper. This has been painted in skin tones, decorated with a copper-wire moustache, and is evidently held in position by a pair of tortoiseshell spectacles that are not merely looped about his ears but actually fastened in a bow about his head. He possesses a pair of fearsome-looking steel hooks in place of his hands and, from the evidence of his awkward, halting gait, might also be missing a portion of leg. Can a man be considered dashing when he is unable to walk smoothly, or shake hands when he wants, and when there is no obvious means of discerning whether he is smiling or not? Lucy does not know, but she resolves not to judge. The Tin Man is smartly dressed and unfailingly courteous. That helps to make up for all the parts he is missing.

"All right," grumbles Coach. "All right now, no crowding."

Her next question is this: is the Tin Man the most freakish of all the funny men? Again, she thinks that he probably is, insofar as he gives the impression of being as much metal as flesh. But then none of the four are altogether unblemished and, even knowing what's coming, she is still taken aback. What a collection they are, with their missing arms, legs and eyes, and their elaborate disguises intended to fill in the blanks. Put them together and you might arrive at one person.

"Hello, you old bastards," Winifred is saying. "Hello, funny men. We've missed you quite dreadful."

Toto says, "Wotcha, Fred, we've missed you too. It's been a shit-awful week, but now the sun has come out. I reckon our little helpers must bring the weather with them."

The Tin Man says, "And what a happy bonus to see that Lucy is back. Of course there's no telling which of our guests

31

will return. One can only be thankful she didn't decide to run away screaming."

"Oh no," she says. "I'd never do that."

"Well, I do thank you, Lucy. You do us all a great service." And now the Tin Man's voice seems to be smiling even if his mouth cannot move.

Take a random group of boys and girls. Throw them together and a hierarchy is established. Each member unconsciously finds his or her own role to inhabit. She has seen it happen at school or on the street and most recently in the bed of the truck, where Winifred is the queen and she and Edith princesses, which leaves poor thumb-sucking John as their subordinate. And here, again, is the very same system laid out anew, because why should the funny men be different from anybody else? Within the first few moments of her opening visit, she recognised Toto as the group's colourful, confident leader and now becomes aware of the other pieces slotting into place. Winifred is correct: the Tin Man is the dashing gallant, full of rueful good humour, at ease in his skin, and never mind that it's not skin, while the Scarecrow takes the rank of cool-headed lieutenant. The Lion, she realises, is the lowliest member. He stands off to one side, with a black patch over one eye and his boyish face clenched. The Lion dislikes company and won't hold himself still. When Lucy walks over, he retreats a few shuffling steps and shouts, "Hello! Hello!" as a warning to her not to draw any closer.

Fred says, "You should be thanking me, not her. I can hardly stand to look at you. I think I'm either going to faint or be sick."

"Give it a rest, Fred," Edith says in a murmur.

"I mean it, I'm not joking. If I start to faint, one of you better catch me. If I start to be sick, it's every man for himself."

There is no picnic on this second trip to the woods. Coach explains that he has been rushed off his feet, he had no time to prepare, and that too much trifle will make the children fat pigs. Instead, he and Crisis suggest hide-and-seek: a spot of exercise to keep them lean and strong. The guests will run off and the funny men can give them a minute or two and then come to find them. At first Lucy worries that they might all become lost, Epping Forest so big and they now far from the road, but Coach reassures her that they have played this game before and drawn up decent rules. None of the helpers, he says, is permitted to run more than a hundred paces in any direction. He is very clear on this score. Anyone who strays further will be disqualified and punished.

He says, "Yes, I'm looking at you, John. No running away."

John nods at the ground.

"Cheating little get. We had to have us some words."

She runs out through the trees, away from the clearing, regulating her stride in order to keep better count. It is a babyish game, she hasn't played it in years – but the very act of setting forth stirs up happy memories and she is somewhat surprised to find herself laughing. She intends to run the full hundred steps and then plop herself down, but she is only a little over halfway when she alights on a clump of bracken and decides this will do just as well and might outwit her pursuers, who will be casting their net further afield. The sun is up but the birds have stopped singing. The forest is still and it feels a good place to be.

After she's been about five minutes in hiding, the Scarecrow passes by. All but the lower part of his face is covered by a mask made from tanned leather. His empty left sleeve has been crisply folded and pinned to the lapel of his coat. She calls, "Well done, you found me. I'm right over here."

The Scarecrow gets down on his heels. "You shouldn't have shouted. I would have walked right by."

"Well, never mind. It's a silly game in any case."

How old is the Scarecrow? There is no way of telling. His hair is dark and his voice is strong; she supposes he may be reasonably young, not much beyond thirty. Looking at him, she is struck afresh by the oddness of these trips. If someone had taken her aside two Sundays gone and told her that this is where she would be and that he would be here too, she would never have believed it, not in a million years.

She says, "It'll be getting dark soon. And then the stars will come out."

He asks, "Is that good or bad?"

"Oh, very good. I love seeing the stars."

From a distance, very faintly, comes the squeal of hysterical laughter. Winifred. Caught.

The Scarecrow retrieves a cigarette from the pack and Lucy helps get it alight. Life must be so tiresome with the use of only one arm. But the silence between them is pressing; it makes her shy and tongue-tied.

She says, "Well, this is very pleasant."

"You find it pleasant?"

"Of course it is. I do like the forest. It feels like we have the whole place to ourselves."

"Then I'm afraid you're mistaken. There are others here too and if we're very unlucky we may even see them. The Kindred of the Kibbo Kift."

"Aha," says Lucy. After a beat, she adds, "The what?"

"The Kindred of the Kibbo Kift. It's an organisation of pacifist boy scouts. They like to ramble the woods on summer nights. Sometimes if you listen, you can hear them singing."

"What a strange name. Are you making fun of me?"

The Scarecrow draws on his cigarette. "No," he says. "If I wanted to tease you, I hope I'd be able to come up with something a bit more sensational."

Lucy fidgets. She can feel that the seat of her dress is damp from where she's been sitting. Next time, she thinks, she'll bring a blanket to rest on.

"If I wanted to tease you, I would say that the woods are full of wolves or bears. I'd say, 'Did you hear that noise? I do hope it's not wolves'."

"Yes, all right. Thank you."

"But there are no wolves. Or bears, for that matter. There's only a band of sanctimonious boy scouts."

Toto shouts, "Found you at last. Now bloody budge up, I can hardly see you in there."

Away from the trail, Toto likes to dispense with the wheelchair and proceed under his own steam. The dwarf has no legs but he moves by wriggling aboard his muscular hips, employing his one good arm to steer and steady himself much as a gondolier might plant his pole in a Venetian canal. In he comes, his head and shoulders rolling. Ideally she would have liked to speak with the Scarecrow longer. Still, there's no denying that Toto in motion is a sight to behold.

"Budge up," he barks at the Scarecrow. "Are you staying or what?"

The Scarecrow says, "All I'm doing is smoking."

"You can be doing that anywhere. Walk about, have a smoke. See if you can round up any more of the tykes."

"Good to talk to you, Lucy," the Scarecrow says.

"Shoo, shoo," says the dwarf. And then to the girl, "Help me off with this jacket, there's a pet. Damn thing gets all rucked up by my pits."

Once, years before, they had hidden in the pantry while her mother went looking. The game in the forest has suddenly brought it all back. She and Tom and their father huddled in the half-light with the door closed at their backs and the jars and tins arranged on the shelves all around. She recalls that the flour had looked so inviting that her father dared her to eat it and see. In the event they each licked their fingertips and dipped their hands in the jar. But the flour was awful, which in turn set them laughing. It seemed strange that the linchpin of all her mother's delicious cakes and breads could taste so revolting in its purest, whitest state.

Later, back at the truck, she learns that some altercation has occurred in another part of the forest. Edith is angry, over-wrought and on the verge of tears. Lucy can't work out the details and feels it would be impolite to ask and yet, unac-countably, it seems the slow, docile Lion is somehow to blame. Edith has climbed into Coach's truck where she sits with her arms tightly folded. She says all that she wants is to be driven back home.

Toto is incensed. Coach and Crisis have barely had time to position him in his chair, but now he wants to set himself down again. He affects to lunge at the miscreant and repri-mands him as though he is scolding a dog. "Lion! You dirty article. Play nice. No rough stuff. Look at her and look at you. You great, disgusting brute."

Lucy steals a glance and is relieved to see that, whatever

offence the Lion has committed, the creature is clearly overcome by remorse. He tries to speak but his constricted throat
won't engage, so instead he turns to clasp his hands and silently entreat the furious girl in the truck.

"Edith, look," says Winifred. "He's saying he's sorry."

"Lion! You great dirty brute."

Crisis says, "It's because he's been drinking. He had a
skinful coming over. He gets too jumpy otherwise. Not that
I'm making excuses for him, mind."

"Can we go home, please?" calls Edith from the truck.

It is left to Fred to make the peace. The girl walks between
the funny men, variously stretching and stooping to kiss each
one goodbye. She leaves the Lion until the end. He shakes in
her embrace and appears to be weeping.

On his way to crank the engine, Coach digs Lucy lightly
in the ribs. "You all right there?"

She nods glumly.

"Attagirl," says Coach.

"Same time next week," the Tin Man is shouting. "It's been
a joy and an honour."

The truck rocks drunkenly on the bridleway. If Coach
dared drive any faster, they might be overturned. The girl
starts tottering, she has not quite found her sea legs – but
when she reaches out for support, the usually accommodating
Edith bats her hand brusquely away.

Lucy back-pedals and comes into contact with John. The
boy has rolled himself in a ball and appears already to be
sleeping. When the truck runs over a branch, it dislodges his
thumb from his mouth.

The night is overcast, full of incoming rain. It is as
though God has run a roller north-to-south across the

sky. Lucy does not like it; it makes the heavens look black.

Fred chatters from the gloom. "Hide-and-seek, they call it. Torture, I call it, when the ground is that wet. But oh no, Coach says hide-and-seek, so hide-and-seek it is. My shoes are completely caked. I think my smock must be as well. And it's all right for Coach." She turns to raise her voice at the rear hatch of the driver's cab. "It's all right for Coach, because it's not him who's playing, he just stands about gassing, miserable bastard." She settles back. "He can't hear me anyway."

Lucy says, "My dress as well. My nan will have kittens."

"If we come down with pneumonia, we'll know where we caught it."

She finds herself peering through the pale stands of trees, at the strips of velvety darkness, and realises that she is looking for the pacifist scouts the Scarecrow told her about, except, of course, she can no longer remember the name. The Kiddo Kiff? The Kiddo Cliff? Something jagged and festive, like a twist of tinsel or a clatter of bells. Her limbs are sore and her lids are heavy and yes, she does worry about the mud on her dress, she can't help herself, it feels like a failing, like she is coming home soiled. As soon as she sat down amid the bracken, she could feel the wetness crawling through the fabric – but what was she to do? The forest is filthy, it scratches, splatters and drips. That's the nature of nature. If one doesn't like it, one ought to stay put indoors.

So far as she can tell, Epping Forest is empty. But maybe it's not. Quite possibly it isn't. There might be a row of boy scouts just five paces away and she would never know because Coach is driving too fast and the trees are too thick and there is no moon out tonight. All the same, she does wish that she could remember the name. The Kindred of the Cliff Kiddos?

"And the other thing that happened, just you listen to this. When the Tin Man found me he got so excited he caught his foot on a root and fell forward on me. And you know, his hooks. I thought he was going to run me right through. En-garde! Like in The Three Musketeers."

"I think I did hear you screaming."

"It's funny now, but it gave me a fright. And him too, he was good about it, but then he's not a bad sort, old Tinny. And he is still my favourite, so there. I shall fight you for him, Luce, and I reckon I'm stronger than you, which means Tinny is mine."

Out of the darkness, Edith says, "They're all horrible."

Fred turns towards her. "You still in a grump, Ede?"

"You should have a listen to yourself. It's pathetic."

"She's only in a sulk because she didn't like the game. None of us did, welcome to the club. Honestly Ede, it's like you think you're made out of glass."

"They're not our boyfriends," Edith says. In the gloom, Lucy cannot make out what the girl's face is doing. "They're horrible. Sunday nights are horrible."

After a moment, Fred says, "Ignore her, Luce. She's in one of her sulks."

At the southern skirt of Epping Forest, the road ascends for a spell aboard steep grassy banks and crosses an expanse of meadow and woodland – and the sensation is that of laborious ascent; it must be how plane passengers feel in the opening seconds of take-off. The land drops away and the night wind whips her ears as the Maudslay travels amid the treetops. And yet to Lucy it seems as though Coach's truck is stationary and

39

the landscape is moving. The trees come streaming past in the opposite direction. She looks out from the bed and watches them run, humped and shaggy, across the meadow at midnight. They are like prehistoric beasts, an army of mammoths in frightened retreat. She fancies that they must be escaping some natural disaster – all of them running, heads down and silent, at the same dogged pace, and then all at once gone. The land bare, the trees streaming away to the north and Lucy sat in the old army truck, left behind to confront whatever is coming up next.

5

THE LONG BOYS are playing inside the Alcazar hall. Their antics have drawn an appreciative crowd. The Long Boys come from Tennessee, which means they are currently thousands of miles from home. Their pockets are lined with ticket stubs and foreign coins and receipts for hotels they have already forgotten. The Old World is new and they're still unpicking its mysteries. Ordinary smells are exotic to them.

The musicians come billed as "genuine darktown entertainers", purveyors of an unruly young sound that has America in a spin. They take the stage one-by-one, loping out from the wings and under the lights, where Ambrose Metcalf reads their names from a card. Ambrose Metcalf has corked his cheeks for the occasion, but the compère fools no one. He is a liverish man in late middle-age. He wears a blazer and a monocle. The night before he called the bingo numbers. He introduces each man with an agonised formality that is unintentionally funny. Midway through his preamble, the audience has divided. One half is applauding the Long Boys' arrival. The other is laughing at hapless Ambrose Metcalf.

Here come the Long Boys and they are itching to play. First from the wings is the celebrated trumpeter, Sunny Boy Bill, a wide-eyed, slender prodigy, barely out of his teens, and trailing behind comes burly George Washington, who blows the trombone. The band's drummer, Rollin' Colin George, claims to be double-jointed and in all likelihood is, while the light-skinned

41

octoroon on clarinet answers to the name of Skinny Boy Floyd and is a notorious tearaway, newly released from Sing Sing. And here Ambrose Metcalf raises his voice and implores the hooting spectators to put their hands together and give the warmest Alcazar welcome to the biggest, longest Long Boy of them all – the boss and the bandleader, Mr Samuel 'Sweetpea' Long. He cries, "On banjo and vocals. Samuel 'Sweetpea' Long."

Out steps Mr Long. Handsome, ageless and painstakingly mild. His hands are clasped and his head is bowed in a pantomime of deference because he is at pains to point out that it is the music that matters, not the lowly creatures who play it. Music hails from heaven; he is merely its packmule. So he says "Good gracious me" and "I am quite overcome". He knows that nothing scares white society more than an upstart negro.

"Ladies and gentlemen. Mr Samuel 'Sweetpea' Long."

The house is full, the audience an even split of regulars and visitors. There is a coach party from Brighton, an arts critic from the Times, and six members of an Irish street-gang from the Islington slums. The critic will later dismiss the evening's activities as "low negro baboonery" and call for the musicians to be packed off back to America, where they regard such behaviour with more tolerance.

Aboard the maplewood stage, the Long Boys take songs that are already unfamiliar and proceed to twist them out of shape, so that a tune that sets forth dressed as one thing changes costumes in the space of a bar, or doubles back on itself, or spins out to reveal a set of outlandish musical cousins who start to chatter and squabble, each vying for attention. They perform 'Good Luck Shimmy' and 'Livery Stable Stomp'. They play 'Heebie-Jeebies' and 'Beale Street Blues' and the down-hearted song about the down-hearted girl who has got the world in a jug and the stopper in her hand. When they play 'Tiger Rag', the noise threatens to take the roof off. The pace is electric; Colin's sticks are a blur. The beat accelerates and accelerates until it reaches a point when the dancers are overtaken and hauled in – where their outmoded dance steps will no longer suffice and they abandon well-worn routines in favour of a drunken tidal surge. George Washington sounds his trombone to simulate the tiger's roar.

Above the throng sits Rupert Fortnum-Hyde, as lordly and distant as a Greek deity. He and two friends have commandeered what the Alcazar presumptuously refers to as its royal box. They have latched the door at their backs and arranged rails of cocaine on the sill at their waists. In the pauses between songs, in lieu of applause, Rupert Fortnum-Hyde dips his dark head and permits a rail of white powder to run into a nostril. The drug excites his senses. The Long Boys excite him too, but Fortnum-Hyde has never been a man to let his enthusiasms unman him. Leave it to the others to clamour and bleat and behave like retarded children. He would rather cogitate at length before delivering his verdict, safe in the knowledge that it is his verdict that counts.

Exactly how many rhythms can the Long Boys sustain during the course of the same ragtime number? He locates three – arguably four – distinct tempos pitted against one another. The songs slalom and careen, but they are not quite a cacophony. They contain some internal motor that allows the melodies to run out for a spell before snapping them back like elastic. It is all rather diverting. The friction is delicious and the music full of pep. Fortnum-Hyde decides that this style of playing should not be called ragtime or jazz; that "pep" suits it better. They should re-christen the music as pep and leave it at that.

At the front of the hall, the set has reached a pitch of intensity, the Long Boys swinging with barely a break into a roiling, loose-jointed tease of a song that conspires to paint a schoolyard jingle with a knowing carnal gloss. This is Sweetpea's cue to abandon the cumbersome apparatus of his microphone and join in the dance. He scissor-kicks himself from the stage and lands amid the first row of revellers. Casting propriety to the wind, he scoops a dancer in his arms and twirls her so ardently that her skirt rises to her midriff. Now vocal duties have switched to Skinny Boy Floyd, a model of beaming innocence as he sings of how he likes to stick his finger in the woodpecker's hole and how the woodpecker says "God bless my soul". Skinny Boy is a wonder. The man is musically ambidextrous. He plays alto clarinet and then sips a breath and begins singing tenor.

"The woodpecker girl gave a sigh and a grin. She said, Turn it round, take it out, stick it in."

This is all too much for the colossal Truman Truman-Jones, surely the heaviest man in the house, who has been manfully attempting to avoid speaking first but discovers he can maintain his silence no longer. Muscle cords straining against his shirt collar, he ventures that the spectacle of the Long Boys puts him in mind of a newspaper cartoon he once saw in which a gaggle of primates invaded Buckingham Palace. It may well be amusing, it is certainly enlivening, but he needs to be convinced that it is art. Is he even saying that correctly? What is the proper collective noun for primates?

"A screech of monkeys," ventures York Conway at his side. "A masturbation of monkeys."

Truman-Jones heaves in like an ocean liner to fortify himself with another dose of white powder. But the tension has undone him. He blurts, "What do you make of it, Rupert? What manner of oddness is this?"

At last, Rupert Fortnum-Hyde is prepared to deliver his verdict. He leans back in his chair and extends his long limbs as though delightedly bored. He says, "Rub-a-dub-dub."

And with a jolt of alarm, Truman-Jones realises he's been caught out. He took a chance and jumped one way when he should have jumped the other, because there is no higher praise than a "Rub-a-dub-dub", and if Fortnum-Hyde likes the Long Boys then that means he must as well. Back-tracking swiftly, he says, "Well, I have to admit it is an astonishing sight."

Rupert Fortnum-Hyde accepts the concession with a cool-eyed smile. "What an incorrigible racist you are, Jonesy," he says.

Full credit to Skinny Boy Bill, who is leading the wood-pecker song to places it hitherto had never dreamed might exist. He is sticking his finger in whatever hole he can find and never you mind who claims it as home, because it is Skinny Boy's home for as long as he wants it. He keeps entering holes to find the one that's the best fit until he enters the red vixen's hole and that is where he gets bit.

At the edge of the stage, Ambrose Metcalf receives this information with an involuntary moue of distaste.

Sweetpea Long is soberly dressed and his short-cropped hair has turned prematurely grey. He could pass for a stiff-backed preacher or a middle-aged country schoolteacher, but this is his disguise and the music is so urgent that the cover soon slips. He dances with a second woman, and a third. Then he rediscovers the first girl and spins her again so that her skirt rises to her waist and her legs are exposed.

At this juncture the dancer's partner feels that he has shared his girlfriend long enough. He pushes Sweetpea, and Sweetpea pushes back. He winds up and hits out and Sweetpea hits him back. The bandleader's punch is well-aimed: it clips the man on the jaw and propels him into another dancer. And this causes a domino effect, so that a sizeable portion of the dancers at the front of the hall lose their bearings and balance and are abruptly falling or fighting or remonstrating and occasionally trying to manage all three at once. Some of the men are battling Sweetpea's corner, while others have taken up the boyfriend's cause. But the majority remain ignorant of the cause of the quarrel and simply mete out punishment to whomever it was who pushed or punched them last.

The woodpecker song squeals to a halt as Sweetpea closes with the dancer's partner. Several of the more rascally members of the Islington street gang have brought knives to the venue and one of these is dropped and kicked and fortuitously fetches up in the banjo player's vicinity. Skipping and shuffling, Sweetpea waves the blade like a wand, commanding his assailants to drop back a step, and in so doing conjures an arc of empty floor between his person and theirs. Still, it's clear that somewhere somebody has already been struck because there are thin lines of wet blood on the scuffed wooden boards.

Now here come the Long Boys. They throw down their instruments and move to defend the bandleader. The musicians launch themselves from the stage and although this should by rights be a decisive act, it proves anything but, because the lighting has dazzled them and they confuse friend with foe. The guests in the hall are swept up in their tempo and now everybody is clawing at everybody else. The women are screaming. There are bodies underfoot and the clicking crocheting of switchblades at work in close quarters. On his perch by the wings, Ambrose Metcalf sinks to his knees, throws back his head and claps his hands to his ears. He could be a ham Othello contemplating Desdemona's handkerchief.

The swaying, breaking, rippling crowd. The screams of women and the exhortations of men. The Long Boys appeared to applause and bow out in disgrace. All five musicians will spend that night in the cells.

In his determination to escape the crush, a slender man in plus fours has begun climbing the full-length curtains which rest against the outer wall. Ponderously he separates himself from the crowd, making a rope of the velvet and bracing his feet against brickwork so as to inch himself up and out by degrees. He clutches and clambers until he is beyond reach of the knives – at which point he turns his head and sees Rupert Fortnum-Hyde sitting in the splendour of the royal box opposite. Their eyes meet across the sea of bodies. The man has clambered so high that he has very nearly drawn level. And the look on his face is so ghastly, so stricken that Rupert Fortnum-Hyde can't help himself: he is poleaxed by mirth. He stares across at this heroic mountaineer who has climbed up the curtains to avoid being stabbed and this is all that it takes for his lordly cool to fall away. The horror. The glory. The garish free-for-all. He finds himself laughing so hard that there are tears on his cheeks. He is laughing so hard that he fears he might choke. Before long he becomes aware of his companions adding their voices to his and the three of them sit with the bolted door at their backs; a trio of cavaliers come to relish the sport. Conway and Truman-Jones are hooting and braying, each engaged in a Herculean effort to outdo the other. Both men have learned, from long years of experience, that Fortnum-Hyde's laugh is an instruction that should not be ignored.

6

I T IS AN era of change, that much is clear. Old things are knocked down to be replaced by new things. On Ermine Street a row of terraced houses is being removed to make space for a depot, and the business of destruction draws a crowd of onlookers. Labourers cordon off the street with a length of twine and the girl stands at the vanguard with it pressing into her midriff to watch the crane swing a ball into the front of the homes. When the frontage falls away, the ball is free to venture inside and nose at the interior. From her place at the kerb she sees the houses laid bare. She sees the rose-print wallpaper of abandoned bedrooms. She sees mounted gas lights, built-in wooden closets, and fireplaces marooned on the walls where a floor used to stand. Is that an oil landscape hung over the mantelpiece? The former tenants have fled. They put their belongings in boxes but decided to abandon the painting, or else looked right through it and forgot its existence until it was too late to return to claim it.

A reverent hush has fallen on the crowd. No one says a word; they might be onlookers at a funeral. The swing of the ball has them transfixed. They find themselves lulled by its lazy retreats and advances, by the way it turns aside and adjusts its approach to nuzzle the brickwork from a different direction. It wanders in like an amiable pig to root and forage among the walls, and each time it leaves it drags a little more of the building with it. The end terrace falls away to reveal a swatch of blue sky. The staircase collapses with a soft bonfire crackle. She thinks of all the people who must have trodden on those steps and wonders where they went next and where those feet are walking today.

Time and again, the ball turns back to revisit its meal. It erases bricks and mortar. It converts the row of houses to dust and this dust spills out past the length of twine to settle on the people who have gathered behind it. Lucy is aware of it in her hair, frosting her lashes and the inside of her lips. It is easy to spot who has been watching the destruction. One by one, they peel away from the cordon and walk back up the street, coated head to toe in grey dust that is fine as talcum powder. The girl slows her pace to let them overtake her. She allows herself to believe that she is observing a collection of phantoms, the ghosts of the people who once lived in these houses, and that the ball has released them and pointed them back towards London.

At a village fête in the west of England, adults and children gather to write messages on a hundred coloured balloons. These balloons are then inflated with helium gas and released. Each bears a homily, or a motto, or a personal dedication of love – although some of the younger children have not quite grasped what is expected of them and one boy's message reads, "I like porridge now". The balloons waft away from the green and bob over the rooftops where the wind begins to disperse them. The villagers raise a cheer and then they disperse, too.

One of the balloons removes itself from its neighbours. It proceeds to travel three miles east, drifting over a railway line and a river and a stretch of private woodland where the nobles shoot pheasant. It comes to rest in the garden of a young widow who lives on a pension with her son. At the very moment it lands the widow is considering killing herself. On seeing its flash of red, she steps from the back door and retrieves the balloon from the privet that has trapped it. The legend on its skin reads, "Chin Up, My Pet".

Later, the widow will insist to herself that she was never actually serious about taking her own life and that, besides, even if that weren't true, she would never have gone through with the deed because of her love for her son. But in her most honest moments she wonders whether the balloon might have saved her; the silly red balloon with its bland message written by someone who does not know her and almost certainly never will. "Chin Up, My Pet". It saved her life – although she suspects that even that is a lie. People find omens when they look for them. Peer hard enough and you can read anything into anything. Unconsciously, then, she was casting about for an excuse not to do it. Were it not the balloon, it would have been the sight of a late-blooming daffodil, or a cloud in the sky in the shape of Bram's face.

But still she is lonely and can find no solace for that. She won't abandon the house because it is her connection to him, even though they only moved here in the first place because she was offered a job. Her mother's in Bournemouth and her sister's in Southampton and both of them claim that they have room for her and the boy and yet she will not leave the house because it was he who painted the walls and put up the bookshelves and replaced the sash windows where the putty had rotted. They used to make love on that rug by the fire. He must have banged his head fifty times on the beam at the top of the stairs. The whole house is haunted. It will not let her go.

Nothing helps, she is sad to say. The loneliness grows more

pressing with every passing day. Of course she ensures that the child is well fed and well dressed and she helps him with his drawing – she supposes he may even have talent – and yet she can hardly bear to look him in the face. The resemblance is too wrenching. It is like being slapped.

One weekend, feeling ridiculous, she attends a church service and positions herself in the back row of pews with her hymn book raised to her chin as though to ward off wicked spirits. The congregation is singing 'All Hail the Power of Jesus's Name' and from the opening verse this strikes her as amusing. In the first place the hymn is slipshod and ramshackle, not built for purpose, and the discordant singing soon cuts it clean off at the knees. And secondly, why should she? Why should she be bullied into hailing a name, and how, pray tell, has its power ever benefited her? Sod him, she thinks. Sod him and his name.

All she feels is emptiness. It is a time of beginnings for those who can make them and this is surely essential; the world must move on. But she suspects that it may well have set off without her. Not yet thirty and she is stuck in amber, stuck in the past, stuck down with the dead. The church is a sham and the child's face offends her and long walks exhaust her body but leave her mind still aflame. What helps? Nothing helps. Maybe she needs to drink more heavily. Maybe she should masturbate more frequently; that might help with her sleep. And into all this fuss and bother comes an idiotic message written on the skin of a balloon that ducks into her garden and says, "Chin Up, My Pet". She does not see this message as being any more profound than that of the verse in the hymn book – yet nor on reflection is it any less so. When the world has been shattered, nothing makes any sense. All hail the power of the bouncing balloon. In the absence of Jesus or him one must accept what one's given.

Grandad is drunk. He thinks it's his eyes playing tricks. When the girl pushes open the taproom door, he has to look over three times. He shouts, "What fresh hell is this? Why've you gone that queer colour?"

"It's all right, Grandad. It's just the dust from the house."

"Thought you were sick." And then, "What house?"

"Just away up the street. Actually more than one house."

"Well, don't walk it in here. Shake yourself off outside first."

"Oh," she says. "Sorry."

"Like a dog, innit?" Grandad says.

Only two o'clock and the taproom is empty, which means he has abandoned his position behind the bar to play-act the role of a carouser instead. He is sat by the window with his boots on a stool, an ill-fitting man who may once have been lithe. His wrists and ankles are too slim for his oversized hands and feet.

"Thought you were sick when it's poor old me that's sick." Theatrically he motions at the empty glass on the table. "Run along and get me my medicine, Luce."

Lucy hesitates. She doesn't know whether she ought to clean herself off in advance.

"Medicine first. Always medicine first. Love of God, can I get some healing here?"

So she splashes scotch from the bottle, regarding him with some interest. "Is that what you want? Healing?"

Grandad grins. He smells of tobacco and carbolic soap. "You, me and everyone. What houses?"

"Those ones up the road. They're not there any more."

He drifts away, comes back again. "Bloody heck, look at you. Go get rid of that dust."

"Sorry." She steps gingerly towards the door. She can't walk any faster; she would leave billowing clouds in her wake.

"Always remember, it's a temple, the Griffin. We can't have people trailing dirt and muck in." Grandad downs half the glass and it's if the afterburn makes him silly, because now he's helpless with laughter and he's not a man who is easily amused. "What we should do, girl, is have the bastards take off their shoes. Put on some white robes. Sit cross-legged on the floor."

"Yes Grandad, all right."

He shouts, "It's our fortune, the Griffin. We must treat it like a temple." Standing on the step, slapping pale dust from her clothes, she can still hear him chuckling inside the taproom.

7

HE HAS BEEN a fat child and a fat soldier and a fat tramp as well. But he thinks he likes himself best as a fat spiritualist. Hello world, the man thinks, I'm a spiritualist. Hello ladies and gents, look at my lovely fat belly. Roll up, roll up, and rub my fat belly for luck. You rub the belly and I'll rub my hands and then my word, bloody hell, we shall see what comes out.

In the town square, the shabby men sell their wares. They lean into their crutches and brandish handkerchiefs and matches. They arrange tarot cards and crystal balls on trestle tables and purport to commune with lost souls for three shillings a pop, despite the fact that none of them hears voices the way he can hear voices and none of them is able to produce the magic he can. The buyers mill about like docile sheep, and he spies a number of child pickpockets darting here and there through the throng, as elusive as ghosts. He admires the pickpockets, whose hand-speed is electric. He has heard that they train themselves by plucking coins out of saucepans filled with boiling water.

He finds a free space in the square and promises miracles. He introduces himself as a fat-bellied firefly and invites passers-by to rub his stomach and then stand back and watch what happens. But his claims are too vague and vulgar; the buyers don't take to him. They remove themselves quickly from his presence, noticing but not noticing, as though they have stumbled into a pocket of bad air. Besides which, he is nervous, which inhibits his gift. He persists for an hour but the flames will not come. An elderly couple eventually take pity and hand him some coppers for food.

For five happy days he was convinced the amulet was his fortune. He would sell it for one hundred pounds and live like a king. He would sell it for ten pounds and check himself into a hotel. He would sell it for one pound and eat until he was sick. But the pendant is worthless. It is cheap costume jewellery, a thing of plaster and paste, and if the first pawnbroker was lying, that meant that the second pawnbroker lied too. And the one after that, and the one after that. So it still hangs off his neck, tapping his chest when he walks. This means that the joke was on him and that he killed Uriah for nothing.

"Oh Uriah," he says. "What a silly-billy I am."

He is what he is: he is God's ultimate bad imp, the Lord's sprightly monkey, the last lonely vestige of an irrational age. Fitfully he sleeps in the draughty nave of the church. Eagerly he positions himself by the bakers, clamouring for day-old loaves, crying, "Look at this big belly. It needs food to fill it". The brim of his bowler is detaching itself. The hems of his trousers have been trod upon 'til they tatter. The odour of stale sweat is coming off him in waves.

It has now reached the stage where he even welcomes the voices. The voices at least speak to him when nobody else can be arsed. He only wishes that the voices would address him more clearly – how nice that would be – or that they would make more sense when they do. Most of the time the voices blow about his brain as an unintelligible murmurous storm. On other occasions he is able to isolate disconnected phrases, although these tend to leave him none the wiser. He is bedevilled by one hushed, feminine voice, which returns at intervals to inform him that she has dropped all of her shopping in a dirty green stream. Another, gruffer voice says, "Chilly out. Chilly out. Chilly out. Chill." He believes that the voices may be those of the dead. He listens for Uriah, but Uriah remains silent.

"Uriah," he cries. "I'm truly sorry I hit you."

"Uriah," he says. "You were like a father to me."

Unable to sleep, he thinks back to the war. Cor blimey, the war – the war always soothes him. Crash bang and wallop, what a wonderful thing. The partridges flushed in droves from the bushes. The horses screaming. All the clowns falling over, like some children's circus. Whenever he's feeling downcast, the war picks him up.

He had been posted to Cambrai and before that to Cape Helles. Cambrai was all right, but Cape Helles was the best. He was given a job disposing of the bodies. Nobody wanted to do it but it really wasn't so bad once you got used to the smell. First he found an old communication trench that had fallen into disuse, lifting his spade to dig into the sand. Next he dragged in the bodies and packed them like sardines, underfoot and in the walls. There were so many bodies there was hardly space for them all. The only problem was the sand, which had a tendency to crumble so that all the dead soldiers slid free or rode up. No sooner had they stiffened than their limbs jutted out. Hard, bony hands extended from the walls on either side. He had a game, he recalls, which helped pass the time. He would walk down the trench, shaking each dead hand in turn, pretending he was a high-born gent greeting a line of dignitaries. He'd grip the hands one by one and cry, "Good day to you, sir!" and "A pleasure to meet you" and

"Upon my soul, you are looking well." It got so he enjoyed stealing back during spare minutes to say hello to the hands and check which new ones had got free.

One morning, after a night of fierce fire, he returned to the trench to find the place altered. Someone had draped the walls, top to bottom, in a thick dark material, like a funeral shroud. This was strange enough as it went, but when he drew closer he thought he must be dreaming, because it seemed that the shroud was made of a living material. It shifted and breathed. It sang in a high, keening note that sounded very nearly human. He narrowed his eyes and stood for a spell, inhaling the odour of bodies and gunpowder and petrol and gas. All those charged atoms coursing through his system. Was it any wonder it had made him light-headed?

After a moment, however, he realised the drapes were not drapes at all. Legions of grubs had evidently hatched overnight and the burial trench was now full of flies. The flies covered everything; he could not see the hands. They were moving and buzzing – several flew up his nose – and when he edged further in he could feel scores of them popping beneath his boots.

Once he took those first steps, he found he could not stop. He walked the length of the trench in a trance, breathing in the stench, thrilling to the murmur of hundreds of thousands of flies. Each of the flies had one hundred and one eyes. Each of those eyes watched the man going by. And then halfway in, as though on cue, the thunder started up again. The gravelly rush of incoming fire. The clap of mortar shells. Everything in noisy flux, everything fizzing and popping, and lowly Arthur Elms stepping like a tightrope artist along the line of voltage, moving through the immensity of the moment, with his thoughts leaking out and atoms pouring in. No wonder he changed. How on earth could he not? The maggots grew wings and the man came out different. Buzzing voices filled his head. His fingers shot sparks when he rubbed them together. It could have happened to anyone. But it had happened to him.

Afterwards when they ran him along to the dressing station, the medic had examined his hands and said it was an atmospheric condition, a temporary reaction; that it would not last very long. But the medic was a fool; he was talking out of his hat. Elms has always struggled to keep track of the dates. Weeks, months and years go by in a blur. He lives in the moment; always has, always will. And yet it seems that the effect has been with him for so long now as to count as permanent, which means that there is no need to worry and that everything is fine. He loves Cape Helles the best because it gave him its gift. Cape Helles showed him that he was destined for great things. Out in the woodland of Kent, Uriah only confirmed it.

Those chancers in the square with their crystals and cards. They haven't a clue; they don't know what he knows. They call themselves spiritualists when what he offers is magic. His fingers create friction and this time they bloom. The day is bright, which makes the flames harder to see, yet still he can feel the warmth against his skin and the sensation lifts him, elates him; his big moment draws near.

"Firefly!" he roars. "I am the human firefly! Come and see what I do!"

"Pipe down, fatty," scolds the matchbox seller with the shattered leg.

"Firefly! Firefly!" He stands in the square with blue flames cupped in his hand. He stands with sweat rings at his armpits and his hat brim come loose. He knows that sooner or later the world will turn and take notice.

8

BARELY A WEEK goes by without Tom stealing fruit from the grocer. The boy cannot help himself – he is touched in the head and nothing attests to his innocence more than his ineptitude as a thief. Dazzled by the sight of strawberries or bananas, Tom will stick out an arm to lift them gently from the stall by the door. But performing this act sends him into a panic. Instead of replacing the fruit, he takes off at a run.

Nan reckons the grocer might be making matters worse, because the more it happens the angrier he grows, and the angrier he grows the louder he shouts, and the louder he shouts, the more likely Tom is to take to his heels instead of returning the fruit. She wishes Higgs could control himself. If one day he could only glance up and say, "Hello, Tom, how you doing there?" she feels sure that Tom would respond in kind and then they would all be spared the same tiresome quarrel, week in and week out.

In the meantime, take cover, because here comes Mr Higgs. His face is flushed, his scalp's gone pink and he is wringing his hands in a manner that suggests he has recently dragged them through nettles. He says, "Mrs Marsh, Mrs Marsh, I must protest yet again."

Nan and Lucy are engaged in washing the windows of the taproom. When Nan breaks off to confront their visitor, the girl makes a show of redoubling her efforts, applying the cloth in a flurry while observing the grocer out of the tail of one eye. Higgs, she knows, is struggling to prop up a failing business, just as her grandfather is struggling to prop up a failing business, just as almost everyone else on Ermine Street is, too. Taxes, bills and the lack of passing trade: it's the same story all over. But it seems to her that the years of anger and worry have made a particularly deep impression on the grocer, leaving him unstable so that he is liable to fly off the handle at the slightest provocation. Somewhere along the line it is as though he has decided that the boy from the pub is embarked upon a personal vendetta, the eventual aim of which can only be to put him out of business. Each time he looks up and sees Tom by the stall, he also sees his own ruin, and possibly the bankruptcy court tucked in close behind.

"Not one banana," he says. "Two bananas."

Nan says, "Mr Higgs, I can only apologise. It is totally unacceptable and he knows that, right enough. And when he comes back, we'll bring him across to tell you how sorry he is."

Higgs, however, will not be mollified. His resistance has hardened with each angry visit. He says the situation has moved beyond neighbourly conversation. The burglary of his produce has become systemic, and he fears that they have now reached the point where the constabulary must be called upon to intervene. He has tried being nice and he has tried being kind, Lord knows he has, but it's a fine line between being kind and being soft, and he realises now that the boy has been laughing at him all this time. It's obvious the lad regards him as an easy mark and in a sense that's his fault because he made the fatal mistake of going all soft when he should have been steely. Well, no more. He's going to be strong from here on. He's going to fetch the constabulary.

Nan says, "Now look. Mr Higgs. Of course he's not laughing at you. The boy runs away because he's scared witless."

Higgs throws a distracted look in Lucy's direction. His scalp shades purple. "I'm having to watch my language because of present company. But there's a word I would use for a boy like that one, a very bad word for a little thief who steals my goods, bold as you please. I'm watching my language here because of the girl."

"Mr Higgs," says Nan.

"Fucker," says Higgs. "That's the word. I'm sorry it got out but there it is."

Lucy puts the cloth in the bucket and turns away from the glass. "I'll go and find him, Nan," she says. "I'll have him bring back what he stole or the money it's worth."

Nan tells her friends that the nurse dropped Tom on his head when he was born and that this is what makes him so slow on the uptake. But then Nan has also been heard to suggest that the exact same thing happened to the butcher boy and the Osborne girl, and once, when a barrel of ale had gone bad without Lucy noticing, her grandmother had shouted, "What's wrong with you, girl? Did the nurse drop you on your head?". This made Lucy think that it was simply a figure of speech; that almost certainly Tom had not been dropped on his head, and neither had the butcher boy or the Osborne girl. Unless they had all been delivered by the same clumsy nurse, and this was surely impossible. The nurse would have lost her job. And besides, Tom was born in St Albans.

All the same, her brother is odd; everybody says so. Like a crystal wireless, he has a habit of drifting away from the signal. Sometimes you can reach him and sometimes you can't.

Lucy throws back the hatch and checks the cellar. She peers

inside the cobbled stalls and behind the door of the gruesome public toilet, but she does all of these things as a matter of course and without any great hope. When Tom's in disgrace, his impulse is to put as much distance as possible between him and the Griffin. Look at me, she marvels. Not five days after playing hide-and-seek in the woods, here I am having to do the same thing again.

She had once asked her mother if there was anything bothering Tom and her mother had told her the birth had been difficult and that he had gone without air for maybe as much as a minute and that this meant that they needed to be patient with him because he always got there in the end. Lucy chose to believe the air explanation rather than the nurse explanation, although even that didn't altogether add up. One, because swimmers held their breath for a minute at a time and never suffered any lasting effects. And two, because didn't babies survive without air for nine months in the womb before the birthing bit began? If Tom could last that long, then what further harm could it do, another minute or two?

Still, the world has always puzzled him. When he walks through a door, the very act of doing so appears to upset his bearings so that he loses sight of whether he is entering or leaving and starts to turn bewildered circles, blocking the way for everybody else. When he's outside he feels overwhelmed and will scarcely speak above a whisper. Indoors he is reassured and over-compensates by shouting. It seems that she is forever telling him to either shut up or speak up.

Everything is heightened. Everything risks being misconstrued. Tom confuses in with out and up with down and someone else's possessions with his own – and then the moment he's put straight, the shock is too great. He is drawn to the fruit, she realises, in the same way he is drawn towards the stagnant water in the horse's trough. Its greasy sheen has the boy entranced; she has seen the way he sidles up and extends a hand to dab at the surface. But when he touches it the ripples alarm him and so he leaps back as if scalded. Lucy loves her brother but she despairs of him too. At school they sit him at the back of the class, with the idiots, and she doubts that the lessons have made much impression. He's only twelve, which means he still has time to improve, and some people are what they call late bloomers. She hopes this is true and fears that it's not, and either way there probably isn't very much she can do. Tom needs a mother, not a sister. And even that, she considers, may still not be enough.

Outside the butcher's, Brinley Roberts occupies himself by making a pattern of footprints in the scattered sawdust. But it is a babyish enterprise, quite beneath his dignity, and he steps hurriedly aside when he sees the girl approaching.

"Where are you going, Lucy-Lu?"

"Looking for my brother."

"If you need a hand, I'm like Sherlock Holmes."

"No, you're alright." The last thing she wants is to be saddled with Brinley.

Lucy heads out. She believes she knows where Tom will have gone, and runs to the parallel street, the arterial road, not quite two hundred yards away and rattling with activity. She can hear the road before she sees it, as a pith-helmeted explorer might hear waves crashing against a rocky beach and know that he has reached the sea again.

The thoroughfare cuts the neighbourhood in two. The road has been widened and resurfaced to accommodate the volume of traffic. No doubt before long it will need to be widened again. She stands at the kerb and takes it all in: the fractious conversation of saloon cars and motorcycles and steam wagons and horse-drawn carts. These contraptions are too different, she thinks; they will never get along. And yet each is under the impression that the road belongs to them alone. In the midst of the melee, a white-gloved policeman is attempting to play the role of mediator, but his presence only serves to inflame the situation. Now the drivers squeeze their horns and the motor vehicles start to blat and squawk like angry geese on a pond.

Then along come the buses, to make the mess even worse. Nan is of the opinion that there are too many buses at large in London, and here is the evidence to back up her case. The red two-deckers of the General Omnibus Company are at loggerheads with the blue-and-green two-deckers from London Transport & Haulage and these in turn are being preyed on by a band of low-slung, six-wheeled interlopers that operate under the banner of Capital Buses and slope out each morning from a set of warehouses in Penge. All of them congregate at the same stops to bicker and honk over the same set of passengers. Something needs to be done; the whole thing is chaos. No one can be entirely sure that the driver is going where he insists he is going. Nan likes to tell the tale of her friend Mary, who boarded a bus to visit a daughter in Romford and looked up from her paperback to find herself in Chipping Ongar instead.

Lucy stands at the kerb surrounded by the din and the fumes, the scaffolding and sheets of tarpaulin and drooping electrical wires. Then she spies a break in the traffic, hitches her hem to her knees and scampers across to the opposite side.

He is in the milk bar, amid the chromium and glass, the

smells of detergent and soured cream. He is staring at the fish inside their dirty tank. The proprietor motions her in with a tilt of his head, the same way he did on her previous visit; they have been through this before. He'd rather the lad bought himself a beaker of something, but life's too short to raise a fuss, plus it's not as if he's doing anyone any harm. Live and let live, that's what the proprietor says.

Softly, so as not to startle him, she says, "All right there, Tom? Have you got those bananas?"

"Ate 'em," he says, without looking around.

"*Sssh*. Inside voice, Tom."

"Ate 'em," says Tom, again, but she wonders whether this is true. She thinks that more likely the guilt overtakes him, and that he panics and offloads the fruit on the first person he passes, or hurls it at stray dogs or hedges in a bid to shake himself free of the crime. It would be simpler if he ate the fruit; it would make no difference to his punishment. And yet a nagging sibling instinct tells her he never actually does.

"Wolfed them both down, did you? And I bet they tasted lovely."

When she attempts to coax Tom outside, he says he needs to wait just a few more minutes in order to see what the fish do next – as if the fish are likely to do anything they haven't done a thousand times already that day, which is basically taking aimless laps of the tank. But whenever she wants him to accompany her anywhere, his instinct is to stall. He seems to feel that whatever comes next can only be worse, and this outlook strikes her as both silly and sad; she cannot think where he gets it from. He didn't want to leave the house, so possibly it all stems from that. He didn't want his dad to die and he didn't want his mum to die, but then so what, who did? Terrible things happen all the time and there is nothing to do but hope that whatever comes next will be brighter and better.

Lucy says that she has a good idea: she is going to tell him what they are about to do. How about they don't walk back to the Griffin just yet? How about they visit some shops and buy lots of fancy new clothes? Then they could take the train into town and catch a show for the night, one of those comedy shows, full of jokes and pratfalls.

"All right, Luce. But first of all we watch the fish."

There are three of them inside the tank. They have black-scaled bodies and lacy grey fins. She does not think they can be English fish. They have been brought in from some warm foreign sea to swim in tap water and eat bread crumbs, butter or grease, whatever the diners see fit to feed them.

"They're like brides."

"Inside voice, remember. Who's like a bride?"

"The fish. It looks like they're wearing wedding dresses."

"Oh yes, I see what you mean. All we have to do is find them each a groom."

"I'm sorry I took the bananas," he says. "I didn't mean to and I'll never do it again."

"Inside voice, Tom." But she ruffles his hair and he briefly turns his face from the tank. His features are drawn and spaced exactly as hers are. You can trace a line from him to her and then to their father and then back to Grandad and then most probably back deeper than that, to his grandad's great grandad, and then maybe deeper than that, all the way down to the dawn of man.

At the counter the proprietor wipes his hands on his apron and says, "One day the pair of you are going to order a drink or a slice of cake and then you know what'll happen? I'll drop dead of heart failure."

"Why?" shouts Tom. This prospect alarms him.

Lucy waves a hand. "We might come by this evening, as a matter of fact, on our way home from the show. Mightn't we, Tom? We'll come in a taxi and tell it to wait outside while we eat dinner."

The proprietor says, "In that case I'll have to reserve you a table. The duchess was meant to be in later, but I'll tell her she can go and boil her head. Why have her sort when we can have you two instead?

"Charmed and delighted."

"She's joking!" cries Tom. "She's joking! Don't really reserve us a table."

But a minute later she hears a clink and turns to discover that the proprietor has poured two glasses of milk and set them at her elbow. He performs this service so discreetly that Lucy is at a loss and finds herself overcome with shyness and is utterly incapable of acknowledging it. Head bowed, she reaches for one of the glasses and hands it to Tom and then takes a furtive sip from the other, enough to know that the milk is cool and good and that it tastes all the better for the fact of it being free. The proprietor stands with his back to her. He is clearing crockery from the table by the door. Lucy turns back, stares intently at the fish tank and risks another sip to clear the frog from her throat. She draws a breath and says, "Charmed and delighted, charmed and delighted. That is to say that my brother is charmed and I am delighted."

"Inside voice, Lucy," says the boy at her side.

Way back when you could still expect a proper sit-down restaurant service at the Griffin public house, the Tottenham Hotspur first eleven stopped by to feast on warm beef, cold cuts, mashed potato and veg. When the food had been served and the guests were eating, Duncan Marsh sat himself at a spare table and scribbled deft caricatures of the best-known players. He drew likenesses of Arthur Grimsdell and Charlie Rance. He conjured James Cantrell into a pious choirboy and made a gurning old man out of stolid Bert Bliss. Marsh was a gifted amateur artist and his pictures generated much hilarity when they were circulated alongside the whisky and cigars.

Also sitting with the squad that day was a man named Harry Norman, who worked as a sports reporter for the Daily Mail. At the end of the meal, Norman took Marsh aside and mentioned that his editor might be on the lookout for cartoonists and that the publican should post a selection of his work to the London office. Flushed with drink, Marsh shook the reporter's hand and politely thanked him for his interest. He added that he had never been the sort of fellow to go cap in hand for work, that was just the way he had been brought up, but that if the editor cared to contact him direct then he would, of course, be open to offers.

Ten years on, he remembers that night clear as day. The saloon bar thronged with hearty, drunken athletes and him sat there too, at ease in their company. Anybody coming in through the door would have taken him for a member of the squad and in a sense he had been, at least for that night. He wishes he had kept hold of those caricatures; he wouldn't half mind having a look at them now. He wishes as well that he had kept on with the drawing. The newspaper editor had never seen fit to contact him with an offer.

Times were good. Now times are bad. He blames the

council and the new thoroughfare. He blames the war and the flu and the weather and the brewery. He blames whatever he thinks he can get away with blaming. Inside the taproom he suffers through halting, circular, borderline incoherent exchanges with his remaining handful of regulars. Week nights it is usually just tragic Mrs Kitteridge and three alcoholic Irish hod carriers whom he has taken to referring to as the Collapsed Catholics, even though there is nobody else to acknowledge the joke. The regulars like to drink and he's grateful for that, but there's hardly enough of them to keep the publican busy. When no one's glass needs freshening, he freshens his own.

In the good old days when the air was sweet, Duncan Marsh relied on Coach to keep him stocked with food. Coach is head groundsman at some lavish estate out near Harlow or Hertford or one of those places – the sort of spread where the swells are always riding to hounds and blasting pheasants with buckshot. So long as their dinner is served at the correct hour every night and they find their knickers freshly ironed by the fire each morning, the swells don't give too much of a toss what their servants are up to. In consequence, Coach and his brother were able to develop a nice little sideline providing fresh meat from the grounds to various restaurants and pubs. The estate had become so clogged with animals, with roe deer, rabbit, duck, sheep and trout, that nobody noticed when a few – or a few score – went missing. Marsh had heard of the poacher-turned-gamekeeper, but Coach had gone better still. He was gamekeeper, thief, butcher and delivery boy, all rolled up in the self-same package.

You had to hand it to Coach: he'd seen business opportunities where nobody else would think of looking. Marsh paid

Coach less than half what he once paid for the same meat at Smithfield, but that was OK because it was straight profit for Coach; all he was giving up was a few hours each week. The arrangement had worked well until the saloon bar stopped taking orders.

He's had no dealings with the groundsman for well over a year when the door heaves to and Coach walks in. Marsh is delighted to see him; he could use some conversation. He pours out a pint and fetches the tobacco for his pipe. When Coach asks how the Griffin is faring, he goes easy on the gloss because what's the point of doing otherwise? His hands play pat-a-cake upon the bar. The taxes. The opening hours. The arterial road. If that wasn't enough, he has somehow managed to rupture himself while walking the barrels from the cellar. For the past five months he has been wearing a truss. He can feel his innards sloshing whenever he rises from his chair.

Mrs Kitteridge, soused on Red Biddies, calls, "Oh give it a rest, Marshy-Moo. We'll have to get the violins out again."

"Shut your pie-hole," the publican says.

Coach sucks his pint, shakes his head and remarks that it's the same story all over. Most of the pubs he once worked with have either gone to the dogs or shut up shop and it's not just the hoi polloi who are feeling the pinch if that's any comfort – the swells are having a rough old time of it too. Up at Grantwood, where he works, the old master has all but given up the ghost and retired to his bed. In the meantime, all of his duties have devolved to the young master, who's prone to hare-brained schemes – he keeps throwing money at fripperies and cutting back on essentials. Anyway, says Coach, you should see Grantwood today. The taxes have crippled it, you'd hardly recognise the place. Half the staff have been let go, indoors and out, while a wing of the main house has been closed off, left to rot.

And the garden, he adds, it would break a man's heart. He and Crisis used to keep the front lawns perfect. You could eat your dinner off the freshly rolled grass. But guess what it is now: it's a fucking sheep meadow. They've let the livestock in to graze. You walk out the door and down the steps and start fighting your way through a hundred shaggy brutes. They shit where they stand and you have to shut all the windows to keep their stink and bleating from sending you half round the bend. It's no wonder the old master has taken to his sick-bed. Coach has half a mind to ask him to budge over and make room for him, too.

"Anyway," he says again. "That's my share of hard times. How about the family? How are those youngsters getting on?"

"The boy's an imbecile," Marsh says. "He can't do a thing except eat, sleep and lift things that don't belong to him. I'd sell him to Canada except the wife would complain. The grandchildren are another cross I must bear."

"The girl seems all right. And quite tidy looking, the last time I checked."

"Ah well," says Marsh. "Maybe she'll get lucky and marry a professional type."

Leaning in, Coach says, "You know I got this other business thing going. The meat trade is dead, it's not worth my while, but I got this other thing going. I might have told you before, we're active in charity work. Over at Grantwood, we look after these chaps. I must have told you before about the chaps we look after."

Marsh nods.

"Poor buggers. Nobody wants them and they don't get out

73

much. But they've money to spend, what with bits of allowance and the charity dances the young master lays on. They don't get out much, for obvious reasons. What they like best is a walk in the fresh air and a spot of nice human company."

Marsh says, "This used to be the finest country on earth. Now, like you say, it's going to the dogs."

Coach explains that he has taken to organising field trips out to Epping Forest every Sunday when the weather is nice. The lads benefit from a change of scene in a secluded spot away from prying eyes, and so much the better if they have some company too. The tragedy of it is that they are still young men, poor buggers, and yet most people won't touch them with a bargepole. One nice thing about youngsters, Coach says, is that they still have that innocence about them, which means they are able to judge the quality of the man as opposed to what condition his hide is in. Just lately he's started tapping up a few of his old clients to see if they could use an extra bob or two and whether any of their offspring might like to help out with the charity. The funny men are grateful and the kids seem to like it, and if they like it then job done, Coach is happy too.

"The money's no great shakes, they don't have much to spare. But I reckon I can stretch to ten shillings a week. That isn't bad when you break it down. Few hours every Sunday evening and home by midnight."

"Ten bob ain't much."

"It's no king's ransom, I won't lie to you. But we're strapped, ain't we? You and me both. The whole bloody country."

Marsh's cigarette has gone out. He relights it in a fumbling fashion and then frowns at the groundsman. "What exactly are you saying here?"

"Use your imagination. Or don't. That might be better. Don't use your imagination. The one thing I will say is nothing bad happens. I personally guarantee the safety of all the youngsters. They are under my care at all times. The other thing I would say is that the chaps are gentlemen. You know me well enough to know I wouldn't have any doings with them otherwise."

Marsh says nothing. He glances over Coach's shoulder to ensure that nobody's ears are twitching. But the Collapsed Catholics are deep in conversation, while Mrs Kitteridge appears to have fallen asleep. Her chin is parked on her chest and her dentures have slid free.

"The chaps are gents and the youngsters are all first-rate. That's the other thing I ought to mention. Polite, respectable. Little angels, every one. It brings out the best in them. They take the work seriously and they can see the good it does."

"And what do you do?" Masks asks, his volume jumping a notch. "You and Crisis, out in the woods. What part do you play?"

The groundsman appears profoundly amused by the question. He requires a moment to collect himself. "Heavens to Betsy. I'm glad you think I still have it in me. Nothing, Mr Marsh. We don't do anything, hand on heart, that's not my bag. I'm shocked you'd even ask me."

"Well, I don't know, I don't know." He draws on his cigarette and discovers it has died on him yet again. In his confusion he has somehow managed to secrete his matches in his seat pocket and retrieving the things proves to be quite the ordeal. "My fucking guts," he says.

Coach pulls a commiserating face.

"I don't know. I'll have to think about it."

75

"One other thing you might want to think about. Last thing, hand on heart. Officially speaking, these men do not exist. So you could say that whatever goes on never actually happened. Whatever relations your youngster has with my chaps do not really exist. And if that's the case then your conscience is clear."

Marsh grimaces. "The ten shillings exists, though, don't it?"

"The ten shillings does exist. Except that this time it's passing from my hand to yours."

"I think I like it better that way."

"I thought you might."

The pints have been sunk and the hour hand has spun full circle on the mantelpiece clock. The groundsman says it's been good to have a catch-up. He explains that he'll call back next week, once Marsh has had time to mull on it awhile. It was just a thought and the money might help, but so far as he's concerned it makes no odds either way. Marsh shakes his hand and says it's not for him. He adds that he's mulling it now and the more that he mulls, the more sick he feels. "Sweet God almighty," he says.

"No harm done. Just a thought."

For all that, the landlord likes Coach and is oddly deflated by the thought of his departure. He doesn't want to part on bad terms; he hopes his old supplier will stop by again. So he walks the groundsman out to his lorry, not even worrying that he has left the bar untended, despite the fact that on several occasions he has returned from the convenience to discover the Collapsed Catholics huddled sheepishly over tankards that strike him as having been recently topped up. Oily bastards, greedy pigs. One day they'll dose themselves so high they'll stumble right off the scaffolding, cement trays and all, and maybe then they'll stop laughing. It'll be good night and lights out.

On the street, blinking in the sun, he says, "I have to hand it to you, Coach, you're a right crafty sod, always something going on the sly."

"I told you. This is charity work."

"Oh yeah, and the other one has bells on. I'm betting you and Crisis get a little taste of it too."

"Barely enough to keep us in socks." He cranks the engine and clambers into the cab.

"Crafty sod. I don't know how you live with yourself. And just the girls you're interested in, yes? Dirty bastard."

Coach shoots him a quizzical look.

"I mean, let's say I said, 'Oh yes, it sounds spiffing' and then offered to throw the little lad in as well. Then that would be twenty shillings each Sunday instead of the ten. But oh no, crafty sod only wants to take the girls on his field trips."

The groundsman pulls the door shut and pops one elbow out the window. "Marshy, calm down," he says, loud enough to be heard over the engine's throb. "As it goes we do have a boy, a nice enough lad, but we don't need another. If you want I can let you know when the situation becomes vacant."

The publican considers his grandchildren. He considers the Griffin and the arterial road. The bills and the brewery and the licensing laws. The six months, tops, he has to turn the whole place around. He has a sudden urge to kick the door of the Maudslay, but instead he staggers backwards, as though the very truck is diseased. His intestines joggle; the truss can't hold him together. "You're a dirty, crafty bastard, Coach. Charity work, is it? It sounds like you're still in the meat trade to me. The more I think about it, the more sick it makes me."

77

Coach nods as if to say that this is right and proper. He says, "You're a good man, Marshy. But the world will ask us questions." Growling and rattling like a living thing, the truck eases its wheels from the kerb and crawls away up the street.

9

I N THE WOODS they lay out their picnics and play hide-and-seek. One day Crisis brings a kite and after a few false starts they are able to get it aloft. Her heart catches at the sight of that bright yellow diamond hanging high above their heads. The string tugs in her grip as though inviting her to let her body go limp and light and be carried along too, and for one lovely moment she is convinced it could happen.

When Coach is in a good mood he lets either her or Fred into the cab to steer the Maudslay on the forest track. Much to his chagrin, John is not extended the same privilege; nor is Edith, although she insists she couldn't care less either way. Lucy knows that the girl is still smarting over her altercation with the Cowardly Lion and hopes that, given time, she will come around. She enjoys sitting behind the wheel, navigating the narrow path, although the Maudslay's power frightens her and she always climbs out with a sense of having just been thrown free of a runaway horse. One evening in the woods she drinks gin and smokes three cigarettes, one after the other, and spends the entire trip back clinging to the backboard, about to be sick. She is always home by midnight. She keeps the door key safely in her sock.

With each fresh visit, it is as though the world shifts and resettles, or it may be that it is she who is shifting while the world stays the same. The visits are odd; there is no escaping their oddness. And yet the more she comes to know the funny men, the less conspicuous and clamorous their funniness seems. She finds herself regarding them almost as children, almost as peers; not really so different from Brinley or Edgar or any of the other noisy, uncertain boys who like to jostle her in the school playground. They only want to be noticed. They only want to be loved.

By now she has come to appreciate the brash, cheerful Toto and the quiet, clever Scarecrow. Winifred is right – the Tin Woodman is dashing and romantic and never mind his appearance because he certainly doesn't seem to, arriving with his morning suit pressed and his hair as oiled as an otter's back. Only the Lion continues to vex her. He is docile with Fred and wary of everyone else. Even the other funny men treat him as a colleague to be tolerated rather than a friend to include. Lucy chooses to think of him as a benign, broken soul – not dissimilar to the blind horse on Ermine Street – and makes a valiant effort to bond with him and have him walk with her for a spell. But when she takes his hands, he shakes his head.

"I'm afraid I'm not much use today," he tells her haltingly. "I'm afraid I'm not much use on any day."

Afterwards she will count even this as a victory of sorts. He let her take hold of his hands. He spoke directly to her alone. She resolves that one day the Lion will come to trust her as he trusts Fred. She does wish he had not set about Edith that time. She hopes that Edith overreacted. Privately she thinks that she probably did.

Out on the trail, the Tin Woodman sings songs. Walking alongside, she picks up the lyrics from ditties and laments to the point where she can provide a pleasing harmony. They sing 'In Dublin's Fair City' and 'Don't Do That To the Poor

Puss-Cat' and 'I Know Where Flies Go', which always strikes her as unaccountably sad. "Lay their eggs and fly away, come back on the first of May. Hatch their eggs and oh what joy, first a girl and then a boy."

The trees are a mystery until the Scarecrow explains them. The pair of them come rambling through thousands of bedraggled, sagging bluebells and he casually identifies every tree in their path, as though naming them on the very first day. Oak and beech are plentiful; they dominate the surrounding land. But the Scarecrow also teaches her how to recognise the hornbeam, the sycamore and the silver birch. He tells her that the trees in the forest are several centuries old but have been kept healthy by a process called pollarding, which involves stripping back the upper limbs. When a tree is top-heavy it will topple or split and very likely crash into its neighbours and bring them down as well. The pollarding prevents that; it ensures growth and progress. He says that every society, however advanced, could use some pollarding every now and again.

Lucy wonders why the Scarecrow wears a leather mask whereas the Tin Man opted for painted copper. She feels it would be impolite to ask. It is another of Fred's Terrible Unmentionables. It sometimes feels that there are too many to count.

Instead she asks who dreamed up their names. If the Scarecrow named the trees, then who named the Scarecrow? By now they are walking back through the clearing. Coach overhears and says that Grantwood House named them and that, in fact, without Grantwood House they would not be people at all.

The Scarecrow snorts, but he admits that what Coach says

is more or less true. "Without Grantwood House there'd be none of us and no trips to the forest. You could say that the Wizard of Oz resides at Grantwood House."

"What's that?" calls Coach.

"I said that Grantwood House made us what we are."

"Now then. That's gratitude for you."

So far as Lucy can work out, the funny men spend virtually all of their time inside a small workers' cottage somewhere to the north of Epping Forest, where they are provided for by a kind – and presumably wealthy – benefactor. It appears that these Sunday trips are their only regular outings, and this pleases her. She feels flattered by the attention all over again.

Crisis keeps a football in the cab and angles for any excuse to introduce it to the party. A game of traditional football is out of the question, what with the funny men's frailties, although they eventually devise a compromise whereby Crisis and Coach take opposite sides and Toto and the Lion are installed as rival goalkeepers, and play is halted every few minutes to allow the Tin Man and Scarecrow to kick from the penalty spot. Fred christens the game "funny football" and it succeeds after a fashion and seems to mollify Crisis, even if the Lion is never entirely at his ease in goal. He has a habit of abandoning his post whenever the players' attentions are directed elsewhere. Time and again Fred must be sent off to retrieve him.

Sunday after Sunday, the weather is fair which surely counts as a blessing. Lucy eats trifle and screws her face in distaste as she prepares to tackle another cigarette. She plays hide-and-seek and funny football and learns the difference between the hornbeam and the sycamore. The forest is teeming with fox and deer and rabbits and owls, but although she strikes out from the clearing in every direction, she never encounters another human soul. Standing still, barely breathing, she listens for the sound of the Kindred of the Kibbo Kift. She hears nothing but birdsong, acorns dropping and the wind in the leaves.

On Lucy's fifth visit, Coach reaches the clearing first, which means that Crisis is late. They stand in the shade and watch the rumbling, rocking approach of the covered truck up the rutted path. He is coming too fast, he risks breaking an axle. "Something's not right," Coach says in a mutter and Lucy looks at Winifred and sees that she's nervous too. And yet Coach's alarm turns out to be unfounded because Crisis is grinning when he steps down from the cab. The reason he's late is down to the fact that he stopped off at the dairy, and the reason he's rushing is that he has bought a silver pail of ice-cream and does not want it to melt. From behind the canvas in the bed of the truck, Toto broadcasts that he is sorry to report that he has already consumed most of it on the drive from the dairy, but the children are laughing; they know that he's joking. Lucy is glad to see Edith and John laughing too. Few people, however committed, can maintain a show of sullen resistance when confronted by a tin bucket filled with vanilla ice-cream.

"But do we have spoons?" Fred wails. "Imagine the nightmare if we didn't have spoons."

"We got spoons, don't you worry."

"Thank heavens for that. I would have had to kill you all off and keep the bucket to myself."

They sit in a circle and pass round the pail. Crisis has done his best, he came as fast as he could and dragged his undercarriage along the forest floor, but inevitably the ice-cream is half-melted by the time it's brought out and proceeds to turn liquid in the minutes that follow. Lucy doesn't mind – she likes it just as well. The taste is sublime, it's like honey from Lapland.

She hands on the pail and observes the diners. John is too greedy. In racing to get the spoonful to his mouth, he dribbles most of it down his front. The Lion's hands twitch but he refuses assistance. He's worse than John, he's a total mess. Coach smokes as he eats – his spoon in one hand, his briar pipe in the other – which strikes her as foolish; it means his attention is divided and his enjoyment, too. She wishes for his sake that he could manage to leave off smoking until the dessert has been finished.

Toto catches her eye. His hands jump as well. "Dinner with the monsters."

"Oh please. Not a bit."

Fred cackles at her side. "Lucy's a nice girl. She's as sweet as ice-cream."

When the pail reaches the Tin Man, he turns away from the circle, puts his back to the children and uses his hook to raise the bottom edge of his mask. Then the Scarecrow takes the spoon and lifts it to his friend's mouth and later applies his handkerchief to mop up the excess. If Lucy leapt up and shimmied to her right, she might catch a glimpse of the Tin Man's true face, but of course she does not. Still, it is hard not to wonder what he might look like. Fred has told her that the reason Tinny wears a mask is because he is the most beautiful man who ever lived, far too beautiful to be gazed at with the naked eye, it would be like staring straight into the sun. What a fabulous notion; she'd love to believe it. But she doesn't, not deep down, and she suspects Fred doesn't either.

84

"One day soon," Toto is saying. "One day soon you'll be able to freeze the back of that lorry. You'll be able to seal off the back and keep the temperature down."

"Who will?" says Crisis.

"You will. What I mean is, you'll be able to buy a refrigerated lorry and deliver fresh meat and fruit and ice-cream all over the country."

"How do you work that out?" demands Coach.

"Stands to reason. Give it a few years and they'll be all over. Refrigerated lorries. Refrigerated trains."

"Refrigerated submarines," puts in the Tin Man.

"I'll tell you, Coach, word to the wise. If I had my time over and was still out and about, it would be the refrigeration business for me, no question."

"What bollocks you talk: refrigerated trains," says Coach. But he says it fondly; he enjoys conversing with Toto.

The Scarecrow is fortunate in that the leather mask does not extend to his mouth and chin. He helps himself to a spoonful and passes the pail and Lucy sees that he too has dripped dessert down his shirt. He says, "Edith, you're the most sensible one here. Tell us about the outside world. Is it ready for the arrival of refrigerated trains?"

"I don't know," Edith says, frowning. "I don't think so. How can you can get electric power to something without using a cable?"

Crisis claps his hands. "Ha! That's you shut-up, Toto. Little Edith just went and took you to school."

The world reaches the funny men in little glimmers, in Chinese whispers. These days they know it only from the newspaper, or from their conversations with Coach and Crisis, or from snatched glimpses through the slits in the canvas as they are driven out from the house. Toto has read that there are now two hundred thousand motorised vehicles on the roads of England. He reckons that the number is bound to increase further still, which will be good in some ways and detrimental in others. There has to be a consequence of all those exhaust fumes; it's going to poison the whole country. The sky is going to fill up like a boil and one day it will burst. The Scarecrow agrees, but the Tin Man feels otherwise. The Tin Man says that the world is big and open enough to accommodate a few extra exhaust pipes along with all the factory chimneys it's got working already. And in any case, the smoke and fumes will simply float up and out of the Earth's atmosphere. Even if the world isn't big enough, the universe is limitless. Let all the poison pour up to the heavens where it can make a few space aliens cough and leave the rest of us to walk in nature and smell the roses at our leisure.

Now Coach chips in to point out that the problem with the traffic isn't poisonous fumes but accidents. Hardly a day goes by when he doesn't witness some collision or other and some of these have been fatal, like that smash outside of Ware last month: the labourers tossed like refuse out of the back of the truck; the woman pedestrian with her head stoved in. What a bloody sight, he still can't shake the memory.

"Lawlessness is what it is," Crisis says. "It's all the same problem. No respect for the road and no respect for anything on either side of the road neither. That's why this country's in the mess it's in, with the king getting barracked and un-employment lines and what-not, and Bolsheviks on every corner. Everybody wanting something for nothing and it's the common working man who's left holding the bill."

The Tin Man chuckles. "Crisis loves the old world. But it's already been and gone."

"Yeah well, what of it?"

"Poor Crisis. One foot in the past. You want to look to the future. Pick up some new fashions. Start learning new dances. Come to think of it, what did the old world ever do for the common working man anyway? At least these days the poor buggers have got a fighting chance."

"Hark at him. We'll have to paint that mask red."

Coach says, "Working men, they call themselves. Peasants, I call them. As soon as you start barracking the king, you've lost your argument. Traitor bastards, I call them."

The Scarecrow says, "Crisis, you idiot. We're all peasants here. We're all wanting the same thing they do."

"My point exactly," the Tin Man says, "It's not red to look on the bright side. It's not only Bolshies who want the future to be better. You know me, I'm the eternal optimist; I like to see the good in everyone. At least these protesters and picket lines are trying to get something done. You have to applaud them for trying at least."

"Amen to that," says the Scarecrow.

Coach says, "Now I know you must be making a sport of us. What do the pair of you know about the future? For fuck's sake, look at yourselves."

Toto raises his hand for calm. "Can we leave off the politics for a bit? It's a lovely night and there's ladies present. On top of all that, it sends my dinner down the wrong way."

Yet later, looking back, she will recall this as her favourite evening in the forest. She will remember the warm air and the cool grass and the delicious melted ice-cream that slipped off the steel spoon on its way to her mouth. And she will recall her delight at being party to an adult conversation that attempted to gather the loose threads of the world and braid them into sense. Fred is always looking for the chance to interject and make a joke, under the impression that this is what is expected of her. But Lucy is content to sit quietly: to absorb all the arguments and weigh up what's said. She thinks she sides with the Scarecrow and the Tin Man, but she cannot say for certain. Her head pinwheels with images of picket lines and car collisions and poor George V in the thick of the mob, his crown all askew, his mouth agape. She needs a moment to knock her thoughts into shape.

"Let's get the refrigerated lorries on the road first of all," says Toto. "Then we can start planning all of our perfect tomorrows."

The world is confusing, but the forest is not. By now the girl has grown accustomed to its Sunday evening rhythms; the movement of bodies is as stately as a waltz. The trucks trundle into the clearing at around seven o'clock, drawing in from opposite directions until the very last leg when they navigate the same lonely trail. The occupants dismount and mingle for a spell and then, at roughly the point where day turns to night, they fan out into the thicket, leaving Coach and Crisis to stand watch at the vehicles. They are like the keepers at a lighthouse, guiding the wayfarers back to port by the orange glow of their briar pipes; Lucy can see them and smell them from the edge of the trees. Finally, when everybody has been safely gathered, the trucks grumble into life, headlights flaring, and take off down the track. The last movement is complete and Monday morning is already idling on the eastern horizon.

The ice-cream has been eaten. The spoons rattle and scrape inside the silver pail and she sees John shoot out a finger to collect one stray globule from the ground. And now, with great ceremony, the Tin Woodman rises to his feet and turns his bronze face to the group. He says, "I'm an incorrigible fellow and I do pray your indulgence but I am hoping I might follow one dessert with another. I now require some gentle soul to escort me on one last lap of the Yellow Brick Road, all the way to the gates of this Emerald City I've heard tell about. Lucy," he says. "I wonder if you might oblige."

10

SIX MILES FROM base, banking low over farmland, Lieutenant Bram Connors is caught by enemy artillery and knows he is lost. The rounds arrive from below and run him through like a sewing machine, punching a line of holes across the wooden frame of the fuselage. His elbow is clipped and turns instantly numb so that his hand slips on the stick and the sky slides through a sick revolution. The engine coughs and catches and then coughs again. And, curiously, what rolls into the airman's mind at this moment is the refrain from the American battle hymn which he has not heard sung for years. *He hath loosed the fateful lightning of His terrible swift sword.*

He has been flying Camels for eight months, thereabouts. By rights he should know what he is doing; he normally does know what he's doing; others think he is good. But now his senses are scrambled and he cannot get his bearings and the Camel has turned on him, just as they warned him it would. Everybody hates the Sopwith Camel. They hate it because they fear it and they fear it because it is high-strung and inconsistent, like a temperamental thoroughbred. It is front-loaded but bottom-heavy. Handle it with too much vigour and it goes into wild oscillations. It's always straining at the reins, desperate to slew to its starboard side. He's heard that as many pilots crash the Camel as are brought down by enemy fire, which is another way of saying that the bi-plane has killed them, that it does Archie's work for him.

Except that Connors doesn't buy it; he has always loved the Camel. He loves its skittish, darting motions; its very weightlessness is gorgeous. You need to hold it lightly, gently, as though you are dowsing for water with a rod of witch hazel, and then when you find it, the response is electrifying. Slide up and under the enemy plane. Catch Archie napping and then let the guns rip. Nothing turns to the right faster than a Sopwith Camel – it is like the welterweight boxer who throws a cold-cocking left hook. Connors loves the Camel and he assumes the Camel loves him back, and maybe it does until the moment it's hit, when it promptly pounces on the nearest person to hand, which naturally turns out to be the man in the seat.

If he can steady himself, he may yet survive; stranger things have happened. He engages full-right rudder to balance the twisting torque of the engine mass. He bears down on the stick, hoping to outrun the danger, but it could be that he has somehow managed to double back on himself, for now he is threaded by another incoming round. This one comes running clean up the hemline, not stitching but unpicking, God's terrible swift sword. The plane porpoises and levels out. Connors has time to draw a breath and then the fuel tank behind his seat explodes. It seems to him that this makes no sound. It registers only as a pulse in his eardrums instantly followed by a hot draft at his back.

The plane is aflame. The engine has convulsions. He turns to starboard and notes that the propeller has slowed to the point where he can identify each blade. His helmet has caught light; he can smell the leather burning. Unthinkingly he unstraps the thing and yanks it loose except that this is a mistake because now his hair is a bonfire, he can smell that burning too. The cockpit flares and the glass blows out of the windscreen frame. Connors does not know whether this is the result of the heat or a fresh artillery strike. He doesn't suppose it matters much either way.

The propeller spins through one last lazy rotation before coming to a halt. He takes his hands off the stick and shuts his eyes on the blaze. The heat is intense. He can feel his lids crisping, while the rinds of his ears have started to prickle; they might be guttering like candle wicks. He has no idea which way he is pointed or what altitude he is hanging at. He has no idea of anything beyond the one salient fact, so glaringly obvious it doesn't even need stating.

Glory, glory hallelujah, he thinks.

The field is waiting and the Camel descends to greet it, gushing flames and trailing smoke and twisting in the final few seconds to present its favoured starboard wing, as though proffering a hand to be kissed. Then the plane strikes the ground and proceeds to undress itself with a series of languid, heavy movements, delivering constituent parts to stage left and stage right. The wings detach and the fuselage collapses. The plywood panels peel off the plane's hide and some are still aflame when they are tossed back into the air.

Inside the cockpit, he feels the impact go through him. He feels it in the roots of his teeth and the knuckles of his spine, and the effect is so immense that it is almost pleasurable. He is a rock that has been slapped by a wave. He is Saul turned to Paul on the road to Damascus. Now it is as though the fuselage is being sent one way while he's sent the other. He is aware his arm has snagged on the wire frame that holds the chassis in place, but before he can turn his head to investigate, the dispute is resolved and the resistance has gone and with that he's thrown free. He comes to rest in wet mud and this puts him out with the swift, unfussy efficiency of a bucket of sand.

Connors stands up and falls down, stands up and falls down. On his third attempt his balance is better and his legs have some strength and he manages three confident strides before he falls down yet again. He draws deep breaths and makes himself wait and finds that it is wrong what they say: turns out it's the fourth time that's the charm.

He thinks of his home by the stream and of his job at the printworks. He thinks of his wife and he thinks of his son. But he does all this with great effort, as though dredging for a dream. He is not the man he was before.

Glory, glory hallelujah. God's terrible swift sword.

During his months in the flying corps, Lieutenant Bram Connors has flown over numerous muddy fields in northern Europe – too many to count and more than enough to know that it is unwise to be caught trespassing in the wrong sort of field. Some fields are good and some fields are bad. To put it bluntly, he does not know which side he has landed on. In the time between being struck and coming down, he estimates that he may have travelled a little more than a mile, but there is no way of telling the direction he was pointed. He decides to strike off in the opposite direction, cross his fingers and hope for the best.

Connors' legs hold him up and he is able to walk. Now his arms are the issue. It is clear that he has been winged on both flanks, one evidently worse than the other; he cannot lift the left limb at all. He also finds that his face or head keeps dripping fluid onto the front of his coat. Some of the fluid is mud, but he concedes that it is not exclusively mud.

He clumps and squelches his way out of one field and then crosses another. The hedgerows stand shattered and the trees have been so brutalised that they barely qualify as trees. He walks past indeterminate bits of the Camel, still smoking and creaking, not quite laid to rest. What he initially takes for a section of plough turns out to be one his propellers poking up from the ground.

But he is feeling good; adrenalin holds him upright. Spying the straight edge of a rooftop, he adjusts his line and comes skidding down a slope towards a distempered farmhouse, shuttered and abandoned. The tap in the forecourt is useless, but there is a fishing lake tucked close behind and a row of horse chestnuts which are still in leaf. All at once he is ravenously thirsty; he could drink the lake dry. The breath booms and catches against his eardrums. His respiration sounds like tidal swells.

His right arm is heavy but it does what it's told. Fresh blood has run down his wrist to pool in his palm. Yet aside from the thirst, he is still feeling quite well. He skirts the building and heads across to the lake, thinking he will remove his clothes and wash off the worst of the mud. He might splash some water on his face, to at least moisten his mouth and his eyes, which have turned so gummy that his lids stick when he blinks.

The world has been grey but now the sun's broken through. The lake laps and glistens; it is a steely bright blue. Connors steps out onto the short wooden jetty and when he looks down to judge the depth, he is startled by the sight of men's faces staring back at him. "Oh," he croaks. "Hello to you." He feels that the world has turned upside down and that it is him in the water, looking up at the land.

The fishing lake is crowded with corpses. Some are uniformed. The majority are naked. He counts nine bodies in the immediate shallows surrounding the jetty although he identifies other bobbing shapes a little further afield. The men have been submerged for some time because they have bloated and their complexions have turned as white as fish bellies. The hair on their heads is buoyant and mossy. Their sloshing genitalia make him think of kelp.

Beneath the surface, the mermen stir. They regard the figure on the jetty with a placid disinterest. For an instant he is tempted to unbutton his clothes and clamber down among them.

His thoughts slide out in all directions. Time skips like a needle on vinyl. And now, incredibly, he is padding along a country lane, hemmed in by hawthorn, following the print of a caterpillar tread. How long has he been on the caterpillar's trail? Surely not very long, although his face has stopped dripping and he senses his features have stiffened. How much further can he walk? Each time he falls over, it becomes more awkward to stand. His stupid arms won't play ball; he has to do the work with his legs. To top it all, he appears to have acquired a stone in one boot, which jabs and nags with every step. He would like to attend to it but his arms are asleep. He would like to check whether he still has his cigarettes, but he can't do that either because his arms are asleep.

"I'm Lieutenant Bram Connors, 70 Squadron," he tells the hawthorn - although what he's actually doing is telling himself. In the course of his travels he has mislaid his ID disc and is dimly aware that this may be a problem. At some point somebody is bound to demand to know who he is. When that happens he wants to be able to give the information straight out: "I am Lieutenant Bram Connors, 70 Squadron". But that won't be possible if his thoughts grow more foggy, or if he keeps sinking to his knees and struggling to get up.

"Ask the men from the lake," he mutters. "They know who I am."

He is a tired shape on a country lane. He's pursuing a caterpillar. He can see its tread at his feet. He can see a church steeple at some distant point up ahead. He is a tired shape with a stone in his boot, but not long ago he had a name and a rank. And not long before that he was something else again: a West Country printer, good with machines. They had put him in charge of the reel-fed rotary press, which the older workers were scared of; they had nicknamed it the Dreadnought. Except that he liked the Dreadnought. He also liked the Camel. It was his skill with the Dreadnought that had landed him first with the engineers. Were it not for the Dreadnought, he would never have flown planes.

When he peers ahead, his eyes gumming, he sees that the lane and the hedgerow appear to have turned onto their sides. Yet when he looks some time later, they are reassuringly upright again.

His thoughts are bleeding out. It has become hard to focus. And before the man was a printer, he must have been something else. Some outraged toddler, shouting for its mother, moving on unsteady legs. And before that something else. A creature unable to speak, squirming on its belly, soiling itself, ignorant of its name. And before that, of course, he was nothing at all.

When Private Harris opens the door without knocking, Captain Jack Bailey of the Canadian Corps is standing on one leg, attempting to balance a rifle upon his raised foot. He has found that if he lifts his toes just a little he creates a natural gully. The rifle can remain there butt-down for as much as a minute or more while he stands, leg outstretched, like some clownish ballerina. Some men would be embarrassed to be caught in such a task. Captain Bailey, for his part, reckons that people can catch him any way they damn please.

He says, "Landsakes, Harris, you went and broke my concentration."

"Sir," says Private Harris. "There is a dead airman spotted over by the church."

Unhurriedly, Bailey stoops to lift his rifle from the floor. "Good one or bad?"

"Bad," says Harris. "Good. By which I mean it's one of ours."

Bailey nods. "By which you mean it's one of yours." The captain is Canadian. Most of his soldiers are not. It is Jack Bailey's fate to find himself playing overseas uncle to a company of Brits.

"Well, OK then," he says. Straightening up makes his aging back crack. "I guess that what we do now is that we go check it out."

They swing out of HQ and trudge across to the church. The town square is a mess of craters and sludge, like some lunar landscape, not fit to be seen. There is a burnt, useless Austin outside the Mairie, a family of feral cats occupying the stone steps up ahead. Bailey says that this is because the French have no civic pride. Why, if this town was in Ontario, it would be treated quite different. It would have fresh macadam laid and the houses brightly painted and flowers blooming in every window box. The town's got potential; it could be passably pretty if someone made an effort. Still, that's the French for you – bone idle.

He shoots the private a sideways glance. "That's a joke, by the way."

"Yes sir, I know."

"Good God," he says. "I'm hilarious."

The Catholic church stands to the north of the square. It is heavyset and functional, as white as a bone and very nearly as fetching. The dead airman is sat on a wooden bench in the yard. He has first sagged and then stiffened, he might have been left there for months. His face is so burned it looks as though it has been turned inside out. Blood has matted and crusted up the length of one sleeve. Few things in this world appear as reassuringly dead as this man. And yet it seems that Private Harris has been misinformed. The sound of their feet on the gravel is such that at the very last second the corpse cracks open one eye. Private Harris can't help it; he skips aside in alarm.

"God's terrible swift sword," the dead airman informs him.

"Oh dear."

The captain barely flinches. Balancing the rifle has helped fine-tune his composure. He asks, "Is that how you respond when one of your fellows ain't dead? 'Oh dear, what a shame'."

"No sir. Of course not."

"I don't believe I'm ever going to understand you people."

"Our people, sir. The men of the Canadian Corps."

"Damn right," says Captain Bailey. "All of us raised on a diet of maple syrup and beef."

As though pausing for breath in the midst of a summer stroll, he plops himself on the bench beside the burnt airman. The man is nine-tenths in the grave; Bailey doesn't think much of his chances. But there's no point being downcast, so he pats the fellow companionably on the knee and asks just where he sprang from: did he drop out of the sky and land right there on this bench? The airman makes no reply. He is sat very still, staring straight ahead out of his one crusted eye.

"OK then. Next order of business. I need your name, rank and squadron."

The figure clears his throat. "You see, I don't know. I think I might have forgotten." He lifts his right arm to scratch distractedly at his scalp.

"Don't do that," the captain says sharply.

With a bewildered half-smile, the man lowers his arm.

All this while, callow Private Harris has been kicking his heels, staring at the ground, looking as sick as a dog. He has not fully recovered; he appears to be keeping his distance. Bailey rounds on the kid with something close to rage. "Hell's bells, private, you waiting for a bus?"

"No sir. Awaiting instruction, sir."

"Then go get a medic. There's your instruction."

As a child his parents had run an unsuccessful smallholding two hours' ride from the market at Brampton. They sold root, grain and berries. What little livestock they possessed became like family members to him. When a cow was sick he would sit watch in the shed. When an animal died it hit him hard. It occurs to him that he has spent a goodly portion of his life watching animals die. Some go out noisy. Some go out quiet.

The unnamed airman draws a ragged breath. He doesn't have very long; the fellow is absenting himself by degrees. Sat on the bench, Bailey decides to at least see how long he can keep the fellow conscious. If they can each hold out until the medics arrive, well then, he will consider that to have been some kind of achievement. It's like his game with the rifle, except this time with a man.

He says, "Here we are, soldier, you've got to pay attention to me. Are you getting all this? Are you with us or not?"

Slight twitch of the head. This shows he is listening.

"OK, here's the plan. I'm going to talk your ear off until the doctor arrives. What happens after that is between you and him. Nothing to do with me anymore."

"Talk my ear off," No Name echoes. The wind moves in the trees. Brown leaves surf the gravel. Bailey estimates that they have approximately five minutes before the medic shows up.

He pats again at old No Name's knee, perhaps the one part of his body that is not burnt or torn. He says, "That's right, that's good. But I warn you, it's not going to be as easy as all that because sat beside you today is an extremely dull individual. Ask anyone, they'll tell you. Even my wife falls asleep at the sound of my voice. So I can't tell a lie, it's going to be mighty hard. But you have to stay focused. Can you do that for me?"

"I'll try my best," says old No Name and attempts another half-smile.

So Captain Bailey of the Canadian Corps sits on the bench in thin sunlight and tells the airman war stories. He tells of ill-starred Bill Jenkins who suffered a serious head injury and regained consciousness to find himself speaking with a crisp German accent. He tells of how alarmed this had made his fellow sharp-shooters and how he, Captain Bailey, had taken it upon himself to explain that it was not Jenkins' fault, it was still old Bill Jenkins and not some hun impostor and that he was on no account to be bayoneted in his bed. Which was what was being discussed, he had no doubt about it.

Then he tells of the cavalry charge, outside Passchendaele, where the riders were picked off one by one only for their horses to continue ploughing forward, hell for leather, as though they were carrying phantoms. Six horses, tails swishing, pouring unscathed through the lines and how he had stood on the ridge with field glasses and watched them keep going. Deep into enemy country; no reason to stop. He leans in, clicks his fingers beneath the man's ruined nose. "Are you following this?"

"I am."

"Well, good work, keep it up." He casts about, wondering where that damned Harris has got to. Time is running short. The man is fading. The balanced rifle drifts out in a gyre; you have to chase it with your foot to coax it back into line. He says, "I've seen some cock-eyed sights in this part of the planet over this past mess of months. Some real cock-eyed sights, soldier. And then there's you."

11

L UCY ARRIVES HOME reeking of rum and cigarettes
and on the stairs is overcome by a swell of sentimentality.
She turns into Tom's room and embraces her brother until he
wakes with a start.

"You stink," Tom says. "Where've you been, anyway?"

She says, "I've been far away. I've been to a magical forest.
I met the funny men out of *The Wonderful Wizard of Oz*."

"Is that really true or are you telling a story?"

"That's for you to say. Maybe a bit of both?"

"I think it's true," he says after a judicious pause. "But *The
Wizard of Oz* is a story."

The smell of tobacco rolls off her in waves. Her speech is
muddy; she has had too much to drink. "The funny men live
very deep in the forest. The Scarecrow can be grumpy, but we
all know he's nice. The Tin Man is charming, but he can be
quite sad as well because he's more metal than man. The Lion
is so scared that he'd rather run away than shake hands. And
Toto is bossy, but that's because he's the boss."

The boy turns his cheek to the pillow. Lucy runs a hand
through his hair.

"At first the funny men are more scary than funny. They
all look very strange. That's why they have to live in the forest.
They need our help and that's why we go there. But they aren't
scary really. They just want to be friends."

"There's a witch as well," the boy points out.

"Inside voice, Tom."

"But there is. There's a witch."

"Not in this story. There are no witches in this story."

"But there has to be. There's a wicked old witch and there's the Wizard of Oz."

"No," says Lucy. "This story's different. There's no witch and no wizard and there isn't a tornado. There's just the lorry that takes us out to the woods and brings us home in time for bed, like right now. There's a lorry and there's me and there are the strange, funny men. It isn't *The Wizard of Oz*. It's a different story I'm telling."

The boy reluctantly accepts this. "But what do you do when you're out in the forest?"

"Well," says the girl. "We have adventures, of course. We explore and have picnics. Sometimes we fly a kite and play football. We learn the names of the trees and make a camp in the woods and you have to know the password before you're allowed to come in."

Tom burrows into the pillow, arranging himself for sleep. Drowsily he asks, "What happens in the end?"

"They all live happily ever after."

The summer term's over, which means she has finished with school. She has hardly been anyway; there have been too many demands on her time. And nobody seems to have cared; so many other children are in the same boat. She attends class on the final day then exits the gate with a skip in her step. She posts her report card, unread, into a drain on the street.

Her school days are behind her, but what exactly comes next? She supposes she'll stay on at the Griffin for as long as it lasts, after which she can move to wherever Grandad finds his next job. So she empties the ashtrays, swabs the toilet, takes the barrels for a walk. She serves the few customers who take a wrong turn into the saloon bar, but the time weighs heavy on her hands to the point where she asks whether she might be needed on other nights in the forest. Nan says, "Oh bless her, so hard-working", but no more comes of this plan. It appears that the travels are booked for Sunday evenings only.

When her hours are free she reads newspapers with a frowning concentration, familiarising herself with an adult world of labour disputes and unemployment statistics. The nation is experiencing hard times, it appears, and this suggests that there must have been a time when it wasn't. At the library she borrows *Sherlock Holmes* and *Three Men in a Boat* and *The Old Curiosity Shop*, which she devours in chunks, conscious of her heart racing. Poor Nell and her grandad. That horrible, horrible Snipe. She re-reads *The Wonderful Wizard of Oz* and is relieved to be reminded that it does all end happily.

One afternoon Brinley drops by in a welter of bashfulness and invites her to accompany him to the pictures that night – his treat, of course. Overcoming vague qualms, she eases the floral-print dress out of the camphor-wood chest. But outside on the street she finds herself regretting the choice. It feels somehow disloyal and the dress is so lovely – it should not be wasted on Brinley, who has plastered his hair with too much pomade and smoked too many Mitchell's Prize Crops to calm the butterflies in his gut. When they sit down in their seats he immediately snakes an arm in behind, except this makes her start, which in turn makes him start, and the pair of them jumping sends the evening off on a tangent from which it never entirely recovers.

But the pictures are glorious so she must not complain.

Once the organist has quit the stage, the lights go down and a smoky beam makes a bridge between the far sides of the hall. Up first is a comedy entitled Spoiling the Broth in which a clownish chef wreaks merry hell in the kitchen, and an equally clownish waiter is sent silly by the cooking wine and starts depositing ladles of scalding soup onto the heads of posh ladies and into the laps of the gents. This is followed by a boisterous animation about a pith-helmeted hunter who confuses a zebra for a tiger and only realises his error when he tries to fit the creature with reins. The cartoon winks out to prolonged cheers and applause. Lucy and Brinley are clapping so ardently that their elbows clash and this makes them giggle and goes some way to erasing the tension between them. They reposition themselves to watch an electrifying drama from the American west where painted natives skulk between the cacti and cowboys are shot dead on dust-blown verandas and young women clutch their faces and shed piteous tears. The world, the world! It is too big and too bright; Lucy cannot take it all in. She needs to suck it up through a straw to regulate the flow.

Afterwards he walks her home. His Adam's apple is jerking and his pomaded hair has come loose. At the door of the Griffin, seizing his moment as a drowning man might grab at a low-hanging branch, he requests that he may kiss her, and she turns her head to allow him to bump his lips against the corner of her mouth. He repeats that he has recently been taken on as an electrician's apprentice and so shall have a little money in his pocket from here on in, which is good. He asks if he might one day invite her to come out with him again and she says that he might. She gestures at the pub and points out that he knows where she lives.

In the kitchen behind the public bar, Nan puts on a pot of tea. She says, "Now that Brinley, be honest. Is he a gentleman or what?"

"Oh no, Nan, he's very nice." She looks around. "Is Tom sleeping already?"

"Well, I'm glad to hear it. He acts like he's nice, but you never know what boys are like after dark."

"And the pictures were wonderful. They had a wild west one."

Nan pours the tea and passes Lucy her cup. "Though I dare say we can aim a little higher than Brinley. He may do for the moment, but we can doubtless do better. Pretty girl like you."

"He's very nice. But I still prefer the funny men."

Her grandmother says quickly, "Oh Lucy, good gracious, don't say that. The very notion, poor Brinley, he'll do quite well for now."

"The Tin Man. The Scarecrow. The Cowardly Lion and Toto."

Nan says, "Never mind all that. Drink your tea, slow-poke. Tom's already in bed."

The girl peers at her grandmother over the rim of her cup. This time she gives the names a little musical lift. "The Tin Man. The Scarecrow. The Cowardly Lion and Toto."

"Drink up your tea. You're acting silly."

She lowers her voice, mimicking Brinley's cracked baritone. "The Tin Man. The Scarecrow. The Cowardly Lion and Toto."

Nan rises from the table and empties her cup in the sink. She says, "Enough of this, I'm off to bed. Good night."

Lucy says, "Good night, Nan. Sleep sound, I love you." She remains in the chair and blows on her tea 'til it cools.

Tom had asked, "What do you do when you're out in the

forest?" and Lucy had told him she flew kites and played games and fashioned camps out of canvas. And all of this is true so far as it goes, except that of course it goes further, and on some subterranean level she has always understood that this is what is required; that this is the real reason why she is brought to the woods. It's for what the boys at St Stephen's called fucking and what Winifred refers to as "the Terrible Unmentionables", which she mostly shortens to Mench, as in "Tinny was absolutely starving for Mench, I didn't know what to do with him" or "the Lion couldn't manage Mench, he only wanted to blub like a baby." And it is Fred who points out what Lucy really should have known all along and what she kicks herself for not guessing: that the funny men are somehow paying for Mench and that the money changes hands behind her back, and that this must be why Coach always trots inside the Griffin to say hello to Grandad but never wants to stop for a drink and a smoke. Except even this can't be right, at least not entirely, because none of the money has ever filtered down to her, and Fred laughs at this and says she's never seen a penny of it either.

"But hang about, Luce. It's not like you get paid for working at the pub."

"Well, no," she concedes. "That's part of my chores."

"There you are then. It's only another way of working for the oldies. Sometimes we're indoors and sometimes we're out."

"But it's wrong, though, isn't it? Isn't it bad?"

"The Mench?" Winifred screws up her face; such moral quandaries exhaust her. "The world's bad. I suppose the Mench could be worse."

There is no preamble, no wind-up, no dance around the subject. If Lucy can say hello to the funny men without bringing up her dinner or running away screaming, then Coach clearly reasons that the Terrible Unmentionables won't spook her either. Having passed the first test the girl is ready for the second – and besides, the whole night has been bought and paid for upfront. The picnic complete, Toto turns to tell her about the little tree over yonder that he swears looks like Edith. After that he leads her out of the clearing, waddling aboard his muscular hips until they find a secluded spot whereupon he drops the pretence and demands she take him in her hand right away. He explains that he is a fellow in ruins and that everything about him is either scarred, broken or missing aside from his old man which is in perfect working order and this shows that he must be blessed and that the Lord God still loves Toto, if only a little. "Here look," he says, "see", and she jumps as though she has trodden on a thorn with bare feet. He says, "Grab hold. Have a look. Tell me how he's looking" and she backs away and straightens her dress and says, politely, "Excuse me, please, I'll be back in a moment."

It turns out that Coach has followed them partway up the trail. He draws on his pipe as he sees her run up. "Where are you off to, little Luce?"

"Oh," says Lucy, suddenly at a loss. She gestures ahead, towards the clearing and safety, although Coach blocks the path so completely she might be pointing at him.

"Not just yet," he says almost tenderly and draws again at his old briar pipe. Lucy looks at him a moment, weighing her options, and then she turns away to retrace her steps.

She goes with whichever of the funny men wants her, whenever they want her, and it is not unusual to attend to more than one over the course of a night, darting soft-footed to various secluded leafy corners until, inevitably, she beats back over old, flattened ground and finds the cigarette butts and wrinkled sheaths left over from previous visits. More often than not she is passed back and forth between the Tin Woodman and Toto, for these two are the most active and demanding, although she is surprised to discover that out of the two, it is the barking, noisy Toto who treats her more gently. The Tin Man is careful to remove his hooks first, and yet he has a tendency to use his stumps and knees to hold her securely in place and this can often leave bruises. It just goes to show, like Nan says, that you never know what people are like after dark.

Or take the Scarecrow, who can be so kind and thoughtful and interested in what she has to say only to turn cold and distant when he requires her to walk with him to quiet places – as if he actually hates what she does for him there and hates himself for allowing her to do it. It makes no sense and it's upsetting because the thing is bad enough as it is. "What's wrong?" she asks and he tells her nothing is wrong, why should anything be wrong? "I'm sorry," she mutters and this makes him laugh, although it is not a kind laugh. She so hopes he will not complain to Coach about her.

One night she is summoned to a stretch of tall grass to work her hand on the Lion while Fred holds his head and strokes his brow. But otherwise she finds she is able to avoid him. Try as she might she can't feel at her ease with the Lion: he gives so little back; he is like a frightened recluse who has turned out all the lights and double-bolted the door.

"Does he ever speak much? He doesn't with me."

"Oh yes, he does sometimes. He once said he has a wife called Beverly but he hasn't seen her in years. He gave me the names and addresses of nice places to see if I ever visit his town."

"Really? How strange. What names and address?"

"I don't know." Fred shrugs, losing interest. "Stockport?"

Occasionally, sitting in the bed of the Maudslay, a troubling possibility will come to her. She wonders whether her Terrible Unmentionables are the same as Fred's, Edith's and John's. Logic tells her they must be and yet the worry keeps nagging. She fears she might be doing something wrong and that the funny men discuss her failings among themselves and then relay their thoughts to Coach, who will listen in horror and tell her that her services are no longer required. Or – worse – he might tell Fred and Edith who would both fall about laughing. Or – worst of all – he might tell her grandad. Imagine that: Coach calling round to explain that the stupid, clumsy girl has been doing everything wrong and that they've done their level-best to be patient but the funny men keep complaining and that enough is enough. She gnaws at her knuckles; she is doubled over with shame. It feels almost as though this mortifying exchange has already taken place.

Finally she is able to bear it no more and conspires to draw Winifred to one side on the walk back to the truck. Fred has been making these Sunday visits for at least a month longer than the rest of them and appears blissfully unburdened by self-doubt. And yet Fred's home situation sounds more precarious even than her own because she says her grandparents have been told they ought to vacate the premises and, in addition to this, her grandad is given to gambling on the greyhounds and now owes thirty-two pounds to an Eyetie called Falconio who keeps dropping in at the pub and threatening to cause trouble. In the rear of the Maudslay she imitates the loan shark's sudden Jack-in-a-Box appearances and her grandfather's abject, oddly operatic attempts to accommodate them.

She waves her hands and rolls her eyes. "Ooh Mr Falconio, please permit me to fetch you a drink on the house," she quavers. "Ooh Mr Falconio, don't be like that, control yourself please. Oh! No! Falconio!" Fred performs this charade with such gusto that John starts rocking on his heels with helpless, silent laughter. He is constantly badgering her for updates on Falconio.

Now Fred dips her head and attempts to take in as much of Lucy's concerns as her attention span will allow. She then assures her that it's perfectly fine, the way Lucy does the Mench, and she knows that it's fine because Coach has told her as much. The driver always collects Fred first of all and she likes to ride the opening leg of the journey alongside him in the cab. She takes the occasional drag from his disgusting briar pipe and in those fifteen minutes they converse almost as equals, or as business partners.

"So me and you are safe and sound. It isn't us who should be worrying."

"What do you mean?"

"Isn't it obvious? John's not pulling his weight."

If the children have their favourites, it naturally follows that the funny men must have theirs. And yes, come to think of it, Lucy has noticed that some weeks John is permitted to remain on what Coach refers to as the subs' bench for the whole of the evening, sucking his thumb while the drivers suck their pipes. His popularity is fading; he wears his misery like a scarf. Toto has explained that the boy's presence is mainly his fault. He developed a taste for his own team when he was playing overseas and he brought this back with him, couldn't seem to shake it loose. Now he believes he might at last be controlling his habit; he might be heading back on the straight and narrow again. The dwarf credits Lucy, Fred and Edith for their assistance in this and then jokingly thanks John for his own contribution. "You could say he's the cure almost as much as the girls. Just look at that face. It proper kills off my appetite."

Fred lowers her voice. "Between you and me, they don't like Edith much either."

"Oh dear, poor Ede." But she's relieved all the same.

"In any case," Fred continues, "it's not like you have to do very much. Just lie down and think of something else for as long as it lasts. It's them that do most of the work, poor beggars, and a lot of the time they can't do it anyway."

Lucy hesitates and then decides that it's best to ask the question right out. "Is it rape, what they do?" The very word seems to jam in her throat.

"How do you mean?"

"The Mench. I mean, if they make us do things we don't like doing. That's raping, isn't it?"

But Fred is bewildered. "What, like, if you scream or fight or run away? That's not what you do?"

"No. Course not."

"Well then, stands to reason. It's not raping, it's Mench. And we get paid for it too, so that proves it's not rape."

The girls come out into the clearing. Up ahead they can see the glowing coals of Coach and Crisis's pipes.

"I shouldn't mind seeing some of that money, though. It all goes to the oldies." Fred sighs. "Then it all goes to Falconio."

The world is bad, says Winifred. As for the Mench, it could be worse. Lucy supposes that she might be right. And perhaps it is this that is the real unmentionable about the Terrible Unmentionables – a truth which strikes her as somehow more dreadful than doing it wrong and being teased by the others; more dreadful even than Coach complaining to Grandad. It is the suspicion that for all the awkwardness, discomfort and occasional pain it entails, the terrible Mench may not in fact be so terrible. Or to put it another way, why should this chore be terrible and her other chores not? At least once a day, for instance, she is instructed to fill a pail from the tap and attend to the most grisly excesses and spillovers in the toilet behind the Griffin, or manoeuvre cumbersome barrels onto the ramp from the cellar. Like the Mench, these jobs are dirty and nasty and she would prefer not to do them. But unlike the Mench, nobody ever looks apologetic about needing her help. Nobody says thank you or asks her afterwards whether she is all right and not hurt. No one teaches her the words of songs, or how to tell one tree from its neighbour. And that is why she reckons the job could be worse. And this is why she worries about her eternal soul and damnation and what that means she's become. Because if there exists anything in the world that is worse than the Mench, it is surely the girl who does not view it as wrong; who subjects herself wittingly and who acquits herself well.

Her thoughts pinwheel and her pulse is jumping. Incredibly, it turns out that there is a more nightmarish scenario than Coach visiting her grandfather to complain about her aptitude. It is the one in which Coach drops by at the Griffin to tell her grandfather that his customers could not be more delighted with the service she provides.

She opens her legs and lets the Tin Man come in. Back arching, breath rasping, he leans the sugarloaf of his forearm against her breastbone and Lucy winces and settles and laces her hands about the nape of his neck, mindful not to disturb the knot of the ribbon which holds his features in place. He endures this for a minute before the strain overtakes him and he shudders and breaks down as though he has been struck from behind. His system is in uproar. She believes he might be weeping although she cannot say for certain. His face is as serene and contented as an effigy in a tomb.

"It's all right," she tells him. "It's all right." And behind the man's head she sees that all the stars have come out.

12

MRS HENRIETTA SHAW has no great desire to receive the fellow who draws up to her door in the trap from the station, but her son is adamant; he says that the man is a marvel. Robert has become regrettably prone to wild fancies since he relocated to London. He runs the risk of embarrassing himself by association with all manner of mountebanks. In the past few months the boy has permitted himself to be beguiled by experimental poets and whisked into a lather by leftist agitators. He has paid good money to witness the antics of a European gypsy who claimed to be able to levitate when he quite demonstrably could not, and became worryingly infatuated by the charms of a dancing negress whose pièce de résistance, so far as Mrs Shaw can gather, amounted to nothing so much as a tawdry striptease. He has been gulled and bamboozled and still seems none the wiser. The Magus, he says, is the most impressive by far.

The Magus, I ask you. Was ever there a name more flagrantly pompous? Was ever there a title so guaranteed to inspire derision? How on earth does one even set about addressing the Magus? Should one refer to him as Mr Magus? Or if that is too formal, may she perhaps call him Gus? Goodness me: she would fall about laughing, were it not so utterly tragic.

Robert rolls his eyes and invites her to go ahead, be his guest. She should laugh all she likes; it would do his heart good to hear it. All the same, he fears that she is fixating on the name as a deliberate distraction. She appears hell-bent on judging the man on the basis of his label as opposed to the achievements themselves, which are considerable, as she will soon see. "Frankly," he adds, "I am a little disappointed in you. I did rather assume that you were bigger than this."

"But the Magus, I ask you. Oh Robert, what rot."

Henrietta Shaw lives in a comfortable house on the fringes of town. The house is called the Vicarage, although this surely counts as another misnomer, given that it has not catered to a vicar in three decades or more. Her husband had been a magistrate before he expired on the links and the sole reminder of his presence is the clotted and dowdy oil portrait over the drawing-room hearth (the artist made his mouth too stern and his eyes half-demented). The house is big and its needs can be clamorous. It is like an energetic Great Dane, always wanting to be walked. She has Steven drop by twice a week to prevent the garden from becoming a Congo. She has Beth in every day (and often overnight) to ensure that the floors are waxed and the clocks wound, and to open and close the curtains at intervals to prevent the sun from bleaching the upholstery. Most evenings Beth will prepare a simple meal of fish and boiled vegetables, after which the pair sit together and talk and sip more port than they ought, and often she will say, "Oh, it's so late, why not just stay over?" If this is old age, it has much to recommend it. Privately she admits that she does not much miss Mr Shaw.

On the morning of the visit she has Beth put out a pot of tea and a plate of ginger cake. For Robert's sake, it would not do to be rude. This is all her son's idea; it is he who is paying. If he is determined to squander his hard-earned wages, it might as well be on a ceremonial magician as on a European gypsy who confuses levitation with the act of star-jumping. But gracious, she does hope the boy will see the light before long.

When the trap pulls up, Beth has the guest take a seat in the library. Mrs Shaw lets him wait for five minutes and then makes her entrance. When she finds the library unoccupied, she returns to the hall. "Beth," she says. "Dashed fellow's not there. Did he leave?"

"No," says Beth. "He's definitely in the library. I'd have seen if he left."

So Mrs Shaw looks again and sure enough, there he is. He is loitering by the drapes at the window; she cannot imagine why she did not notice him before. She blinks and composes herself and nods a curt greeting. She says, "Mr Magus, you'll forgive me if I don't shake your hand. I have an injury which troubles me in damp weather."

"I understand," says the Magus. "You fell and broke your right wrist as a child."

"Not a bit of it," Mrs Shaw retorts. "It was a sprain in the garden. And it was only last week."

Up steps the Magus, dressed in rabbinical black. His jacket is unbuttoned, exposing some kind of gaudy scarab pendant, while his head is topped by a bowler hat that he seems at no pains to remove. He has the faint tinge of the Jewry about him, but she suspects that this is for show, a cheap disguise, and that he follows no particular creed. He is pale and obscenely fat and has applied liquid kohl to his eyebrows and lashes in a pathetic attempt to add definition to his bland, creamy features. He less resembles a wizard than a vaudeville comic whose notion of entertainment is to split the seat of his trousers or plant himself upon a rubber horn which simulates the noise of breaking wind. But he treads softly, lightly, with a grace that for some reason strikes her as doubly repulsive. His accent and bearing mark him out as a member of the lower orders – whatever that means in this topsy-turvy age.

When she invites him to sit he sinks like a feather to the chair opposite hers. In the absence of Beth, Mrs Shaw pours the tea. She says, "I should really apologise for a small untruth. I fell on stone steps and fractured my wrist as a child."

"Madame," he says, "please don't mention it."

"Although I must say, if you had known it was an untruth I do believe you might have pointed it out."

"Perhaps I was being polite," says the Magus.

"Or perhaps you were bluffing and could not say one way or the other."

He collects the teacup and saucer with a delicate motion, his little finger cocked as if to balance its weight; not a single drop spilt on its way to his mouth. He drinks and smiles and lightly smacks his lips. "Madame. Sometimes I perceive things and sometimes I don't. Sometimes I'm defeated and sometimes I'm not. If your wish is to catch me out and make sport of my errors, then I can promise you that the next hour will pay . . ." He gropes for the correct term. "Handsome dividends."

"I am delighted you admit it."

"It will be like Christmas morning for little children."

Mrs Shaw returns his smile and collects her own tea. "That does rather strike me as an admission of defeat."

He says, "What a lovely house you live in, Madame. When I've made my own pile, I should reckon to get myself a house very much like this."

Mrs Shaw once had two sons and now has only one. She supposes that one was defeated and the other was not, although if she were asked to select the natural victor between Robert and Richard she knows which one she would choose every time – Richard had always been her favourite. But the fates felt otherwise and duly acted, as fates will, with their own perplexing, irresistible logic. It just goes to show that you never know what is coming until it is hard up against you and you can feel its hot breath in your face. She sips her tea and shakes her head.

Now this fat, foolish fellow is merrily purporting to lay out his credentials. She attends with half an ear as he explains that sometimes he will see things and sometimes he won't and that lost souls sometimes speak to him and that sometimes he is able to bring comfort to those loved ones left behind. Every time he says "sometimes" he puts a stress on the word, as though he is cautioning an imbecile not to set their hopes too high, and each time he does this his eyes widen, which makes his kohl brows waggle until it is all she can do not to ring the hand-bell and have Beth come and show this man to the door. She catches herself wondering which cabbie drove him up from the station. She prays it wasn't the younger fellow because the younger fellow gossips and it might cause a stir in the town: the tale of the obese painted buffoon who called in at the Vicarage.

Once, long ago – he says – he was prospecting in Egypt and searching out the truth regarding certain ancient mysteries. He was travelling with a learned man, a seer of sorts, and out in the desert they uncovered the tomb of a pharaoh. All of this took place before the most recent discoveries, the ones the newspapers are so excited about, and he was left with the impression that this particular tomb was older by far. Inside, he found the fabulous Eye of Thoth-Amon – the very amulet he is wearing today. The talisman, he explains, was fashioned in honour of an ancient deity and it invests the wearer with a power both beautiful and terrible.

She scrutinises the pendant. It is blue-green, ostentatious, with horny protuberances. It puts her in mind of a sickly stag beetle. She says, "He doesn't mind that you stole it? Your old deity, Cough?"

"Thoth, Madame. And no, he wouldn't, because I treat its powers with respect and only in the service of bringing peace to the afflicted."

"And lost souls send you messages by way of the pendant?"

"Sometimes they speak and sometimes they don't. We mustn't be discouraged if they choose to stay quiet."

"Why, bless my soul, that makes you a telephone. Perhaps this is how you regard yourself. As a walking, talking telephone."

The Magus helps himself to a slice of ginger cake. He appears determined to maintain his happy smile as he eats.

Mrs Shaw watches him. She says, "I am going to be entirely frank with you, sir, because it would do us both a disservice were I to be otherwise. I hope you won't take offence at what I have to say."

"Madame."

"I believe you are a fake, Mr Magus. Which is to say that I don't believe a single word of your fabulous story about hidden tombs and buried treasure and a grand deity called Cough."

"Thoth."

"I have no doubt my son has paid you handsomely for this session and I am therefore prepared to witness your charade and to witness it for what it is: a little one-man circus, designed to fool the gullible and amuse those who are blessed with a more sensible outlook. I do hope it's amusing. It's rather good so far. Still, it would be remiss of me not to lay my cards on the table. You are a fraud, Mr Magus. In my opinion, I am minded to say that you are more sham than shaman."

In the hush that follows, she is aware of the ticking of the clock on the mantel. "Madame," he says.

"Please understand that I have no objection to small, shabby men making a living for themselves. I am aware that we live in difficult times. One might even go so far as to commend you on your ingenuity and pluck."

The Magus swallows his cake and says, "Your eldest son, Richard Shaw, was killed by a German shell in May 1917. His disc was recovered but the body was not. That's not unusual. I was in Cambrai myself. It happens all the time."

Mrs Shaw bridles. It is her son's name that does it. "Would this be before or after you discovered your Egyptian tomb?"

He raises a chubby hand and appears to be concentrating. His eyes are shut and his face screwed tight. She has to fight a silly urge to rise silently from the armchair and steal out of the room. It would serve him right to open his eyes and see her gone, the horrid little clown.

A full minute goes by. The carriage clock tick-tick-ticks in her ear. Finally his face clears and he says, "When the shells explode they leave a hole in the ground. The hole is round and as big as a room. It is about the same size as the room we are sitting in now, though not nearly so nice. You wouldn't like it, Mrs Shaw. There's no door, or walls or bookshelves. There's no table or tea, and no window to look out of. Sometimes—"

he waggles his brows "—the hole contains nothing at all. Sometimes it contains smoking bits of flesh and bone."

She says, "Mr Magus, I am fully acquainted with the horrors of the battlefield."

He blinks. "Well that's jolly good. Is that so? Are you really?"

"I am."

He says, "Richard Shaw met his end in a hole near Arras. It was early morning, May 4th. He was twenty-five years old, a captain in the 62nd Division. There were others with him; none of them survived either. Afterwards, the next day, they were all gathered up and buried together in another hole, a different hole that was dug for the dead from all over. That's where he rests, Richard Shaw, in a mass grave beside a village or hamlet that is either called Pipurdie or Lepurdie or something like that, I wish it were clearer."

If she lifted her teacup he might see her hands shaking. "Oh dear, what a shame," she says brightly. "Pipurdie or Lepurdie, I do so wish it were clear. Still, one must not be discouraged. Pipurdie or Lepurdie: what a wonderful comfort to know."

"Madame, just a moment. I am getting further word besides."

"Goodness. How splendid."

"Richard Shaw," he begins and that is as far as he gets. She cannot stop herself, it is all too much, the sound of that name on those wet, smacking lips. She is abruptly furious with Robert for press-ganging her into receiving this belly-crawling slug of a man and furious with herself for allowing herself to be press-ganged, and furious, most of all, with the detestable invertebrate who has quite obviously squeezed Robert for information and then embroidered the information with his own foul flights of fancy. That's how these people operate. It is how they pull the wool over innocent eyes, but not hers, thank you, the charade is preposterous. Her voice lifting, she says, "That will do, Mr Magus, I'm not interested in hearing further words, particularly if those words are emitting from you. I request you to wait outside, or you might prefer to simply walk back to the station. I hope the weather holds. I confess I have played along for quite as long as I'm willing."

"Richard Shaw rests in a mass grave near the village," the man says hurriedly. "But not all of him is there."

"Stop saying his name. Our conversation is over." She rises from the chair.

Speaking very quickly, he says, "Not all of him is there, only most of him is there. Some of him is still in that round room in the field. Every last bit could not be collected. So he leaked into the earth and the hole has grown over by now."

"Get out." But when he hops to his feet it is only to ensure that he maintains eye contact. They confront each other across the inlaid glass table.

He says, "But not all of him is there. We still have more parts to account for and the parts are all precious, aren't they, Mrs Shaw? You know that better than anyone, don't you, Mother? Don't you, Mum?"

When she moves for the door, he moves alongside her, blocking her exit. "You are acquainted with battle, but are you acquainted with rats?" At this he scrunches his nose and bares his incisors. "The rats," he says. "The rats, the rats. Down south had the flies but the north got the rats. Out in the trenches they grew big as otters, big as badgers, some said, because there was so much meat to tuck into. And when they gobbled themselves on human flesh it made the fur on their faces turn white. We all saw it happen, it was a right peculiar thing. We could see their white faces in the dark, getting closer and closer."

Again she darts at the door. Again he cuts her off. "Beth!" she shouts. "Beth!" She feels physically ill. His eyes won't leave her face; she cannot break his gaze.

"Richard Shaw. Richard Shaw. Excuse me for saying his name. I can't help myself, it's like he has me possessed. Little parts of him are in a ruined barn. Little parts of him are moving still. He's been passed about between a good number of rats. Then those rats fucked and made more rats and those rats fucked and made more rats and each one of them carries a small piece of your son. Listen to the Eye of Thoth-Amon. Lay your head up against my breast. Listen to the Eye and you can hear him scratching and squeaking as he runs about in the barn."

"Beth!"

Now the Magus laughs. He could be a close friend who has just shared a joke. He says, "What a jolly nice house you own, Mrs Shaw. And how kind of you to allow small, shabby men to cross your threshold. Fully acquainted with the horrors of battle. Cor blimey, but the war was lovely. You should have come along, Mrs Shaw. Me and you together! It would have been capital."

The door bangs open. Beth blows in like a springtime squawl, her cheeks flushed from running and her hair come undone. She sees her mistress totter and swoops just in time to steady her. "Oh, what?" she exclaims. "Is it something about Richard? Did he tell you something about Richard?"

The Magus leans forward and shouts into Beth's face. "Richard Shaw is food for rats!" With this he brings up one hand and makes a curious motion, rubbing the pad of his thumb across his index and middle fingers. It is the sort of gesture a trader will make when he is demanding a re-calcitrant customer pay him what he's owed, although Mrs Shaw barely has time to conclude that this makes no sense, that Robert has paid him already, before this whole hideous morning pitches into nightmare. She has no explanation for what happens next and yet it seems to her that this horrible specimen has somehow conspired to strike fire from thin air. Flames spark and gutter about his fingertips. She can feel the warmth against her cheek.

"Richard Shaw is food for rats! Burn the fucking barn down and you may just bring him peace."

The housekeeper's knees unhinge. Mrs Shaw senses more than sees the redoubtable Beth collapse to the floor. She turns, unthinking, and her hands find the table and the cup half-filled with tea. She grips the handle and flicks the contents, almost certainly intending to put out the flames except that her nerves are twanging and her aim is awry. The tea goes in the Magus's face and makes his kohl lashes run. Then, as quickly and inexplicably as they appeared, the flames are gone and the Vicarage library is a library again. The man stops rubbing his fingers and swabs at his brows, pinches the bridge of his nose. All at once he appears startled by the recent run of events. His obscene relish has left him; gone the same way as the flames.

"We got carried away," he mutters. "I really ought to say sorry."

The housekeeper is down but Mrs Shaw remains upright. Summoning the last of her strength, she backs the man towards the door.

"I'm leaving," he says. "I've been paid, don't you worry."

"The Lord is my shepherd," Mrs Shaw says. "I shall not be in want. He makes me lie down in green pastures. He leads me beside quiet waters." She wants this man vanished. She wants the memory of him expunged. Night after night, kneeling at the foot of the brass bed in her room, identifying white faces in every patch of moonlight, she will pray that, as long as she lives, she never sees him again.

13

S TAND STILL. BE quiet. Hold your breath and you can just hear it – that faint, unearthly singing swimming out of the trees. Voices harmonising in a distant corner of the forest – but is it really so distant? Off the road, in the dark, the dimensions telescope and collapse until the figure at your side can feel a hundred miles away while the invisible sources of faraway sounds seem near enough to touch, were you to pluck up the courage and stick out a paw. And if you can hear them, then they can surely hear you. So be still, stay quiet. It would not do to alert them, the unearthly singers in the deep, dark woods.

They have erected tents and kindled a bonfire. Look closely and you can make out its red glow. And side-by-side, the girl and the Scarecrow discover themselves being reeled in like fish, dragging back on the line to delay their approach, testing the ground with their toes for twigs that might snap. "Softly," he says. "Slowly. Imagine we are the trappers and they are the bear."

Out here the forest is honeycombed with clearings – some large and some small, some oblong, some round. The Maudslay trucks sit cooling in one while the magical singers make heat in another. As the girl draws closer she hears them more clearly. They are singing of the old ways and the ancient land, when the forest was not confined to this small parcel of Essex but ran wild across Britain so that the kestrel looked down on a mossy blanket of treetops extending all the way to the western sea. They are singing of the creatures that once lived in the forest: the elves and the centaurs, and the sons and daughters of Adam, who drank clear water from the streams and slept in cool shade and were untroubled by dreams. Hey Nonny, they sing. Hey Nonny No. Now dress up your daughter in green garter and bow.

"Will you listen to that," the Scarecrow says in a whisper. "The sanctimonious little shits."

Lucy is beside herself. "Is it really them?"

"It is," he says. "The Kindred of the Kibbo Kift."

Hidden behind ferns, she can peek out and see them: a set of small hooded shapes gathered by the fire and, beyond that, an outer circle of tents that appear to be decorated with Red Indian markings. She wants to investigate further but this would be perilous; she should be grateful that she has seen them at all. The Kibbo Kift are skittish and elusive. They are reputed to ride out to the forest every summer weekend, a good ten or twenty in number, but they are careful to keep to remote corners, and they cover their tracks when they leave. They melt away into the undergrowth and ensure that the land where they camped is made virgin again.

The Scarecrow has explained that this is a pacifist group, an antidote to what they regard as the tub-thumping war-mongering of Baden Powell's scouts. He says they are led by a man called John Hargrave, also known as White Fox, and that the organisation is divided into lodges and tribes. Inductees must hand-stitch their own robes of Saxon cloak and tunic, and they learn woodcraft and folklore and how to respect Mother Nature. The Scarecrow can't abide them. He says there are few jokes more amusing than the moral superiority of children. But their singing is gorgeous and glacial, like vanilla ice-cream, and Lucy believes they might be beautiful. She would like to stay put. She would like to hear more. She rises with great reluctance when she feels the Scarecrow's tap on her shoulder.

They retrace their steps and find somewhere to sit. The bonfire fades to a dull stain at their backs and the Kibbo Kift's singing regains its ghostly old tint. She says, "Do you want to do something?"

"We are doing something."

"You know what I mean."

"We are doing something. Maybe later we'll do something different. But right now I'm enjoying this particular something."

She helps light his cigarette and they pass it between them. He asks how she has been and she finds herself telling him a little about her life at the Griffin and her parents who died and her brother who steals but whom she loves all the same. He asks if it was her granddad who made the arrangements for her trips to the woods and she nods and coughs and hands the cigarette back.

He shakes his head. "It's none of my business, Lucy. But I reckon you might want to look into getting yourself a new set of grandparents."

"He's a nice man. He means well."

"Lucy," he says. "He doesn't. He's not."

From far away, through the stands of pollarded trees, comes the crystalline sound of that extraordinary singing. The wind must have shifted: it has brought it to them.

"The Campswarden met the Tally keeper and the Gleeman had his say," sing the unseen children of the Kibbo Kift. "Then all set sail in a coracle and cried, 'We won't return 'til May'."

Turning the tables, she says, "I've always wanted to ask. Why does the Tin Man wear a copper mask when yours is made of leather?"

"I tried it with the copper mask. It aggravated my skin. It drove me half-mad. The leather is better."

"Fred says the reason the Tin Man wears a mask is because he is too handsome to look at. She says he does it to protect us from how handsome he is."

The Scarecrow snorts. "And what do you think?"

"I think she's joking."

"I think you may be right."

The four funny men had each been hurt in the war. This knowledge steals up on her incrementally, imperceptibly, until it strikes her as strange that there was a time when she did not know it. Nobody ever goes so far as to state it aloud; certainly the funny men have never discussed their history except glancingly in rueful asides or in a private, playful language she does not fully understand. And yet through the very act of circling the heart of the matter they eventually put a frame around it, as wary ice-skaters navigate the rotten centre of a frozen pond, scoring marks around the edge that only make the middle gleam brighter.

She gathers that the Scarecrow, the Tin Man and Toto were variously shelled and cut and shot down while in France, although she has not yet managed to work out what happened to whom. And she realises now that the Lion's wounds are internal and that he suffers from a disease called "neurasthenia" that affects some soldiers who have spent too long under fire. This accounts for his disposition, for his closed, boyish face, and it explains why he rarely speaks and won't look you in the eye and why he is liable to start at the sound of a tumbling acorn or a squirrel in the tree. She reasons that he is only cowardly today because he was too brave in the past, and she wishes he could trust her as he so obviously trusts Fred. Once she asks the Tin Man why the Lion attacked Edith and he tells her that most times the Lion doesn't even know what he's doing. That he sleeps at odd hours and often screams in his bed and occasionally wets it as well. That he is constantly trying to do away with himself – can't look at an oven without wanting to stick his head in it, the big eejit. He says the Lion means no harm but that he is all out of sorts. He's more Humpty Dumpty than lion; he can't be put back together again. The Tin Man adds that she should count herself lucky to have three chivalrous escorts to keep the Lion at bay. They might have been Humpty Dumpties as well and then where in hell would she be?

The wind turns again and drags the singing away with it. Or could it be that the songs are now finished and the Kibbo Kift boys are readying themselves for bed? She likes to picture them untying their cloaks and crawling into their tents and hopes that one day she herself will have the chance to sleep under canvas. What would the boys say if they spotted her in the woods? Would they be delighted or scared? Would they consider her pretty? She experiences a queer stab of loneliness, sitting out here in the dark.

The Scarecrow lifts the dropper from his pocket and applies saline to his eyes, which have a habit of crusting over and causing discomfort. Seeing him preoccupied, she decides she can risk one further question. "Don't you have any family?"

"No family," he murmurs, his head tilted back. "I'm as free as a bird. I flew off into battle and I never came back."

Later she will use her hand on him and on balance she thinks

131

that she prefers it this way. She would rather not stare into his moistened brown eyes and feel his tobacco breath on her face because this only makes her realise that they are not close when they're close. Of course they are not close when she uses her hand on him either, but at least the anger is not there and they both go at it in silence, secure in the unspoken understanding that she is performing a task and providing a service.

How strange this all is. The only times he truly feels close is when she does not touch him at all, when they are walking and talking or sharing cigarettes, and at these times it is as though she has known him for years. She doesn't even like it if his fingers brush hers when he passes the cigarette over because it reminds her of the times when he is pressed up against her, when he detests his own frailties and appears to view her as the cause. It makes little sense but there it is, and she can do nothing about it. Everyone has their limits and these limits conspire to keep the world at arm's length.

"We all fall into darkness," the Scarecrow says, as if picking up on her thoughts. "Even the Kindred of the Kibbo Kift."

In the bed of the truck on the long road home, Winifred amuses herself by making animal noises. At intervals, quite softly, she will say, "Mee-ew" and then giggle. She sounds like a peevish house cat that is being subjected to some minor indignity, like having its fur washed or being made to swallow bitter medicine.

"Mee-eew," she says and then waits a few seconds. "Meee-ew."

Previously half-asleep, Lucy props herself on her elbows. "What are you doing?"

"Eee-ew."

"Yes," says John, "what are you doing, Freddie?"

"You all have to guess. Edith has to guess too."

"Cat!" blurts John.

"I don't want to," says Edith.

They ride on through the night. It seems that the game might have finished. Sleepily, Lucy says, "I always look up to see if a plane is going by. They fly every day to Paris and then back again. One day I'd really love to go up in a plane."

"It's very expensive," Edith says. "Flying up in a plane."

The headlights pick out a sign. They are driving down Turpentine Lane. They come past the Wesleyan church, a huddle of houses, civilisation at last.

"Eee-eew!"

"Cat!" says John.

Now Fred's mewling has gained a little volume, turned a degree more insistent. What began for the creature as a mild concern has apparently bloomed into an active nuisance. "Ee-eeew?" she says. "Eeugh!"

"Give up," John says.

"Lucy?" she says. "Edith?" Lucy shakes her head. Edith says nothing.

They turn off Turpentine Lane and hit the main road, the arterial road, that unwinds like a ribbon right into London. A motorist blasts past them, heading the opposite way, and when the noise of the engine has faded, Fred says in a light, casual tone, "Me and Toto were walking back to the clearing. I mean to say. I was walking and he was, you know." She plants one arm between her bare knees and wiggles her hips. "Anyway, there we were, walking along, when we went by a big bush that looked like it was alive, it was shaking that much and kept making these noises. I must admit I was rather scared. I was petrified."

John has been laughing. "Do Toto walking again."

"Anyway," says Fred, "I said, 'Oh my stars, what's inside that bush?' And Toto – " she wiggles her hips as a concession to John. "Toto says, 'Don't worry about it, I think Tinny's in there with one of your little pals'."

Lucy flicks her eyes at John. But the boy is bemused; he grins in encouragement.

"Eee-ew!" says Fred. "Eeeew!"

A silence descends on the children in the truck. Lucy is aware of the back wheels that roll immediately beneath the place she is sitting, she can feel the road's vibrations in the joints of her spine. Looking over the board, she sees they have arrived at the half-timbered houses, the spacious outer suburbs, which means they must be making good time and she will be home before midnight.

The tension has become unbearable. Seeking to break it, she says, "We saw the Kindred of the Kibbo Kift," and at the exact same moment John says, "Do Toto walking again" and at the exact same moment Edith springs at Fred and the two start pummelling at each other and Fred goes off into peals of hysterical laughter. One instant the girls are employing their hands as fists, the next as claws, then as fists again, as though each is bent on murdering the other. Edith is on top and Fred underneath, which puts Fred at a disadvantage and yet she will not stop laughing. She shrieks, "Oh! Oh! Falconio!"

"Stop it," cries Lucy. "Both of you. Stop it!"

Their legs are pistoning, their fists are flying. "Oh Falconio! No Falconio! You Falconio! Please Falconio!"

Without a word, John tosses himself overboard. Lucy's attention is so fixed on the fight that she sees his departure too late to prevent it. He places both hands on the running board, braces his legs and is gone. She stands, tottering, but the skies are covered and the road is black and she is unable to see where the boy might have landed.

"Oh! Oh! Falconio!"

Now Coach slams on the brakes and she is catapulted forward onto Edith and Fred. The driver is out of his cab before she can disentangle herself. "What the fucking hell?" he says.

They find the boy about fifty yards back. He has rolled to the bottom of a short weedy embankment. He has twisted an ankle and can put no weight on his foot. When Coach and Lucy walk down, he is sitting sucking his thumb. He is entirely calm and appears already to have made peace with his injury, perhaps regarding it as a reasonable price to pay for a ticket out of an intolerable situation.

John is fine; he nods his big head. But he does not want to return to the truck. He says he doesn't like to see fighting. Please don't make him watch any fighting.

"Don't worry," Coach tells him. "You can sit up front with me."

At the top of the slope they meet a youngish couple on a late-night stroll: the woman quite handsome, the gentleman gawky and with too many teeth. Lucy can tell from the scent that they have been drinking and the alcohol has turned them garrulous and solicitous, so that they lay on a great fuss for the poor, stoical youth who tumbled out of the truck. The man assists Coach in carrying him back up the road. John suffers these ministrations with a placid half-smile, his eyes wide and moist, his thumb permanently docked in the corner of his mouth. Lucy has the impression that he is rather enjoying himself.

The woman says, "Poor beggar. And out horribly late. Did he fall asleep and roll out the back?"

"Something like that," says Coach.

"Poor little trooper. How old is he?"

"He's twelve," says Coach.

"I'm fourteen," says John from around the side of his thumb.

"You know what you want to do?" says the man. "You want to make sure grandad has that back gate secured. You tell him, 'Grandad I'm not getting in there again until you check that back gate is secured'."

They come wheezing and shuffling up to the truck. Lucy notes that Edith and Fred have now positioned themselves at opposite ends of the bed. Edith has been crying. Fred stares at the sky with a merry defiance. Her forehead is scratched and her hair stands at angles.

"Lawks," says the woman. "Even more broken children."

"I want to go home," Edith says to Coach. "This is the last time. I'm not coming again."

Coach makes no reply; he is out of breath and deeply relieved to deposit John on the passenger seat. Meanwhile, the drunk man has drawn back and briefly massages a bicep. He glances from Edith to Lucy and then over to Coach. His good-humoured grin has slipped slightly on one side. "Heavens," he says. "What sort of night have you had?"

Coach says, "They just want to get home."

The man tries a laugh that is only part-way convincing. "If I was a detective I'd say there was something fishy afoot. If I was a detective I'd wonder if you were holding these children against their will."

Coach shuts the passenger door and hastens around to

the front of the truck. Lucy smiles a vague farewell at the woman and prepares to put her foot in the stirrup and climb into the bed.

"Yes," says Edith, as clear as a bell. "We are being held against our will."

The man's smile slips further. He shoots a questioning look at his wife. "Oh Mick," she says, and then nervously laughs.

"Don't listen to her," snaps Coach. "She's a right spoilt bitch."

"Yes," Edith says. "He is holding us against our will."

Fred says, "Shut up, Ede." She rolls her eyes at the man on the road. "Everything's all right. She's having one of her sulks."

By now Coach has cranked the engine and put himself behind the wheel. Lucy barely has time to get up over the gate before the truck finds first gear and begins jerking forward.

"Well, I'm glad to hear it," the man calls to Fred. But his smile has gone; he offers a limp little wave. "You all look after yourselves."

"We will! Thanks ever so much!"

The drunk steps to the side and takes his girl by the arm. The Maudslay pulls away from the verge, picks up speed and engages second gear. And still Edith is not ready to let her complaint rest. On hands and knees she scurries the length of the bed until she has reached the tail-gate. She stares behind at the diminishing figures. She outstretches both arms. She screams, "Yes! Yes! We are being held against our will! We are being held against our will! Oh, you fucking stupid bastard! We are being held against our will!"

14

T HE PUB IS shut mid-afternoon but the way the bar door is rattling you'd think it was seven. Somebody has urgent business with the Griffin. When the door does not budge, they slap open-palmed at the glass.

She is seated on a bench reading a library copy of *The Secret Garden*. She's just reached the part where annoying Mary Lennox has discovered the crippled little boy crying alone in his room. She is disappointed to be plucked out of the tale at such a critical juncture, but dutifully turns the book face down and trots to the door.

Higgs has worked himself into a terrible lather. His collar is open. His bald head is puce. His eyes are over her left shoulder, scanning the empty bar. He barks, "It's happened again. I want to see Mr Marsh."

Her father died first, in the war, then her mother followed not quite eighteen months later. When Lucy told this to others, they would perform a swift mental calculation and assume she had been carried off by the flu. After all, the Spanish flu killed more people than the Germans, although she's heard it said that without the Germans there would have been no Spanish flu. The disease was hatched in the mud of the trenches, and the Armistice released it. It filled a person's lungs with glue and turned their skin as purple as Higgs's scalp, and the soldiers spread it like butter. They couldn't wait to get home, and they took the thing with them. They threw open the door and walked into the house and killed off their loved ones with a kiss and a hug.

Just how many people did those sick soldiers kill? Nan said it was tens of millions, all around the world, except that couldn't be right, surely there weren't that many people in the world to begin with. There would be no one left; Nan has always exaggerated. But the flu killed a lot, that was certain. It accounted for three children in her class at school. It killed Winifred's mother and Edith's mother and her Uncle Peter and her cousin Jo. And she knew her mother was scared it would come for them too, because when the children in class began to fall ill, Lucy was taken out of school and the three of them spent a whole week indoors and did not leave the house once. She remembers standing at an upstairs window looking out at the empty street and wondering whether everyone else was hiding, or if they were dead, and if so, what that meant. They might step out the door and find the town empty. She remembers thinking she could walk into the confectioner's and help herself to bon bons. They could move all of their belongings into that nice house with the wisteria over the door.

About a month after the epidemic blew through, Lucy and Tom were out with their mother when a small girl ran to the side of the pavement to shout a greeting to a friend who was seated on the upper deck of a bus. June Marsh stepped off the kerb to avoid colliding with the child and was struck by a cyclist, scattering her shopping and banging her head on the ground.

Lucy and Tom saw the accident unfold, and it seemed to them their mother was not especially hurt. The cyclist helped her collect her provisions, after which she sat upon the kerb and waited for her head to clear. The shouting child made her exit and the double-decker bus pulled away up the street. After enquiring three times whether she was really all right, the cyclist remounted his cycle and then he left as well.

Five minutes later Mrs Marsh was still feeling giddy. She laughed at her frailty when she tried to get on her feet. Then the Lambs drew up at the kerb and suggested she run herself along to the hospital. Mr Lamb would drive her while his wife took the kids home.

At St Bethesda's Royal Infirmary, Mr Lamb helped her onto the bed and it was there she lost consciousness. The fall had caused extensive bleeding in her brain.

After it happened – after their mother died – the adults debated where the children should go. The paternal grandparents were the most likely choice, not least because Mrs Marsh's mother had grown frail in recent years and it was whispered that she kept mislaying her marbles; she might not have many more rattling around.

One evening, still at the Lambs', Lucy sat down and composed a painstaking letter to her Aunt Nell in Ramsgate. Aunt Nell wrote back to say that it broke her heart but that she could not have them. She said she was still getting to grips with her husband, and Jo. She said if it was just her and not Tom then that might have made a difference. She said that she loved them and that they must stay in touch. One week after that, they moved into the Griffin.

She rubs a forefinger across the wood grain and eavesdrops on the back-and-forth. Higgs wants restitution or he is walking to the police station without further ado. Mr Marsh retorts that if that's what he's decided, he should look lively and do it, not keep yacking on and on about it. But Higgs suspects that Mr Marsh is trying to brazen things out and that if push came to shove, the landlord would rather not have the police involved. Higgs says it is not so much the cost of the fruit, it's all the aggravation that comes along with it. The loss of labour, the hassle of it all. He is making himself ill running after that lad. He leaves the shop unattended. He's not sleeping right. He wants some proper restitution or he is going to the police.

Marsh looks up from wiping the taps. He feigns jovial surprise. "Bloody hell. Are you still here?"

"Right, that's it. Have it your way."

"*Ach*," says Marsh. "What do you want from me? It's nothing to do with me."

"I want ten shillings."

Marsh hoots with laughter.

"I want five shillings."

"Well, I haven't got it. I'm all cleaned out."

"Five shillings," says the grocer. "Else I shall be seeing your grandson in the juvenile court."

"Can't do it. Haven't got it."

The grocer points with a trembling finger. "You've got it in the till there. Open the till, give me the five shillings I'm owed, or I'll be seeing that boy in the juvenile court."

Marsh is amused all over again. He snorts and he grins. He points out, as a teacher might to a particularly dense student, that the till in the bar should not be confused with his wallet. The till contains money, but his wallet does not. But the money in the till has all been accounted for, which means he can't go dipping into it every time someone barges in with a full head of steam and demands five shillings to shut him up. "Bloody hell," he adds, "it's no wonder your business is up the Swanee if you can't tell the difference between your wallet and your till."

"Who says it's up the Swanee?"

"Everyone does. Everyone knows it."

Higgs weighs this up. "I want my five shillings," he says.

"I told you. My wallet is empty."

All this time Lucy has been rubbing her finger along the wood grain at the bar. She says, "You do have it, Grandad. I know you do."

Both men turn towards her. Her grandfather frowns. He was shamming surprise with Higgs, but this time it is real: he had not even noticed his granddaughter standing in the room. "How do you mean?" he says.

Addressing Higgs, she says, "I earned ten bob for him last night. He won't have spent it all already."

Higgs claps his hands. "There we are. Simple as that."

"You can take the five shillings and leave my brother alone."

Her grandfather fixes her with a look that is so knotted and unreadable it defeats her. She drops her gaze and returns to the woodgrain. "Well, fancy that," she hears him say. "My little granddaughter knows my business better than me."

Inside the saloon bar, the sun pours through the window and skewers the room with bars of drifting dust. She arranges herself on the bench, lifts the book to the beam and attempts to find her way back to the safety of the story – but it is no use. She's like Mary Lennox, she can't locate the door for the ivy. What had seemed so urgent just a few minutes before has become no more than a series of black-on-white blocks; words on a page, criss-crossed by dust motes. She keeps thinking of Edith, hanging over the tailgate and crying out to the drunken man on the road. She redoubles her effort to return to the book, and now she has read the same paragraph three times over. Come to think of it, where is Tom? He must have run away to the milk bar again.

In another hour or so she will devise an excuse to stand up at the window, or at least in its vicinity, so she can check on the progress of the old shire horse. But not yet, it's too early. Those crossing dust motes have swept her up as well. She is restless, can't settle. She should go and look for Tom. She remains on the bench.

If she wrote to Aunt Nell again, what would happen? It's been several years since her last request. She's nearly grown, which means she could look after Nell as opposed to the other way around. She could take a job and pay bed and board. She could care for Nell, and for Tom besides. If she wrote again and said all of this, Nell might relent and say they could come. Then again, she might say no and that she loves her and that she must be sure to stay in touch. Would it have made any difference if she had?

Something has been left on the linoleum, by the wall. The bar of sunlight picks it out where previously it had evaded her cleaning. With a grimace of distaste, Lucy sees that it is not one item but two: a complete set of dentures, upper and lower plate, laid in such a fashion as to give the impression that the owner vanished mid-sip, leaving them to drop unattended to the floor. Furthermore, she fancies that they have been watching her for a while. Any instant now they might come scuttling across the lino like some prehistoric crab, meaning to clamp shut on her feet, devour her toes one by one. She vows to pick them up before the Griffin reopens, but for the moment it is all she can do to even look at the things. She wonders whether she is sickening with a fever. She was feeling quite fine not a half-hour ago.

Grandad is bent over the supply book in the kitchen. But he is not working. He is just like the dentures: he has been lying in wait. When he sees her walk in, he glances up fiercely. "Right you are, Lucy, let's have it all out on the table."

She stands before him, hands clenched. She must be sickening. She does not feel herself.

He says, "Come on. Come on. If you've got something to say, let's be having it." The bars of sunlight don't penetrate the kitchen at this time of day, so the light is all at the man's back. It casts his face in shadow but makes his big ears glow amber. George drums his tail on the floor as a welcome.

"Someone dropped their teeth in the saloon bar."

"Is that it? That's what you want to say to me."

She moistens her mouth. "I don't think my dad would like it. You sending me to the woods."

He says, "I don't think your dad would like it, the fact I had to. The fact that I did it and the fact that I had to. I don't reckon he'd like either of those things very much."

Lucy stoops to pet the dog's Brillo-pad back. George thumps his tail in a flurry.

"And that's it, is it? Got that off your chest?"

"I suppose."

"You suppose," scoffs her grandfather. "You think you're the only one who knew him? You think I don't know what he'd make of all this? He'd choke on it like poison, that's what I think. He'd think, 'My poor little daughter' and he'd think, 'My poor old dad'. Isn't it obvious that's what he'd think?"

"He's dead," she says.

"Yeah, he's dead. So he'd be thinking 'Poor me' as well.

144

'Poor me, I'm dead. Poor old world. Everything buggered'. And fair play, he's right, but where does that get us? Me and you and the rest of them, where does that get us? It's down to us to keep going."

Lucy splays her fingers in order to part the dog's fur and expose the pink skin. She realises that unconsciously she has been checking for fleas.

"He still wouldn't me want to do it, though."

"Come on, girl, what do you want me to say? You want me to say sorry? Right you are, then, I'm sorry it happened for whatever it's worth. Wish it could have been different. But there we are and that's how it is. Wish it could have been different."

She nods at the dog and rises to leave. In the doorway another thought strikes her and she turns back to face him. "What if one of them . . . ?"

Sat at the table, his ears irradiated, he shoots her a look of impatient inquiry.

"What if one of them puts me with a child?"

This brings him up short. "Have they?"

"I don't think so."

He laughs. "Bloody hell, girl. Why mention it then?"

She figures there is probably an hour to spare before the horse trundles by, although all of a sudden she feels it would be no great loss if she were to miss it. Upstairs in her room, she slides under the covers without removing her shoes and pulls the eiderdown up so that it covers her head. That traps her own heat and she can feel it banked around her; there is nowhere for it to escape to. If it is true that she is running a fever she decides she will sweat it out on the sheet and then fetch the soap powder and boil some water. There are chores to attend to but these can wait for a spell, for she is extremely busy sweating the sickness from her pores. And if her grandparents want her, well, they can shout her name up the stairs and then she will walk down as though she is perfectly happy to help. She will lie in bed until they call her name. Only then will she walk down and tackle her chores.

15

E VERY SO OFTEN she catches sight of little Frank Perry, the post boy, except that little Frank Perry isn't little any more. He has filled out, turned portly; apparently he has some clerical job in the town. She has seen him sat among friends outside the Angel public house. He always tips his cap when she passes by. One day she will stop and marvel at how much he has grown. She will say, "Why, it's never Frank Perry, you are looking so well. How's work? How's the family? When are you going to move away and find a new job somewhere else? Or better still, why not die? That would suit me best of all."

Back in the day they had all hated Frank Perry, the diminutive post boy who haunted the village. He wore a midnight-blue uniform and rode an oversized bike. She recalls he had to extend his toes to locate the pedals, so that he would come listing and weaving up the lane like something infected, on the edge of control; a rabid old bat that was about to expire. Nobody wanted to be passed whatever it was that he carried, and this invested the post boy with a terrible power. She had heard tales of children who came to exalt in that power, or who would play malign games to distract themselves from the task in hand. They would ring their bells in a frenzy, or they would feint to ride up one driveway only to swerve at the very last second to target the house opposite. Or they would shout, "I've got a message for you!" at the solitary pedestrian and then add,

"Whoops, sorry, wrong person." She understands why they did it. Frame the world as a joke and it is like taking gas at the dentist. The drill's vibration becomes a tickle. All the same, she is glad that Frank Perry was never that way inclined. Frank Perry regarded the job as a torment and aimed to perform it with the minimum human contact. And she is grateful for that, although she does seem to recall that one unfortunate consequence of his efforts to avoid looking a woman directly in the eye was that he tended to stare fixedly at her breasts instead.

The poor, pathetic post boy. The poor, pathetic wives and mothers he called on. He had called on Margaret and he had called on Jean and she knew beyond a glimmer of doubt that he would one day come and call on her as well. This was not what he wanted and it was hardly his fault. He jingled a mortified warning on his bell as he walked his bike through the garden gate.

"Oh my, yes," she will explain to the youths at the Angel. "I have known Frank since he was a rabid little bat. I've known him since he was the most hated boy in a five-mile radius. I've known him since he stared at breasts all day long. Surely he's told you of the time he stared at mine too."

Except that this would be foolish, and what possible good would it do? She has nothing against Frank Perry, aside from the fact he's Frank Perry and had once brought her a message she did not wish to receive. And now the tables have turned and it is her haunting him, because she thinks her presence serves as a sour reminder and he looks faintly nauseous when he glances up from his tankard and lifts the cap from his head. And perhaps the thought flashing through his mind is just a mirror of hers. Why won't she move on? Why won't she drop dead?

And besides, who's to say that they haven't already moved on? The world keeps turning and it has carried them with it. In this way, the teenaged post boy becomes an office apprentice with a regular berth at the pub and a starched white collar that he irons each morning. The boisterous bride becomes just another young widow, one in two million, who supplements her pension with three days' secretarial work. Michael, formerly a baby, celebrated his eighth birthday last month, while the fiery young man who once worked as a typesetter and dreamed of bigger things is now bone meal in the ground, with his job at the printworks passed on like a baton. The replacement typesetter has been recruited from Taunton and his name is James Winter. He is in his mid-twenties, keeps a cottage in the village and instructs the local children in football every Saturday morning. When Michael fell on the pitch and dislocated his shoulder, James Winter returned the joint to its socket and carried the boy home in his arms. On another occasion, she saw him drop a banknote on the road and then embark upon a quite comical pursuit, trying to secure the note with his shoe. Some shift in the breeze brought it over to her and with one easy motion she was able to trap it. "Pick a foot," she said boldly. "Fifty-fifty chance."

In the back garden next door, the neighbours' dog is barking. She dislikes the neighbours; marvels at their cruelty. They keep the wretched creature chained up there all hours. She should go and do something, except she has turned more timid of late.

These days the streets are patrolled by spiritualists. They travel door-to-door, claiming to speak for the dead. Margaret has admitted that she has sat with two of them, which probably means that she has sat with four or five, and she swears blind that one of these frauds told her things about Jack that nobody could have known. She says, "Come on, Aud, there must be a part of you that wants to give it a try. I would have thought that you'd at least keep an open mind about such things." Margaret says this with a tone of tender reproach. But the whole thing is enraging; she wants no part of it.

Instead she thinks that one day she will take a boat out to France. She's read of a travel firm that arranges excursions to the field. Relatives stroll through the old trenches as if they are tourists at San Marco. They pay their respects at mass graves and eat picnics while sat on ammunition boxes. They munch sandwiches and stare at the overturned tanks and the bald, branchless trees. The prospect once struck her as ghastly, but it now seems less ghastly than sitting down with a fraud. In the early days of their marriage they often walked in the woods on the Mendips. They would find a high place to eat lunch and watch the clouds scudding by. The notion of the French trip is macabre. If undertaken, it may prove masochistic. But it nonetheless involves the breaking of bread and the contemplation of a view. It might drag the wheel full circle and bring resolution to see the place where he fell. One bittersweet holiday to put all the others to bed.

By nine-o'clock the boy is asleep and James Winter taps on the side door where he won't be observed from the green. He is more nervous than she and in those first blundering moments he rather resembles a child himself. He is too big for the room: he collides with the furniture, treads on her foot. The rows of books on the shelves seem to further alarm him. It is as though she has set him some fiendish challenge, although she explains that they are mostly Bram's books, left over, and that the truth of it is that they have sometimes challenged her too. She must never forget what a stiff-backed snob he could be. His love was so sweet, but it was at least partly dependent on her utter devotion to him. He viewed himself as her superior and yet – here we are, fancy that – it is she who's left standing.

Teasing, she says, "Work must be dreadful for you. To be so bothered by books."

"It's a waking nightmare. They rustle their pages at me."

"And you worry that they mean you harm?"

"Mental harm. Only mental harm. I'm not bad at the printing. I'm not so good at the reading."

"Well, you see, there's the difference. I think he saw printing and reading as all part and parcel."

In avoiding the shelves, James Winter finds himself ambushed by the small framed photograph beside the curtained window. "Oh," he says. "And here he is."

"Yes," she says. "There he is."

"Lying in wait."

"Turn him to the wall if it makes you feel safer."

She decides that, yes, she does like the replacement typesetter. Or rather, she appreciates the qualities she might previously have regarded with amusement or scorn. She likes his athletic build, his square face, his open, innocent air. She likes the fact that he is younger than her. It makes him seem freshly sprung, an elastic green sapling, untainted by anything. It is even a faint relief that the bookshelves distress him.

And as for Jim Winter, well, he likes her too. He says he likes her shape and her voice. He has found himself charmed by her unguarded, mobile features and bewitched by her boldness – the way she trapped his money with her foot and made him pick a shoe. He confesses that he was engaged back in

Taunton but that the girl broke it off and that this was surely for the best; he is well over it now. He says that he likes little Michael as well. He says he's an all-round good lad, a credit to his mother, a youngster you can trust. "A disaster in goal," he adds. "But still an all-round good lad."

Below the old photograph sits another framed item: a shrivelled pink skin, mounted on card and pinned behind glass. "Bloody heck, what's this?"

She cranes her neck. "It's really nothing. A silly thing."

"Ignore me, I'm nosy."

"No," she says, "It's a balloon. Or it was a balloon. It was important to me once. It's not any more."

"A balloon," he says. "Well that does make more sense." But a flush has risen on the back of his neck and she realises with a start that he had initially mistaken the balloon for something else. That for one upsetting moment he believed the lovely, lonely widow kept a spent, used preventative framed on her living room wall. She has to bite down on her lip to keep the laughter locked in.

At about this time of night, the village ducks go insane. They abandon the water and congregate on the green where they proceed to fight and fuck for hours on end. Stepping out to investigate, she has witnessed a number of avian gang rapes in which the hen is held down by one drake so that the others can run up and work at her hind quarters. She has seen assaults so violent that they can only have resulted in the death of the combatants. It is impossible to reconcile the cheerful, bustling ducks of the day with these nocturnal carousers. She can hear them now through the window, they yap at one another like dogs. The neighbours' mongrel takes the day watch and the ducks take the night.

Presently she will sit him on the settee and allow herself to be kissed. She shall gently explain that they should go slowly because she is shy and has not been with a man since the last time with her husband; that inconsequential old lie. And yes, it was true when she said it to Mr Lincoln the schoolmaster, but then it was naturally untrue in the months and years after that. It was false when she said it to the asthmatic electrician and then again to the married quantity surveyor, and the un-married gamekeeper who became so stirred by the claim that he lost control of himself before she could get his flies open, and it is false to repeat it to handsome Jim Winter whom she has decided she likes a good deal after all. What would happen, she wonders, if these men were somehow thrown together? She pictures them all on the back seat of a stalled country bus, passing around a bottle, confessing their sins. But that would never happen: too many coincidences. She suspects she is safe.

And when she sits the man on the couch and tells him her trifling untruth, this is his cue to tell her his in return. So Jim Winter will say that if she's not ready it's fine, that he is happy to wait, because it is not so much this night that matters as all the nights to come. And that this is because he has come to adore her direct gaze and her expressive face and the way she has shouldered her loss and raised such a fine son. And so, he confesses, he has started to hope for a future in which she has some small part to play, assuming she is not too appalled by the prospect, and she accepts that he might even believe what he says, at least in those minutes when he is sat on the settee with her turned to face him and the bed immediately over their heads. That is one benefit of an uncom-plicated man. They live on the surface and act themselves into being, so that by telling a lie they manage to make it become true.

When Margaret is drunk, at the Angel or in this very room, she has a habit of beating back over recent years and bemoaning all the ruin she finds. She leaves lipstick smudges on her glass and wine stains on her teeth. She drops cigarettes in her lap and needs help to retrieve them. Margaret has become an embarrassment, with her loud voice and her drinking and her parade of spiritualists. Respectable types have begun to avoid her.

But in the midst of her lament, this poor, drunken woman will invariably turn imploringly towards Audrey and Jean and say, "And what was it all for?" Meaning the war. "What was it for?" – her big coup de grâce, her unanswerable question. Then she and Jean will shake their heads and pull commiserating faces and there endeth the lesson. When all the while what she really wants to do is to point at the wine glass and at the stray cigarette and say, "What was it for? This is what it was for, you dozy, miserable cow. It was for you to be able to sit here and get sloshed and be sick and repeat the same tired sentences again and again. It was for me to take a man I barely know by the hand and then lead him to my bed. It was for some people to live and for some to be killed, the same as it ever was; that is how the world works. And if our husbands are dead then that means we have survived and what we've won is this moment and the next one, this night and the next, to do with what we want, to drag it down or to raise it up. What we have won is our lives and there is no greater prize, there is nothing more precious. So there you go, that's what it was for. And what more do you want, you dozy, bleating, drunk cow?"

She instructs the typesetter to tread on the inner edge of

each step, to prevent the stairs from creaking and disturbing the child. She does this to let the man know that she is a responsible parent and that the boy's welfare and stability are her primary concerns. She does it to show she is first and foremost a mother. She does it to ensure that this man takes her seriously. The truth, however, is that Michael typically sleeps like the dead and that when the child is out he is out until morning. Once inside her room, with the door closed behind them, she knows she can be just as loud as she likes.

16

FRED CLAPS HER hands and clears her throat. "Ladies and gentlemen, we have a sorrowful announcement, please try not to cry. Miss Edith has decided not to join us this evening. She wanted to attend but her sulk got too bad, it took a turn for the worse. Oh ladies and gentlemen, please do try not to cry. It is all very sad. Miss Edith has gone. She will not be coming again."

It's the hottest day of the year so far, they might as well be marooned in the Spanish interior, and when Coach pulls away she can feel the whole of Edmonton in her lungs: the smell of baked horse dung, dust and tar, and the aroma of old cooking that has no space to escape. And undercutting it all, the exhaust fumes from the Maudslay, which appears to be poorly. Coach has to crank the handle for several minutes before the engine turns over; he thinks the plugs need a clean. The omens are ill ahead of their last trip to the forest.

"Fucking cocking contraption," says Coach.

To pass the time on the drive, Fred suggests that they share treasured memories of their former co-worker. For her part, she says she'll never forget the night Edith fell down in that puddle and made such a scene, or the time she claimed that she couldn't manage the Mench because her monthlies had come on, or the sound she made in the bushes, howling like a cat. But these are just her memories, and she is sure the others have theirs. Edith may be gone but she brought so much joy to the world.

"She had quite a long nose," ventures John with a frown.

"She did," says Fred. "She did have quite a long nose and we shall always remember her long nose with a smile. Thanks for that, John. What a nice contribution." She turns to Lucy, adopts a businesslike air. "Actually, this is good for us. I've been thinking it over and we should ask for a raise. If the funny men are still paying the usual amount, then we need to get more otherwise it all goes to Coach."

Lucy is unconvinced. "But if we get a raise it only goes to the oldies."

"Only if they know about it. We ought to talk to Coach and Crisis. We need to see how we can work out a deal. If we're doing more Mench we should be paid more as well."

They come through the suburbs and onto Turpentine Lane. Ancient oak and beech pile up all around and the birds are excited; they keep dive-bombing the truck. The funny men have arrived bearing gifts. They carry thick glass jars filled with fortified wine that has the consistency of treacle and leaves the mouth full of grit. The weather is such that she would prefer to drink water, but she accepts the wine all the same, which immediately makes her lightheaded. The Tin Man's mask grows so hot that it sticks to his face. He turns his back and has Crisis undo the strap and employ the mask as a fan to take the worst of the heat from his skin.

This operation complete, Coach lifts his jar in a toast. He says: "To the continued good health of the Grantwood estate. Without which none of this would be possible."

"To the Grantwood estate," Toto says heartily.

"Outside it's all beggars and Bolsheviks. Everyone wanting something for nothing. But still, never mind. As long as the sun keeps on shining on the Grantwood estate." He appears to lose his thread; the wine is working its magic. "May the sun never set on the Grantwood estate."

"To the Grantwood estate," says Crisis.

"Too fucking right," says Coach.

It is perhaps not the ideal moment to raise a matter of business, but Winifred has never been one to keep her counsel. Now, without preamble, she lays out her case. "I was meaning to say, me and Luce want more money. It stands to reason that if Edith's left we're working much harder. If we have to work harder we should be getting more money."

Crisis guffaws. "What were you saying about the Bolsheviks, bruv?"

Coach says, "I don't see you working. I see you drinking our wine."

"You know what I mean. We're going to have to work harder."

"I think Fred's right," blurts Lucy. She glances to the Scarecrow for support but he is looking elsewhere.

The Tin Woodman, by contrast, is enjoying himself. He says, "Dear me, poor Coach. Here's your very own labour dispute on your very own doorstep. Poor old Coach, he thought Grantwood would protect him. Vive la revolution! Wheel out the guillotine. Poor old Coach, don't you see, the irony's priceless."

"You know what I mean. And you should pay us, not the oldies."

"Hark at this one," Crisis marvels. "Little Miss Bolshy."

Coach says, "Yeah, I know what you mean. Little Miss

Bolshy, wanting something for nothing. Greedy little brat who don't know she's been born."

Toto chips in. "You have to admit, the girl has a point. Either you pay them more or we pay you less. That's basic accounting. Don't be chiselling us now."

And all at once Coach finds himself outgunned. He scowls at Toto and then back to Fred. He says, "Fair enough, you've had your say, we can sit down and talk about it properly later." But his temper is flaring and his muscles are twitching. He promptly drops the glass jar, which splashes his shirt front, bounces off his belly and shatters on a rock. And now his fury breaks cover. "Look what you fucking made me do!" he shouts at the girls, after which he rounds on the Lion, who is only trying to help. "Leave it! Leave it! Don't pick up the pieces, what the fuck are you doing?" For a second, Lucy fears he might be about to turn violent.

The Tin Man says, "What an ill humour we are all in this evening. Might I recommend a quiet walk in the woods?"

And so when the wine has been drunk and the sun has dipped, Lucy helps the dwarf into his wicker chair and pushes him for a spell along a crooked forest trail. The moon climbs from the trees, vast and full, and it makes the place look so beautiful, like a fairytale illustration. It could almost be daylight, except that all of the colour has been drained from the world. Those darting shapes to the side must be a family of deer. The creatures overhead are either squirrels or owls. And here once again she is struck by the wonder of life. When the light hits it differently, even familiar places turn strange. She supposes this is why artists return through the year to paint and repaint the same favoured landscape.

Afterwards, in the clearing, she learns that the Lion is

missing. No one saw him go. Fred explains that she has been occupied with Tinny, while it transpires that the Scarecrow and John stayed with the groundsmen at the trucks. The Lion is not given to wandering off on his own and his absence sparks rueful amusement among the remaining funny men, who pretend to regard Coach and Crisis as being somehow to blame. Toto jokes that first off they lost Edith and now, bloody hell, they have mislaid the Lion. One loss might be forgiven, but a pair looks quite careless.

Coach says, "Oh yeah, very good. Please be sure to speak up if you've got anything useful to say."

They post Toto and John at the trucks and trudge out through the trees. The Tin Man suggests that they spread out in order to cover more ground but Coach won't hear of it. He says he doesn't want anyone else getting lost, for Christ's sake. He adds that if Tinny spreads out and takes one of the girls along with him then who can say what might happen? What with all that temptation, they probably wouldn't see him for another hour or more. He says he knows full well what Tinny means when he talks about spreading.

"Ugh, that's disgusting," says Fred. "But mind you, he's right."

"The big dirty get," says the groundsman with a grin.

They call out for the Lion and before long they locate him. He is sat beyond the clearing with his back to a tree. The Scarecrow takes Lucy by the shoulder and attempts to turn her away. "Don't look at him," he says.

She tears herself free. She needs to see what has happened. The Lion sits with his back to the trunk, with one leg bent and the other laid straight. He has taken a shard from Coach's broken jar and he has used it to open the veins in his wrist.

His clenched face has loosened and whatever disturbed him has now departed for good. The blood has run out to drench the ivy at his side. In the gentle lunar cast, it is possible to believe he has dozed off and spilt what remained of his fortified wine.

Dimly she is aware of Winifred's hiccuping sobs. Crisis says, "Well now, fuck me, what a ballsed-up sorry mess."

"Don't look at it, Lucy," the Scarecrow says again.

"Heavens above," the Tin Man says softly. "I do hope this isn't what happened to Edith as well."

"How can you joke?" she cries. "Oh God, what a thing." And now amid all this confusion, she senses the presence of further figures behind her. She thinks it must be Toto and John but instead sees two boys, a year or two younger than her, bizarrely got up in bright hooded cloaks. They have been drawn by the shouts or by Winifred's sobs. Their faces are pale and they are on the brink of flight.

"Fetch Great Crested Owl!' shouts one scout to the other.

Coach runs a hand across his face. "Fetch what?" he says faintly and to no one in particular. He resembles a man freshly shaken from a dream.

"Fetch Great Crested Owl!" And with that the boy scouts turn on their heels and dart away through the trees.

Working together, the men gather up the Lion and begin hauling the body to safety. Coach is breathing hard; Crisis appears to be giggling. But they are barely into the clearing before Great Crested Owl is upon them. He arrives in a tumult, like the trooping of the colour. His bracelets are jangling, his headgear is flapping. The two hooded figures snap at the scoutmaster's heels. "Explain yourselves, gentlemen!" bellows Great Crested Owl. "I demand an explanation!"

"Sir, please," gasps Coach. "I'm having myself a fucking heart attack here."

The Owl's voice is thunder. "What has befallen this man?"

"He's tried to do it before, many times," says the Tin Man. "This time he got lucky."

Eventually they are able to load the Lion's body into the back of Crisis's truck. They push it over the gate and let it drop out of sight. Coach, Crisis and the Scarecrow are liberally printed with blood. She notes that John, on witnessing their approach, has folded himself into a foetal position on the grass and that even Toto appears to have turned his wheelchair away so that it is facing the trees. "Oh Toto," she cries. "The Lion is dead."

"Get out of it, quick," Coach mutters to Crisis.

But the Great Crested Owl is still moving among them. His embroidered cloak billows. His tail-feathers rustle. He demands to know where they are taking the body; he wants them to notify the authorities this instant. He wants to ride in the cab with Crisis and be deposited at the nearest constabulary.

One of the scouts peeks through a slit in the canvas. "Malcolm, step back," the Great Crested Owl scolds him. "You must at all times show respect for the dead."

Lucy sees Coach draw his brother to one side. He instructs Crisis again to get out of it, quick. In a whisper, he tells him to lay up and wait down on Turpentine Lane. He shall follow on with the kids when he can.

Crisis nods and turns away. He gestures for the funny men to climb up in the back.

The Owl says, "Memorise these registration plates, boys. These men are intending to evade justice."

The Tin Man attempts to intercede. He says, "Sir, please try to remember that we have lost a good friend here tonight. We're all quite upset. I don't doubt you mean well but some sensitivity, please."

"Into the truck," says Crisis.

Lucy and Fred help Toto out of his chair and into the cab. The Tin Man and Scarecrow clamber in the back with the body. Then Coach cranks the handle and Crisis peels out so fast that the back wheels dig out a fan tail of dirt.

"Memorise that registration plate, boys!"

The Maudslay jumps across the clearing until it finds the rutted trail. They can hear it crashing through the brambles like an elephant in retreat.

"It's from the Grantwood estate," reports the scout named Malcolm. "They had it written on the side."

The Great Crested Owl appears to weigh up this information. Lucy sees that beneath all the bangles and plumage lurks a four-square middle-aged man with outsized dentures and an undershot chin. The Owl looks so fearsome from a distance and so unimpressive up close. She reaches across and squeezes Winifred's hand. In the hush that follows the lorry's departure, she can hear Coach still toiling to get his breathing under control.

"Why are they wearing masks and things?" asks the second scout.

Instead of replying, the Owl rounds on Coach. "Of course, you must realise I know what goes in these woods. Were you honestly under the impression that your activities had gone unnoticed? If so, you must be a more stupid man than you look. But this is doubly shocking. Are we to believe this is how Grantwood conducts itself now?"

The groundsman winces. "Sir, hang about. I don't know what you're thinking, but it's not as bad as all that."

The second scout says, "Why did that one have a mask and some hooks?"

"He was hurt in the war," Lucy explains in a murmur. "They all were."

Without turning his head, the Owl says, "Do not speak with these girls. They are both prostitutes."

The scout stares at Lucy and she quickly drops her gaze.

"What's prostitutes?"

Malcolm says, "He means that they're tarts. They kiss the soldiers for money."

Coach tries again. "Sir, hang about, there's an important thing I would say. A bloody tragedy has happened to us here tonight. But there is one important thing I would say to you now."

"If a man has died by his own hand, the authorities must be informed."

"Yes, sir, and they will be, much good it'll do. But the trouble is, sir, that the poor fellow in question is already listed as dead. All the rest of them too. They're officially listed as dead."

The Owl shakes his headgear. "What nonsense."

Winifred pipes up. "You know what you look like? In that feathery hat?"

"Hand on heart," Coach continues. "I'm telling the God's honest truth."

"You know what you look like? Go on, have a guess."

The Owl says, "A man has died. That is the salient fact."

"But hang about, sir, I am trying to explain. It's true enough, what the little boy says, Grantwood House looks after these men. And swear to God, the authorities couldn't be more happy that we do. It's part of our help for the heroes. But this is the important thing I would say to you now. Officially speaking, these soldiers are dead."

It falls to Winifred to break the silence that follows. "Big Chief Pig's Arse," she says.

On Turpentine Lane they come upon Crisis's truck. Coach draws up at the rear and the brothers gather on the verge for a moon-lit conference. The upshot, explains Coach, is that the arrangement is over and that the Sunday nights in the forest have now run their course. No question, it's turned out to be a right fucking mess and they are all sad about the Lion – he was all right, the Lion – but that is only the half of it. He says he's willing to bet that the scoutmaster will alert the authorities and that the authorities in turn will alert the young master or maybe even the old master, which would be worst of all. If the Lion had only seen fit to do away with himself in the comfort of his room, or even in grounds, they might have got out with minimum fuss and bother. Or how about if the boy scouts had managed to mind their own fucking business? Well, then that probably would have been all right as well. But it was not to be, so here they are. It never rains but it fucking pours.

Lucy says, "But what about the Lion?"

Coach throws her a distracted look. "What about him?"

She points at the truck. "What happens to the Lion now?"

"Dig a hole in the grounds. Put some dirt on the top. What does it matter? What's done is done."

"Oh God," she cries. "Did you not love him at all?"

The Scarecrow says quietly, "It's not as easy as that."

"Well, I loved him," says Fred. "You bastards. I loved him."

But Crisis is anxious. He says time is pressing and here they are gabbing and that there are houses close by, which means they might be overheard. They must now say their goodbyes and put the whole sorry business behind them, once and for all and without looking back. Coach is in agreement. He concludes that it was nice while it lasted and that everybody benefited, but what's done is done. He adds that if you take a shit in the woods, you don't hang about smelling it, you get away from the thing as fast as you can. He says he might go back to Epping Forest when the scouts are full grown and not scouts any more. Until that happy day he is giving the place a wide berth.

In the midst of this exchange, Lucy takes the chance to step away from the group and look under the canvas. The Great Crested Owl had felt that Malcolm was disrespecting the dead and this was probably true in his case, but it is less so in hers. The Lion is laid on his side facing the opposite way and he registers only as a black shape in the gloom. The girl kisses the tips of her fingers and touches her hand to his shoulder. "Lion," she says.

Crisis calls, "Wrong vehicle, darling. You're wanting the one over there."

And yet when Coach attempts to round up the children, it turns out to be John who's the most reluctant to leave. All at once it's as if the consequences of the Lion's death come crashing in on his head and it is imperative that he speaks to Coach right away. He says he enjoys his trips to the forest and would be quite keen to return – if not next week then why not the Sunday after that? He explains that he loved the Lion and is ever so sad that he died. But he says that he loves all the other funny men just as much.

"Get off out of it," barks Coach.

The Scarecrow is beside her. "Goodbye," he says. "We treated you badly. You deserved much better than this."

"Oh don't say that," she says, finding herself suddenly choked. "Don't say that. It makes it sound horrible."

He looks into her eyes. "Lucy," he says. "That's what it was."

"And is it true what Coach said? That you've been listed as dead?"

"I'm afraid it is," the Scarecrow says.

Coach cranks the handle and the engine turns over. "Farewell, sweet helpers," the Tin Man is calling. Lucy moves to climb up behind Fred, but she sees that John has turned stubborn and won't leave Coach alone. The boy says that he needs the ten shillings each week or his stepfather gets upset. He says Mr Parnell is counting on John to earn the money each week. He says he loves the funny men and wants to keep on seeing them.

"Will you at hark at this one," Crisis marvels. "Hardly says a word for weeks on end and now tonight of all nights we can't shut him up."

"Fucking hell," Coach says. "He was boring when he didn't say anything and he's twice as boring when he does. Get off out of it."

John says, "If I don't earn the money, Mr Parnell will be cross. Please Coach, I want to keep earning the money each Sunday. Please Coach, it's not our fault, is it? If I can borrow a bike I can get here on my own."

"John," says Lucy. "It's all right. Come on."

The boy spins on his heels and fixes her with a look of pure loathing. "Shut up!" he shouts. "I'm talking to Coach not to you!"

"Fuck off out of it," Coach says. "Useless little get."

At the end of the lane, Crisis's truck swerves away to the north, carrying its load of the dead, official and actual. Coach points himself to the south, in the direction of London, the children huddled in the bed for their last ride on this road. John is lying prone with his face in deep shadow, and seeing him in this way reminds her of the Lion. Stare at the boy long enough and she might start to believe that she climbed into the wrong truck after all. She is numb, desolate, and so she raises her head and focuses on the landscape instead. Who on earth knows the time? It must be well beyond midnight. Here come the Tudor suburbs. There is not a light in the houses, they might just as well be abandoned.

The soldiers who are dead when they are not really dead. The dark empty homes and the bright empty stars. She cannot process it all. Her brain is exhausted.

"So that's that," Winifred says. "Goodbye to the forest. Goodbye, funny men. Goodbye money, more's the pity."

John says in a monotone, "I'm going back there next Sunday. You see if I don't."

"You can do what you like. Won't be nobody there."

"You see if I don't. I'll go there on a bike."

The truck strikes a pothole. The children briefly leave the bed and return with a bump.

Fred says, "Poor old John knows he's about to get battered."

"Shut up, you."

"Old Mr Parnell's going to come at him with a stick."

Lucy says, "All right, don't tease him."

"I'm not teasing," Fred retorts. "I'm feeling sorry for him."

"All right," says Lucy. "But do leave him alone for a bit."

Instead, defying this instruction, Fred gathers John in her

arms and plants a kiss in his hair. Lucy is braced for his furious response. But tonight of all nights the boy is full of surprises, just like Coach said, and he accepts the embrace without a word. He docks his thumb in his mouth and stares beyond and through Fred to watch the night sky overhead. The pair's intimacy is such that Lucy feels abruptly excluded. From her place by the gate she hears him mumble something about his new house and his step-brothers and about Mr Parnell.

"Well, I won't let that happen," Fred reassures him. "Wicked old bastard'll have to get past me first."

Around the sides of his thumb, he says, "I don't know what to do."

"Then I shall show you," Fred says with a matter-of-fact air. "Will you promise to do exactly as I say?"

Lucy guesses that the boy must have nodded or given some sign of assent, because then Fred tells him, "Tap your feet together and repeat these words after me. Tap your feet together and say, 'I wish I was at home'."

In the darkness of the truck, above the noise of the engine, she hears the knock of John's wooden clogs. Tock-tock-tock. "I wish I was home."

"Louder," Fred tells him. "And take that thumb out your mouth."

"I wish I was home."

"Louder."

"I wish I was home," John says. And in this way the truck delivers the children to town.

THE HOUSE

17

GRANTWOOD HOUSE HAS stood in this fold of rural Hertfordshire since 1625, and there is no reason to suppose it will not still be standing three centuries from now. Its porticoed entrance is set back and shielded by gabled sandstone wings, which in turn are bookended by a pair of cedar trees, older even than the house itself. In fair weather, the sun glints off mullioned windows. In winter, blue woodsmoke streams from a symmetrical arrangement of chimneys. Whatever fierce storms bedevil the nation at large, the weary traveller is assured of safe haven behind the doors of Grantwood House.

If, for whatever reason, the traveller is unable to gain access to the house itself, he may console himself with the fact that Grantwood's hospitality extends beyond mere bricks and mortar. Grand though it is, the manor is merely the centre-piece of a five-thousand acre estate that rolls out on either side of the River Lea, crawls for half a mile into Essex and incorporates forest and farmland and the village of Brent. And it might be argued that the borders of Grantwood extend even further than that, because the family holdings also include a sugar estate in Jamaica, twelve London townhouses and an ongoing stake in the British South Africa Company. The current Lord Hertford has been heard to remark that his earldom exists as a set of core principles as much as it exists as a physical plot. He says that if a house does not stand for something, then more often than not it risks falling for anything.

None of which is to imply that the earldom of Hertford is an unbending institution, some calcified relic of a feudal age. History records that the seat was originally created to accommodate one of Charles II's bastard sons and this vibrant mongrel pedigree remains much in evidence today. Critics have joked that there's an obvious reason why Grantwood hastens to make common cause with the more roguish strains of modern British society. Like calls to like, some are minded to say. One set of bastards instantly recognises another.

What the house stands for, specifically, is social justice and progressive politics. As a young man, Lord Hertford lobbied for improved living conditions for factory workers in the coke towns of the north, and since inheriting the estate from his own wayward father, he has for the most part maintained his youthful idealism. First he shocked observers by establishing a minimum wage for Grantwood's agricultural workers. Then he shocked them again by holding his farmers to the terms of the deal after cereal prices collapsed and most of the fields went for grazing. The Brent residents were goitrous from dipping their pails in the pond. Lord Hertford ensured they had drinking water piped in.

Casting further afield in search of fresh challenges, Grantwood installed itself as a base camp in the campaign for female suffrage. It set up a charitable arm – the Grantwood Foundation – to provide support for disabled war veterans. More recently it has added an annex to the local hospital (the Grantwood Wing), built a theatre for the Bluecoats school and funded an ambitious programme of musical performances (New Productions of Lesser-Known Operas) that has been touring town halls between Aberdeen and Truro. To his supporters, Lord Hertford is a hero to the masses, enlightened and kind. To his detractors, however, he's the reviled "Pink Earl": an addled eccentric; an establishment radical. It has been said that he cannot see a liberal cause without ransacking the coffers and throwing good money after bad.

On the last Monday in August, an Essex sedan rounds the Palladian lodge and begins its ascent of Grantwood's gravelled drive. Inside sits Sir William Hunt of the Department of War Casualties. Sir William tips the scales at thirteen stone, but he feels roughly ten pounds lighter than he did leaving London. The weather is brutal: the back seat of the closed car is as intense as a greenhouse, and one cannot wind down a window because the roads are all topsoil and billowing dust, which means there is nothing to do but simply sweat oneself thinner. Given the conditions, he ought not to be overly surprised when he glances up from his papers to see a North African camel loose in the grounds. Nonetheless the sight still makes him start. There is a camel blocking the drive of the Grantwood estate.

Sir William leans forward and peers over the top of his spectacles. "Burton, I wonder if you'd be so good as to clarify a small matter."

"Sir," replies Burton. "It looks very much like a camel to me."

"Jolly good. So it is. Thank heaven we are able to solve the mystery between us."

When Burton sounds the horn, the camel moves on. Its pelt is matted and its flanks are heaving, but it picks and plants its hoofs with a fastidious air. The very set of its head speaks of overweening contempt. As the beast makes its exit, it takes the attendant horseflies a moment to regroup and catch up.

Burton adds, "As to why they keep a camel, sir, I'm afraid I haven't a blinking clue."

Lord Hertford is awaiting his presence in the Italian garden. A butler takes Sir William's coat and escorts him under the barrel-vaulted ceilings, past the garish abstract by that young brute, Picasso, and across a marble-floored ballroom. At the back of the house they descend a set of crumbling steps, which opens onto a thicket of plaster pillars and potted plants and the speckled statues of Grecian gods. Looking up, he can see that the west wing of the house has been dust-sheeted and is no longer in use. Sir William has heard that Grantwood's fortunes have taken a turn for the worse and that the estate may be as much as forty-thousand pounds in debt – and all at once, this astronomical figure seems entirely plausible. Taxes have throttled the noble families of England. The place has faded and faltered since he visited last.

Gesturing ahead at the sunlight, the butler says, "My Lord, the Earl of Hertford."

Beside the ornamental pond sits a lanky, sand-coloured specimen lacking any obvious demarcation of sex. He has pale eyes and big teeth, and his hair is so long that only his earlobes remain visible. A valet has seen fit to attire Lord Hertford in pristine tennis whites, although Sir William very much doubts he would strike a ball with much mustard. More likely the outfit has been deliberately chosen to project an image of youth.

He says, "My Lord, an honour" and hears something flop and resettle in the syrup-brown water of the ornamental pond.

The ninth Earl of Hertford responds with a vague smile and an unfocused gaze. He says, "I think of you as Pluto. The emissary from the Department of War Casualties. Prince of the underworld. And one day I suppose you shall come for me too."

Sir William tries a laugh. He says, "Only the Almighty Himself would dare to take on such a task."

"One of our statues bears the likeness of Pluto. Is it this one? Is it that one? Raine," he says, "which of these statues bears the likeness of Pluto?"

The butler says, "One moment please, my Lord. Let me ascertain."

Sir William draws up a chair and plucks a crease from his trousers. He does wish the butler would provide a jug of water; his mouth is dreadfully dried out from the drive. Yet it is apparent that Raine is now intent on appraising the statues, and there are quite a number of statues so it may take him some time. Sir William clears his throat and says, "Lord Hertford."

"One day I suppose you shall come for me too."

"Lord Hertford, I am grateful for your agreeing to receive me and I do apologise for having to trouble you at home. As I have mentioned, my visit concerns the unfortunate demise of a gentleman in your care, one Daniel Calder. Hopefully this need not take up very much of your time."

When the Earl dips his head, Sir William takes it as his sign to continue. He explains that ordinarily he would have processed the paperwork himself and the entire matter would have ended there. It is simply that on this occasion the issue was first raised by a member of the public – a scoutmaster, no less – and the complaint had landed on the desk of a junior clerk who was new to the role and unaware of the details of this particular case. The clerk then took it upon himself to make a grand song and dance about it. The first thing he did was to contact the Home Office, which in turn called Sir William, who in turn marched down to the junior clerk's desk to discover the boy busily drafting letters to all four widows explaining that, despite being listed as dead, their husbands were gadding about in Epping Forest as recently as two Sundays ago. Had Sir William arrived half an hour later, well, jig up, game over.

This monologue has taxed his parched larynx. He concludes, "I did so hope I should not have to involve you, Lord Hertford. But this is precisely the situation we have been so mindful to avoid."

Implacably, the Earl sifts all this information. "Dear me," he says. "You have embroiled yourself in the proverbial pickle."

By this stage the butler has returned from his errand. "If you'll excuse me, my Lord. I believe it to be that statue over there."

"Which one?"

"There, my Lord. Perhaps ten paces."

"And the likeness? Is it especially striking?"

"I beg your pardon, my Lord."

"Does the statue of Pluto resemble our guest?"

Raine appears to give this question his deepest consideration. Finally he says, "My Lord, I do not believe that I can honestly say."

Again something stirs and splashes in the ornamental pond. Lord Hertford says, "Quite so, quite so" and reluctantly turns his gaze back to the man in the chair. He says, "I dare say we should be rather disappointed in you. There is no denying that a delicate situation has been somewhat handled with thumbs. Still, I remain satisfied that the department is functioning to the best of its ability in what must be trying circumstances. I suggest we put this incident behind us and move onward, ever onward."

With a jolt of alarm, Sir William realises that Lord Hertford feels that he has now had his say and therefore considers the meeting concluded. He says, "Ah, thank you, my Lord, that's very generous, of course. But we do need to ensure that provisions are in place to prevent something like this from occurring again. In fact, I would argue this is the very least we should do."

He sees a look of faint strain cross Lord Hertford's sandy features, but presses on regardless. "I feel this request is not entirely unreasonable. Of course, in sanctioning and supporting the Grantwood Foundation we are also implicitly condoning the more – shall we say? – shadowy side of its charitable enterprise. However, we are only able to do this for as long as it remains, as it were, in the shadows. If you recall, Lord Hertford, we did have an agreement. The gentlemen were to remain on the grounds at all times."

To the butler, the Earl says, "I rather think the department objects to our helping the heroes."

"Not at all, perish the thought," Sir William returns. "If Grantwood is willing to provide sanctuary for the few poor souls who have felt unable to reclaim their place in society, then we applaud you for it. It is a noble endeavour."

Lord Hertford accepts the compliment with a gracious incline of his head.

"However," he continues. "However. You must understand that we need to avoid reaching the point where the department is forced to deny all prior knowledge of this unorthodox arrangement. Or worse, a situation in which we find ourselves accused of participating in a systematic cover-up, no matter how noble the intentions behind it. Furthermore, I must point out that if this latest incident had been drawn to the attention of the press . . ." He draws a hand across his brow. The brutal weather has quite sapped his resources. He really does think the butler might have offered to pour him some water.

"Calamity," Lord Hertford suggests. "Headless chickens running hither and thither."

Sir William nods. "And then I'm afraid there is the related matter. The scoutmaster's accusation of public indecency."

Stationed at the Earl's shoulder, Raine interjects. "Sir William," he says. "Lord Hertford would prefer not to be troubled with related matters. The daily management of the Grantwood Foundation in fact falls to the viscount, his Lordship's son. Such has been the case for these past several years."

"Forgive me. Then perhaps I might presently speak with the viscount as well."

"Indisposed," Lord Hertford remarks. "Off gallivanting."

Some subtle shift in the Earl's posture informs Sir William that he risks outstaying his welcome. Lord Hertford is a genius at conferring favour and then withdrawing it. He has shot down harrumphing statesmen with a single stony aside; doused revolutionary firebrands with a half-turn of his shoulder. The head of the Department of War Casualties is no match for him.

Making one last effort, Sir William says, "Lord Hertford, I believe we have managed to keep a lid on this scandal. God knows the Loughton constabulary has no desire to make mischief. However, we do require some assurance that this was an isolated incident and that it will not be repeated. Moreover, the department would like to be informed of what has become of the unfortunate gentleman."

Lord Hertford is bemused. He looks to the butler for assistance.

"He is referring to the Lion, my Lord. To the late Mr Calder."

"Oh ho," chuckles the Earl. "Of course, Pluto wants to know what became of the body."

Raine says, "Sir William can rest easy that the body rests easy. But Sir William should also be aware that my Lord has been unwell these past months. I fear that this interrogation carries with it the risk of exhausting him further."

Sitting parched in the sun, Sir William dutifully rejoins that he is extremely sorry to hear it. He does hope that the ailment is a minor one.

"Merely the fatigues of age," says Lord Hertford, directing his words more to Raine than to his guest. "Old Pluto will have to wait a little longer to claim me."

One last time, the creature in the pond rolls itself on the surface. Sir William supposes the pond must contain carp, but the water has reduced to a thick brown broth which keeps its occupants hidden. He does not like this sunken garden. He is already braced for the long journey home.

He says, "Upon my arrival, a most extraordinary sight. I witnessed a North African camel, just as bold as you please."

The Earl looks straight through him with his milky stare. At his back the pond-water kisses the stone sides and settles again.

Raine says, "The camel is one of the viscount's recent acquisitions."

"But why?" says Sir William. "Whatever for?"

The audience complete, Lord Hertford proceeds to organise his features into a benevolent smile. "What an abundance of questions you have brought with you today. We have scarcely begun to address one when back you come to jolly us with another." He chuckles indulgently. "It occurs to me this is a sign of the times. Everybody is asking questions these days. I propose fewer questions and more statements of intent."

He remains beside the pond as Raine leads the guest on the reverse trip through the house and to his car outside on the gravel drive. He does not move a muscle. He is as tranquil as the statues; as still as standing water. A horsefly swoops in to alight on one white-cottoned knee. A dragonfly brushes a wing against his bright breast. It seems to him that the butler has been gone for merely an instant and yet look, here he is, magically reappeared. He announces, "My Lord, I believe it is time for your nap."

With a confidence born of practice, Raine stoops to gather the ninth Earl of Hertford, who entered his sixty-second year last December and is suffering with cancerous tumours. The butler places his left arm under his Lordship's thighs and his right against his Lordship's back and he lifts him so gently that the motion barely ripples the man's tumbledown yellow hair.

As though retrieving the thread of a sentence already in motion, he says, "Of course the progressive agenda is forced to contend with doubters and nay-sayers. It is always easier to ask questions than provide statements of intent."

"Indeed, my Lord."

"While all around grey little men say it can't be done or that it should never be done. They ask 'Why?' and 'How?'

when what they are really saying is 'No, God forbid' and 'Please, not on your nelly'."

"That is very true, my Lord."

Locked in tender embrace, Raine and the Earl come out of the sunlight and into the house's marbled cool. They arrive at the hall in which two grandfather clocks are locked in endless dispute over each passing hour. And here the butler repositions the Earl in his arms and prepares to ascend to the upper floor.

Lord Hertford says, "Some men will say no and cast about for reasons to fail. Other men act and fashion the world in their image."

"Indeed, my Lord." His knees buckle only slightly as he takes the stairs.

"It is my fate to find myself drawn to the men who say yes. To the Alexanders and Hannibals. Heroes of that stripe."

Inside the main bedroom, the butler sets the Earl upon his four-poster Queen Anne and draws the curtains across the three mullioned windows. Lord Hertford's arms lie folded across his brilliant tennis whites. His eyes have hooked shut; he might be unconscious already. He says, "The impossible is impossible until the very moment it is not. It is my fate to be drawn to the nation's Alexanders."

Raine says, "Very good, my Lord," and pulls the door to at his back.

18

THE STORM ARRIVES at half-past noon. Black clouds spill upwards against the pale sky. Lightning clangs in time with the thunder. Two inches of rain are dumped in the space of an hour. The River Avon has burst its banks. The Wiltshire water meadows have gone to swamp. They're up to their ankles in the village of Britford. They're up to their waists in Charlton-All-Saints.

The Eastleigh locomotive recommences its crawl through the sodden green woodland. Salisbury is at its back and Gillingham somewhere up ahead, but the going is slow because the conditions are bad. The conductor explains that the delay is principally due to a pair of trees on the line. The trees blew down earlier, he says, but it has been a devil of a job clearing all of the branches, and as a result the service is backed up; you know how it is. The conductor advises that they simply sit tight, stretch out, they'll get there when they get there.

Mrs Kemp is unimpressed. As soon as the conductor has slid the door closed, she says, "Get there when we get there. Ever so helpful, I'm sure."

Jim Ferguson leaves off fussing with his pipe. "Let him be, why don't you? It's not his fault, poor bugger."

"We are in imminent danger. That is the point I am making."

But Mr Ferguson will not be drawn. He says, "Well, you've made it already. You keep on bloody making it."

There are five passengers inside the first-class compartment. The narrow space is thick with smoke. Perched at the window, facing the direction of travel, garrulous Mrs Kemp dominates the conversation to the point where it cannot truly be counted as a conversation at all. First she drew murmurous Mr Carmody into her drama of missed connections and thunderbolts. Then she snared the bulky Scot, Jim Ferguson, whose impatience with her mounts with every suck on his pipe. Now she glances across, seeking to inveigle the remaining two gentlemen. But here she suspects she has her work cut out. The quiet, smiling young fellow will not meet her gaze, while the last occupant – a dilapidated old chap with a high bony forehead – has spent the past hour or so in a state of deep slumber. The old man's snores are so noisy and varied they make Jim Ferguson laugh.

The rain slaps the glass. The trees shake their plumage. "All I am saying," Mrs Kemp continues, "is that if two trees can topple, then others can too. And was it this gusty when the first trees came down? Well now, you see, I don't think it was. And that is why I'm saying we're in imminent danger."

"My dear woman," says Mr Carmody, "either you feel that we should not be running late, or you feel we should abandon ship altogether. I would venture that you need to choose between these complaints. You cannot have them both running in tandem."

Ferguson says, "Buggered if I'm abandoning ship. Have you noticed how cold it is out there?"

"Language," says Mrs Kemp. "And for goodness sake, will you stop laughing at the gentleman. He can't help his breathing, poor soul. I dare say you sound much the same when you're sleeping."

"Not like that, I don't."

"Well. Well. Even so."

"Not like bloody that."

"Now then," puts in Mr Carmody, "let us all make an effort to finish this journey as friends."

At this point the smiling young man shakes himself from his daydreams. "A-ha," he mutters. "We're moving again."

The carriage noses through the woods. The old man grunts and resumes his snoring. But Mrs Kemp is only briefly cowed. She keeps her counsel for a tense two minutes, after which she abruptly announces that if a third tree came down it would smash straight through the roof. Try as she might, she can't shake the thought of all those trees overhead, either side of the train, bent by the wind, on the brink of losing their balance. If one came down now, it would shatter the compartment; they would be dead in an instant. Jim Ferguson rejoins that at this precise moment he might almost welcome it and Mrs Kemp says, "Oh yes, very amusing, I'm sure. Let's see if you feel differently when a tree crashes through that roof."

"My dear woman," says Mr Carmody, and at this the young passenger grins distractedly around the compartment and says, "Oh fucking hell, so much talking today."

"Language."

"Get your pal to stop snoring," Mr Ferguson says. "Then we might leave off talking."

"Will you ever let that poor gentleman be? Or at the very least, put out your pipe, or open the window. It's your smoke that has caused it. Your smoke makes him snore."

"Open a window? Arseholes to that."

Seated over by the door, the young man offers a brief, barking volley of laughter before falling silent again. He is still in no rush to join the conversation. The three travellers regard the young man with some interest.

"He smiles and laughs because he's nervous," Mrs Kemp explains. "It stands to reason, what with the wind and the trees. Isn't that right, sir? You're just as anxious about this as I am."

"He's not getting involved. I like that about him." Ferguson reaches across to cuff the man's shoulder. He says, "You got the right idea, just pay the lady no mind," and the man starts and grins and says, "Oh Christ, here we go."

Mrs Kemp says, "I also wonder whether he is not slightly deaf."

The train picks up speed and there comes a sudden break in the woodland – barely enough to reveal a drenched, rolling field and a small cluster of habitations – before the foliage rears back and the window goes dark. That cluster of buildings: it could have been the outskirts of Dinton, or Timsbury. It could have been Brigadoon.

Mr Carmody says, "One thing to point out about our young travelling companion. You do realise he passes himself off as a spiritualist."

"A spiritualist. Fancy."

"This man," he says, extending a finger, "this man has become quite the sensation of late. They call him the Magus, or perhaps he calls himself that. He performs at village halls, private homes. Small venues are best. They suit his hand-skills"

"Any good?" asks Ferguson.

Carmody smiles. "His spiritualism, I'm afraid, is not quite up to snuff. Anyone with sense can see through his act in minutes. Also the man lacks confidence and authority. Maybe, dare I say, he lacks sensitivity too. People aren't minded to trust him and without the trust of an audience, well, your success will be limited. But never mind that. He has another string to his bow."

While the passengers' focus is now on the young man, the young man himself gives no sign that he's heard. He rubs the heels of his hands into his eye sockets and resettles his rump against the green upholstery. Outside, the wet woodland crawls incessantly by.

"Fat little chap, isn't he?" says Ferguson.

"Mr Ferguson. Please."

Carmody says, "Our young friend is a freak of nature. He possesses the ability to make flames rise from his fingers, or perhaps it's more accurate to say that the ability possesses him. Either way, it is quite a sight. I've heard that customers pay to sit through his hogwash simply to watch him make flames."

Ferguson remarks that he has half a mind to hand out a few shillings right now. He adds that this journey has bored him half out of his wits. He could use some entertainment to make the time go faster.

"Feel free to ask him, but I'm not sure it's much use. I have the sense he's not keen to acknowledge our company."

"Oh yeah, I get it. Too good for the likes of us."

But here again Mrs Kemp stands ready to correct him. She insists that this is not it at all. The boy would like to join in and be included in their gathering and this is why he's smiling. But his very ability sets him apart and makes him lonely. One must be careful even shaking hands for fear of setting the other person alight. "Just look at him," she says. "See the way he is smiling."

Carmody says, "I believe there is a great deal of truth in

that. Also one would do well to remember the boy is damaged goods. Some might go so far as to call him unsound."

Mrs Kemp nods eagerly. "Sometimes I worry about him, it's true."

The line turns to the south amid dense woodland and the train slows, either to take the bend or because there is another train up ahead. But for whichever reason, the train is slowing; it is losing speed by the second.

Against the squeal of brakes, Carmody says, "Flames burn out. Mechanisms wind down. And the sad truth, I suspect, is that our young friend is a glitch. Or the consequence of a trauma. When the world suffers a trauma, as indeed it has these recent years, then it follows that certain energies are temporarily released. They spark and misfire. But these effects are short-lived because they are not natural, you see? Now some of these fires have made themselves a hearth of this boy. But what becomes of him when the fire burns out? Well now, your guess is as good as mine"

Ferguson asks, "If he's got so much energy, how come he's so fat?"

All at once it is as though the young passenger has rejoined them. The train's movement has roused him; he turns to stare at the rain-spattered window. "Oh Christ," he blurts. "Are we stopping again?"

Mrs Kemp says, "The train is stopping but the wind is not. If it blows any harder it will bring another tree down."

But it is not just the young passenger that the train's movement has stirred. When the brakes engage, the jolt is enough to wake the dilapidated gentleman in the corner. He comes to consciousness in a flurry of limbs, his snore aborted mid-breath and he proceeds to flash a sheepish greeting at his fellow travellers. His mouth is wide and wet, crowded with yellow teeth. "Hello!" he booms and then, when his eyes alight on the young man in his midst, "Dear boy! Hello!"

"You were snoring like a saw mill," Ferguson informs him.

"Was I? Dear me, what a shame, I suppose that I was."

Mr Carmody allows the old gentleman a moment to collect himself and take in his surroundings: the first-class compartment; the swaying branches outside. Then, leaning in, he says, "We were discussing this fascinating young fellow. But I believe the pair of you are already acquainted."

"Indeed, yes," says the man, pulling his embroidered robe tight around him. "He is a dear friend, that is true, a most remarkable boy. Fifty-eight years I have walked on this earth. And I have never seen anything remotely like him."

"Fifty-eight years," echoes the fat passenger and then laughs.

Mrs Kemp ventures that she does wonder if he might be a trifle deaf, although the dilapidated old man insists that he doesn't believe that this is the problem. He admits the boy has other problems. But being deaf is not one of them.

"Why is he always smiling?" asks Ferguson. "And why do you reckon he's so fat?"

"Shut up," shouts the boy.

"And there is one further prospect that concerns me," Carmody puts in. "When his wiring burns out – as it indeed it soon must – what becomes of the rest of us? We are travelling with him too, you know."

The train heaves and stutters. Mrs Kemp stares at the window. The woman is of the opinion that the recent turn of the conversation has now run its course and is awaiting the chance to nudge it back on its rightful track. She says, "I must say, I have some experience of what a strong gale can do. Last year it tore a pair of heavy bags clean out of my hands. It sent all of my shopping into a dirty green stream."

"Shut up," the boy shouts. He clutches at his knees in an effort to make them stop jumping. His belly joggles against his lap. The smile has become a stricken leer. "Shut up. You're just a bunch of buzzing flies."

"Come to think of it, this fellow has something of mine," the old fellow is saying. "He stole it from me and I would like it returned."

"Here," says Ferguson, "what did you steal from him, little bastard?"

"My amulet."

"Shut up!"

"Your what?"

"A glitch in the system. A remnant of stale air."

"Enough!"

"Amulet, I said. Amulet."

The passenger doubles over as though he is about to be sick. He cries, "Shut up, shut up, for Christ's sake, some peace!" And just as the train lurches forward to resume its painstaking journey, the door slides open and a uniformed figure appears in the jar. The conductor's gaze rakes the compartment. He sees the chubby young man bent double in his seat. He asks, "All right there, sir, have you been taken unwell?"

The passenger peers back. His moon-face is white; his eyes are wet raisins. He croaks, clears his throat and says, "Have I been taken what?"

"Unwell, sir. I thought I heard you call out. Are you feeling unwell?"

The moon-faced man looks at the conductor. Then he

throws a glance at the window. "No," he says. "No, I'm fine."

The conductor nods shortly, eager to be away on his rounds. Privately he is of the opinion that the solitary man in first class is some way short of fine. But this trip has been gruelling enough as it is, what with the trees on the line and everyone blaming him. He dearly wants to be home, so why go in search of fresh bother? He says, "Glad to hear it, sir, and thanks again for your patience. Sit tight and stay put. We'll have you there in a jiffy."

But this sad, sorry fellow appears to be too busy wool-gathering to follow what's said. His smile is ghastly and uncomprehending. "In a what?" he asks.

"In a jiffy," says the conductor and closes the door with some haste.

The continental visitor has brilliantined hair and a long grey topcoat that is almost a cloak – it extends to his ankles because his legs are so short. He dips his head with deference and he is constantly nodding and bobbing because his English is poor and he is always having to show up uninvited and he hopes this display will put his hosts at their ease. He is bobbing now as he pushes the door and steps apologetically in from the street. The publican shudders to see what fresh hell he's been served.

"Oh," he says, "you." He cannot think what else to say.

Bowing and scraping, the little supplicant removes his hat and places it carefully on a peg. Then he clasps his waxen hands as though it is cold outside and he is desperate for warmth. "Mr Lloyd-ah, such joy. How is you and the family?"

Mr Lloyd makes no reply. He draws a deep breath; he is composing himself.

The little man is a working man and he offers assistance to the needy. His daily rounds have carried him the length and breadth of north London and they have worn him out; he has too many years on the clock. Experience has taught him that the gentlemen he assists are seldom happy to see him and he counts this as his misfortune, an awkward cross he must bear. He circles the tables, contemplating a seat, and he could rightly sit anywhere because the taproom is deserted. But he knows he is not welcome and he has further errands to run. So he redoubles his bowing and scraping and says, "Mr Lloyd-ah, my friend. I have an interest in you."

He says this with an earnest, open sincerity and his words seem to have the desired effect. The publican is so moved that he promptly bursts into tears. His shoulders heave. His Adam's apple strains at his shirt collar. He has to grip at the bar to steady himself.

"Oh please, Mr Lloyd-ah. Please you don't cry. I have kerchief in my pocket." With this he hastens behind the bar, fishing in the confines of his billowing topcoat. He is mortified to witness the publican in such disarray and stricken by the knowledge that he has somehow been its cause. He holds out a crumpled cotton square. "Here! Look-ah!" And out of the corner of his vision he notices that the connecting door has swung open and that the publican's granddaughter has joined them. He nods a diffident greeting. "Oh-ho," he murmurs. "Bellissima."

The publican shakes his head at the cloth and tries to speak through his sobs. He says, "I can't, I can't, I can't, I can't."

"Please, Mr Lloyd-ah. Please understand. I have a big interest in you."

"Oh," says the girl. "Spaghetti-oh."

Behind the bar, Mr Lloyd makes a Herculean effort to collect himself. But it's no use, it's beyond him, and when the man takes his hand he only sobs all the louder. He says, "I'm so sorry. I can't."

The girl at the door has been observing these proceedings with a sober concentration. Now she says, "Oh Falconio. No Falconio. Please Falconio."

The little man's eyes widen in wonder. "The bambina?" he enquires. "She is making joke out of me?"

Mr Lloyd throws his granddaughter a desperate look. "No, Mr Falconio. Never."

"You Falconio. Me Falconio. We Falconio. Please Falconio."

Now the Italian makes a series of sweet, simple movements. His right hand dips into his pocket and returns in possession of a medium-sized hammer. His left tugs the publican's arm out straight. Next he applies the head of the hammer to Mr Lloyd's downturned elbow. He does this so cleanly, so smoothly, that he is able to reel off three swift strikes before the man can draw breath to scream.

"Oh," says the girl over the publican's racket, "oh, oh, Falconio."

Falconio releases the publican's hand and allows him to drop heavily to the floor. He now turns his attention to the bottles lined behind the bar, breaking each in turn with a single tap of his hammer. He spies his reflection in the large frosted mirror, ascends on tiptoe and delivers a blow to that too.

The publican lies on his back, staring up at the ceiling. He screams, "I'm sorry, I can't. I'm sorry, I can't." But the din of glass is terrific and it drowns out his words. The girl flies into the hall in a state that one observer might take for terror and another for joy and there spies her grandmother huffing and puffing on the stairs. The old woman has planted both hands on the banister to make sure she stays upright. She says, "Fred love, what is it?"

And in a shrill falsetto, her pulse racing, Winifred sings, "Oh Falconio. No Falconio. See Falconio. Be Falconio."

"Your grandad, Fred! What's become of your grandad?"

Winifred grins and shrugs and points to the taproom at her back. "Falconio," she says.

Early Sunday morning she takes the boy for a walk, away from the cottages and the infernal barking dog, to the low wooded ridge above Tucker's Lane. Michael has it in his head to sketch the rooftops and road. He says from the ridge one can see the entire village laid out. His drawing improves by the week; she cannot think where he gets his talent. The last time she drew a horse it came out as a hippo.

She is learning to recognise the good moments in life. This morning, she decides, counts as one of those moments. The air freshly laundered, her son at her side and the wind only bothersome until they find a sheltered spot between two raspberry bushes, which opens to reveal the land down below. She has brought a tartan rug to lay out; they might remain here for hours. She might even nod off, how nice that would be.

One thing they're not short of in the house is bright, white sheets of paper. Michael clips them to a board and lines up his pencils. He likes to rough the lines with hard lead and then move to soft. The wind picks at his hair. The nape of his neck's caught the sun. He says, "Doing the houses is easy. What's more hard are the trees."

She tells him she thinks drawing is like a different way of

seeing. It sharpens the eye or throws a new light on a scene. She's been living in this village for year upon year. If she were able to sketch, as he can sketch, she would probably see things she hadn't ever noticed before.

He says, "I'm going to draw every single old machine in Mr Lewis's garden."

"Now those I have seen. Those I could actually do without seeing."

The road below is still waking up. She spots a horse and trap taking the turn to the church; a number of stick figures embarked on non-urgent errands. From this distance, however, she struggles to make out who they are.

With the thin wooden board propped against his bare knees, Michael puts in roofs and chimneys, a pedestrian on the road. She has noticed the boy has a tendency to be tentative in these early stages, scared of making a mistake that will leave a telltale smudge on the page. But after a few minutes his movements start to loosen. The pencil moves faster, the strokes gain authority. It does her heart good to see it. The trees are in leaf, which means he doesn't have to agonise over the way the various boughs meet the trunk. Instead, he reaches for the soft pencil and drops them in as plumes of smoke, joyful explosions. She wishes she'd remembered to bring some green crayons. She finds herself wanting to colour the things in.

The last time Bram was home they walked up here together. Michael was a toddler; he had to be carried up the slope. They had sat in pretty much the same spot, on the exact same tartan rug, and he had leaned over the boy's head to kiss her lightly on the lips. He joked that it was odd to find himself in the air but overlooking his house. He said, "Most of the time I'm looking down on French towns."

"I hope you think this is better."

"No doubt about it. That's our little kingdom down there."

This time, it transpired, it was her turn to kiss him. And then, after Michael had excitably announced the arrival of a woodlouse, she had drawn a breath and recounted what happened so recently to both Margaret and Jean. And she had stressed, seemingly for the umpteenth time, that she was absolutely determined it would not happen to her. Because it would kill her. Because she wouldn't be able to cope. So her conclusion, she said, was that he must bring himself back safe and sound. He could come home and rest and they could take more walks like this one. They would put the whole business behind them and proceed with their rest of their lives.

"Aud," he said gently, "I'm fine, I'll be careful. And honestly, it's better in the sky. I have more control. I can keep out of harm's way."

By now she was on the brink of tears. She had whipped her head angrily so Michael wouldn't see.

"Promise me you'll come back to me."

He reached for her hand. He had lovely hands; long and strong. He said, "I'll do my very best."

"I'm sorry, but no. That's not good enough."

So then, still holding her hand, he set himself on one knee, as if about to propose marriage all over again. He looked her straight in the eye and said, "Aud, yes. I promise" and the solemnity of the moment was such that he had to fight back a smile. And the worst of it was that he'd broken his word. He had made her a promise and then gone and broken his word. She remembers the feel of his hand against hers and the way he had been trying not to smile – or possibly checking to see if she might smile back. She thinks a great deal about what that smile might have meant. Had he known even then that he would let her down?

The wind flutters the pages and it's 1923. In the time she's spent daydreaming, Michael has completed one picture and embarked on the next. She remembers that they are all booked in to have lunch at Jean's house, with her jolly solicitor husband parked at the head of the table. Afterwards they may repair to the park, kick a ball back and forth. The good moments, she thinks, are coming more frequently. She loves her son deeply. Probably she loves Jim Winter as well. String enough good moments together and they might make a good life.

The boy's neck is so reddened, she will have to dab on some cream. She says, "Base camp to Mick. Your presence is required."

He grins back at her briefly. "Twenty more minutes. I want to get this one finished. It's better than the first one. The first one was rubbish."

"Twenty more minutes." Audrey has to restrain herself from planting a kiss on his head; she knows how much it annoys him. She says, "Twenty more minutes and then we need to move out."

19

THEY NAMED SODDEN trenches after grand London streets and mapped the city upon the farmland of France. But somehow the layout had been shaken in transit, so that Piccadilly sat on the firing line to the east, with Regent Street running parallel close behind and the Mall conspiring to connect the two. And linking all three was a narrow, shallow scar, lined with splintering duckboards and butt ends, which had no name at all. Mr Pritchett told her that he started calling it Ermine Street and that this label caught on. Mr Pritchett joked that his French Ermine Street was only a degree or two worse than the real Ermine Street.

On returning from the front, Mr Pritchett had taken up his old job at the furniture warehouse and celebrated each payday with tankards at the Griffin, his clothes pungent with linseed oil. So far as she can tell, he has been able to darn himself back into his previous life so completely that one would have to look very closely to see that he had once been torn out. And she is aware that Pritchett is not alone. All around, in shops and offices and on factory floors, thousands of men have cast off their adventures and rejoined the throng and you would never guess where they'd been just a few years before. They might feel different inside but this makes no odds because the change doesn't show.

But not everyone is like Mr Pritchett. Some are not so robust, or else they had suffered in ways Mr Pritchett had not and their adventures have bent them out of shape. She has seen them out in Edmonton: the halt and the blind and the overwrought; the servicemen who appear to have only half made it home. They can't return to their old jobs because the work is beyond them, so they get by on war pensions or sell trinkets and matches. Some of these men are outright abject while others are at pains to maintain a front of good cheer. Either way, she has the sense the world has passed them by. They would prefer to be elsewhere. They would prefer to be in different bodies than the ones they are trapped in today.

Like Mr Pritchett, Lucy Marsh has survived her adventures and taken up her old duties. Like the men on the street, however, she would rather be somewhere else. Having previously disliked school and avoided it when she could, she is faintly surprised to find that she misses the place. School at least provided a framework that she could either rely upon or kick against. Now her days at the Griffin stretch out endlessly, unvaryingly, with nothing to look forward to except her birthday or Christmas – both of which she will in all likelihood spend working. To make matters worse, she has lost her appetite for reading. It is all she can do to pick up a book – the stories are too rich and too thrilling. The events they describe strike her as too far away and the vast yawning gap is enough to make her heart ache.

Instead, when alone, she tries to recall the songs she was taught in the woods. She sings to herself about the man who danced with a girl who danced with a boy who danced with a girl who danced with the Prince of Wales. She sings the one about the poor puss-cat and the poignant one about the flies. "Lay their eggs and fly away, Come back on the first of May. Hatch their eggs and oh what joy, First a girl and then a boy."

"The taxes," says Mr Marsh, playing pat-a-cake on the bar. "The licensing laws. The arterial road. If it weren't for the drunks, we'd have no custom at all."

How strange her brain is: she can't work herself out. For instance, she fervently wishes Brinley would ask her out again, as he promised he would; she even catches herself mooning over the memory of him during quiet moments in her bed in the eaves. And yet when Brinley does eventually drop by to see if she is free on the following night, she tells him she's not, that she is working through a heavy summer cold and that she ought by rights to be tucked up in bed. She is so short with the youth – so sullen and disinterested – that one would never know she had ever liked him at all.

Her window on the world frames fifty yards of Ermine Street. She can see Mick's Bric-a-Brac and the café with its white painted lettering advertising "Dinners & Teas", and the bedraggled butcher's shop, forever leaking sawdust on the pavement. But the elderly man and the shire horse have stopped walking by. One day they are there and the next they are not, and though she stations herself at the glass out of habit, she never sees them again. She supposes that her grandfather was right and the tottering beast was finally rendered for glue. This is what she had feared would happen all along, what she kept vigil for each afternoon to somehow safeguard against, and yet – horrible though it is to admit – she doesn't pine for the horse as much as she assumed that she would. One would think she'd be devastated instead of merely downcast, but there it is. The anticipation of the act is what caused her distress, whereas the execution provides something close to relief. Sometimes a murder is necessary to clear the path for fresh traffic.

Four Sundays after her last trip to the forest she glances up from her barstool to see that a girl has materialised in the empty saloon. The girl is dressed in a crimson blouse and a navy-blue skirt and her hair appears to have been recently set. It takes Lucy a moment to place her.

"Oh God," she cries. "Fred."

Winifred grins in acknowledgement. All at once it is as if the sun burns brighter and the air tastes sweeter and the noise of the street takes on a musical lilt. Right there, that second, Lucy is convinced she has never been so delighted to see anyone ever.

Fred says, "Poor Lucy, you really ought to have said. There was I thinking the Ring-o-Bells was a dump. This place is worse. This place is rank."

Lucy rises from the stool and then sits down again. Her legs are a-quiver. She says, "What on earth are you doing here? You look so pretty!"

In a booming stage voice, Winifred says, "Believe me when I say I am your fairy godmother. I came on a pumpkin to take you away from this place. I came to tell Cinderella she can go to the ball."

"Seriously Fred."

"Seriously Luce, no word of a lie. You're coming with me and it's all been decided. While you've been sat in here twiddling your thumbs, the gentlemen have been talking and everything has been sorted. Although I'd say your grandad should take whatever he's given and be grateful for it, but that's up to you, my grandad's getting nothing. All for me." She cackles like a pirate and gestures at her clothes and clean hair. "All for me and not for nobody else."

Lucy shakes her head. She has been thirsting for news and

conversation, for friendship and action, and now it arrives in a flood; she is bowled over and drenched. She has so many questions she cannot think which to put first. "What gentlemen?"

"Coach and your grandad, in the taproom. Come on, Lucy, get with it. Have you been drinking or something?"

"No," she says. "But I don't understand."

And so it is that Winifred, after an exasperated harrumph, proceeds to explain in her Winifred manner. Inside the gloomy saloon bar she lets fly a flurry of information, augmented throughout by extravagant hand motions and vaudevillian dumb-shows. She explains that the Eye-tie Falconio broke the old bastard's arm with a hammer, after which he only went and broke up the whole pub, at which point she thought, 'Well, to hell with this, I can do better elsewhere'. And then she remembered where they lived, out in the country, because Tinny had told her, except that she had no idea at the time it was in the middle of nowhere and she had a devil of a job, what with three different buses and then a walk on the road. And who was to say they wouldn't turn her away? But luckily for her they didn't turn her away, especially as she had no cash to get home, even if it was her home, which it isn't of course, probably never was. But anyway, where was she? Oh yes, she remembers and now she has been there a week and they've put her up in the cottage and she eats pink salmon from the tin and bloody hell, the whole place is totally out of this world, they've got an African camel, no word of a lie. She says she earns a pound a week which really isn't too shabby because the bed and board's free, but she's told them she is prepared to come down to fifteen bob if they get Lucy along too and pay them fifteen bob each. And really that's not bad either because the bed and board's thrown in, or did she say that already?

"Stop, stop!" orders Lucy. "You're still making no sense. Go with you where?"

"To Grantwood, you idiot, I think you must have been drinking." She throws her arms wide. "There's this massive old mansion, very nearly a palace, but we're not allowed there because the nobs wouldn't like it. Tinny and the rest live in a little house on the grounds and that's where we stay and I said I was bored and I wanted you there as well and they said all right, because the more the merrier and besides, they always did like us more than they liked Edith and John."

"But wait. Go for how long?"

"Miles and miles. I told you already. I had to take three buses and then walk on the road."

"No, how long do they want us to stay?"

Fred scrunches her face; the question has thrown her. She has never been a girl to think more than two steps ahead. "A week, I don't know? Stay as long as you like. I've been there a week and I'm going back for another."

And sitting dazed on the edge of her stool at the bar, Lucy realises that at this point she has just two further questions, at least for the time being: all of the others can wait. First she asks, "Why me?"

"Because I like you, stupid, even when you have been drinking. And because they like you too and there's enough Mench to go round. Also I get bored, so why not bring a pal?"

Next she asks, "When?"

Winifred hoots. "See, that's why I like you, that's the Lucy I know. Edith would say, 'Ooh, I don't know, my monthlies have come on'. Bloody Luce says, 'When? Let's go'. No time like the present, that's what I say. Run and pack some things. You don't need much."

And yet upstairs, alarmingly, she finds herself worrying that the whole thing was a joke. That she will return to the bar, dragging her packing case, to find Winifred in peals of laughter. Or worse: that she will haul her case into the bar to find Winifred gone, vanished like the old man and his horse, never to be laid eyes on again.

"No," she murmurs. "That'd be too cruel."

She wants to tell Tom what has happened but the boy is away on his wanderings. And so, horribly conscious of the time, she scribbles a note. She writes that she is off to earn money and will be away for a few days or a week and that when she returns she'll bring him something nice. She tells him she loves him and to stay away from Higgs' shop. Then she clatters her case down the stairs to find Fred standing with her grandparents in the hall by the door.

Her grandmother says, "How long will you be gone?"

Her grandfather says, "You send that money straight here. They got postboxes up there."

She assures Mr Marsh that she will bring it with her next week. A moment later, staring at the linoleum floor, she adds, "I'll bring the money for Tom. But I'm keeping half for myself."

"You what?"

Winifred cackles again. "She's working for herself now. We both are."

Mr Marsh stares at the girl with a violent distaste. "Oh yes," he says. "There's a word for the job that your sort do."

Outside on the road, big as life, the old Maudslay. Coach has the engine cranked and is so keen to be off he barely tips her a nod. Lucy has the impression that the groundsman has been somewhat deflated by recent events. Either that or he's feeling excluded. If the funny men have been paying Winifred direct then it follows that Coach is no longer brokering any deals. The current arrangement must be a humiliation for him. In one stroke he has been reduced to the role of driver, of servant.

Adding to this indignity, Fred cries, "Onward, dear Coachy. And don't spare the horses."

"You post me that money," Marsh shouts from the kerb.

"For Tom," she shoots back. "Not for you."

And so it is that not forty-five minutes since Lucy looked up from her study to find Winifred in the bar, she is out and gone, the Griffin receding and a fresh adventure before her. She sits in the bed that once held four children but now contains only two, and the truck comes rolling down the length of Ermine Street, which is a better road than its namesake in France but not significantly so – at least not for Mr Pritchett and probably not for her either. And perhaps for the first time in her life she sees the place plainly, as though she is studying a two-dimensional frieze or a formal tableau. Its furniture has all been arranged for her scrutiny; the inhabitants summoned to the kerb to bid her an oblivious, unseeing farewell. She spots the hapless Higgs, his back half-turned as he labours to construct a pyramid of green apples. She sees callow Brinley Roberts, engaged in lighting one cigarette from the stub of another. She passes Dinners & Teas and the three collapsed Catholics and finally, sitting alone on the wall beside the church of St Peter, she sees her brother Tom. His head is bowed and his boot heels drum the bricks as his sister glides by scarcely five yards away. If he glanced up he would see her and if she called out he would hear her, but it is as if the boy's name has temporarily stuck in her throat, and anyway, what could she say in those few seconds that she hasn't already spelled out in her letter? You don't shout 'I love you' in public places. It is dangerous enough to write the words on a page.

Ermine Street unspools, winds out and is gone. Winifred says, "Oh yes, my pretties. Oh yes indeed. There's a terrible name for the job that your sort do."

Now Coach presses the pedal and they rip through the industrial skirts. Here come the brickworks and chimneys and the tangle of silver tracks where the goods trains run. They flash past Mrs Ghoulardi who operates a spiritualist stand. She is sat on a stool behind her thumb-marked crystal ball. The rip tide of the Maudslay is such that it tears the patterned scarf from her head, so that Mrs Ghoulardi has to abandon the stall and pursue it out into the open road. Lucy wants to shout an apology, but the engine is loud and they are moving too fast.

At her back, Winifred says, "Independent traders. That's the name he was looking for."

The awful truth is that she is glad Tom didn't see her. She is relieved to be able to leave him behind; it's like shaking a burden. With each turn of the road and every jouncing pothole she can feel her chest loosen – and now the balance has shifted because it is Fred who turns quiet whereas she wants to talk. Lucy asks about Grantwood, and whether there is really a camel on the grounds. Excitably she points out that spot in the suburbs where John jumped that time. She'd thought he was dead. Thank heavens he wasn't.

She says, "You know what this lorry is, don't you? I was just thinking about it and I know what it is."

"Hunk of junk is what it is."

"It only looks that way on the outside. But what it is, Fred, it's a time machine. And when it's out on the road it's like it's travelling through time."

"Madness," says Fred. "Lock her up, the girl's gone potty."

"Think about it. I know I'm right. Back there is the past. Up ahead's the future. And that's what we're doing, we're travelling to the future."

Coach bypasses the forest and points his truck to the north. Presently the girls look over the side to see that they have entered a rolling rural country of timber mills, grain silos and rust-coloured meadows. Mountainous horse chestnuts stand shackled in ivy. Blue wood smoke drifts against a distant scarp. This far afield, the land still risks running wild. A man might go to ground, forage for his food and not be seen for weeks on end. And when the roads are this clear the motorists can't help but go faster. They bear down on the pedal and hit the fauna so hard that the fauna explodes, so that the tarmac is decorated with smeared foxes and badgers and rabbit and deer. It is a joyous, murderous country and it leads all the way to the gates of the Grantwood estate and the long shingled drive behind the Palladian lodge. The past is at their backs and before them is the future, where the girls will discover their lives changed and their fortunes improved, and will consider themselves blessed, if only for a spell.

20

S HOULD A GUEST choose to investigate the land immediately to the rear of Grantwood House, his route would
lead him on a gentle descent of sandstone steps and through
the sunken Italian loggia where the classical gods stand watch
and the carp stir the primordial soup of the ornamental pond.
From here a raked gravel path separates the kitchen gardens
from the apple orchard and then extends past the rolled lawns
of a tennis court, which has in its time been graced by no
fewer than four Wimbledon champions. At the back are the
stables and behind these an iron gate in the wall, which creaks
open to reveal a set of interconnecting workshops and service
cottages clustered conspiratorially about a cobbled yard. The
cottages have pitched roofs, small windows and low doors.
The first is occupied by Coach and Crisis and Coach's wife,
who works as a housemaid and is up and out before dawn.
The middle building, empty for years, has been given over to
storage. Its rooms are packed with mouldering books, broken
furniture and stacks of antique oil paintings that have been
judged as outmoded and therefore not fit to be shown. Some
of these oils should by rights be sold off or thrown out, although others retain a certain sentimental value. A buttery
likeness of the sixth Earl of Hertford hangs askew in the
gloom above the sitting-room hearth.

The funny men live in the third service cottage and
they have been assured it is theirs for as long as they wish.

Grantwood provides for servicemen whose injuries were so severe that they are now in need of constant care. But it also provides for those whose wounds were such that they took the decision to spare their families fresh torment and set themselves apart.

The Grantwood Foundation, established by Lord Hertford and then passed on to his son, might be counted as one of the few truly successful ventures in the family's extensive portfolio. Disabled veterans rattle buckets in the shopping districts of every English city. There are collection boxes inside church vestibules and fund-raising dinner-dances at costly London hotels. The head office occupies the ground floor of a town house in Hanover Square where a team of accountants channel the funds to hospitals and soup kitchens and community projects in remote rural pockets. And while it's true that, unbeknownst to Lord Hertford, some of the funds have lately been diverted to plug outstanding holes in Grantwood's other accounts, this remains a small, ring-fenced percentage, easily covered under general administrative costs. It is therefore not so different from the Foundation's other hidden expenditure: a small weekly stipend for the unfortunate souls who live behind the main house.

Coach told the truth, that final night in the forest. The funny men went missing in action and were promptly listed as dead. Each has decided he prefers it this way. They have forgone disability payments to ensure widows' pensions go directly to their wives. They have settled their accounts; they have severed their ties. Were it not for Grantwood they would be all alone in the world.

No doubt the land is full of similar casualties; men who slipped briefly off the map only to be relocated later. No doubt most were quick to make sure that the error was corrected and their families informed. But there remained, in the end, a handful – maybe more – who peered into a mirror in search of a face, or dabbed at a blanket where their legs used to be, and concluded that they were not the same men they had been before. They did not look the same or move the same or think along the same lines as the men who went into battle. They had been so transformed that there was little point going home. It would upset those who had known them; it would disturb the world's balance. The Bible does not record what happened to Lazarus after Jesus raised him from the tomb and threw him back on his family, beyond suggesting that the Jewish priests were scandalised and wanted the stone rolled back into place. The Scarecrow thinks this sounds about right and that Lazarus's family might have wished the same thing. The initial thrill of reunion would be overtaken by an undertow of consternation and then a creeping kind of horror.

When the Maudslay turns off the track and honks its horn, the funny men gather in the courtyard to welcome their guests. Lucy is delighted to see them and it takes but a minute to show her the cottage. What was once the sitting room has been given over to Toto, who can't manage the stairs. Instead, they all gather in the kitchen, which opens onto a back garden that ends almost as soon as it begins at a dark yew hedge as high as a man's head. The Scarecrow's bedroom is a tumult of papers and books and laden ashtrays, but the Tin Woodman's next door is almost comically neat. The bed is so crisp and ordered it looks as though it has never been slept in, as if the Tin Man simply props himself in a corner and flicks a switch at his back. Lucy has an urge to tease him about this, but there is something so intimate about being shown into his room that she finds she can't do it; she feels awkward and shy.

The girls are to share the third room, at the back. It contains a bed and an armchair, and a modest chest of drawers. The window is uncurtained, but the view is lovely: over the top of the yew hedge to fields and woodland beyond. Lucy puts her packing case on the floor and takes it all in with a glance. She doesn't need to be told that this was the Lion's room once.

"One important rule," declares Coach when they are back in the yard. "You don't go up to the main house, ever. It's not for the likes of you. Don't even walk in that direction. If you have to walk, walk the other way across the fields at the back. Even then my advice is to go early in the morning or late at night when it's dark. Your best look-out is to stick around here."

Crisis is keen to have his say too. "The other big rule: clean up after yourselves. Come to think of it, clean up after us and the fellows to boot. You'll have to earn your keep and we have plenty of jobs you can do. There'll be enough time for dirty business. Time enough, I'm sure."

Crisis is right. In the days that follow there is time for dirty business of every kind. Working in tandem, Lucy and Fred clean the cottages, prepare shepherd's pie and wash dishes after dinner. They launder clothes and peg them to dry on the drooping line in the yard. They shovel the stables and wash down both lorries until the vehicles could pass for new if you squinted your eyes and stood at a thirty-yard distance. And they perform these duties without complaint. Winifred explains it is a great opportunity and that they are basically employees of the Grantwood estate and this means they've pulled themselves closer to the aristocracy than either their parents or grandparents managed to do. She says running away from the Ring-o-Bells was the best decision she made. She says she can't believe Edith and how stupid she was. Poor Edith jumped ship just a moment too soon and if she had only stayed put she might be here with them today.

Scrubbing tiles in the kitchen, Fred spins exuberant fantasies of where Edith is now. She says she saw Edith dancing for pennies outside the Ring-o-Bells. She has heard that Edith has taken a part-time job with the organ grinder, standing in for the monkey when the monkey is sick. She says that Edith recently got married to the fat widowed father of a fat boy in her class and that both the boy and his dad take it in turns to have Edith in bed, and that they both crush her with their bellies and have unfeasibly small cocks. She hears that Edith recently gave birth to a baby. It has a very big belly and an unfeasibly small cock.

"For heaven sake, Fred, she's only been gone for a month."

"Maybe it wasn't Edith," Fred says thoughtfully. "Maybe it was John instead."

If the evening is cool, they sit with the funny men in the kitchen and play a card game called Bumble and Buck, or such a version of it as their various impediments allow. If it is warm they drag the chairs out into the yard and pass the bottle between them, like al fresco revellers on an Italian piazza. The funny men are not fussy, they favour rum, gin and scotch. Lucy decides that she likes the gin best of all.

"Oh Falconio, Falconio. I'm drinking like an Eye-tie and I'm so far from home-io."

Crisis heaves up his bedroom window. "Last time, I swear it! Keep the fucking noise down!"

The Tin Woodman waves this complaint away with his hook. "Who is this chap anyway? Falconio."

"Little Eye-tie fellow. Bookmaker. Money-lender. He broke my grandad's armio."

Toto says, "We'll get him for you. We'll rough him up."

"Oh leave him alone, poor little Falconio. Best thing that could have happened, if you ask me."

The Scarecrow says, "What a vicious kid you can be. I shouldn't care to get on the wrong side of you."

"You're a fine one to talk. You killed people in the war, the whole lot of you. How many did you kill in the war?"

"Conservative estimate?" says the Tin Man. "Six hundred, at least."

"Three bears and a tiger," the Scarecrow confesses.

"Put 'em up. Put 'em up. I'm seeing red which means you're dead."

"See what I mean? Vicious."

"But that's why we love her," the Tin Man explains. "She's our little spitfire. She's our wildcat. She's one of the best I've had and by God, I've had a few."

Fred dissolves. "Oh Tinny, you bastard. Always thinking of Mench."

Toto says, "Pass that over here, you've been at it too long. And anyway," he adds, "where does that leave our Lucy? What's Lucy's special appeal?"

"Don't," she pleads. "I'd rather you didn't."

The Tin Man says, "Lucy's appeal is that she's the nice one. Men lust after the bad girl and they dream of the nice girl. It was always that way and it always will be."

"So you're saying we've got the ground all covered?"

"Indeed I am," the Tin Man says. "What I'm saying is, we're living in paradise."

She does wish that Crisis had not called it dirty business; it seems an unnecessarily mean thing to say. It reminds her of what Great Crested Owl had said on that last night in the forest, or her grandfather's remark when she was leaving the Griffin. And immediately he said it, it felt as if he'd sent her off on the wrong foot, like a long-jumper who stumbles on his run-up to the board. Because it was not long after that, on her first day at Grantwood, that the Tin Man took Winifred with him upstairs and Toto requested she join him in what used to be the sitting room. And on this occasion the procedure felt strange; it was bothersome and uncomfortable in a way it had never been in the forest. Even with the curtains drawn, the day outside was far too bright and she was conscious of either Coach or Crisis clumping about in the yard. There was a framed picture on the bedside table of a woman she supposed was Mrs Toto, and a pair of spectacles he would put on to read the newspaper. The pillow smelt of his hair tonic, and once he had installed her beneath the sheet, he had her help him remove his shirt and his vest, which meant that she could see clearly where his arm had been torn off and his side pierced by sharp objects. And while this sight did not repulse her as she might have assumed beforehand, it did make her sad and breathless and she thought she might have to leave, it was looking that bad. But then she demanded some scotch from the bottle by the bed and drinking calmed her anxieties, or certainly softened their edges, and after that it was the same as before, or very nearly. She does not like the scotch so much as she likes gin. Still, she has discovered that all have their uses and, lucky for her, there are plenty of bottles to hand. All those years at the Griffin, surrounded by bottles. Only now does she discover what a comfort they can be.

On Saturday morning Coach says that he might drive down to London to pick up provisions and that if she were to give him six shillings she could ride along too and drop by at the pub. She says, "Why should I pay you six shillings if you're going there anyway?"

"Five shillings then. Don't chisel me, girl."

"But you just told me you were going there anyway."

"I only said I might be. In any case, it's off my regular route."

She weighs this up and says, "Maybe next Saturday." If she gives Coach five shillings and her grandfather five shillings then that obviously leaves only five shillings for her.

Another thing that bothers her: while she is called to Toto's room and the Tin Man's room, she is never called to the Scarecrow's room. Winifred shrugs that she hasn't been either, but that it makes no odds so long as the Scarecrow pays up at the end of each week and that it is common practice in business to pay to keep the goods on reserve whether you use them or not. She adds that the Scarecrow is probably drinking too much and that this has made him too sick and dozy to manage much else. But Lucy is unconvinced. The Scarecrow has never struck her as remotely dozy and she doesn't believe he drinks any more than Toto and Tinny. If anything, he drinks less. Most mornings he is up and working while the rest lounge in bed. He has set himself up in the workshop across the yard, where he likes to repair the broken furniture from the middle cottage and construct cutlery that can be used by men with one arm. Some of these items could be sold

216

in a shop, they are that impressive. She is particularly taken with a combined knife and fork that operates on a hinge. But he has also made a spoon with sharp sides that cuts the food first so it can be lifted to the mouth. The Scarecrow says that the only task beyond the power of a one-armed man is taking the top off a hard-boiled egg.

Finally the suspense grows so great that she resolves to confront him. She pads to the workshop and asks him outright when he is going to ask her upstairs and he glances up from his varnishing and informs her, quite shortly, that this will not be an issue. He adds that he is prepared to pay for her and Fred to be here, but that what happened in the woods was wrong, and will not be repeated. Then he returns to his work and leaves her standing there like a fool.

Close to tears, she says, "It makes no sense. Why are you cross with me?"

"I'm not cross with you," he snaps, which of course makes him sound more cross than ever. "Why must you be so deliberately dense?"

Dismissed, feeling hurt and confused, she turns on her heel. Mrs Coach eyes her froggily from the bench in the yard.

And there is one last thing that bothers her. When the money changes hands she sees that Winifred has lied. The lie is not especially great, but even a middling lie is a lie nonetheless. Fred had explained that she earned one pound in her first week at Grantwood but had agreed to cut her fee to fifteen shillings to ensure Lucy's inclusion. But when the banknotes are passed over it becomes apparent that Fred is still on her regular rate, which means that she is being paid more for the exact same work. Lucy takes the view that this is wildly unjust. She is careful not to cause a scene in public but rounds on Fred when they are alone in their room.

"Lucy, Lucy," Winifred says soothingly. Then she abruptly changes her mind and adopts a different tack. The girl leaps onto the bed and brandishes her pillow as a shield. She screams, "Don't hit me! Don't hit me! My lawks, Lucy-Goose, I've never seen you this way."

"It's not funny, Fred, I'm really angry about it. It's really bad form."

With faint reluctance Fred lowers the pillow. "Business problems. We'll sort it out. But don't you be getting all het up with me about it."

"How will we sort it? I thought it was sorted."

"Christ, Lucy, simmer down. And anyway, how was I to know they were going to still give me a pound? I was as surprised as you were. But what should I say? 'Oops, sorry, you've given me too much. Here, take it back and have the next one free of charge'?"

Lucy says, "I just think we should be paid the same."

"We will be," Fred says. "I'll have a word with Toto."

Standing alone in the cobbled courtyard, she can see the gables and chimneys of the big house. She could open the gate and walk there in three minutes but of course she does not, it would send Coach apoplectic, so she has learned to appreciate the house from one remove. Hardly a night goes by without the place throwing some kind of revel. The dark air brings bright noise. Men's laughter booms like distant thunder. Excited women shriek like fireworks. From time to time a band will play and the songs are wanton, exultant and thoroughly foreign to her ears. She has never heard music that bears even a passing resemblance; she suspects it might not strictly be counted as music at all. She wishes someone would see fit to throw up the windows and open the doors. She would dearly love to be able to hear the music more clearly.

The obvious consequence of consuming too much rum, scotch or gin of a night is that she has developed a tendency to wake early and then is frequently sick. Winifred is more hardy, she rebounds like a ball. The trouble is that Winifred snores and spreadeagles her limbs and it is all Lucy can do to maintain her berth in the bed. She wants to requisition a spare mattress from the storage cottage, but the days keep slipping past her and she has not got around to it yet.

One bright, balmy morning – perhaps the last truly warm one of the year – she hauls herself upright shortly after eight, which means she has slept for a good deal less than five hours. But when she descends to the kitchen she sees she has company; the Scarecrow is up too. Despite their last fractious exchange, she supposes she is still glad to see him. She likes him best of all the funny men.

He says, "Can I pour some tea? Or would madam prefer to vomit first?"

She accepts the tea and gingerly sips. "What are you reading?"

He turns the cover to face her. *The Island of Dr Moreau*, by HG Wells.

"Is it good?"

The Scarecrow nods. "It's not bad. I think *The Invisible Man* is better."

"This tea. It's not bad either."

Her studies her face. "I'm glad to hear it. That said, you remain a quite interesting shade of green."

"I think I'll be alright. I just need some fresh air."

They find a gap in the hedge and strike off through the field, following the route that Coach has instructed is the only one she can take. Along the way he runs her through the plots of *The Island of Dr Moreau* and *The Invisible Man* and she resolves to read them both because she is sorely missing her books. The mist is rising off the grass and a kestrel has stationed itself as a fixed point overhead. She feels less sick; stretching her legs has worked wonders. They circle the woodland, which is really not much more than a copse, and the return leg affords them a perfect view of the house. It stands warm and golden in its fold of green valley.

"My God, what a thing. And Fred says they have a camel too."

"That's true, they do. It's not very friendly, though."

"Who cares if it's friendly? I just want to see it."

Sheep graze the meadow beside the house's west wing. And in the middle of the meadow, amid the sheep, the servants have erected a medium-sized marquee. She assumes the marquee has been put up to accommodate the excess guests from the various parties and if so might have stood here all summer. The Scarecrow tells her that the marquee is made out of Indian chintz. The sides have been painted with crimson flowers. Each one is far larger than any flower has a right to be.

"How do you know it's made out of Indian chintz?"

"Coach was saying. He called it 'Indian Chink', but I worked out what he meant."

"I love it," she says. "Don't you think it looks beautiful?"

The Scarecrow grimaces. "I don't know, it's alright. I'm afraid it reminds me of a tent I once spent too much time inside. A small field hospital overseas." A moment later he adds, "Naturally that one was also made out of Indian chintz."

"Seriously?"

"No," he says. "Not seriously."

When they head down to explore, the sheep part like the Red Sea to allow them to go through. There is no sound from within the marquee, the last guests would have departed sometime before dawn, but the interior is still pregnant with the revels of the night before. The air is so fragrant with cigar smoke and alcohol that it feels thickened and sweetened, like condensed milk. Embroidered cushions and silks have been scattered and heaped along the sides. White trestle tables carry laden ashtrays, overturned magnums and champagne flutes marked with the prints of noble thumbs and fingers. She identifies a pair of Turkish hookahs, a discarded top hat and a sequined shoe with a broken heel. Sunlight illuminates the fabric walls, which gently bow and ripple as though the marquee is sleeping; as if it inhales and exhales in its own steady rhythm. And standing there inside the rippling skin, Lucy decides that ghost stories need not always be dreadful and that some haunted houses are significantly better than others. The marquee is at rest after its nocturnal exertions. It is a place of old enchantments and merry shades.

She says, "If I was rich I don't think I'd even want to live in a castle or a mansion or whatever. I think I'd be happy living in a place like this."

The Scarecrow has found an unsmoked cigar. He sets it between his teeth and is able to get it alight. "Only in the summertime, mind," he says indistinctly. "You just see what this place feels like in November."

"In November," she says. "In November I should have the thing taken down and shipped to the West Indies. Then I

221

would have it put up on the beach. Each morning I'd open the flap and step into the sea for a bathe. In the afternoon I'd throw in a hook and pull out something for dinner."

The Scarecrow coughs. "And where would you cook it – this fish you caught?"

"Oh well, that would be the servants' problem. I can't be doing with cooking, you see."

"Fair enough, it sounds splendid. I'm relieved to see that you've properly thought this through."

Out of the tail of one eye, she sees something stir. She supposes the breeze is at play against the fabric again. Then, with a rush of alarm, she realises the source of the disturbance is lower down, among the piled cushions and throws, a portion of which now tumbles away to reveal a tangle of honeyed limbs and abundant hair. The marquee is not empty. It contains three prostrate figures in a dizzying state of undress. Two gorgeous young women frame a tall, dark-headed young man. They are tucked in so tightly that they might almost be one creature.

Lucy freezes. She takes in the sight with a horrified stare. And while the fairytale dryads remain securely asleep, it is apparent their prince has been roused from his slumber. He extends one long arm and dislodges the woman at his front. He peels himself free from the naked breasts at his back. Lucy judges him to be a handsome gentleman in his early thirties, although arguably his mouth is too small and his eyes too widely spaced. He is barefoot and elegantly ruffled. His shell-pink shirt has been unbuttoned to reveal a muscular stomach and a tanned, hairless chest.

Her paralysis breaks. She shuffles behind the table and seizes the Scarecrow's hand, which means he cannot retrieve the cigar which still sits in his mouth. "Lucy," he mutters. "It's all right. Don't worry."

The young gentleman props himself on one elbow. He blinks and squints, dazzled by the sunlight pouring in through the chintz. On registering the intruders, he manages the notable feat of arranging his face into a simultaneous smile and scowl. He looks from Lucy to the Scarecrow and back to Lucy again. Then he clears his throat without hurry and says, "Rub-a-dub-dub."

21

T HE MAN LOLLING amid the cushions and silks inside the enchanted marquee is none other than Mr Rupert Fortnum-Hyde – although this is merely one of his names. Coach refers to him as the young master and his friends variously address him as King-Roo and Kanga-Roo and sometimes as Woody, after Grantwood, which is his preferred nickname. More formally, he is known as the Viscount of Hertford and stands to inherit the estate upon the death of his father, assuming the Treasury doesn't strip him of the lot. Fortnum-Hyde for his part plans to live to one hundred. Moreover, he intends to live every one of those years to the full. He has been blessed with authority, charisma and pristine self-belief. He possesses the loose, lordly confidence of a man who has never been thwarted in his pursuit of whatever he wants at any given time.

Naturally he has been raised as a child of privilege – the cherished heir of a titled family, succoured and sated by parental adoration. His mother would trill with delight whenever he so much as walked into a room. His father was constantly on the look-out for proof of ability and succeeded in finding countless bits of evidence which might have eluded those with a less discerning eye. It mattered not that the boy was an indifferent student, bored by books and drawn towards devilry. His boundless energy had already marked him for greatness. His gallant activities attracted a gaggle of admirers. Friends knew that wherever Fortnum-Hyde went, the adventure would follow.

It is said that, while still a pupil at Eton, he stepped into the ring for a bet and within seconds proceeded to knock a prize-fighter on his tail. In his early twenties, on the grass at Grantwood, he had conspired to split the opening four sets against ironclad Arthur Gore, that old titan of lawn tennis, and was only trailing by a break in the fifth when Gore ran into the net post and had to be carried to his chair. He believes that this should therefore go down as a technical victory.

The war did not move him as it moved other people. He served as a staff officer at brigade headquarters and King George himself had pinned a medal to his breast. All the same, he was at pains to point out that he did little to earn it and knew of many chaps who had sacrificed rather more. In fact he had only had cause to visit the line once in three years and had not been overly impressed by its dismal, dirty tone. Every other Friday he was able to board a boat out of Calais and could be found dining at his Mayfair club before eight. He allows that most of the other poor sods were not nearly so fortunate, they had a lousy old time. He says that the Grantwood Foundation is about setting the past right.

After the Armistice, against his father's wishes, he spent six months in Paris and refers to this now as a life-changing experience. In the bars of Pigalle, he drank alongside the likes of Brancusi and Picasso, Modigliani and Picabia and even tried his hand at painting a few nude studies in a cavernous rented attic with a picturesque leaking roof. The act of painting the nudes did not interest him nearly so much as the nudes themselves did. But above even that – above even the nudes – was the pure thrill of discovery, the bright rush of fresh knowledge, the sense of standing at the very centre of something that could only strengthen and bloom and turn the world on its head.

. If the man has a failing it is that he is a hedonist, a spendthrift and a gadabout. He drinks too deeply, enthuses too wildly and is drawn like a moth towards sensation and risk. He enjoys smoking opium and injecting morphine, but in recent years has developed a taste for cocaine, which he carries with him at all times inside a screw-top glass vial. He holds the opinion that opium and morphine are the drugs for dreamers whereas cocaine is an agent of the twentieth-century: a drug for action, a drug for doers. He has always regarded himself above all as a doer.

Rupert Fortnum-Hyde, then, has grown up with the conviction that he is able to do whatever he chooses to do. And what he has chosen to do is to think big and act boldly. What he wants is nothing less than the future itself – or, at least, his hand on its tiller, or his valise in its state room. The nation, he knows, is in a state of horrid confusion. This is because it is mired in the past, centrist and timid, in thrall to antique ideas and institutions. He pictures a future that is lean and hard and unafraid of extremes. To this end he is determined that Grantwood should be a friend to the new. It must be a seedbed for radical notions, a haven for anyone in flight from mediocrity, a home for heroes of every stripe, for outsiders and rebels. These are the men he feels a kinship with. These are the men he will nurture and promote. On this balmy morning in September, rolling half-drunk and hungover from a night amid the cushions, he fancies that his mission is already well underway.

Six hours later, Coach comes trotting through the side gate

in some agitation. He says that the young master desires to speak with both Winifred and Lucy at the earliest opportunity. He says they need to freshen up and run to the house right away. He says the young master is waiting by the pond in the loggia. He says that they are to remember their place at all times – and not to breathe a word about anything that he, Coach, may or may not have done in the past.

"What's loggia?" demands Winifred.

"Italian garden. Just follow the path."

"Ooh," she says, "Falconio."

"Shut up now. Shake a leg for God's sake."

But at the gate an amusing thought strikes her and she turns back to the groundsman. "What do you reckon he'd do if I said you got me pregnant?"

The man's start is so violent he nearly clears the cobblestones. "You what?"

"Ooh please, your Lordship. Coach put me with child and I'm only fourteen years old."

"Get the fuck," he says. "You're a nasty piece of work alright."

In the intervening hours the viscount has changed into a lemon shirt, bright white slacks and two-tone brogues. A homburg hat is set back on his dark head. He is lounging at a table and regards their approach with a kind of glorious bored amusement. He says, "Miss Lucy, isn't it? And the name of your fiery-looking little friend?"

"Winifred, sir."

"Winifred." He yawns. "I like it."

The butler glides in, pours three glasses of wine from a decanter and then glides out, as stealthy as a stoat. Lucy sips from her glass and attempts to hold her gaze steady but she is entranced by the place. What with this and the marquee, her head is positively spinning. She keeps catching sight of the cream-coloured gods. She is terribly conscious of the proximity of the house itself, separated from them by no more than a run of stone steps and some trailing bougainvillea. It is all she can do not to stand up and gawp.

In his unhurried fashion, Fortnum-Hyde says, "Indirectly you have each provoked quite a scandal."

"Oh," she blurts, "I'm so sorry."

He raises a hand. "Relax. I am assured that it wasn't your fault."

"Or mine," rejoins Fred.

He says, "I must add at this juncture that I had not the faintest idea what Coach and Crisis were getting up to out there. They are a pair of fucking troglodytes, the both of them, and we are still to decide what their punishment should be. It was wrong and it was dangerous. And I would stress that Grantwood in no way condones such activities."

Lucy stares fixedly at the rim of her glass. She feels a flush rise on her cheeks and dearly hopes it won't show.

"All that being said," he continues, "if you desire to visit with our house guests – of your own free will, of course – then I see no particular reason why you shouldn't do that. And removing the groundsmen from the equation, I see no particular reason why you shouldn't also make yourselves a little money from the opportunities provided."

"Independent traders," Winifred says.

"Independent traders." Rupert Fortnum-Hyde snorts; laughter lines etch his cheeks. "I do like this one," he tells Lucy. "This one has got spunk."

There is something fascinating about the tall man at the

table. He might have recently winged in from some neighbouring galaxy. The antics of humble earthlings are a source of entertainment to him; enough to provoke a mild, casual interest. But his thoughts are directed towards higher matters.

Plucking up her courage, she takes a gulp of wine and asks if it was he who named the funny men after Dorothy's companions in *The Wonderful Wizard of Oz*. He grins and says, "I believe that was more my sister's doing. Do you disapprove?"

"No, sir," she says. "Of course not." She is thrilled by the news that this man has a sister.

The meeting in the loggia appears to have concluded. But when Lucy and Fred get up to leave, Fortnum-Hyde lifts his tanned hand and the gesture is so commanding that it fixes them both in a semi-standing position. He reaches for his glass, appraises the girls with a fetching frown and says that he likes to fill Grantwood with unconventional people. In the house alone, he explains, he is currently playing host to an avant-garde painter and a political playwright. A group of negro musicians. All kinds of types.

Fred interrupts. "We've heard the musicians. My stars, what a racket."

Fortnum-Hyde appears tickled all over again. "I shall have them make that the title of their next composition. My Stars, What a Racket."

By now Lucy's knees are aching. She lowers herself to the chair and nods at Fred to do likewise.

Fortnum-Hyde says, "What I look for is people who gamble and chaps who take risks. I must say I'm half-minded to throw your gentlemen friends in amongst that number. That is why I pay their costs. That is why they will always be welcome on my estate. You should be aware that your fine fellows are heroes to a man. They are men of action. They are stone-cold killers, or at least they were. And of course they are outcasts besides. All of which makes them hunky-dory with me. These, you see, are the individuals I like."

"Yes sir," Lucy murmurs.

He reaches into his pocket and removes a glass vial. Next he instructs the girls to each hold out their left hand and make it into a fist. The man judges the breeze, leans into the table and expertly applies a hillock of white dust to Lucy's hand and then to Fred's.

"What is it?" says Fred.

He says, "You can call it a lot of names in a lot of languages. I have heard it called dowser and I have heard it called bouncer. And a friend of mine likes to call it a secular sacrament. That's rather good, I think – a secular sacrament. Take it quickly, before it blows away."

And yet when Lucy obediently sticks out a tongue, her response sends Fortnum-Hyde into paroxysms of mirth. "No, don't eat it, you dope. Sniff it up your nose. Oh foolish child, lapped it up like a dog. Would you believe it? Is she always like this?"

"Most times," nods Fred. The girl applies one nostril and is then forced to pinch the bridge of her nose to prevent herself sneezing.

But Lucy has collapsed against the back of her chair. Her face is glowing and her mouth is fizzing. Her lips inflate like balloons. Her teeth are colossal. She is feeling utterly out of sorts. She vows that next time – assuming there is a next time – she will be sure to follow procedure and sniff the powder instead.

Still chuckling, the man asks how she is faring and she

nods and beams to let him know that she's fine. He asks what she thinks it tastes of, the powder, and she shakes her head because she has not the slightest idea. The dust tastes almost citrus but it has a dry, savage edge. It prickles and rasps. It might be crushed human bones.

"Think about it. What does it taste like to you?"

"I don't know, sir."

"Think about it. Take a second."

"I don't know."

Rupert Fortnum-Hyde grins. "Then I shall tell you, my child. That taste is the future."

22

IN THE COBBLED yard by the cottage, Fred says, "And we had yellow wine and everything and we just sat there in the Italian garden, fancy as you like, and anyone who walked down the steps and saw us would probably have thought we were his sisters or his nieces or something like that."

Toto says, "He's a proper gent and he's done us proud. You'll have no argument from me about that."

"And he gave us this amazing dust to sniff, only Lucy licked it and that made him laugh. And he's quite spiffing, I like him. And wait, best of all, he really likes us all too. He said we can go up to the house just whenever we want. So that shows how much Coach knows, he can't tell us what to do." She adds, "I might go up there tomorrow. He's throwing another party, because he likes parties best of all."

Round and round the bottle goes. Above their heads the stars are bright. This has become their nightly ritual. It takes an extremely cold evening to drive them into the kitchen, which is narrow and oppressive and fills too quickly with smoke. The yard suits them better, and they genuinely do try to keep the noise down. Each time they argue or joke it sends Crisis quite demented.

It is shortly before midnight when Lucy's sense of balance becomes strained and her stomach flip-flops and she excuses herself to run off and be sick. When she returns it is clear that during her five minutes away the conversation has petered to a halt. The funny men stare silently at the heavens. She rather believes that the Tin Woodman might have fallen asleep. She stands among them, breath misting. It is as though she has walked in after several hours away.

Winifred says, "Come along chaps. I might as well be talking to myself."

The Tin Man stirs. "Poor little Fred. Someone tell her a bedtime story."

Toto says, "Roll the bottle this way if you please."

"Only if you have a bedtime story to tell."

"Well, who knows, I might at that. Roll the bottle this way and we'll see what comes out."

He takes a deep drink and explains that right now his head is foggy, which means he can only think of one particular story. He says it is chiefly about a soldier he once knew by the name of Reggie Cooper and he may not have the exact details down pat but what the hell, he'll give it a go; old Reg isn't around to complain. Toto says that it was a well-known fact that some soldiers had been born lucky and that whatever rotten things were about to happen would always happen to other men and not to them. It got to the point where this level of good fortune made the soldier the most prized possession of his regiment. They became like those sacred white cows you can see in Calcutta – all the natives following them about and patting them on the back in the hope that some of the magic might rub off.

That's what it was like for Reggie Cooper. Of course it didn't hurt that he was a popular and sociable lad to begin with. He had the common touch, the gift of the gab, and that always helps. But word of how lucky he was soon got around and before you knew it he was practically mobbed, everyone crowding around him in the firing line. They believed they were as safe as houses so long as Reggie was there. Nor did it matter that he occasionally liked the boys as much as the girls. A good many soldiers would have had a problem with that, but they didn't mind what Reggie did, they reckoned it was best to let Reggie do as he pleased. Even those lads who would never dream of letting themselves be involved in that sort of thing would often make an exception when Reggie came calling. Maybe they thought that if they rubbed themselves on Reggie they could grab a little of his sparkle.

The Scarecrow says, "You've had that bottle long enough. Pass it over here for once."

Absently Toto does so. His thoughts are all elsewhere. He says, just how lucky was Reggie Cooper? Well, one time they were all sitting around and having a drink, much the same as tonight, and they were burning waste material on a brazier to keep warm. Toto was watching him, this Reggie Cooper, and he was perched on a packing crate smoking a cigarette and when the cigarette was finished he hops up to cadge another off a fellow standing by and in the moment he was up a private called Fitzpatrick sat down on the crate. What nobody knew, of course, was that the waste on the brazier contained a live bullet too. When the bullet ignited it went straight through Private Fitzpatrick's eye. It was a stupid, pointless accident; the war was riddled with them. But it could have happened to Reggie, and by rights it should have happened to Reggie. He had been sitting in the exact same spot not ten seconds before.

Anyway, says Toto, one night four men were sent out to strengthen the wire and they came under shelling and three of them were killed. Back in the trench we could hear the fourth man screaming and he couldn't get back. So Reggie being

234

Reggie said that he would go and fetch him. And everyone agreed that this was a terrific idea because they knew that Reggie was lucky and they knew they were not. So off sets Reggie, bold as brass, shimmying along on his belly through the mud and barbed wire and bits of dead bodies. And he's about fifty yards out when he hears the sound of an incoming shell, like gravel rattling inside an old tin can. And he thinks 'So what?' because he has the sparkle, you see? But then he realises he's been hit and that his right arm has been torn and that he's been filleted all up under his ribs and he thinks, 'Well now, what's this? This wasn't in the script'. So he crawls and rolls a bit more and decides that he had better take shelter under this burnt-out blasted tank. He can still hear the fourth fellow screaming for help and he reckons that once he's got his breath back he can start calling out too. And this would normally have been a sensible plan. Except that no sooner has he dragged himself under the tank when another shell hits and this takes out the tread on one side of the vehicle and makes the undercarriage drop so that it sits good and snug upon Reggie's legs. And when he tries to call out he is a bit shocked to find he can barely make any noise because what with the arm, legs and ribs he never even noticed that his face has been nicked too. And all at once, clear as day, Reggie Cooper knows that he's not lucky at all and that there is no luck and there is no sparkle and all there is is the accident. For two whole days he lies there trapped under that tank, every now and then sucking water from a puddle and retying the suture at his shoulder to stop himself bleeding into his drinking water and he thinks, 'There is no luck, only accident'.

The bottle has come to Winifred. "What happened to him then? Reggie Cooper?"

Toto laughs shortly. "Do I have to spell it out, kid? He died of course."

They sit for a spell, each chasing the tail of their own thoughts. Lucy attempts to smile at Toto and catch his eye but the yard is dark and he will not look up. Presently the Tin Woodman says that he has been mulling over what Toto was saying about accident and that while he supposes it's true he would still rather reject it. He thinks it's a bitter pill to have to swallow. He points out that he was raised Catholic and that the idea of a moral universe has been drummed into him, although obviously he has strayed from the path, bloody hell how he's strayed. But he says that it is hard to shake, the whole idea. Sin and repentance. Divine retribution. A man has to hold to some higher power because if that isn't there then, shit, what is?

"Nothing's there," Toto says. "Isn't that what I've just been telling you?"

But the exchange has jogged the Tin Woodman's memory of a chap he was on passing terms with who went by the name of Alan Hughes. He explains that while he did on occasion knock about with this Hughes, he is not about to defend the man. The sad truth was that this Hughes was an incorrigible rogue and a bounder. He drank to excess and fucked too many girls without a thought for his wife. In fact, whenever he was able, he beat a path to an Abbeville brothel where for a few drunken hours he could indulge all his whims. Hughes wasn't the sort of chap you'd care to meet on a dark night – as will soon become apparent.

The Abbeville brothel was situated on a long, crooked street called the Rue Mathieu. A blue light had been rigged above the door, but the blue light meant that the house and the beds and the prettiest girls had all been set aside for officer use. The common soldier had to move on a few paces and look for the red lantern, which directed him to the back of the building and a set of stone barns. Naturally the girls in the barn were not nearly so fine, but they would do at a push provided a man was not fussy. Alan Hughes prided himself on the fact that he had never been fussy.

On the night in question, however, he arrived to find that the queue for the barns extended across the yard and past the house where it doglegged into the road itself. This, it goes without saying, was nothing short of an outright disaster. Hughes had no wish to stand in line until dawn, by which point the raddled lovelies in the barn would no doubt be too fatigued to meet his requirements. First he decided to knock on the door beneath the blue lantern and plead for clemency and a little human understanding. He said that he was more than happy to pay whatever the officers paid, but this cut no ice with the peasant thug on the step who ordered Hughes in mangled English to rejoin the others or risk spending the remainder of the night gathering his teeth on the street. Next he hurried around the yard as though embarked on an urgent errand and merrily insinuated himself near the head of the line. On this occasion several punches were thrown and although Hughes was able to deliver a few decent blows in return, he was eventually knocked down and dragged off and found himself out on the Rue Mathieu with the line even longer than it had been when he came.

It is important, you see, to understand his state of mind at this time. He had arrived at Abbeville in anticipation of a night of revelry. He had, moreover, been looking forward to it all week. And for his trouble he had been bellowed at and abused and made to feel second-rate. He had been cuffed and kicked and dragged over concrete by his heels while perhaps as many as forty men jeered and hooted and told him he was scum. And to top the evening off, it had started to rain.

The Tin Man pauses for a good while and then noisily draws a breath.

Moving swiftly on to the nub of the matter, let us picture our hero walking back up the road in quite the high temper. The rain's falling heavily and he has nowhere to go besides back to his barracks. He turns onto another street that is more crooked, more rustic, and passes a cottage with a barn tucked in beside. A young woman has emerged from the cottage and is engaged with securing the catch on one of the downstairs shutters. Let's assume that the screws have come loose and the shutter has been rattling. Whatever it is, it's kept her awake.

Hughes carries a knife in his pocket and he uses this knife to direct the young woman across to the barn. He has no intention of hurting her, he would simply prefer her not to cause a scene and he is confident he will not inconvenience her for long, he just needs what he needs, every man will understand. When he opens her gown he sees that the woman is wearing a cross and this is very nearly enough to make him stay his hand. But by then he has come so far that it is easier to complete the task than to set about unpicking the damage, and a few seconds later it is over and done with. On departing the barn he tells the woman he's desolate, which is as close as he can get to the French word for sorry. And this is true – he is desolate. He knows right off the bat that there is no excuse for what he's done. Afterwards it will strike him as somehow doubly dreadful that he did not know the woman's name or anything of her life and was not even able to see her face clearly between the dark of the street and the pitch-black of the barn. At least with the red lantern whores, he would always ask them their names.

The Tin Man pauses once more to gather his thoughts. He says, rest assured that this ugly tale has a happy ending of sorts. Alan Hughes' punishment was already in the post and it arrived two days later. Out in the field he stooped like an idiot to clear some wreckage from his path and when he put his palms on the wreckage it became an inferno. It obliterated his hands and took a chunk from his leg. It lifted his features clean off of the bone.

"Fucking hell," says Winifred.

"Exactly," the Tin Man says.

At the field hospital, in the bed next to Hughes, there lay a second soldier who was even worse off than him. This soldier's head was swaddled in bandages and he lay so still and silent that Hughes assumed he was dead. Days drifted by and the soldier never moved. One morning the medic sauntered up to Hughes' bed and said he had good news and bad news and which one should come first?

"Bad news first," replied Hughes. "Always bad news first."

With apparent good cheer, the doctor said, "You've lost your forearms and you've lost your face. If you ever get up off this bed you're going to walk with a limp. Children in the road are going to run away screaming."

"That is bad news," agreed Alan Hughes.

"The good news is that you're not actually dead. That was the assumption. and a letter to that effect has already been sent. Your family thinks that you're dead which means that they're in for a lovely surprise, because here you are sitting up in bed and yakking with me."

At the end of this speech the man in the next bed – the other dead man in the field hospital – abruptly began laughing. He still did not move but he did start to laugh. His throat had closed from underuse and so the laughter began as a growl and then gained in pitch to rattle and shriek in a horrible way. His head was all bandaged and the life had left his limbs and yet the doctor's good news was the best joke he'd ever heard. Hughes lay on the cot and listened to the rising, unearthly sound and in that moment was convinced that some higher power – God, if you like – had briefly descended to inhabit the corpse at his side and was using this vessel to celebrate his defeat. He thought it was God laughing to see him so roundly punished for the abject, sinful life he had led and for what he had done to the girl in the barn.

"Fucking hell," says Winifred again.

The Tin Man chuckles and shrugs and inclines his bronze face. "Your turn now, Scarecrow."

"Please not another war story," Lucy puts in hastily. "Those two were just awful."

The Scarecrow says, "I can't think of any at the moment. So I'll tell a story from before the war."

He reaches for the bottle to fortify himself, although he assures them this story won't take much time to tell. He says that one hundred miles from here lived a man named Bertram Connors, Bram for short, who fell deeply in love with a local woman called Audrey and discovered to his delight that Audrey liked him in return. On the day after their wedding they went for a walk in the woods beyond town. They wandered along the river where the wheels of the mill stirred the still brown water, and finally up a steep embankment and out onto the single gauge line that the quarry trains used.

"Can I get the bottle? I'm parched like a pheasant."

"Shut up, Fred," Lucy says.

"Desert, I mean. Parched like a desert."

Just at the point where the track went into a bend, a man lay unconscious. His head rested on the rail and he had turned himself sideways so that one arm lay across it and one foot hooked beneath it. The man was a vagrant and had probably stumbled because he was drunk. The smell of cheap whisky clung to his clothes and his hair. Somewhere along the way he had lost his jacket and shirt. His bare torso was spattered with grit from the track.

The newly-weds shook the man by the shoulder. He groaned at length but would not wake. And then, inevitably, as Bram stood leaning down he became aware of a thrumming on the rails that signalled the approach of a train. The quarry cargoes do not travel fast but the driver is perched high up in the cab, which restricts his vision. The forest was thick and the bend was a tight one. There was no doubt at all that he would run the man over.

Audrey and Bram tugged hard at the man but his foot was securely hooked about the rail's underside and his heel had dug itself a nest in the gravel and although they were able to swing him out onto the verge it still seemed that the weight of the train would bear down on the track hard enough to cut him off at the ankle. Audrey half-stood, meaning to run ahead around the bend and attempt to flag down the driver, but by this point the chances of success had grown slim. The train was approaching more swiftly than usual.

They redoubled their efforts to free the trapped man. Audrey got herself on the ground and began working her fingers into the dense nest of gravel. Bram took the fellow under his arms and proceeded to swing him vigorously from side to side and at the very instant the train sprang out of the trees – as heavy and clamorous as a New Year's Day hangover – the foot left the rail like a cork leaves a bottle and all at once all three figures were rolling and tumbling down the embankment to safety.

Fred says, "Hurrah, hurrah. I'll drink to that."

The escapade had roused the victim sufficiently to cause him to open his eyes and briefly remonstrate with his rescuers. This completed, he tottered into the woods and settled himself to continue his nap. The day was chill and the man's chest was bare and so Bram took it upon himself to remove his own coat and fit the fellow's arms into the sleeves and button the thing all the way to the neck. There was a small sum of money in the coat pocket, but he figured he might as well leave that there as well.

Please remember that we are dealing with newly-weds here. Allowances must be made. And on this, the first full day of their marriage, they should perhaps be forgiven for feeling sentimental, sanctimonious, and somewhat in love with the notion of their being in love. Walking home through the woods, Audrey and her husband came to the conclusion that what had transpired was the best wedding gift of all. It was true what they said: it was better to give than receive. Furthermore, the greatest good deeds do not draw attention to themselves. On their first outing together they had saved a man's life and nobody would ever know except themselves. Even the man they had rescued would eventually wake none the wiser – left only with the mystery of how he had acquired a coat with ready cash in the pocket. For some foolish reason they began referring to the vagrant as Sir Lancelot Coombs.

They devised a whole history for him. They said he was a noble who had been cheated of his birthright and framed for the murder of his brother's champion race horse. Foolish stuff. Lovers' talk. But crucially they made a vow that their good deed would stay between them. It was their personal treasure, the act that bound them together, more so even than the ceremony inside the church of St Peter. They swore they would never mention it to anyone else for as long as they lived.

"Never told it to anyone," Toto says in a murmur.

"Never told it to anyone." The Scarecrow smiles. "Although I suppose they must have told it to me."

Inside the cottage she readies herself for bed. She sheds her outerwear and slips under the blanket and is almost asleep when Winifred steals in to explain that she will probably have to spend the rest of the night in Toto's room. She says that the dwarf has had a good deal to drink and that the more he has mulled on the stories, the more they have upset him. He has worked himself into a right old lather; she has never seen him like this before. He has requested she stay and so what can she do?

"All right," says Lucy muddily. She counts it as a blessing to have the single bed to herself. Guiltily she wishes that Toto would work up a lather more often. But afterwards she will regret the fact that Winifred was not there – because this is the night she is visited by the Devil.

Her sleep is not restful. It is tacky, loose and ill-fitting, like the linoleum at the Griffin. Dreams scurry across its surface and it seems to her that each dream drags with it the mangled remains of the stories from the yard. In one, her brother Tom is trapped beneath an upturned steam wagon. When she pulls at his hands he implores her to stop, because his face has come loose.

"Your face is fine, silly. I'm looking at it right now."

"Please stop," says Tom. "If you pull me out from the wagon it will slide clean off of the bone."

An hour or two before dawn she wakes with the sense that somebody has just very quietly crept into the room. She thinks it must be Winifred and then she thinks that she must be mistaken. The room is perfectly dark and entirely still. Under the blanket, the only sound she discerns is the metronome pulse of the vein behind her ear. She wonders whether she might need to be sick. After mentally assessing the damage she decides she can hang on until morning.

Lucy is about to roll over and resettle when her attention is caught by the very faintest of movements. No, she thinks, I was right. Unless she is still dreaming there is something in the room. By now her eyes have adjusted enough to make out a concentration of darkness. It is away in the corner by the little ladder-backed chair.

She props herself on her elbows. "Who's that?" she asks.

"Who do you think it is?" replies the concentration of darkness.

The voice is pitched low; it is barely a murmur. But she knows it's not Fred.

"Tinny?" she says, but the shape makes no sound.

"I don't know," she says. "I don't like it. What do you want?"

The shape says, "I have come to see where the bad girls play. I've come to see where they play with monsters."

"Who are you?" demands Lucy. "I don't like this at all."

"Isn't it obvious? I am the Devil."

"Nonsense." Thank heavens her eyes have adjusted, her vision has marginally sharpened. A hunched, shortish man has positioned himself on the chair, not five feet from her bed, close enough to reach out and pinch her toes through the blanket if he chose to do so. She considers crying out – or would that put her in more danger?

He says, "Dear Lucy. The Devil rides out in search of pastimes that amuse him. With all the amusements that take place in this cottage, did you honestly believe you would escape my attention for long?"

Under the blanket her legs have gone cold. She tells herself she is safe and that she has the protection of Grantwood and its handsome young master. She tells herself that the funny men and Winifred sleep peacefully in the other rooms. But she worries the hunched black figure might have called on them first and come for her last of all.

"You're not the Devil. He doesn't exist."

"Who am I then? If I'm not the Devil."

Lucy says, "I don't know. Some horrid little man."

The figure bends and appears to smother a giggle with his hand. He says, "Do try to enjoy yourself in this shabby little cottage with the monsters all around. I'm sure it's an education for you. I'm sure you are making big pots of money. But never forget what happens to bad girls in the end. The Devil rides out to claim them and then he carries them to Hell."

"Get out," says Lucy, her voice lifting.

"Then it's into the furnace. Then it's into the flames." And at this very second a corona of blue flames erupts in the black air before the girl's upturned face. Through its liquid licks and curls she has the fleeting impression of fat, piggy features and moist raisin eyes. Her terror is such that she can feel her heart lurch.

He says, "Now do you believe that I am what I say?"

"Yes, I do," she says in one exhaled breath. "You're the Devil, you're the Devil, if you want, you're the Devil."

23

ARTHUR ELMS IS not the Devil, although it pleases him that others might choose to see him this way. In recent months he has established himself as a spiritualist and a performing magician. He has played tatty town halls and private homes and boarded at well-appointed hotels where he flicked his fingers in the grate to set his evening fire alight. But the constant travelling has come to weary him and the nightly shows are a chore, so he is more than happy to take up a position as one of Fortnum-Hyde's entertainers inside Grantwood House. All the same, it gives Lucy a start to see him mingling so freely with the ladies and gentlemen inside the Regency Room.

He grasps her hand and gives her a wink. "I'm the Devil," he says and laughs.

The avant-garde painter has departed for an exhibition in Hove, and the anarchist poet has mysteriously quarrelled with one of Fortnum-Hyde's friends. But Grantwood operates a revolving door policy, which ensures that departures go unnoticed and the numbers stay largely steady. It is the last party of the summer, or the first of the autumn; the end of the revels or the start of fresh ones. More than fifty guests have driven up from the city or leapfrogged across from neighbouring estates. These include the film actress Chrissie White and the government minister Sir Horace Hughes-Robert, whose hardline social policies are energetically decried by his left-leaning wife, who writes a weekly political column for the Times. Patrick Foster is a respected wit and intellectual, best known for a scandalous novel entitled *Nervous Rex*, while that uproarious drunk in the throng is the Earl of Huntingdon, an old friend of Lord Hertford and a reliable jester at every social occasion. Departing for home the next morning, the Earl of Huntingdon will spin his car off the road and shatter his pelvis – an injury from which he will never fully recover.

Still stubbornly sober, York Conway orders that his glass be refilled before his night turns to ash. Parked at his side, Truman Truman-Jones explains that he is boarding at Grantwood House for a week before he heads overseas to take up the governorship of Bombay. Confidentially he adds that he rather fears he should be in situ already. He has received several intemperate letters.

"Oh," says Lucy. "Fancy that." She is convinced she has never met so daunting a figure as Truman Truman-Jones, who looms well over six foot and is so deep-chested and wide that he blots the light in a doorway. From a distance, he could pass for a storybook giant or troll. But the closer one draws, the less forbidding he becomes. Truman-Jones's face is as simple and sunny as that of a good-natured child. She cannot imagine how he will fare as the governor of Bombay.

Fortnum-Hyde extends one long arm. "We are joined this evening by the lovely Miss Winifred and the equally lovely Miss Lulu, our little friends from the cottages. And behind them, it's true – your eyes are not playing tricks – is the Scarecrow, the Tin Woodman, and legless Toto makes three. It is our heroic ex-soldiers. It's the glorious undead."

"Bless my soul," exclaims Samuel "Sweetpea" Long. "Would you take a look at this curious sight?"

With a shyness that strikes Lucy as uncharacteristic, the funny men draw out of the shadow and into the chamber. The Scarecrow pushes Toto aboard his wheeled wicker chair. The Tin Man appears to be intent on concealing his hooks at his back. But their wariness is unfounded. The funny men are welcome; everybody is delighted they've come. Truman Truman-Jones is bellowing "Splendid! Splendid!" while Patrick Foster declares that these new arrivals put the rest of them to shame. He says that he for one is proud to stand among men who have made the ultimate sacrifice for king and for country.

"Penultimate sacrifice," the Scarecrow points out, which prompts Foster to chortle and say, "Indeed yes, quite correct, and thank goodness for that."

In time she will become aware of Grantwood's other occupants. There is the sonorous butler, Raine, and the under-butler, Colvin. The Earl and his son each possess a valet, and ranked below these are any number of footmen, cooks and maids, one of whom she recognises as frog-eyed Mrs Coach. All, it seems, are under the command of Mrs Cleaver, the sour, heavy-browed housekeeper who has reportedly been at Grantwood since Lord Hertford was a boy and has managed each sway of fashion with the same cold-eyed efficiency. The Tower has its ravens; Grantwood House has Mrs Cleaver.

"What a place," says Winifred. "It's not the Ring-o-Bells, I'll give it that."

York Conway stoops to explain in hushed tones that Grantwood is not so much a place as a state of mind. Or better yet, he adds, it is a champion of modernity. He explains that his great friend, Fortnum-Hyde, has ambitious plans for the house. Grantwood has a long and noble history as an agent of social change, but it is now preparing to take that extra step. It is ideally placed to sound a bugle-call to the nation – to show how it can better itself and to lead by example. He says that ten years from now, historians will write about Grantwood and conclude that this was the wellspring and that the future fountained from here.

"Oh my," mutters Fred. She checks over one shoulder to assure herself that yes, this lordly young gentleman is really talking to her. For perhaps the first time in her life, she is quite lost for words.

At the back of the room the musicians tune their instruments. Fortnum-Hyde declares that he is overjoyed to have hired the Long Boys as Grantwood's official house band. He first encountered the Boys during a memorable show at the Alcazar ballroom – what a frantic night that was – after which he was impelled to engage his own lawyers to ensure all the charges were dropped. At present, then, he regrets that England is too stuffy, too shackled to the past, to properly respond to the Long Boys' wild style. But he insists that one day it will be and that he has made this his mission. In fact, Grantwood is currently arranging to fund and promote a national tour. He plans to establish a musical publishing house too. Raising an elegant hand to quiet the musicians, he explains that the Long Boys are the leading, most radical purveyors of an exciting negro sound that is still finding its range. He says some refer to this as jazz while others call it pep but that these are mere quibbles; the details and the name can be ironed out in due course.

"I've heard them," Winifred says, on safer ground now. "Cover your ears. I've heard them already."

Fortnum-Hyde says, "So yes, the Long Boys. The Long Boys are the thing."

In response to a nod from his master, Raine brings his white gloves together. He announces, "Grantwood House is a place for marvels and magic and for radical prose. But tonight, first and foremost, it is a source of new music. Ladies and gentlemen, we present for your entertainment, the Long Boys from the American state of Tennessee."

And now, inside the faded splendour of the Regency Room, the band launches into a self-penned composition entitled 'Come Back Up to Bring it Down' - a surging rip tide of a song, heavily reliant on George Washington's trombone. Stone-faced footmen circle the guests like dancers, carrying bright silver platters. Some of these platters are arranged with champagne flutes. Others contain rails of the astonishing white powder.

The music is electric, ecstatic; it will not be denied. "Oh," exclaims Lucy. "I've never heard anything like it." It must be amazing, she thinks, to be able to conjure such songs from thin air. The musicians that can must truly count themselves blessed.

She abandons the funny men and spins for a spell amid the servants and guests. On the way she pauses to help herself to a dose of the powder, sniffing it gingerly and feeling it fizz in her nostrils. The band runs through four songs and then breaks for a drink. During the intermission Fortnum-Hyde calls for Arthur Elms to amuse the guests by flicking flames from his hands and then - after Elms, for reasons perhaps known only to himself, finds himself unable to oblige - he has Patrick Foster read aloud from a copy of *Nervous Rex*. So far as Lucy can judge, *Nervous Rex* is a tale of ruination and thunder; a mountain castle toppling upon unwashed villagers in the valley below. It is a novel of long words and breathless sentences. She wonders whether she ought to add it to her list of books she must read.

The girl circles back towards the Scarecrow and the Tin Man. Both are standing apart from the crowd, paying close attention.

"That castle's going to fall into the valley again," the Tin Man remarks softly.

"You could be right," the Scarecrow replies. "But what about the honest villagers who live down yonder?"

"All fucked," says Tinny. "Even the ones that are wearing hard hats."

On and on the reading goes. The castle goes down; the village is buried. Yet when Clarissa Fortnum-Hyde makes her entrance, the effect is so galvanic even *Nervous Rex* can't compete. Lord Hertford's daughter arrives on the arm of Julius Boswell, a rising playwright and stage actor who specialises in polemical dramas about modern working conditions, usually at north-country mills or corroded coke towns. Boswell has a reputation for being strident and combative. Yet tonight he too is content to play a more diffident role.

All heads turn towards Clarissa Fortnum-Hyde, a vivid young woman in her thirtieth year. Her honeyed hair bounces with each manly stride. Her flesh-coloured nylons are deliciously suggestive of nudity. The electric lights play against the sequins on her dress, so that when she turns to survey the room, they send flights of Tinkerbells across the ceiling and walls.

"Wotcha fellas," cries Clarissa in the gap between passages when Patrick Foster comes up for breath, throws a despairing glance at the room and prepares to take another dive. The young woman is fully aware of the effect that she has, to the point where she no longer pays it any mind. Her charisma has become as natural to her as brushing her teeth in the glass.

Caught gawping, Lucy hurriedly stares down at the flagstones. Then she takes herself off for another lap of the Regency Room while the recital of *Nervous Rex* gallops on without pause. But either her orientation is wonky or the guests conspire against her, because she has not walked ten paces before she runs into the woman again.

"Hallo," Clarissa Fortnum-Hyde says. "You're one of the girls from the cottage."

"I didn't mean to be staring," she apologises. "All of this is very new to me."

"I fear it might be new to all of us. The music, the readings. My dear brother can be positively crackers at times."

"I mean all of it. The lovely house and grounds. All of these important people. It makes me feel foolish."

"You're no more foolish than the rest of us. I mean, have you met Truman-Jones?" At this Clarissa Fortnum-Hyde lets fly with a deep-throated laugh. She adds, "People are people. That's the incontrovertible truth."

"Yes. Thank you. I know that, of course."

They draw nearer the door so that their conference will not further disturb Patrick Foster's reading.

"Actually, come to think of it, that's not entirely true. There are right people and wrong people, regardless of money or class or outmoded rubbish like that. If you're the wrong sort of person we'll soon weed you out."

"Of course. I know. I hope you won't."

The woman leans in to lightly punch Lucy's arm. "Don't worry, alright? I have a strong sense already that you are the right sort of person."

Clarissa Fortnum-Hyde was once engaged to be married to dapper, dashing York Conway. She is currently engaged to be married to Julius Boswell. But she somewhat fancies that this match will not take either, and that this time next year she will in all likelihood be engaged to someone else. In the meantime, she says, she comes and goes as she pleases; she keeps a flat in Kensington, and suggests that Lucy should feel she can come and go too. Lucy excitedly admits that she knows what she means. She used to live with her parents and then with her grandparents and now she supposes she lives in the service cottages with the funny men from the war. But who can predict where she will be dwelling by Christmas? Nobody knows, that's the beauty of it. Everyone is embarked on their own adventure.

"Arthur Elms would claim that he knows more than most. You might ask him nicely where you will be by Christmas."

"Excuse me, ma'am. Who is Arthur Elms?"

"The spiritualist fellow. The discount Aleister Crowley. The chap who was trying and failing to get his fingers to spark."

"Excuse me for saying, but I don't like him much. He broke into the cottage and scared me half to death."

Clarissa frowns. "That is not good behaviour. We shall have words, he and I."

"No wait, please don't. He didn't cause any harm."

How long has she been conversing with this extraordinary woman? It might be five minutes; it might be five hours. Her sense of time has become unmoored.

"I am going to look after you, Lucy. You will be quite safe with us."

"Oh yes, thank you. I know I will. And I am very happy."

Spotting a silver platter at her side, she dips her head to sniff another rail of the powder.

"And it was you who named the funny men. Tinny and Scarecrow and Toto the dog. I do think that's lovely."

"Go easy with that stuff," Clarissa tells her kindly. "It plays mean tricks on the brain."

Patrick Foster says, "And even those who chased death did find it fleeing from them as a timorous cat evades the attentions of the curious child, all the while leading him further from the path until he is lost and the cat turns to face him and he notes through stupefied eyes that it is no longer a cat."

York Conway and Truman Truman-Jones break into applause. The other guests replace their champagne flutes and obediently follow suit.

"Rub-a-dub-dub," remarks Rupert Fortnum-Hyde.

"It certainly does sound like an excellent book," Lucy says but when she turns to her right she notes that Clarissa Fortnum-Hyde has vanished and that Winifred has replaced her.

The girl says, "You'll never guess the name of the man who painted that picture over there."

"Fred, how should I know? It's as much as I can do to remember my own."

All the same, she turns to study the framed portrait. It depicts a grotesque-looking figure in an aquamarine dress. What appears to be a lute perches where the figure's head ought to be and discarded newspaper sits on the floor at its feet. A picture (a picture within a picture) sits on the wall at its back. Lucy stares at it with mounting alarm. Is the painting a riddle? If so, she can't solve it.

"Pick-Arsehole," says Fred. "I'm not even joking. Pick-Arsehole."

It is high time for the Long Boys to resume their set. York Conway tells the guests that if they peer very closely they will spot a cameo appearance from someone they might recognise. This, it transpires, is Rollin' Colin George's cue to cede his drum-kit to Rupert Fortnum-Hyde. The young master's appearance generates a fresh storm of applause together with a few good-natured catcalls, all of which he acknowledges with his combined grin and scowl. The band play Honeysuckle Rose and Darktown Strutters' Ball and the accelerating, locomotive lift of Heebie Jeebies. Rupert Fortnum-Hyde leathers the drums with a furious concentration.

Lucy lets her gaze follow Rollin' Colin George as he sniffs from one platter and collects a glass from another. Presently his wanderings bring him past the framed poster promoting New Productions of Lesser-Known Operas and across to the Scarecrow and Tin Man.

He tips his glass in casual greeting. "Man," he remarks, "you people are something."

The Scarecrow smiles. "We're certainly something. We're still trying to work out precisely what."

"Hurt in the war, huh? That's rough."

The Scarecrow is holding his cigarette up for the Tin Man to smoke. He says, "This must be unusual for you. Having to sit out the set while his Lordship bangs drums."

"Don't bother me any. So long as I'm fed, watered and paid, the man can do as he please."

The Tin Man says, "Is it just me or is our friend Rupert a little bit off the beat?"

Rollin' Colin shoots him a wry, appraising glance. "No, sir, not at all. Mr Woody's doing fine. That man has got skills."

The three men, all outcasts, stand together in companionable silence. The Long Boys play 'Beale Street Blues' and 'China Boy' before wrapping the set with the lovely, lilting 'Tar Paper Door'. Sweetpea – his eyes closed, his face serene – sings of the heaven which lies across the river and beyond the hill, where a man may throw off his irons and run free as the west wind. He sings that this is where he is going and that he is no longer afraid. His forefathers have sprinkled a trail of grey pebbles to lead him to their door. Lucy is rapt, transported. Involuntarily she sways and spills champagne down her front.

From somewhere close behind she hears the Tin Man remark, "No doubt about it. Completely off the beat."

After that come more platters, more powder. The night slips in and out of focus. The merriment extends all the way until dawn. At one stage Chrissie White breaks down in tears for no apparent reason. At another, York Conway and Truman-Jones remove the fire extinguishers from the wall and, purporting to check that they work as advertised, proceed to direct foam upon the guests standing to either side. A conga line rampages through the downstairs chambers. A naked woman has either leapt or been pushed into the ornamental pond. All told it is judged to have been a most satisfying party.

Come and go as you please, Clarissa had advised, and this is what she elects to do. Most evenings, after a tea of tinned salmon or rabbit stew, she finds the gate in the wall and takes the path to the house where the silver platters contain powder and the crystal flutes are always full. Some nights the funny men come dragging behind. More often than not they remain drinking in the yard. They are guests of Grantwood and yet they still know their place. The house with its noise and finery is not their natural habitat.

The Scarecrow, having finally managed to light his cigarette, calls, "Do let us know what becomes of the cat. The cat that was only a cat until the time it looked back."

The Tin Man says, "I've started to look a bit askance at that cat. Frankly I've started to wonder whether it's really a cat."

At the gate she shakes her head and tries a smile. She says, "At least the men in the house do things with their lives. What do you do? Besides sitting here drinking scotch every night."

Toto chuckles. "She's got you there. One-nil to Lucy."

Outside his cottage, Coach scrapes dried mud from his boots. He shouts, "What are the little doxies up to now?"

Fred says, "We're going to the house, so you can like it or lump it. We've been invited. Have you been invited?"

Coach considers this, still scraping at his boot. "Mercy," he says. "Hark at Fancy O'Mally."

The groundsman once mattered. He does not matter anymore. He has become a minor irritant, a grumbling distraction, forever fussing about in the yard or agonising over the root rot that's eating the trees in the orchard. Eventually she supposes she will have to negotiate a price for him to drive her to town. She has money to deliver and she is yet to spend a shilling. But she finds she has no great desire to drive out past the Palladian lodge. Grantwood House has the girl in its grip. It enthrals and enchants. It bolts the gate on the outside world.

In the space of a fortnight the Griffin has faded. The pub has become absurd and unreal in a way that the camel is not. The legends are true: the camel exists. She and Fred have observed it on the lawns beside the great house, standing unconcerned amid the grazing sheep. They tried to approach it but the beast is standoffish and haughty and they've been warned that it spits. Fred christens it Edith and is delighted to find the name adopted by the others. Within the space of a day everyone is referring to the camel as Edith. How's Edith getting on? Where in hell has Edith got to? Is she feeling the cold? Lucy asks why the camel was brought to the estate to begin with but Fortnum-Hyde laughs and replies that he hasn't thought that far ahead. He has a habit of buying items that snag his interest and then sitting with them a while to discover the role they will play and precisely where they fit in. Invariably, he says, his instinct is correct. But he has yet to decide what he should do with Edith. If it turns out to be nothing he can always offload her onto someone else. In the meantime she's happy, which means that he's happy too.

What an incredible place Grantwood House is. How astonishing that she should come to be here at all. She has to keep pinching her arms to prove she's awake and not dreaming and then pinch herself again just to double check. She canters in and out of the cobblestone yard, grabbing at her forearms until she raises red welts.

"Stop that!" the Scarecrow barks from the doorway to the workshop. "Honestly, Lucy, don't keep savaging your own flesh."

"I can't help it, I can't help it. I'm just too happy to be here."

The girl is embarrassed by her clothes until Clarissa takes her in hand. The flower-print dress from the camphor-wood chest has frayed at the neck and tattered at the hemline, but the lady flings open the doors to her own dressing room. Clarissa says she sees no reason why Lucy should not dress like a lady; she says that Lucy's more lady than most of the real – as in titled – ladies she knows. The girl ought to dress and act the way she wants to be and that way, with a little good fortune, she can make it come true.

She says, "The world is full of people who'll try to tell you you're one kind of person. It's up to you to say that you're not. Tell them often enough and they'll come to believe it."

"Yes, ma'am."

"Take those friends of yours from the cottage. They regard you as a plaything when you are jolly well not. You don't have to be what they want you to be. You don't have to do anything that you don't want to do."

The girl nods uncomfortably. "Yes. Thank you."

"Lucy," she says, "you can be whatever you want. Believe you me, the clothes are just the start of it."

Clarissa's dressing room is a marvel. It is like a department store on Oxford Street where all the colourful goods are strung together on rails. Now Lucy and Fred trip through the loggia in pageboy tunics and last season's shoes. They wear translucent nylons that peel off like snakeskins. Fred's string of beads is so long she has to loop it three times round her throat and even then the last coil extends below her navel.

These are the good times, before the leaves turn. During the day she prepares lunch and dinner and is sure to keep the cottages clean. She joins Toto in his room and the Tin Man in his and arranges herself on the bed so that they may each attend to their business. But she performs these tasks automatically, almost listlessly, and rather has the sense the funny men do as well. The onset of autumn has cooled their ardour. They were at their hungriest in the summer, in the woods. These days they appear to be preparing for a long winter sleep. The Scarecrow leads the way. He is spending more time in his workshop, or away with his books. Never once has he requested that Lucy accompany him upstairs, although he continues to chip in his share at the end of each week. She resists pressing the point about the difference in pay. Were she to ask for more money they might reasonably demand that she did more to earn it.

Fred fidgets in bed and complains that her bladder is full. They have mislaid the pot which means she must step outside to the yard.

"Go and use the toilet then. You're keeping me awake."

"The amount you put away I'm surprised you're not dead. Besides," she adds, "it's too cold in the yard."

"Oh do get it over with. If you fall asleep now you'll end up wetting yourself."

Fred says, "Wouldn't it be good if we had rooms in the house? Do you think they might let us? Clarissa's taken such a shine to you and there's easily enough space. One wing is shut. They could open it up."

"I don't know. What about the funny men?"

"Who cares? I'm tired of the funny men."

"Ha," Lucy scoffs. "Do you think the young master would pay you for the work?"

"He might if I asked. Even if he didn't, I'd probably do it for free. Or he could set us both up in one of his houses in London. Imagine that. Me and you living like ladies in a big London house."

Lucy turns over and gets one arm under the pillow.

Fred says, "What an idiot Edith was. She could have been here with us now if she wasn't so stuck up and stupid." A moment later she says, "Bloody hell, I need to pee."

"Then good heavens, go and do it. You're driving me spare."

But it seems as though Fred has barely left the room when Lucy becomes aware of her screaming outside in the yard where the shared toilet stands. The girl tumbles from bed, her senses in uproar, and flings open the door to the landing. She knows all too well who was lying in wait. The horrid little man who claimed to be the Devil.

Fred climbs the stairs at speed. Her head is down. "Is it him?" cries Lucy. "Is it Mr Elms?"

Fred snaps, "No, get inside. I'm alright. Shut the door."

And yet Fred is not right, something has rattled her. She pulls up the chair and wedges it beneath the door handle; almost knocks Lucy over in her dash to the bed. A moment later come footfalls and the footfalls are followed by a hard tap at the door.

"Freddy," calls a familiar voice. "Don't take on. It's only me."

"Go away!" Fred shouts.

"Come on, Freddy, I'm sorry. I didn't mean to surprise you."

"Go away!" They can hear the man's laboured breathing on the far side of the door. Eventually he turns and limps away on the landing.

Fred whispers, "I don't know why I put the chair there anyway. He can't turn the doorknob with those fucking hooks."

They huddle together, the blanket pulled up to their chins. The cottage has settled. All its inhabitants have returned to their beds.

"Are you really alright?"

"Yes," says Fred. "It gave me a fright."

Lucy nods sympathetically. "He needs to use the toilet as well, you know."

"Then he should get properly dressed when he does," Fred says. "He really, really ought to put on his mask when he does."

She weighs this up. "He probably thought it was safe. It's so long after midnight."

"Feel my hand. Is it shaking?"

Lucy does; it is. "Fred. You knew what they were like. The funny men from the war."

"The funny men," says Winifred and then laughs.

24

THE CLOCKS IN this house all tell different times. Electric bulbs burn in some rooms but do not work in others. The upstairs bathrooms are imperfectly plumbed, so that the taps release brown water at intervals, on a whim, no matter how tightly they have been turned. The telephone in the entrance hall rings so feebly that it is only heard by accident, if a figure happens to be passing the mahogany table. One evening Clarissa Fortnum-Hyde discerns its trill and cups the device to her ear.

Into the mouthpiece, she says, "Hallo."

As through from an inordinate distance, a faint voice says, "Hallo."

"This is Grantwood House. Who is this on the line?"

A moment later the voice returns. "This is Grantwood House. Who is this on the line?" The woman replaces the earpiece with a queer sense of vertigo. She feels as if she has spoken across many miles to some doppelgänger, standing in the hall of a cavernous house in a parallel world.

The trees in the valley turn coppery orange and chimney-pot red. Storm clouds of starlings draw patterns in the sky. A heron targets the pond and devours the carp, and this infuriates Raine who has tended to them all year. The mercury drops and the estate shrinks in sympathy. When it grows too cold to sit out in the loggia, the guests retreat first to the Regency Room and finally, in October, to the grand drawing room with its crackling hearth and velvet wall hangings and its heroic, life-sized oil portrait of Lord Hertford's son. Each time Lucy and Fred are shown in, they find its occupants spreadeagled in armchairs or lying prone on the sofas, already in the grip of cognac or cocaine.

Fortnum-Hyde regards their approach with languid amusement. He says, "Here they are. The pleasure dolls."

Spacious though it is, Grantwood House is unable to accommodate rival writers of stature. Patrick Foster has taken his leave, which means that the Scarecrow and the Tin Man will never discover what became of the cat that was not really a cat. Even Julius Boswell appears to remain only under sufferance. The playwright is still officially engaged to marry Clarissa, but her interest in the matter is on the wane and she has begun to direct her attentions – in a playful, unfocused fashion – towards Sweetpea Long. At regular intervals Arthur Elms will try and fail to get his hands aflame, burble an apology and then return to his seat. And Truman Truman-Jones explains that he needs to depart for India by next week at the latest; he has recently been forwarded a quite vexatious telegram. He shifts his immense bulk and makes the furniture squeak. He adds that by rights he should have been in Bombay by June.

"Tell them to fuck off and stop bothering you," York Conway advises. "Why do you want to be governor of Bombay anyway?"

"I'm not convinced I do, quite."

"I'll do it," Winifred volunteers.

"Don't be preposterous, child."

"Oh, let her do it," Rupert Fortnum-Hyde snorts. "Let Fredo go to Bombay and whip the natives into shape. They'd never know what hit them, poor devils."

"I think I'd be good," Fred says.

As a result of the incident in the yard, Fred informs Lucy she has made an important decision. She'll continue to provide Toto with Mench – every now and again, should he ask her nicely – but she will no longer consent to lie down with Tinny. The Tin Woodman is too disgusting for words. She keeps recalling the sight of his face in the yard and feeling sick to her stomach. She can't believe she ever went with him to begin with. She cannot imagine why he was ever her favourite. She will go with Toto, assuming of course that she is in the mood to be kind. But she has resolved to have nothing further to do with the Tin Woodman. Even when he is wearing his mask she can hardly stand the sight of him because she knows how revolting he really is underneath.

Lucy thinks this over. She recalls her conversation with Clarissa in the dressing room. At length she says, "They're all disgusting, that's the truth of it. I'd rather not have Mench with any of them."

Fred nods excitably. "They've had a good time with us until now. But enough is enough. I might not even do it with Toto."

Lucy has an absurd urge to reach over and shake Winifred by the hand. This feels like a breakthrough or some thrilling escape – more significant, even, than her flight from the Griffin. Still, she is concerned about the money and would prefer to avoid a confrontation. If they were to tell the funny men outright that the old arrangement was over, the funny men would almost certainly then demand that they leave. And she does not quite know how she would feel about this.

Fred says, "They can keep paying us to cook and clean for them. But if they don't want to do that I'm moving up to the house."

"We can't live in the house. You just try it and see."

"I will," vows Winifred. But Lucy detects a note of defiance and wonders if the girl might not also have her doubts.

At first all fears of a row appear to be unfounded. Previously garrulous, the Tin Man has become passive and shy. The encounter in the yard has upset him more than Fred. In the days that follow he does not request Mench and neither does Toto; maybe the dwarf is shy, too. When the evenings draw in, the funny men retire to the cramped kitchen to drink and play cards, leaving the way clear for the girls to slip past them unnoticed. It appears that the confrontation could be avoided or at least forestalled, except that the lack of resolution chafes at Winifred's spirit. She is not a girl to leave things unsaid. She cannot identify a crisis without trying to cure it. She can't see a calm without whisking it into a squall. On departing the cottage, lavishly decked out in scarlet chiffon, Fred pulls up short in the hall, pivots on her heel and cries, "By the way, Lucy and me had a very interesting talk. None of you are getting any more Mench out of us."

"What's that?" barks Toto.

"Lucy said you're disgusting and I reckon she's right. You've had your fun. It's over now."

The Tin Man steps hesitantly to the kitchen door. "Freddy," he begins.

"You can take your mask off if you like, we don't care any more. No hard feelings, but we're not giving you Mench."

"You're not giving us anything," Toto shouts from his chair. "Last I checked, you're earning one pound every week."

Brightly she says, "Is that the time? We must really be off. See you tomorrow, funny men."

"Now hang about, for God's sake. You can't land us with something like that and then run away."

The girl treats him to a corrosive smile. "Then chase me, Toto. Chase me up to the house. Let's see how fast you can go in that little chair."

Outside, by the tennis court, she says, "Dirty bastards. I'm done with them,"

"I think you might also be done with your pound every week."

The girls dart out of one drama only to pitch headlong into a second. When Raine opens the door to the draped drawing room, he puts a finger to his lips and won't let them in until he is confident of their silence. Lucy gathers that they are interrupting a private performance of Julius Boswell's latest play. A sofa has been shifted to clear a stage by the hearth. Boswell has taken the role of the corrupt factory owner; Fortnum-Hyde the young firebrand, hailed as a hero by his downtrodden co-workers.

He says, "You ask what became of the honest working man? He fought at the Somme and he learned vital lessons. His college was built out of mud, blood and gas. He educated himself there. He learned he had worth and that he should not be mistreated. He learned that he controls the means of production and he understood that this makes him of greater value than you. You ask what became of the working man? Well, here he is, Mr Doncaster. Do you like what you see?"

"I do not care for it one iota," Julius Boswell thunders in return. "I do not see a working man. What I see before me is a dangerous Red."

The performance has been deemed to be of such importance that the master of the house has been coaxed from his bed. Lord Hertford is enthroned in an armchair, a blanket over his knees, his noble head tottering aboard a sinewy neck. This is the first time Lucy has laid eyes on the man. He has unkempt yellow hair and a pinkish, unhealthy cast to his skin. He puts her in mind of a venerable pet hare, twitchy and unfocused; the poor creature made so irascible by a combination of old age and coddling that the children are advised not to stroke him because he would in all likelihood bite.

Cross-legged on the floor at his feet sits his daughter, Clarissa. Her skirt has rucked and ridden to reveal her garters and her limbs glow golden in the banked firelight. Lined shoulder-to-shoulder on the adjacent sofa, Sweetpea Long, Arthur Elms and Truman Truman-Jones are ostensibly transfixed by the urgent drama unfolding – yet they each take turns to shoot darting, hungry glances at the woman on the floor.

The butler waves the girls to a pair of footstools. A silver platter glides by at eye level. Lucy has time to pinch a nostril and take a polite sniff before it moves off again on its tour of the room.

She watches the play. It is extremely exciting. Julius Boswell clears a frog from his throat and says, "If you persist with this course of action, it goes without saying that it spells ruin for all. The factory floor stands empty. The production line does not move and the workers won't eat. And how does that serve your Bolshevik revolution?"

Fortnum-Hyde scowls at his paper. He says, "That is where you are wrong, Mr Doncaster. A strike does not mean inaction. A strike is a strike. A strike is a blow. A blow against the old order. That is why we are striking – to knock down the factory and build a new one in its stead. And in this new factory there will be no division between management and labour. There will only be workers and they will work for themselves. That is why we strike, Mr Doncaster, and that is why you fear us." He lowers the sheet and says, "And so on and so forth. You get the general gist of the case. It's not bad, I'll admit, but it is boring me now and I'm in need of refreshment."

Boswell is perturbed. "Come on, King-Roo. There's only a page or two left."

"Yorky can do it." He motions for a footman to bring the platter across.

The performance halted, the Earl of Hertford stirs. His tendons strain. He says, "I suggest we resume at a later date. Mr Boswell's scenario is raw and rather crude and yet it is not without merit. And I must say you fared splendidly as the upstart young gentleman."

Fortnum-Hyde accepts the compliment with a complacent shrug. He rubs a dab of white powder from the side of his nose. "Rumours that the role was written with me expressly in mind are merely that. Merely rumours."

"It does play to your strengths, that much was clear. I dearly hope I live long enough to see you take your place as an MP."

"But not for the Liberals," the playwright interjects. "Please, Woody, I wish you'd reconsider."

Lord Hertford says, "The Liberals and Tories are the natural parties of government. Of course, given the choice, he will sit with the Liberals."

Fortnum-Hyde lowers himself into a vacant armchair. "I go where I'm able to make the greatest impression. If this country needs leadership, let the natural leaders provide it." He grins wolfishly. "But, I'll concede, no one would ever mistake me for a typical Liberal. And if they think I'll toe the line, I am bound to say they do not know me at all."

"Hear hear," roars Truman-Jones.

"By God, I mean to shake some trees when I'm there."

"Hear hear."

"Shake the trees like a red-arsed baboon. Shake the trees until the fruit falls out."

When the door opens to admit the funny men, Raine is initially reluctant to remove himself from the entrance. The drawing room, he protests, is crowded enough as it is. He has already had to turn away both Colin George and Sunny Boy who are regarded as the lowliest Long Boys – rude and rowdy, unfit to be sat amid polite company. But Lord Hertford insists the funny men be waved in. He is delighted to see them, the fellows from the cottage. Grantwood prides itself on being a house for heroes. And if it is good enough for the rest of them, it is good enough for Toto and his friends. Indicating the dwarf, he points out that this man spent two days in no-man's-land, trapped underneath a disabled tank. Who among them can say they spent two days under a tank and survived?

Toto manoeuvres himself into the room. His chair swings into a turning circle and he has to reach across to correct his course. He says, "Thank you, your Lordship, you're very kind. We don't like to interrupt. It's just that we were wondering if we might have a quick word with the girls. It's about, um, a small business matter."

"Let's do it later," says Fred. "We're enjoying ourselves here."

"Shame on you, Raine. Not letting this man in. What were you doing when he was trapped under that tank?"

"I'm sure I don't know, my Lord."

"Yes," scoffs the Earl. "That does sound about right. Weak little men are always sure they don't know."

"Steady, old stick," placates Fortnum-Hyde. "Raine fought with us too, you know."

"Strength and courage. Those are the qualities that I admire."

Then, with a sudden hoot of laughter, Fortnum-Hyde points out that even Clarissa did her bit. He is determined that his sister should not be left out. He says he is so proud of his sister, who volunteered as a nurse in the dressing stations of France. She brought great glory to Grantwood; the soldiers were lucky to have her.

Now all eyes are on Clarissa. She unfolds her long legs and leans back, supporting herself on her hands so that her honeyed hair almost touches her father's knees. She responds to this praise with a crimped, mirthless smile. Once again Lucy is struck by her beauty. The features that have gathered haphazardly on Fortnum-Hyde's face have found their perfect symmetry on that of his sister. Lucy could look at this Clarissa all evening and yet she remains terribly conscious of the funny men at her back. She wishes they had not followed. She wishes they'd leave.

Fortnum-Hyde says, "Tell them about the time you forgot to sterilise the instruments."

"Don't be an idiot."

But Fortnum-Hyde is enjoying himself. The play did not rouse him, but this is an improvement. "I believe she was known as the Angel of Death. She'd walk into the tent and they would scream for their mothers. They knew as soon as they saw her that the jig was up. She'd lean over their beds

272

and the poor bastards thought they saw heaven. But they knew what that meant and they screamed for their mummies."

"Man, I tell you," chortles George Washington from his seat on a stool. "That lady can lean over my sickbed any day that she please."

"Starch whitey uniform," says Skinny Boy Floyd. "Damn right, lean on in. Just kill me right now."

"She will," hoots Fortnum-Hyde. "She did."

By now Julius Boswell's perturbation has bloomed into outright distress. "Gentlemen, please. This is my fiancée, remember."

"Fuck off the lot of you," his fiancée retorts.

Fortnum-Hyde helps himself to another dose of white powder. Playfully he says, "Tell them about the time you got the saw stuck in a bone."

At this Clarissa rises unhurriedly to her feet. She announces, "That's it for me. It has been terrific fun but I'm going to bed."

"She did, you know. She got her saw stuck in the bone and couldn't pull it out."

Following Clarissa Fortnum-Hyde's exit the guests appear at a loss for a fresh source of entertainment. Responding to the tension, the footmen pick up the pace and send out the platters. Winifred sniffs and then sneezes, which affords a shared burst of amusement, but this is over too soon and it is abundantly clear that the conversation has faltered. The guests look to one another in search of assistance. York Conway remarks that, well, one early night might not be such a bad thing.

"Freddy," says Toto from his perch by the door. "Maybe we ought to think about going back to the cottage."

"Nonsense," booms Lord Hertford. "You are very welcome to stay."

But Toto's interjection has given the room a new focus. Where the guests once stared at Clarissa, they now swivel in their seats to study the funny men at the rear. Prompted by a sudden unease, Lucy considers getting to her feet and bidding everybody good night. But then the platter is there and it seems rude not to partake.

"Excuse me for asking," she hears Skinny Boy say, "but one thing's been nagging on me. How you pick your nose with those hooky hands?"

The subject has been broached; the Rubicon crossed. The musicians succumb to a prolonged fit of the giggles. Finally Sweetpea Long says, "Isn't it apparent? There's no mystery here. He has his Scarecrow friend do the picking for him."

"No, that ain't it," chips in George Washington. "He ain't got no nose so there ain't nothing to pick."

"Gentlemen, please," protests Julius Boswell.

Standing at the door, the Tin Man holds his hooks up for calm. Amiably he says, "No offence taken. In fact I'm bound to say that Mr Washington is right. I have no nose because I have no face."

Lord Hertford frowns. "You would do well to remember that these men are war heroes. That fellow in the wheelchair spent two days under a tank. The fellow beside him is a decorated airman. I currently forget the provenance of the third man in their party."

Throughout this exchange, Winifred's thoughts have evidently been elsewhere. All at once she sits up and says rather loudly, "Do you think me and Lucy could sleep over here for the night?"

Fortnum-Hyde blinks and then smiles. "I think not," he says blandly.

"Yes," continues the Earl. "I have momentarily forgotten the provenance of our third honoured guest."

Lucy is aware of Fred resettling on the stool. But now her attention has been caught by the horrid man. Arthur Elms, who appears to be angling for the chance to play his part as well. In her time at the house she has come to detest Arthur Elms. Everything about him strikes her as somehow off-kilter. He has a habit, she's noticed, of closing first one eye and then the other, as though each eye reveals a different image. He rubs his fingers in a fury when he thinks nobody is watching. He doesn't speak a great deal, she supposes he's nervous, but he makes an effort to roar with approval whenever Fortnum-Hyde makes a joke.

Now, for the first time this evening, he means to make himself heard. He smacks his wet lips, traps his squirming hands in his lap. He says, "You say this bloke was a decorated airman?"

"What's that?" barks Lord Hertford.

Skinny Boy Floyd rides roughshod over the pair of them. Attempting to reroute the exchange to its original track, he says, "But sweet lord above, I still can't figure it out. How you wipe your old ass with them hooky hands?"

"Why don't we have him wipe yours?" the Scarecrow says. "You can find out for yourself."

"His Scarecrow friend does the wiping for him!"

The Magus coughs and tries again. "Sir. Sir. Are you telling me you were a decorated airman?"

The Scarecrow ignores him. He is awaiting Skinny Boy's response.

"Aw, simmer down. We were just kidding with you."

"Excuse me for saying, you don't sound like an officer, you don't sound like these fellows. I thought the flying corps was for officers, by and large."

"That's true enough," the Scarecrow says shortly.

"Well then, there we are. All I'm saying, you see, is that you don't have the accent. Me neither, of course. But then I was never an officer."

"Freddy," calls Toto.

"Some airmen started out as engineers," the Scarecrow explains. "When there was a shortage of officers we were allowed to fly planes."

"Freddy."

"Shut up," says Fred.

Lord Hertford says, "The gentleman we refer to as Scarecrow is a majestic war hero. He rose through the ranks. He shot down many planes. We are honoured to have him as a guest at Grantwood."

"Well said, old stick."

"Of course, there's no denying that it is untoward: a young engineer ascending so high. And perhaps it is to be avoided because it invokes other hazards. I confess that our Scarecrow puts me in mind of Icarus. He flew too close to the sun and sadly melted his wings." Abstractedly he turns his pale stare in the butler's direction. "Raine," he says. "Those statues in the garden."

"Sir?"

"Icarus," says Lord Hertford with a sigh. "Never mind. It is of no great importance."

The Scarecrow draws on his cigarette. "Your feeling is that low-born men should know their place."

"No," says Fortnum-Hyde. "That's not what my father is saying."

"My feeling is this," explains the Earl kindly. "Mobility and equality – these are things I will always support. And yet it follows that mobility is most effective and lasting when it is properly regulated. This is why we look to sensible, progressive members of the ruling class. To ensure there is free movement and proper fairness for all."

"I see," says the Scarecrow, although it is obvious from the tone of his voice he does not. This is apparent to Lucy – even in her current foggy state – and it is also apparent to York Conway, who has become quite agitated by the direction the discussion has taken. And so over the next minute and a half, his voice trembling with emotion, Conway says a great many things about impertinence and ingratitude and the natural order of things. Indicating Lord Hertford but addressing the Scarecrow, he says, "Let me state it quite plainly. Men like him have done more for men like you than men like you have ever done for yourself."

Arthur Elms pipes up again. "Anyway, never mind. A pilot in the war, what a wonderful thing. But then the whole war was wonderful. Crash, bang, wallop, I can remember it now." He beams delightedly about the room. "Cape Helles. Gallipoli. Who else was at Gallipoli?"

When the platter comes by, Lucy drops her head for a refill and discovers too late that she has exceeded her limit. Her temperature jumps and her heart thumps at her ribcage. The walls press in; the velvet hangings are like spun sugar. Usually the powder provokes not much more than a pleasurable tingle. This time it causes her to recoil so forcibly that she slips from the edge of the stool. And now it is as though the ceiling descends more than half the height of the room, so that she feels she might touch it were she to reach up from the floor.

She hears Fred guffaw. "Whoops-a-daisy. Lulu's down."

The ceiling drops a further notch. She tries to join in the gaiety but her head is too fogged. Then the Scarecrow swings into the diminishing gap and drags her to her feet. She totters alarmingly like a newborn fawn. "Lucy," he tells her.

Looking about, she notes venerable Lord Hertford regarding her with faint but genuine concern. "The young lady," he murmurs. "The little girl."

"I'm alright really." But her heart is still skipping and she can feel fresh sweat on her skin. She wonders if maybe she might have passed out for an instant.

Now Lord Hertford has turned to his son to remark that honestly, he does worry the cocaine has a detrimental effect on the system. He has been observing its influence on those guests who have consumed it and has decided that the drug both inflames the blood and quickens conversation. He confesses that everybody has been speaking at such a motorised rate that he has found it difficult to follow precisely what has been said. Even during the recital of the play, the entire exchange went by him in a blur.

Fortnum-Hyde gently insists he has nothing to fear. All the powder does, he explains, is separate the weak from the strong. It is no more than a stimulant and, as such, allows men of great strength to achieve their true potential. He leans over his father and plants a tender kiss in his hair. He says, "Please remember, old stick, I take this stuff by the lorry-load. And look at me. I have never been better."

"Hear hear," says Truman-Jones.

And yet when Lucy continues to stumble, the decision is

taken that the girl has had more than enough. Raine suggests that the funny men return her to the cottage and Conway airily motions that Fred should go too. Outside, the night air hits her like a draft of cold water. Her knee joints have gone liquid; she almost topples again. Painstakingly the Scarecrow walks Toto's wheelchair down the short run of steps. Unwilling to wait, she runs ahead into the Italian garden and loses herself amid the plaster gods. Her thoughts are so antic she fancies the voices at her back are emanating from them.

Hermes says, "Well played, Lulu, ruining the night for the rest of us. So what if she has to be sent off to bed? I don't see why I have to go home as well."

Beside the pond, Poseidon leans into his trident. He says, "You're getting yourself a fucking attitude, girl. And watch it, watch it, these fucking steps."

"Lucy!" calls Artemis. "Hang about. Don't run off."

To the gods she shouts, "Leave me alone, the lot of you! None of you are real at all!" Her cry rouses the heron, which takes off from the pond in a great pale commotion.

At the loggia's far end sits another run of stone steps. She scales these at speed and doglegs around to the western wing of the house where the rooms are unoccupied, their effects swaddled beneath dust sheets. Up ahead, in the gloom, a hundred sheep stand immobile. She draws a breath of night air and starts to stagger towards them.

From a distance, Artemis calls her name. She turns and sees that the Scarecrow has outstripped his companions. Here he comes, a lanky shape on the darkened field.

"Leave me alone." But she's not up to running and he overtakes her with ease.

"I told you I'm alright. Can't I walk in peace?"

He matches her stride. "You've been taking too much of that stuff. And you've been drinking too much. You're all over the place. A good amount of the time you don't make much sense."

"What do you care? It's none of your business."

"I do care. That's why I'm telling you."

She rounds on the Scarecrow, properly furious now. "You don't care. You don't like us. You just like to fuck us. And the oldies don't like us, they just wanted us fucked. I know that very well – am I making sense to you now? And Edith was right, that's the worst of it. Edith was right – you're all horrible." Can it be that she is suffering with a cold? It seems that each time she breathes out she blows balloons of wet snot.

He says, "Lucy, it was wrong. The whole thing was wrong. There is no excuse for it. That's why I stopped."

She laughs in his face. "Oh jolly well done. Well done to you. Will you be wanting another medal for that?"

She dearly hopes that he will leave her, but he elects to keep pace. In the black field the sheep loom like apparitions. This is their land and they are comfortable in it. But they step silently aside to allow the walkers to pass.

At length the Scarecrow says, "Look at us, Lucy. It might be hard to believe but we are all young men still. We had wives, we had families. We all had big plans. Now all that's left is a kind of crippled half-life."

"Fuck off back to your families then. You can be their problem for a change."

"I don't want to be a problem. I don't want to have her help me in and out of my clothes. Tell me it's alright. Force herself to look at my face. I don't want that. I couldn't do it."

"Ha," says Lucy. "You're not heroes, you're cowards. I don't like you one bit." She definitely has a cold. She blows out more mucus. "Edith was right," she says raggedly. "Edith was right and if I ever see her I'll tell her."

By now Grantwood House is a good way behind them; they are striding towards the copse on the hill. The night air is a tonic, it has helped clear her head. All the same she wishes the Scarecrow would let her be.

Before the trees they arrive at a small mound of earth. A rudimentary wooden cross has been set at its head. The sight of the cross is enough to bring the girl up short and make her snuffle again. She says, "Oh you bastards, poor Lion. You didn't love him at all."

He hesitates. "I don't know that we did, that's the horror of it. Men died all around, every day of the week. It gets so that another one is just another one." A moment later he adds, "By rights he was dead. So it was as if the official word became more real than he was. He shouldn't have been here to begin with and maybe that's how he saw it as well. He didn't love us much either."

"Very good," she says. "It's so easy for you. Pay schoolgirls to fuck you and then joke when a friend dies." She bends to straighten the cross; rubs her face on her sleeve.

He says, "I'm sorry. There is no excuse for what I did. It's too easy to say that we came back as beasts. We were beasts to begin with and then the war brought it out."

She makes one final effort to shrug him off. Echoing Winifred, she says that there are no hard feelings, what's done is done. It was dreadful and embarrassing and painful while it lasted, but it never really lasted very long, did it? From now on they will be spending much more time at the house. She does like the house. She may one day move in.

The Scarecrow considers this. He says, "Be careful of that place. Those people aren't honest."

"Ha," says the girl. "How much worse can they be?"

Liberated at last, she loses herself in the trees and emerges on the far side. Walking still further afield she looks back and sees the distant hull of Grantwood House, becalmed like an ocean liner, the smatter of sheep arranged like whitecaps on water. And she is struck all afresh by how her fortunes have changed and how she has come to be here, the guest of such wealthy hosts. It used to be that she regarded the trips in the Maudslay as a journey into the past, with Epping Forest installed as the primitive final destination. But now she knows there is a land beyond even that – a place of sunken gardens and rolling lawns and graceful, handsome demigods – and she supposes this must count as a heaven of sorts. It is certainly closer to heaven than anything she has encountered in her life before now.

She stretches out on cold ground to study the cosmos overhead. Ideally she would like to pass the night here and not return to the cottage at all, and yet privately she accepts that the chill will drive her in before long. The stars fill her vision; they could be multiplying by the minute.

Lying on her back in the truck she had once wondered aloud if her father was living on one of those stars and Fred told her that was stupid while Edith wasn't sure. And then again, in her first days at Grantwood she had briefly entertained the idea that this might be true after all, or some twisted version of it, and that her father had not so much died as simply dropped out of sight, because if this had happened to some men it had surely happened to others. And she had thought that maybe Grantwood House was not unique and that there must be other places of shelter hidden in green folds of the country, where masked men sat in wheelchairs or propped themselves up on crutches and played games of Bumble and Buck deep into the night and felt they could never return home because they were too proud and pigheaded, or because they feared that they weren't loved quite enough. Then she would picture herself finding one such place of rest – perhaps a thatched, whitewashed cottage behind an ivy-clad wall. She would ease open the gate and scrunch her feet on the gravel and there in the garden she would discover her father. She would know it was him, however much he had changed. When she called to him he would start and turn, re-setting his sticks on the lawn as he circled to meet her. "Dad," she would cry. "It's Lucy." And her face by now is wet with tears.

But these thoughts are perilous and have too much momentum. She cannot control their trajectory and they shake her loose. At the very point when the scenario begins to accelerate, rushing her urgently towards its happy conclusion, the fabrication tatters and she sees it for what is – a painted mask, like the Tin Woodman's – and understands that there is nothing behind it, or rather that the only thing behind it is death. Because in all likelihood there is no thatched sanctuary; there is only the service cottage at the back of Grantwood House. The strange, funny men are all alone in the world, which in a sense means that she is all alone, too. The past has been cleared and the dead swept away to one side and there is nothing more to be done except to keep walking forward and resist the urge to look back. Wherever he went, whatever he became, she hopes that her father remembers her kindly. She hopes he recalls the time they hid inside the pantry and ate flour from the jar. She hopes he does not judge her too harshly for all the things she's done since.

The autumn ground has gone cold, she feels it crawling into her chest. But still she lies on her back and gazes at the sky and supposes that up there, perhaps, is a land beyond even heaven and that it has been lit top-to-tail by a million balls of burning gas. "Dad," she says. "It's Lucy. I'm here."

25

H ERE HE COMES, the rag-and-bone man, perched atop his loaded cart. He calls "Rah-boh!" to the roofs and windows of the houses ahead. Repetition has twisted the call into lilting calypso. His cart is home to a broken wardrobe and a box-spring mattress. It carries pale woollen blankets, a tractor engine and a stack of rust-spotted placards advertising Pears soap, Ideal milk and holidays in Bridlington and Sutton-on-Sea. An unprepossessing armchair faces the road to the rear. The owner had sat down and died in that chair. Nobody could bring themselves to use it after that. But the rag-and-bone man doesn't judge, he is content to take what he's given. Bring it all to the cart. He wants the things that you don't.

What becomes of these items, the boy wants to know, and the rag-and-bone man explains that he is transporting them all to the Land of the Lost. His plan, he says, is to carry them through the water meadow and over the Billy Goat Bridge to the Land of the Lost. Once there he gives the items to the goblins and the goblins either eat them or repair them, he is always too polite to ask which. Then he winks at the boy's mother to include her in the joke.

She asks, "Do you think he's telling the truth?"

The boy shrugs, embarrassed.

"Come on," she tells him. "You know there are no such thing as goblins."

The pair have arrived with bundles in their arms. These,

she explains, are her husband's old clothes, not worn for years but in decent condition. He clears a space beside the blankets and she says that she has a number of books that can go too, if he can wait a few minutes.

"Madame," he says proudly. "I will take anything that you can throw at me."

He steps down from the cart and turns up his toes so as to stretch his hamstrings. As he does this, a butterfly – out late in the season – drifts in to sit briefly on his forehead. The rag-and-bone man is wearing mismatched socks and a pair of clogs he collected from a Warminster church. His regulation grey overalls once belonged to a plumber. The name "Matthews" has been stitched above the breast pocket.

The woman and her son return with the books. This requires several trips because there are so many of the things and only two of them. He has to lift the tractor engine onto the chair to clear space in the cart. He says, "Why didn't you mention that you'd been running a library?"

"Again," she says, a little out of breath, "these are my husband's books." When he reaches to take the first batch from her hand, he senses a momentary resistance before she hands them over. It's the same all over; he encounters this all the time. One thing people never understand about the rag-and-bone trade is that it has more in common with undertaking than with refuse collection. Every item has a history and some are hard to part with.

He says lightly, "So is he going to raise a ruckus, your husband, when he finds all his books have been thrown out for scrap?"

The woman shakes her head shortly. She is red-haired and youngish; too thin for his taste but handsome in her way. If

286

her face was less stern, if she looked less wrung out, she might pass herself off as a beauty "No," she replies. "Not a bit."

"Come home and shout, 'Oi missus! What have you gone and done with my bleeding library?'."

"Still no. Not even close."

He says, "Well then, ma'am, I reckon we can probably let them go. More room for everyone when they're out of the house."

"More food for the goblins," the boy says with a grin and the rag-and-bone man laughs and admits that the kid is dead right, they can have the books for their pudding.

In a back garden nearby, a dog is incessantly barking. He thinks it would send him spare, having to listen to that yapping all day, but he is not about to point this out to the red-headed woman. She may have reached the point where she does not hear the dog anymore. If so, having him remind her is hardly going to help. It's like when somebody asks whether you are aware of your own tongue in your mouth, or how often you breathe in and out in a minute. All of a sudden you can't think of anything else.

The cart is overloaded, which means that the journey will be slow. He reaches down to collect the last lot of books. Play-acting a bus conductor, he says, "Ding-ding. Room for a few more upstairs."

The woman retreats to the kerb and takes her son by the hand. "Ah, what a shame. Now it's too full for us."

"I'm afraid so, ma'am. This here cart is for the cast-offs only. You and your boy don't look like cast-offs to me."

"What's a cast-off?" says the child

"Things that aren't wanted anymore," she tells him. "Mostly if they're broken or old."

287

She comes forward, her hand extended, empty this time for the man to shake. And when he leans down she squints at the name on his chest. "Mr Matthews," she says. "Thank you for your help. It's appreciated."

And the rag-and-bone man grins, shakes hands and thanks the woman right back – and never mind that the overalls are hand-me-downs and his name isn't Matthews. He says, "Look after yourself, ma'am" and gives a thumbs-up to the boy and then he's off and away, with that infuriating dog still barking at his back. The horse strains in its harness and the wheels throw up dust from the macadam. Up on his high perch, the man sings "Rah-boh! Rah-boh!" even when the village drops behind him and the green hedgerows press in and there is nobody to hear. Glancing down he sees that the butterfly has returned and appears to have taken up residence on his shoulder. He tries to hold himself steady so as not to disturb it.

His cart contains an engine and a mattress, dark clothes and pale blankets. Broken wardrobe, tin placards. Forty-two books and a haunted armchair. He calls out "Rah-boh!" as he comes over the bridge and dips out of sight. He carries his cargo to the Land of the Lost.

26

YOU WOULD NOT think it to look at him, but he moves with a dancer's silken grace. In the hours before dawn, unable to sleep, he wanders the house, barely parting the air. The house is colossal, it feels without end. It seems to expand in the night and contract in the day. One room opens onto another and onto another after that. He is constantly finding nooks and crannies that had passed him by before. He treads lightly, gliding in and out of handsome chambers where the guests lie sleeping. He prides himself on his ability to pass unnoticed. He is God's last little imp, the Almighty's bad monkey. He has always felt most at home in the dark.

It occurs on some semi-conscious level that he may be searching for an escape. If he steals along enough corridors and prises open enough doors the opportunity will present itself – and when it does he'll respond. So much in life depends on recognising the right door. So much depends on knowing when to stick and when to twist and he suspects the time to twist and cut loose is now drawing near. His status is slipping; his position has turned tenuous. His heightened sensitivity has been born out of a lifetime of slights.

"I've grown bored," Fortnum-Hyde says. "Entertain me. Impress me." But the only response he can muster is a stricken grin and a stammered excuse. Sit him amid the gentlemen at Grantwood and he exhibits none of the grace he has when he is alone on the move. He is a gauche, stumbling, inadequate creature. Buckets of merriment are draining out of his system. He sweats too much and he is far too fat. Kohl runs into his eyes and it makes them smart.

Before long everybody comes to bore or frustrate Fortnum-Hyde. That is the nature of the man, or the nature of a world which turns at a slower pace than his tastes dictate. Yet no one has come to frustrate him so quickly and so comprehensively as bouncy, beaming Arthur Elms. He supposes this may go down as his one claim to fame.

Could it be he has already stayed put when he should have moved on? It might have been better to have absconded swiftly, silently, a whole week before, when Fortnum-Hyde was still dazzled and York Conway impressed and when the Long Boys edged anxiously aside whenever he stepped into the room. Heaven knows his first night at Grantwood had been a triumph. The voices screeched in his head and fire jumped from his fingers and Truman-Jones was so startled that he broke wind like a thunderclap. Whatever he requested at that moment would surely have been granted without complaint. He was put up in a south-facing bedroom with a four-poster Queen Anne and a deep copper tub in the adjacent bathroom. He was sat next to the young master at dinner and lavished with pink steak and red wine. The second night was almost as successful and by rights he should have asked for money then (one hundred pounds! two hundred pounds!) because he has blundered and failed on all the nights after that. The last time he flicked flames was when he crept into the cottage and gave the girl such a fright. His gift is horribly unpredictable. It tore in out of nowhere. Now it has skipped out without so much as saying goodbye.

Elms wonders whether the cocaine is partly to blame. He

ought to lay off for a spell; it makes him ruffled and distracted and that can only hinder his skill. And yet the platters keep being passed round and when everyone else is partaking it feels silly not to join in. So he bows his head and applies a nostril and the powder helps drown the swelling chorus in his head. And now when Fortnum-Hyde remarks that he's bored and demands his pet conjurer put on a show, Elms attempts to brazen it out and splutters that the conditions aren't right, there is disquiet in the room. He must be reassured that they are all of one mind and one breath and that their hearts beat in time.

Fortnum-Hyde lifts an eyebrow. "The conditions are right when I say that they are. Don't be a mouse. Stand up straight, be a man."

York Conway says, "Unless of course it was a trick all along. I have come to the opinion that this man is all smoke and mirrors."

"Obviously it's a trick," adds Boswell the playwright. "Odourless spirit and a few concealed match heads. It's a perfectly fine trick, but it is a trick all the same."

The jazz singer, for his part, confesses that he remains of two minds. On the one hand the man is a trickster, in which case he is playing them for fools. Or on the other he's real, in which case he's worse. Because if the man is real then it follows, says Sweetpea, that he's no man at all but something unnatural, unearthly. They ought to shoo him away before he curses them all. At this the other musicians offer a rumble of assent. Elms guesses that they have already debated this matter among themselves. The Long Boys hate the imp. He allows that he probably hates them in return. The Long Boys are his rivals for Fortnum-Hyde's attention. And there is no doubt the Long Boys have gained the upper hand.

Find the right door and disappear into the night. Grantwood House contains treasures; he can snatch something and run. York Conway has mentioned that King-Roo paid a small fortune for the jagged, freakish composition that hangs in the Regency Room – yet the instant he steals in to check how well it's secured turns out to be the one where he is finally clocked. Mrs Cleaver rises early. It is as though she has been lying in wait. Her shadow falls across the canvas so that he twitches and pivots. He fears that his smile gives away his intentions.

"What a lovely painting that the young master picked up. Who did you say the artist was again?"

The housekeeper regards him with a dry contempt. "I didn't, sir."

He splutters, "A friend of Rupert's from over in Paris. I wish I could remember his name."

Another significant pause. "I'm sure you do, sir," Mrs Cleaver agrees.

The simple truth is, he despises them all. He hates the scurrying servants who have evidently decided that they are better than him, and the noble young gentlemen who know full well that they are. He hates neat, nimble York Conway and Truman Truman-Jones (so unnaturally large, he must weigh half a ton), and he has developed a particular aversion for Lord Hertford, forever lecturing his staff on the evils of social inequality. The simple truth is, he hates them all, every one.

Not King-Roo.

This objection brings him up short. It is as though one of the voices has spoken, very loud, directly in his ear.

No, he allows. Not King Roo. Fortnum-Hyde is exempt. Even now, despite all his humiliations, he remains under the man's sway. Such boldness of vision. Such sweeping authority. He marvels at the way King Roo holds court with such ease. How he sits on a chair as though it's a throne in the Palace, with his legs spread wide and his hand sculpting the air as he speaks. Someone should write down what he says. He is pointing the way to the world up ahead.

Gesturing for the butler to relight his cigar, Fortnum-Hyde says, "The twentieth-century has no room for mediocrity. It is a time for true courage. It is a time for good men to stand up."

He says, "The nation needs leadership. But all I see around me are rabbits and sheep."

Lolling back in his chair, wreathed in aquamarine smoke, he cries, "The future is coming, boys. Either jump on board or bail out." It is all purely thrilling.

"Am I a part of that future, Roo?" Elms had excitably asked during his first week in the house, at which point the young master had favoured him with a smile and said, "You are indeed, Elmsy" and he had spent the rest of the evening replaying the exchange in his head and wondering precisely what this future would be like. But of course that was when he was still able to make flames, when there was a point to his presence. Were he to ask the same question today, he knows what Fortnum-Hyde would reply. And that, probably, is the worst of it – the knowledge that he has disappointed the man he most longed to impress.

Oh but he needs to get out – and sooner rather than later. It was half-true what he said: Grantwood House has taken on a disquieting air. He knows it, he feels it, he picks up on tremors that get by others unnoticed. The guests gathered in the drawing room resemble pots and pans arranged on a stove, coming steadily to the boil. The lids are just now beginning to rattle.

His magic has left him. The voices, however, continue to roll up in distracting waves. The gruff Scottish fellow reports that it's chilly outside and the garrulous woman chips in to complain that she has dropped all of her shopping into the dirty green stream. The others remain at a distance, he cannot discern what they say, but he is nagged by the sense that their numbers are growing and he catches a mental image of shadowed figures standing in lines, with the gruff man and hushed woman at the vanguard and then row upon row behind that. And it could conceivably be that each of these rows has begun an incremental advance, like timid soldiers or schoolchildren playing a game of grandmother's footsteps. He fancies that several voices are screaming in the lines near the back. If they draw any closer he fears he might lose his mind.

He needs to get out. Grantwood House is unhealthy; it is making him ill. If he cannot steal the French painting, then perhaps he could make off with some jewellery instead? The drawers of the dressers must be clogged with the stuff. The beautiful sister walks about festooned with trinkets; she is brought in like a fucking Christmas tree every night. He could grab a handful and slide away through the dark – except that he has had bad luck with jewellery in the past. Each time he walks, the amulet taps his breastbone to remind him of his sin. And if Grantwood House is a fake then it surely follows that its contents will be fashioned out of crystal and paste. Only his magic is real – and even that's not real any more.

Hunched on his armchair, his belly resting on his lap, Arthur Elms catches himself staring for long periods at the velvet wall hangings. He has to battle the ridiculous urge to pull the hangings apart, to check they don't conceal some shadowy figure or secret door. The drapes fascinate him. They remind him of something. He can't think what it is.

Fortnum-Hyde yawns and extends his long limbs and with a tilt of his chin orders the platter sent round. "I've grown bored," he announces. "Entertain me. Impress me."

Poor Julius Boswell has toiled through the day revising his one-act play and still the young master remains unconvinced; he decides that on balance it does not quite pass muster. Hulking Truman-Jones should by rights be in Bombay and yet here he sits, showing no inclination to leave. Even the once lively Long Boys are becoming lulled by the house. They have medicated themselves on alcohol and cocaine and will only consent to perform when ordered to several times. Fortnum-Hyde has come to regard them as recalcitrant offspring. He loves them so deeply but they need to buck up their ideas. He demands they compose another song in the manner of 'Come Back Up To Bring It Down'; it vexes him to see the musicians sitting on their hands. Fortnum-Hyde has always considered himself a friend and supporter of the negro race. He confesses he almost counts himself as a spiritual cousin; it has even been remarked that his own features are faintly negroid in nature. But this naturally means he expects something in return. It means he holds them to the same lofty standards that he sets for himself. And besides, how will the world learn to love pep if they won't crack on with new songs?

George Washington asks, "What's this pep he keeps talking about?"

"He means jazz," York Conway explains. "It's his Lordship's word for the music you play."

George Washington exchanges a look with the other Long

Boys. He says, "All due respect. He can call it pep until his ass falls off. Ain't never gonna happen."

Elms camps out in the chair, only stirring when the silver platter appears, determined not to attract attention. On the other side of the crackling hearth, Fortnum-Hyde casts about for a fresh line of attack and alights on his sister, draped in her evening finery. He reminds her again of the time she stuck her saw in the bone and enquires whether she kept score of all the soldiers she killed. But Clarissa has come armed, she gives as good as she gets. She asks in turn about Rupert's own wartime score sheet. She cannot imagine he managed to kill any soldiers, he was that far from the line. From what she has heard, he chiefly shot grouse. His hunting prowess was legendary. He must be the only officer in history to be awarded a medal for his skill at riding to hound and shooting grouse from the sky.

Fortnum-Hyde grins and scowls with the same contorted expression. Through an indulgent chuckle, he says, "Why you dopey cunt, that shows how little you know."

"Easy, King-Roo," protests Julius Boswell.

Elms stares fixedly at a vertical fold in the velvet hangings. If he were to hook a hand around its corner, would he find the wall immediately – or would his hand keep extending until his whole arm disappeared? Would he be able to step into the fold and escape the room and its people? And what might he find on the other side, through the portal – something better or something worse?

The door opens at his back to admit a draft of cold air. "Ah," says Fortnum-Hyde. "The pleasure dolls."

The girls take their footstools; the magician steals a glance. The shorter girl is brash and depthless; she does not interest him in the slightest. But the other one is more intriguing. She is a little like him: she keeps herself to herself. He regrets that he started off on the wrong foot with this one. He wishes he had not crept into her bedroom. What was he thinking? He is at the mercy of mischief. Half of the time he does not know what he is doing, or what prompted him to do it. He is a mystery to others – yet he foxes himself most of all.

Clarissa says, "Lulu and Ferdinand, what a blessed relief. Please come and save me from these tiresome bores."

"I'm sure they will be more than willing to oblige," Fortnum-Hyde says. "They are good at providing relief, so I'm told."

Now Sweetpea leans forward to study the new arrivals. He is dressed in a shell-pink polo neck which is on loan from his host. A Panama hat sits aboard his narrow head. He is a fine-featured man with a calm, courtly manner. "Gracious," he says. "Seems to me those crippled soldiers have their refreshment on tap."

"Rub-a-dub-dub. The pleasure dolls. They look like butter wouldn't melt, bless them. But each would suck you dry without batting an eyelid."

Clarissa says, "Shut up, Ru. Lulu and Ferdie are friends of mine."

"I like them as well. I think they're tremendous." He turns to the others. "They're outlaws. They're buccaneers. A fine addition to the house. Heavens, who doesn't love Ferdie? She's a hellcat, that one. And then there's Lulu. Sweet little Lulu."

The taller girl is staring, embarrassed, at her feet.

"She looks like a veal calf. Don't you, Lulu? Like a beautiful veal calf."

"I don't know," murmurs Lucy.

"God damn those cripples," exclaims Skinny Boy Floyd. "We're sitting up here with nothing. They got all the action they want."

York Conway, very drunk, says, "I must admit, the darkie has a point. Whatever became of all the girls that were here? There are too many men in this room. I sometimes have the impression I'm in the bloody trenches again."

Clarissa says, "When were you in the trenches, Connie? Did Rupert give you time off from beating the bushes for grouse?"

It is at this point that Fortnum-Hyde risks losing his cool. "Stop talking about the fucking war. The war's in the past. What interests me is the future."

"Grouse season. Or is that over already?"

Winifred pipes up. "If you want to shoot something I think you should shoot all the sheep. I've been thinking it over. I think they're bothering Edith."

Fortnum-Hyde ignores this and returns to his sister. "I suggest you go up to your room and take Sweetpea with you. The man needs some relief. And you've been rather leading him along."

"Now then, excuse me," says the playwright.

"Go boil your head, Ru. I'm engaged, don't you know?"

Yet Fortnum-Hyde is enjoying himself now. He has happened upon the line of attack that he wishes to pursue. He says there is no call being prudish and that he personally recommends the dark meat. Last year he spent six months in Jamaica, supervising the sugar refinery when it had all of its problems – and my God, what a life. The music. The people. The sun constantly blazing. The women were as hot as the sand at midday. Clawing at his back like untamed tigresses.

The sweet, wet suction of their loins against his. He confesses that he is half-minded to return to Jamaica, though it is perhaps wisest he did not. He suspects he may have sown his oats just a little too freely. He would be barely off the boat before he was accosted on the quay by half-caste toddlers of uncertain parentage.

This talk of West Indian women has a curious effect on Truman Truman-Jones. His stare goes glassy. His mighty limbs start to tremble. When Fortnum-Hyde describes the sweet, wet suction of negro loins, he responds with a low, involuntary groan, as though invisible doctors are subjecting him to some invasive medical procedure.

"Did you ever jigger a sheep?" George Washington asks the party.

"Do what?" says the playwright.

"Oh my, yes," chuckles Sweetpea. "This is a favoured pastime of our country cousins. When you cannot find a lady, the livestock must do. It causes no harm to the sheep, or so these young fellows claim."

Skinny Boy nods earnestly. "Stands to reason. Inside of a sheep's no different to the inside of a woman. Like putting your hand inside a good suede glove."

George Washington says, "Forget jiggering a sheep. Did you ever jigger a camel?"

"Now there's a notion. Can't say that I did."

Fortnum-Hyde retrieves his goblet of cognac. "The glorious undead have no need of sheep. From where I sit, they have more appropriate entertainment to hand."

"Not any more they haven't," says Winifred.

Again he ignores her. Conway asks what she means by that, exactly.

"We're having nothing to do with those chumps anymore. We're going to make our money elsewhere, aren't we, Lu?"

Sweetpea's serene face registers delighted amusement. "Oh mercy, listen to this. Good little girls grow up and be bosses."

"Sure enough, it's the way of the world," George Washington agrees. "Soon as they can, they start cracking the whip."

"Independent traders," says Fred. From his berth in the chair, Elms sees her lean forward and make a remark, under her breath, to Fortnum-Hyde.

The viscount responds with a laugh that is more air than noise. He asks, "How old are you, child?"

"Very nearly fifteen."

"Then I think not," he tells her. "The last time I was with a fourteen-year-old girl was when I was a thirteen-year-old boy."

But it becomes apparent that some haggling transaction is now underway. The haggling is being treated as a joke for the moment, although Elms wonders whether some of the jokers have a more serious intent. Skinny Boy asks out of interest about the girls' going rate and the one they call Ferdie replies that she typically charges one pound a time. This provokes great merriment and mock outrage, with Skinny Boy protesting that she must have misunderstood. He wasn't asking to hire both of the girls for an entire fortnight. He wasn't asking them to do all of his laundry as well.

Through tears of laughter, George Washington explains that a pound is a discount. These ladies are ruthless. They usually demand a man's limb for a jigger. He points out that the cripples weren't cripples until the pleasure dolls came to stay. The first night they said, "Oh, pay us with a leg." The second night they said, "Oh, pay us with an arm."

Skinny Boy splutters. "Man, I knew that's what it was. And the one with the tin mask, he don't know when to quit. He says, 'Take my old face and leap up in that bed. Take this old nose, I don't wanna pick it no more'."

The shorter girl makes an effort to join in with the laughter. She cries, "His face looks like something that's been left outside in the rain. I honestly thought I was going to throw up my dinner."

"But what did you do with the face, pleasure doll? What in hell did you do with the poor soldier's old nose?"

"I reckon she ate it. She's telling you that was the dinner she ate."

Conway's clear tones cut through the gaiety. He says, "It's a fine attempt by Ferdinand. But the general consensus is that a pound is too steep."

"Ten bob then," says Winifred. "That's our final offer."

But this latest figure is not nearly so amusing. Conversation stops. The guests shift and scratch. When Truman-Jones, arriving late to the joke, cries, "I've heard of charging an arm and a leg but I never imagined it would be literally true", Fortnum-Hyde frowns to let him know he has spoken out of turn. A footman sends out the platter once more. But, perhaps for the first time, no one pays it any mind. The room's attention is all on Fred.

Conway says, "And so we arrive at the nub of the matter."

Sweetpea says, "It's a fact, men need to scratch their itch on occasion."

Elms looks from Sweetpea to the girls and then on to Clarissa, who has a policy of refusing chairs to sit cross-legged on the floor. The young woman is bent forward, half-turned from the group and has busied herself with picking at a loose thread on the fringe of the Afghan rug. He can see a pale dusting of freckles across one exposed shoulder and a honeyed down on the nape of her neck. He glares at her furiously; her very beauty is scalding. Clarissa has absented herself because this exchange is beneath her. It belongs to a different world from the one she inhabits. How much would a man have to part with to secure such a creature? He could offer one hundred pounds and his limbs and she would still laugh in his face. He could offer his face; it would still not be enough.

Coal slips and settles in the grate. Skinny Boy says, "Ten English bob. I do believe I can work with that."

Winifred looks at the man for an instant and then drops her gaze. She mutters, "All right then. Ten bob."

"Fred," says the other girl, abruptly alarmed. "Wait."

In a rush, Truman-Jones says, "Do you know I must say I'm rather tempted myself. Fancy that, but there it is. What a hilarious thing."

The big man's announcement helps lift the tension. Fortnum-Hyde explains that his friend can be quite the dark horse sometimes, while Conway chips in to say that this isn't correct, he's more like a dark elephant and will surely obliterate the poor girl. Skinny Boy points out that either way, horse or elephant, the gentleman will have to wait his turn because he booked her first and plans to take his time. She'll be tired out afterwards; he can guarantee them that much.

"It's a present to myself," Truman-Jones tells the group. "It's a small goodbye present before embarking for Bombay."

Winifred stands up, tucks her hair behind her ears in a matter-of-fact manner. "All right," she says. "If we are going to do it."

"Fred, wait. Stop."

"What an occurrence," Fortnum-Hyde marvels. "And top marks to the pleasure dolls. I'm sure you agree, they have managed to enliven a very dull night."

Still tugging at the loose strand on the rug, Clarissa says, "Forgive me. I am finding all of this just a trifle unseemly."

Her objection passes all but unnoticed. Skinny Boy takes Winifred by the hand and together they pick their way through the furniture and out the door. Fortnum-Hyde sees them off by instigating a round of applause.

"Oh poor girl," Conway says. "First the darkie and then the elephant. There'll be nothing left of the child by the end of the night."

"Nonsense," Fortnum-Hyde rejoins. "Ferdinand is going to eat them both alive."

"Ten bob for the other one," Arthur Elms blurts. The words are out of his mouth before he knows what has happened.

Here a thick silence falls on the room. The imp's outburst has taken everyone by surprise.

"Now then," Fortnum-Hyde says at length. "Our broken tinderbox exhibits faint signs of life."

The girl grips her knees. Addressing the young master, she says, "I don't want to, I'm sorry."

"Why ever not, child?"

"I don't like him, that's all."

Fortnum-Hyde frowns. "Nobody likes him, that's beside the point. The man is a dung beetle. He's a waste of everyone's time. But it may be that you can rekindle his fire. God knows, he needs something. I have just about given up."

"Leave her alone," says Clarissa.

The thing about his sister is that she can always make him laugh. "Leave her alone to do what? What else does she do?

We all know why this young lady is here, but it is only you who likes to pretend she is something she's not. Ferdie and Lulu are the pleasure dolls. They are good at their job and that's why we love them." He turns back to the girl. "Go on," he says. "Get."

When she continues to hesitate, Conway moves to resolve the impasse. He says, "The viscount just gave you an order, my child. It would be rather ungracious if you forced him to repeat it."

In the half-light of the great hall, Elms is aware of her casting about to see where her friend has got to, no doubt aiming to overtake the girl for some whispered consultation. But the only figure in the vicinity is the housekeeper, Mrs Cleaver, standing against the far wall with her hands tightly folded. Mrs Cleaver is as impassive as the Sphinx. She prides herself on her skill at revealing no more information than is strictly required.

Placatingly he says, "I reckon they will both have gone upstairs" and then trots behind as the girl makes her ascent. He calls, "But I don't know what room the skinny negro is using," and this is true, he does not. He has heard that the musicians like to swap rooms on a nightly basis. He supposes the Long Boys are roving gypsies at heart. They try each room for size but have a horror of becoming too comfortable, too stuck. They are convinced the next room will mark an improvement on the one they are in.

He says, "Actually I lied. I only want to talk to you. And I don't have ten bob as it is. In fact I am completely stony broke."

For the first time she speaks. "That's all right," she says faintly. "I only want to find Fred."

But the corridor confuses her; she scrutinises each door in turn.

"Maybe this one," suggests Elms. He turns the handle and puts his free hand at her back. Inside the big bedroom the lights have been lit. A fire burns in the hearth. The branches of the cedar stand black against the uncurtained windows.

"No, not this one," she says.

"No, this one is mine." He closes in behind her and positions his bulk at the door jamb to prevent her escape. "Don't worry, I mean it, I just want to talk. Sit down for a moment. You're safe as houses with me."

It is abundantly clear he repulses the girl. Elms does not mind. He has accepted his role as an object of revulsion. He repulses high-born ladies and well-to-do widows, and now it transpires he can add schoolgirl tarts to the list. This particular tart has no compunction about bedding down with legless cripples and half-dead men in masks, and yet show her healthy Arthur Elms with his proud belly and she says, 'Oh please no, I don't like him'. How amusing that is. It merely confirms the imp's status as the lowest of the low.

Trying again, he indicates the amulet on his chest. He says, "I can't pay you with money, but I can pay you with this. This was taken from a pharaoh's tomb, it's called the Eye of Thoth-Amon. It's worth more than ten bob, I can tell you that much."

"I don't want it."

He slips the chain from around his neck and immediately feels lighter; he has come to hate the amulet. "Take it as payment. I just want to talk, it's the only thing I can manage. Take it, miss, please. It's worth ever so much money."

Unwillingly she reaches out and gathers the chain in her hand.

He says, "I killed my best friend to get ahold of that thing."

"Oh take it back," she says, shocked. "I don't want it anyway."

"Too late, it's yours. Put it in your pocket. Do you believe what I said? That I killed my best friend."

"I don't know," says the girl. But all at once her resistance crumbles; it may be the old amulet has some power after all. She steps into the room and bonelessly drops on the chair by the fire where she proceeds to wrap the chain about one slender fist, pulling its coils so tightly that her flesh stands out pink. He expects her to weep at this point and is momentarily thrown when she doesn't.

Elms pulls the door at his back. He takes a perch on the edge of the four-poster, poised to glide onto his feet if his guest attempts to escape. His thoughts have been chaotic but the girl's presence works wonders. She possesses a still, quiet quality, which is entirely at odds with her line of business. She appears to stand apart from the rest of Grantwood's occupants. He does not even mind that he repulses her so long as she is able to provide him with solace.

"Queen Anne," he says.

"What?"

"This bed. Queen Anne." He pats the eiderdown with one white hand. "But don't worry, I mean it, I only want to talk." He thinks it might help if he were to unbutton his flies and present her with some tangible evidence of his harmlessness and good intentions. In this moment it feels important that the girl, alone out of everyone, understands the situation. He cannot produce fire. He cannot be aroused in her company. So he sits here before her, a flaccid, hollow man. Whatever he once was has now departed for good.

Instead he leaves his right hand on the bed. He says, "It's true what I said. I killed men in the war, but of course that doesn't count. But then I killed my best friend Uriah to get ahold of the amulet and an old nag I could sell. I wish that I hadn't. I'd take it back if I could."

"Take it back then. I don't even want it."

"Ha," he says. "What's done is done."

But the truth of the matter is that he feels very nearly content. It is the happiest he has been in many months, perhaps the happiest he's been since his final night in the woods, beside the shallow, rocky river, when they cleared timber from the lean-to and listened to the rain tapping the metal roof overhead. Afterwards he will recall the feel of the eiderdown against the palm of his hand and the soothing sight of the girl in the chair by the fire, her face half-turned to the hearth as he tells her of his life. He has paid for her time, which means that she must sit and be quiet until he has said his piece. It does not concern him that she would rather be elsewhere. They have an understanding, she and him. She cannot leave until he lets her go.

He cocks his head, squints his eyes. "Your mum and dad are both dead, I think."

She says nothing.

"Yes," he says. "Both of them dead. All very sad. Do you want me to contact them for you?"

"No." The very notion appals her. "Please don't."

"I can, you know. I can do it for free."

She shakes her head dumbly.

"Very well. Never mind."

The voices in his head have gone silent. Maybe they're listening too. Then, speaking unhurriedly in a measured tone he has never been able to master when inside the drawing room, he explains that he first stole the amulet because he wanted to sell it, but then began to use it as Uriah had used it, as a part of his costume – a stage conjurer's accessory to augment his real magic. He tells her about his time as a spiritualist, purporting to commune with the dead and bring comfort to the living. He says that being a good spiritualist is much like being a good detective. You need to lay the ground, do your homework and keep an eye out for clues. After that, you dim the lights and shuffle the ingredients and spice up your story with a few harmless white lies. But really what you are doing is leaving a trail or a bait as an invitation for the client to come and meet the spiritualist halfway. And when that happens, you've won. The client winds up doing most of the work for you.

The girl leans in to add nuggets of coal to the fire. She says, "So it's all a lie. It's all a fake."

He shakes his head, irked. "You're not understanding. The lie tells the truth. It comforts the afflicted. That's what makes it magic."

"But a lie is a lie. A lie's always wrong."

"Not always, though. That's what I'm saying."

"And that trick with the flames. That's not real either."

"No, that was always real, a reaction to the war. And then it burned out. I can't do it anymore."

"Why not, if it's real?"

By now his fingers have left the eiderdown and begun to probe at one another. He is conscious of a growing agitation. He wishes the girl would keep quiet and simply let him speak. He clears his throat and prepares to tell her about his time in the trench. About the rats and the flies and the charred human flesh that smelled like cuts of roast pork and about how he came away without so much as a scratch, which proves he is blessed – so much more blessed than her pathetic friends in the cottage. He is speaking in a rush; his fingers rush and grope; they have a life of their own. Downstairs, at a distance, the first grandfather clock chimes the hour of midnight.

He says, "Your crippled friends in the cottage. I used to bury those men every day of the week."

She says, "Show me how you do the trick."

"It's not a trick. It's real. I don't know how I did it."

"That's stupid."

He says, "The world is stupid, that shows how much you know. Nothing makes any sense. Things just happen, that's all."

He rubs the pads of his fingers but it's no use, he is spent. His energies are exhausted and the magic has wound down. He stares at the lost, lonely girl on the chair by the fire and thinks how nice it would be if they could both leave together. They might take their trade on the road; she could be his assistant. He would treat her so kindly. He could be her saviour.

He urges his hands to stop their writhing. He attempts another laugh. "Could you ever love me, Lucy?"

"No," she replies without hesitation.

This time his laugh feels looser, less false. "What about like? Could you ever learn to like me?"

"No."

"No," Elms says with a sigh. This is what he suspected. The second grandfather clock strikes; the third will follow shortly. Indistinct voices leak back into his brain and now he is convinced that there are screams from the back rows. Something terrible is approaching, it draws closer by the hour. There is nothing to do but sit tight to one side and see what form it will take.

27

T HE LAST FULL day of Lord Hertford's life arrives bright and cold on a gust of brown leaves. The sheep on the lawn are becomingly ruffled. The camel sets forth to seek shelter in the woods. Somewhere in the house an unfastened window is banging. The acoustics are such it takes the servants a half-hour to find it.

The earl awakens to the weight of a breakfast tray being set upon his lap. He eats a poached egg and white fish and permits his valet to dress him. The night has been an uncommonly restorative one. The autumn light is so splendid that it cajoles him outside. In his wheeled wicker chair he can feel the wind's whip and drag. His sandy hair is a tumult and his woollen scarf streams out and then up and then across his long face. "Raine," he complains. "I am temporarily blinded."

Several gods have been toppled but the butler is quick to reassure him that no lasting damage is done. They come scrunching up the raked gravel drive that leads to the orchard where the groundsman has been summoned to report on the state of the trees. Gesturing with his briar pipe, Coach shows where the root rot is at its worst and where the saplings have failed. Lord Hertford replies with a series of commiserating grunts and then requests an apple be plucked for his inspection. Root rot aside, the fruit appears to be healthy. Perhaps this weekend he will have Cook bake a pie.

Migrating birds wheel overhead. When his chair is turned

back towards the gate in the wall, he idly asks whether the two little girls are still boarding at the cottage and Coach scratches his ear and says he believes that they are.

Lord Hertford smiles. "Dear me, they have been with us an awfully long time. I rather think that quite soon they might prefer to go home."

He lunches on a whim in the kitchens and has Raine fetch Mrs Cleaver to join him at the table. And perhaps he knows he is pointed towards death because he is preoccupied by his legacy and what will follow in his wake. He reminds the housekeeper of the labourers' summit that these kitchens once hosted, and of the angry farmers whom he brought into line and then set upon a higher path, ensuring they maintained a living wage for those who worked on the land. He recalls the suffragettes and their supporters who employed the house as base camp, and concedes that even she, Mrs Cleaver, has played a small role in shaping British history. That her reward is the ballot and that she must use it wisely.

And he is concerned that these achievements should not be forgotten. The liberal course is almost – not quite – Sisyphean in that it requires a constant, steady hand to nudge the boulder uphill. Relax the pressure for an instant and so much social progress risks being rolled back. Such is the way of the world, and of capital, and of the basest urges of human nature. But he has performed his role as best he could and it now falls to the viscount to take up the challenge. He truly hopes that he will; the evidence is encouraging. If anything, the scope of Rupert's ambition surpasses even his own. The boy is energetic and bold, almost to a fault, although is that really a problem? The world demands boldness or else nothing ever gets done.

His long features twitch. His blue stare has gone milky. He

says, "He is an impressive figure, is he not? I dare say he has given us cause for concern in the past. But he has blossomed into a man of true stature, I think."

"He is a credit to you, sir," Mrs Cleaver agrees.

"My one wish is that the tax officials leave him just a little to play with. He is not obviously suited to managing diminishing resources. He has been built to lead an advancing army as opposed to one in retreat."

"I am confident," says Mrs Cleaver and then appears to trail off.

Lord Hertford says, "The world appears to me to be shrinking. And yet of course that's not true. Rupert understands the situation rather better than I."

The valet runs his bath. He soaps himself and retires for his nap and when he awakens the October brightness has faded and it is very nearly winter. The clocks introduce the evening with a whirr and a clang. And this is how the day ends for Lord Hertford: installed in his upstairs drawing room, with the fire laid in the grate and a modest supper set on the claw-footed table. He reads fifteen pages of the *Life of Disraeli*, after which he requests that Clarissa join him for whist. They play three hands in near silence; he keeps dropping his cards. At one stage, losing interest, he gets it into his head that Rupert's musicians should come up and perform. That would be rather agreeable – a private recital – but Clarissa explains that these particular musicians possess a limited repertoire. They exclusively play jazz, which she knows her father dislikes. The Long Boys, she adds, are slaves to modernity. They have no appreciation of history. They might as well all have been hatched yesterday.

"The modern world," marvels Lord Hertford with a laugh.

In bed, deep asleep, he is returned to a summer he passed many decades before, navigating the mountainous interior of the Peloponnese. He is a handsome man, lean and trim, striding between hard light and black shadow, or swimming alone in a lake cradled by high granite walls. This was the summer he turned twenty-one and the land about him felt younger even than that, like some glistening newborn, altogether comical in its blinking, stumbling savagery. The cobbled streets are so steep that they invite him to run, and so he canters to eat dinner at the ramshackle tavern where he is circled by garrulous Greek urchins who want his leftover goat stew. And then on to his room where he likes to sit up and drink ouzo and write urgent political tracts, the import of which he can hardly bring himself to believe until he puts it down in black ink and realises that it is all true and that every letter, each word, is like a lick of bright fire. This is the summer he spends in the Peloponnese and the experience transports him and erases all of the years in between, so that when the butler heaves open the door to let the light pour into the room the earl rises up in exaltation to claim it. "Raine," he exclaims. "You put me in mind of the sun god Apollo."

Climbing the long slope to the east, Winifred turns to take her bearings and spies two match-stalk figures edging up the path from the garden. She says, "Who's that in the wheelchair? It's not Toto, is it?"

"No," Lucy says. "It's the old man. The earl."

"Oh yes, so it is. Look at him, the poor bugger. He's not long for this world."

They forge on up the hill, calling out to the camel to play with them awhile. But the animal does not care for company.

It throws a contemptuous glance over one bony shoulder and shows them its hindquarters again.

The pursuit has become hopeless. Fred loses patience. She picks up a stone and hurls it at the camel. When the first stone drops short she casts about for another.

"Stop it, Fred, you're being cruel."

"Bloody hell, call me Ferdie. Everyone else calls me Ferdie."

"I'm not calling you Ferdie. What's wrong with you today?"

"Oh my stars. Ask me that one more time and I shall throw a stone at you too."

Twice that morning the girl has asked how Fred is feeling. The previous night was so strange, she wants to be certain that her friend is unhurt. Both times Fred has replied in shrill tones that of course she is fine, why shouldn't she be? She cannot for the life of her imagine why Lucy is acting so gloomy. Fred points out that last night was the night she made herself thirty bob. Lucy does not appear to have done so badly herself. She walked away with a priceless old necklace; it must be worth almost as much as the Pick-Arsehole painting. If that's being hurt, they should get hurt more often.

"Fair enough," Lucy says. "Have it your way."

By this point, however, the camel has fled. It maintains its course up the hill. Assuming Edith has the wherewithal to stick with this line, she will presently ascend clear out of the valley and cross into woodland. Beyond the woodland, Lucy has heard, sits the village of Brent, which contains a grocer's, a post office, a Saxon church and a pub. She thrills to the prospect of the camel escaping Grantwood and continuing her ill-tempered progress through the home counties of England. What might people make of the sight, if Edith wound up walking right up Brent high street? They would think that the woods had sprung monsters, or that some prophecy had come true.

When they turn to go back, the house fills their vision. The morning sun slaps its sandstone sides and turns its windows into smelted silver oblongs. Smoke streams sideways from the chimneys; the coloured pennants are flapping. It is a fabulous place, a storybook house. It is a fairytale palace; it can make all dreams come true.

Fred says, "And when the old fellow has croaked, it will all go to Rupert. I mean," she adds breathlessly, "it will be sad when that happens, but come on, own up, won't it be wonderful too?"

The sad truth, however, is that this precious kingdom is in decline. The agricultural crisis bites deep, land values have collapsed and the Grantwood estate is tens of thousands in debt. The house and its grounds have both seen better days; there used to be double the staff to keep the wheels smoothly turning. Now the ones that remain come scurrying through the faded rooms, their hands made raw from scouring powder and their necks and elbows damp with the patchouli oil they use to mask the smell of old sweat. When the groom of the chambers is found lying dead on the stairs, the servants are informed that he will not be replaced. This inevitably means that they must all work harder still.

It breaks Lord Hertford's heart to have the west wing shut up. It feels like an amputation, a permanent break with the past. Now the whole place is haunted by apparitions in dust sheets. The faces of long-dead relations sit in gilt frames on the walls. Bars of weak sunlight pierce the gaps in the shutters and provide enough illumination for an intrepid explorer to pick his way through the ruin, although he would be advised to tread carefully; there are various hazards to hand.

Hastening across an upstairs salon, Arthur Elms catches his pocket on the exposed arm of a chair and in twisting to free himself succeeds only in tearing his trousers clean across the seat. His thoughts are unsound and his trousers are useless. Prompted by some residual sense of decorum, he removes them entirely and proceeds on bare legs. On and on he walks, past portrait after portrait. Avert your eyes, ghosts, if the half-naked guest causes offence. At least the voices don't mind. They are keening and buzzing. He believes they have never been this loud in the past.

It dawns on him that he has finally found his way to the very heart of the house. All that time he spent searching for an exit when what he really should have been doing was directing himself not outward but inward. Here in the shuttered west wing resides the source of all power – the wellspring of history and its burial site, too. Nothing dies in the wing. It is merely put under sheets, awaiting someone to unveil it.

Up ahead, another door. It is the door he has been searching for. He prises it open and enters a long narrow chamber that is empty except for a bronze bust draped in white linen. He peels back the dust sheet and underneath is Uriah.

"Hello Uriah. I haven't seen you in ages."

The bronze head has large ears, a full beard and a furrowed brow. Its eyes are deep-set and suggestive of sadness and yet there is a rueful set to its mouth which makes it plain that it regards the world with as much amusement as sorrow. The bronze head is not that of Uriah Smith, who made no great impression and passed away quite unnoticed. And yet nonetheless the resemblance is striking. In the half-light of the west

317

wing, one dilapidated old man looks very much like another.

"Uriah," he weeps. "I'm sorry I killed you."

And how might Uriah respond if the bust were Uriah? The magician decides that his former friend would be kind. He might say, "Oh my dear boy, think no more about it. As you can see, I have been returned to full health."

"I'm glad, Uriah. I have missed you so much."

And Uriah would say, "But just look at you now. The guest of nobility. It makes my heart swell to see it."

"Thank you, that's kind. I wish that you had come too."

"But where is my amulet? What, pray tell, have you done with the Eye?"

By this point his tears are flowing freely. He reaches out to stroke the man's weathered cheek. He says, "I'm sorry I hit you. I'm sorry I took Queenie and your amulet. I don't have it anymore, I gave it to a whore. I don't have anything anymore. Even my magic has gone."

Except that this would only make Uriah laugh. "Nonsense," he would say. "You have mislaid it, that's all. Don't forget what you are – you are God's ultimate imp. The magic is there. You need to think hard and find it."

He nods his head in a frenzy. "Thank you," he says. "For believing in me."

"The magic is real. But it is inside, not out. Reach down inside yourself and you shall find wonders."

Bare-legged he kneels and puts his thumb to his forefinger. And now at long last he thinks Uriah may be right and that some force still remains, knotted and trapped, like the water behind a kinked garden hose, or a hornets' nest inside a cavity. The daylight has now faded. The room is entirely dark. He rubs his fingers together and whispers, "God's ultimate imp."

"What's that, my boy?"

He says, "That's what I am. God's ultimate imp."

It is Fortnum-Hyde's custom to limit his cocaine use during daylight hours so as to reward himself more fully when the evening rolls in. Typically he will ration himself to a morning tonic on waking, a few lines over lunch and a pick-me-up ahead of his afternoon tea. But today the viscount has broken with form – the early morning tonic is merely an aperitif. Once that has gone in, he unleashes the hounds; he treats himself to both barrels. By mid-afternoon he is what the Long Boys would describe as comprehensively baked.

His house guests are not baked and this is vastly annoying. In the velvet-draped chamber he demands they catch up and has the platters sent out. He laments the fact that it always falls to him to lead and the rest to follow. Such is the nature of the world and of natural selection, but it remains a trial all the same. He sits in his armchair with beads of sweat on his brow and his temples twanging like a double bass and orders his guests to pick up the pace and step up to his level. He is up on the mountaintop and he is waving them in. He outright refuses to be the only baked goods in the room.

When the footmen reload the platters with cocaine and cognac, he drags his gaze left to right and makes a mental note of the absentees. Clarissa, it seems, is still upstairs with Old Stick, while that skunk Arthur Elms has yet to make an appearance. But this makes no difference. His sister's an irritant and Elms is a crook; Mrs Cleaver has advised they check his luggage when he leaves. He orders that the others drink deep and sniff at the powder for all they are worth. The two pleasure dolls should join in if they like. He decrees that tonight shall be a time of fun and games. There has been too much chatter and indolence for his taste. Too much lounging about. Too much jawing about nothing. The hour has come for a little action instead.

Hauling himself from the chair, Fortnum-Hyde decides that now might be a good moment to lay out his credentials – to remind his guests exactly what kind of man walks among them. Then, brandishing the poker, he demonstrates the drop-shot which forced the great Arthur Gore to collide with the post. Adopting a pugilist's stance he revisits the blow that sent a prize fighter to the mat. He throws back his head and says, "Look at me now, I've reached the mountain, my friends. Climb up to the top and I shall show you the promised land."

The night unfolds in a merry blur. First Fortnum-Hyde arm-wrestles Skinny Boy Floyd into grinning submission. Then he directs hulking Truman-Jones to get down on all fours so he might ride him like a horse. On a whim he dispatches Raine to fetch the crippled soldiers from the cottage. He explains that what he has in mind is a monster hunt.

"What's a monster hunt?" says Winifred.

"She asks what I mean. Then I shall tell you, my child. A monster hunt is like riding to hounds but with the monsters as foxes and the baked goods in pursuit."

Skinny Boy asks, "Where's the Elmsy-man at?"

Fortnum-Hyde throws him a distracted look. "Who cares? All I wish to discuss is this monster hunt."

Before long Raine returns with the crippled soldiers in tow. They look reduced and forlorn amid the room's finery. Fortnum-Hyde freshens himself with a further rail of white powder and explains that they are all about to play a game and that he requires three volunteers to brave the chill and

320

run into the grounds. The rest of the group will count to one hundred and then chase them down.

"It's a monster hunt," says York Conway. "We have all been getting very excited about it."

But it seems his enthusiasm is not shared by the cripples. From his wheelchair, Toto laughingly points out that running might be difficult. He very much fears that those days are behind him.

The Tin Woodman raises his hooks and addresses the girls. "Oh Lucy and Fred," he says, "I thought you were our friends."

Finally it is the Scarecrow's turn. He says, "If it's all the same to you, I think we'll sit this game out."

"Nonsense," rejoins Fortnum-Hyde with a scowl.

Winifred says, "It's going to be ever so much fun. It will be like when we all played hide-and-seek in the woods."

York Conway cocks his head. "I should remind you that the only reason you're here is due to his lordship's largesse. If he decides he wants to play a game, you ought to count yourselves lucky that he has seen fit to include you. It certainly isn't your place to whine and complain."

Truman-Jones claps his immense hands. He cries, "Monster hunt. Monster hunt."

Out in the hall, they line up for the game. Fortnum-Hyde beats the Long Boys' drum kit to keep count, setting out at a leisurely pace and then quickening the tempo so that the final fifty beats roll out in a thunder.

Gallant Toto has pulled himself from his chair to proceed on his hips with his gondolier's waddle. He moves as fast as he is able but the stone steps to the loggia prove to be his undoing. The dwarf has to tackle them one riser at a time and is barely at the bottom before the count is complete.

Fortnum-Hyde and Conway overtake him at the gate to the garden. They kick away his supporting arm and jubilantly roll him along the ground. The hunters are intoxicated, on the outer edge of control, and the capture of the dwarf sparks loud celebrations.

"Monster hunt! Monster hunt!" By now even Lucy is joining in with the chant.

"Don't hurt him!" shouts Julius Boswell. "He has no legs, for fuck's sake."

Fortnum-Hyde leaves off his kicking to seize the dwarf by the collar. "Toto, that was pathetic. Make some effort at least."

"Oh Toto," cries Lucy. "I hope you're not hurt."

"Monster hunt!" roars Truman-Jones and jostles her so forcibly she almost loses her footing.

"I'm fine. Never better." But it is obvious the adventure has made Toto dizzy. When his collar is released, he tumbles onto his back.

"Ridiculous," Fortnum-Hyde tells the group. "I'm sure we agree it was a dismal show from the dwarf."

Attention now turns to the remaining two targets. The hunters fan out through the gardens, trailing lunar shadows across the plaster gods. Running at the rear, Lucy spies York Conway and Fred take the stone steps at the side and quickens her pace, meaning to catch them both up.

Fred is shouting, "Monsters, watch out! We are coming to get you!"

They dash up the steps out onto the lawns. Up ahead, in the gloom, sits the sagging summer marquee; nobody has seen fit to dismantle the thing. Lucy calls out to the others but they are some distance ahead and she suspects they can't hear. She hesitates for an instant and then alters her course.

The marquee, like the house, has fallen on hard times. It feels very different from the last time she visited. The autumn wind has unpicked several guy ropes. Its tropical chintz is plastered with dead leaves. The girl pulls back the fold and inhales the cold scent of mildew. The interior is so dark that she collides with the table.

"Monster hunt!" she shouts. She more senses than sees the figure standing inside.

"Well done," says the Scarecrow. "How brave and resourceful you are."

Something in his tone dampens her excitement. She says, "Don't be in a grump. It's only a bit of fun."

"The careless fun of the idle rich. But congratulations all the same. You've caught your monster."

"I thought you liked fun. Isn't that how this all started? You wanting some fun?"

The Scarecrow snorts. "You can walk me back now. I'll tell them how you caught me."

Only the Tin Man is at large, although he does not remain so for long. The hunters run him down at the front of the house. When he turns to surrender he is instantly knocked over. George Washington expresses a desire to see whether he does have a nose and so Fortnum-Hyde decrees that his mask be removed. But the Tin Man is reluctant and scrambles onto his front. "Mercy, like an eel," exclaims Sweetpea Long and now they are all clutching at the Tin Man, pulling him this way and that. Truman-Jones plants his feet on the flagstones and, following shouted orders from Fortnum-Hyde, is able to lower his square buttocks upon the cripple's chest so as to better hold him in place.

"Mercy me, like an eel," says Sweetpea again.

The laughter is infectious; the game has reached its crescendo. Skinny Boy is able to remove one of the hooks while Conway takes the other and together they use them to prod and hit the Tin Man – and sometimes Truman-Jones for good measure, not entirely by accident. And now there is blood on the hooks and on the flagstones at their knees and on the collars of their coats and spotting their faces as well. The Tin Man bucks and wriggles so violently that it is close to convulsions. The hunters press in, Truman-Jones shouts "Hurrah!" and the monster hunt winds up in a state of joyous disarray.

Lucy and the Scarecrow pick their way across the darkened lawn – the girl out in front and the airman trailing. Neither says a word; they are no longer friends. They said all they needed to say on their night in the copse. Lucy has decided that if she never speaks to him again that would probably be for the best. Her life has moved on and it has left him behind. All she wants is to shake him loose and get indoors, in the warm.

The draw up to the house, the huntress and her trophy, and she realises with elation that a welcoming party awaits her. It is out on the lawn beside the abandoned west wing and it hoots and applauds when it sees what she has brought. Winifred is sat astride Truman-Jones's shoulders. "Monster hunt! Monster hunt!" Skinny Boy is shouting.

And there at the centre is the Tin Woodman himself, returned to full strength, merrily conducting the cheers. When he steps forward to greet her, he moves with an easy grace – his copper face smiling, his greatcoat billowing. He says, "Rub-a-dub-dub. Little Lucy, our hero". Then, when he is almost at her side, his right hook detaches and drops to the earth with a thump and at the cuff of his sleeve she sees his unblemished brown hand.

"Oh Tinny," she says. The shock is terrific. But at her back, very loudly, the Scarecrow shouts an oath.

"Tinny?" she says.

In a rich, full voice, he says, "My child, behold a miracle. A spot of rough and tumble has worked a wonder on me."

The Tin Man takes a further step up and this time his spectacles unfasten and his copper mask comes loose – and behind it is the grinning, scowling face of Rupert Fortnum-Hyde. He says, "Lulu, have courage. It is only I."

Winifred is beside herself. "You should see yourself, Lu. I thought you were going to have a heart attack then."

The Scarecrow says, "You fucking idiots. What have you done with him?"

He has been left on the flagstones beside the front steps. They skirt the side of the house to collect him. Sweetpea says, "The man's fine, don't take on. He's simply catching his breath."

Fred shouts, "Get up, Tinny. You can sleep it off later."

He lies splayed and still, like a cat's offering to its owner. His out-flung arms end below the elbows which has the effect of making him appear to be a much smaller man – as though this figure is not quite the Tin Woodman either. Lucy has always recognised her friend by his hooks, by his voice and by his handsome copper face. Try as she might, she cannot reconcile the Tin Woodman she knows with this mangled thing on the ground.

"Mercy," says Sweetpea. "Not so fine after all."

They gather at a distance. The celebrations peter out. Finally Fortnum-Hyde says, "Truman, you brute, you crushed our monster to death."

He is about to add something further when the Scarecrow

325

lunges forward. The viscount discerns his intent and neatly blocks the blow. He then goes into a shuffling boxer's dance, circling the Scarecrow, who appears to be half out of his mind. Fortnum-Hyde ducks and bobs and reaches out to cuff the man smartly on the side of his head. He has the measure of the Scarecrow; his long reach is sufficient to keep his attacker at bay. He moves with ease and precision and it seems over-confidence is his only foe because when Fortnum-Hyde risks a sideways glance to see how his display is being received by the ranks, he lowers his guard for an instant – and this allows the Scarecrow just enough time to strike him hard on his left cheek.

Fortnum-Hyde falls straight-backed, like a tree. The impact of his landing runs through Lucy's heels. Were it not for George Washington's immediate intervention, she believes that the Scarecrow would have gone on to close with Truman-Jones next.

Now a melee erupts beside the steps to the house. The Scarecrow, outnumbered, joins Fortnum-Hyde on the flag-stones. When Lucy rushes to protect him, a forearm slams her nose.

"Oh jolly well done!" the playwright is screaming. "Why stop at one? Why not kill them all?"

When it is judged the Scarecrow presents no further danger, his assailants leave off their kicking and cluster about the young master. The Scarecrow's blow has caught him square; Fortnum-Hyde is out cold. His mouth is agape and his eyes show the whites. They haul him up the front steps and across the threshold, shouting for the servants to bring smelling salts and brandy. The door bangs shut at their backs and Lucy is alone in the darkness between the two fallen figures.

"Tinny," she cries. "Scarecrow."

Eventually the Scarecrow is able to get to his feet. He clutches his head and repositions his mask. "Is he dead?"

Lucy cannot reply; her breath hitches. And this, she supposes, is all the answer he needs.

The Scarecrow nods grimly. Then, a little unsteadily, he begins climbing the stone steps. When she shouts for him to wait, he gives no sign that he's heard.

Lucy gathers her senses and moves to catch him up. But the entrance hall is empty and the oaken doors closed. The grandfather clock whirs and clicks. She finds the telephone on the table and cups the earpiece to her head.

"Operator" she says, "I need to speak with the police."

Her words fly off down the wire and then boomerang back. "Operator," says the earpiece, "I need to speak with the police."

She has always arrived via the rear of the house. The entrance hall is alien territory; she does not know how it connects to the other rooms. Selecting a door at random she pulls it back and uncovers Mrs Cleaver, the housekeeper. In that instant it occurs that whichever door she had chosen would have had Mrs Cleaver standing behind it.

She stands long and straight, in charcoal smock and white collar. Her severe slot-mouthed face is softened only slightly by the dandelion fluff of her hair.

When Lucy explains that the telephone isn't working, Mrs Cleaver impassively looks her up and down.

She says, "What do you require the telephone for?"

"Mrs Cleaver, please listen, the Tin Man is dead. They left him lying outside. We have to call the police right away."

The housekeeper blinks. "Who says that we must?" And then, when Lucy does not immediately reply, she says, "I take

327

my orders from the masters and the mistress. What gives you the impression that I am here to serve you?"

The girl wheels back on her heels, tries another door and discovers herself in the Regency Room with its high vaulted ceiling. She flies past the Picasso, aiming for the stairs, intending to seek out Clarissa, who will know what to do. And here at last luck runs in her favour. The lady of Grantwood has just that moment come down.

Clarissa gathers Lucy without ceremony into her freckled arms. She says, "Oh Lucy, how awful. Did you see the whole thing?"

"They killed the Tin Man. He's lying outside."

"I know, Connie told me. It is utterly awful."

"We have to call the police. But the telephone doesn't work."

Clarissa has them both sit on the bottom step. It turns out that Lucy's nose has been bloodied from the struggle outside, when she was either hit or ran into somebody's forearm, and she now sees she has stained the lady's immaculate green dress. It is one further crime to add to all the rest and she attempts an embarrassed apology. But Clarissa is unconcerned, tells her not to be silly. "I mean, good God, Lulu. Isn't that the least of our worries?"

She rubs at her nose and finds further blood on her hand. The under-butler, Colvin, crosses the room carrying a bottle of cognac. His eyes skip sideways, registering the distraught pair on the step, but he proceeds on his errand without missing a beat.

"They killed him," she sobs. "Why?"

Lowering her voice, Clarissa says, "The trouble with Rupert is that he never grew up. He's like a spoilt little boy pulling the wings off flies. Everyone in this house is a plaything to him." Again she reaches across to pull Lucy against her. "For the moment, however, I am most concerned about you. I promised I'd protect you and then this horrid thing happens. No child should witness what you've seen tonight."

"If the telephone doesn't work, we can take a car to the village."

Clarissa hesitates. "Let's not get ahead of ourselves, Lu. I confess that at present I'm most worried about you."

They embrace on the steps and the wind bangs the shutters. Lucy weeps and gulps and then weeps some more. And for one brief, jumbled moment it seems that the night may not quite be lost after all, because a door is pulled open to allow the mountainous hulk of Truman Truman-Jones to lumber out under the wash of electric light. Spotting Clarissa on the step, his ruddy face cracks into a grin. It is apparent that the man has come with good news.

"Disaster averted. He's not dead, he's alive."

Lucy is up on her feet in a trice. "Tinny?" she cries. She can hardly believe it is true.

"King Roo," confirms Truman-Jones. "He is conscious at last."

"But Tinny?" she persists. "What about the Tin Man."

When Truman-Jones's gaze alights on the girl, his euphoric grin buckles under the strain. It is as if he has been presented with a complicated maths problem. The task proves beyond him and he turns to Clarissa for help.

She says, "You dopey, murdering bastard, Tru."

"King Roo just woke up," he says. "Can't we all make an effort to look on the bright side for once?"

Beside the steps in the forecourt he meets a fabulous creature. Its face has no features and its arms have no hands. In the moonlight its flesh gleams like Venetian glass, while its midriff appears to have been stuffed with a compound of clotted blood and dead leaves which has now leaked out across the flagstones. Elms decides that the creature is either sleeping or dead, although he knows that these two states are often separated by nothing more than the width of a cigarette paper. That's how it was out at Cape Helles. That's how it is all over, no doubt.

He crouches over the thing and regards it with tenderness. "Bloody hell, poor old chap, you should be buried in the sand."

The creature makes no movement; it has nothing to say. Elms squats at its side for a minute, drawing deep breaths and marshalling his strength; he knows exactly what he needs to do. So he leans in, drags the body to his breast and braces his bare legs. Then he carries the Tin Man on a halting ascent to the house.

28

I T IS THE measure of a man how he responds under
pressure, and Rupert Fortnum-Hyde is renowned for
his leadership skills. Stretched full-length on the couch, he
replenishes himself with a goblet of cognac and gathers his
supporters about him by the simply trick of pretending to
ignore them. The playwright's hysterical complaints are an
idle distraction, and he is blithely unmoved by the rage of
his sister. Finally, with an exaggerated yawn, he tells his good
friend York Conway to keep an eye on the Scarecrow. If the
cripple stirs up further bother he will require restraining. He
has the sense that everyone in the room has become a degree
too excited. They should look to someone like Raine and
follow his example. "Please promise me, Raine, that you are
not excited as well."

"Certainly not, sir."

"Look at that," he says blandly. "My fucking butler puts
you all to shame."

He risks a glance about the room, performing a quick
mental inventory and ranking its occupants in order of their
importance. At the top he places Conway, Truman-Jones, his
tiresome sister and her idiotic fiancée. At the bottom sit the
surviving cripples and the pair of pleasure dolls. Toto has
reached out and is gripping little Ferdinand's hand; the events
of the night have exhausted them both. He fancies he will have
no trouble with those two, or with tearful Lulu, who is too

sweet to make a scene. But the Scarecrow has a temper; that's why he must be watched.

Sweetpea Long fidgets at the door. The singer is not quite an equal and yet not quite a servant – and Fortnum-Hyde rather respects him for that. But Sweetpea sheepishly explains that the other Long Boys have fled. Washington and Skinny Boy rounded up the drummer and the trumpeter and told them what transpired. Anyway the upshot is that all four musicians have now cut and run; they did not even make time to collect their instruments. Sweetpea adds that the dead man had them spooked. They figured it was best to make themselves scarce before the authorities were called.

Fortnum-Hyde receives this news with an amused show of disgust. "What authorities?" he says. And then with more confidence: "I'm the authority."

"They are like little children," Conway says. "No doubt they'll become tired eventually, and turn back. They'll find it is quite a long walk through the dark to the village."

Sweetpea shrugs. "I have to say I'm tempted to follow on, too. The sad truth is that we have a dead body outside."

The viscount's head is still ringing but the cognac has helped. It would not do to show weakness; it would encourage further dissent in the ranks. So when Julius Boswell demands that the police be notified, he raises his voice to shout him down. Fortnum-Hyde points out that calling the police would only add to the confusion. So far as the authorities are concerned, the Tin Man does not exist. One might make the case that he was dead to begin with. In the morning they will have the groundsmen dig another hole. The Tin Man can go right next to his friend.

He turns to explain. "We had a fourth cripple who decided to do away with himself. A sad state of affairs, although perhaps it's to be expected. One way or another, these fellows never last very long."

When the Scarecrow jumps forward, Truman-Jones is prepared. He puts the man on the floor and twists his wrist behind him.

"Leave him alone!" Lucy shouts. "Don't keep hurting him!"

Fortnum-Hyde smiles. "Don't hurt him," he scoffs. "Please remember this is the same chap who attacked me for no good reason outside. Later, perhaps, we can arrange a rematch. And I assure you the result will be rather different next time."

On the floor, the Scarecrow writhes and thrashes. He resembles a rat that has caught its snout in a trap. Truman-Jones applies his knee to the small of the man's back.

"Beating up a one-armed man," Clarissa says with a sigh. "Is there no end to your heroism?" She motions for Raine to relight her cigarette.

Toto cries, "Scarecrow, calm down! This isn't doing us any good."

The viscount waves his hand. "What has happened is in the past. Let us now make an effort to look to the future."

There is so much more Fortnum-Hyde would like to explain to them here. He wants to say that when accidents happen, they happen for a reason. That sometimes it is necessary for old, broken items to be laid to rest and for weeds to be uprooted and for the blackboard to be cleaned. It is his view that this onerous task falls to the young and the brave. Men who aren't afraid of getting their hands dirty and who know that true progress is impossible when one is saddled with outmoded old luggage. He would like to tell them all this and more besides, but his cheek is still smarting and his head hasn't cleared and he is therefore forced to be brief and trust them to fill in the blanks. "So it's all good," he says. "The future."

The butler dips to attend to Clarissa's cigarette. Truman-Jones adjusts his knee upon the Scarecrow's back. Julius Boswell clears his throat to present a further objection. And it is at this point that the door behind them rips open, hard enough to smack the wall and make Sweetpea Long start. He says, "Jeepers, what's this?"

Into the room staggers Arthur Elms, an agent of chaos, the last of his kind. His bare legs buckle and his head is thrown back and he strains under the weight of a burden it takes the onlookers a moment to recognise. He comes reeling forward, aiming for the vacant armchair by the fire only for the cargo to slip from his grasp in the final shuffling steps. It lands on its side and turns its face to the room. The sight jumps through the guests like an electrical current.

Clarissa's cigarette drops into her lap. "No," she begins. "This is not right." But her words are leapfrogged and laid low by Winifred's scream and Toto's cry and by the side table that is toppled when Raine mislays his composure and scuttles for cover.

In the room, by the fire, Elms toils for breath. He lists and weaves drunkenly. His trousers are missing and he has cobwebs in his hair. He turns in full circles as if his bearings are shot.

"No," Clarissa says. "For God's sake, get it out."

But Fortnum-Hyde has swung his long legs off the couch. Alone of the group, he is choked by amusement; it does not even matter that he has been interrupted. "Elmsy," he splutters.

334

"Oh Elmsy, you chump." His gaze leaps from the corpse by the fire to its knock-kneed delivery boy and he brays happy laughter. He gasps, "Mr Elms, you have surpassed yourself. We have no further need of your usual party trick. You shall never be able to top an entrance like this."

The man completes his final circle and finds himself pointing at the couch. He is still out of breath but manages to join in with the laughter. "Look," he calls to Fortnum-Hyde. "I can still do it, you know. It's my gift to the house."

He does not rub his fingers against his thumb. He snaps them with a crack and it's as though the magic he thought was spent had merely been trapped like intestinal gas - bunched up and knotted all the way to his torso. Now it unlocks and tears out like a jack-in-the-box and the flames are not blue but briefly, brilliantly white. They fry the hair on his wrist and catch the sleeve of his robe, and the shock sends him backwards so that he lands on a couch. He looks up dumbly, registering the stricken faces of the guests in the room and opens his mouth to reassure them that he is not too badly hurt, except that his robe has strayed onto the couch's cushions and he's abruptly aware that these too are aflame.

As though from a great distance, he hears Sweetpea say, "Jeepers."

The flames are not natural. They burn too fiercely, too fast. They devour his robe and crawl into the upholstery which has been primed, as though in readiness, by a month's worth of spilled cognac. The entire couch seems to draw a breath and then cough - after which it becomes a bonfire. When the heat is too much, Elms staggers back to his feet. He turns another full circle and moves to extinguish himself against the velvet hangings. Too late, the Scarecrow shouts for him to stop.

335

"The tanks of foam," Clarissa cries. "There are two of them by the kitchen door."

Raine and Truman-Jones run to fetch them. But the tanks are no longer beside the kitchen door. Both had been emptied during that final frantic summer party and the canisters later deposited in dustbins. And so Elms loses himself forever amid the soft velvet folds, and scraps of burning matter drift out through the room.

Hauling himself upright, Fortnum-Hyde sees flames run up the drapes and fan out across the corniced ceiling. He decides his show of unruffled disinterest has now run its course and that it is better to swiftly remove himself from harm's way. He knocks Lucy aside in his dash from the room.

If the drawing room door had been shut, the fire might have been contained. But the door is left open and the corridor fills with smoke. The carpets catch light and the wood panelling blisters. Grey figures jostle and grunt as they press towards safety. Outside the Regency Room, Fortnum-Hyde runs full-bore into Raine.

"His Lordship, sir! His Lordship upstairs!"

"Then for God's sake go and get him. Or what's the fucking point of you?" Ahead, he spies several servants breaking for the front exit and it is enraging to think that they are at the vanguard and he's bringing up the rear.

On departing the drawing room, Clarissa angles towards the back door that leads out to the gardens. Julius Boswell initially believes that he is following her lead but these closed quarters have become thick with fumes and it is possible he has taken a corner when he should have continued straight on. Somewhere far behind he can hear Sweetpea exclaiming

"Hellfire". His throat is grating. His eyes are streaming. He wanders blind through the smoke, holding his hands out before him.

What began by the drawing room hearth has spread out to explore the adjoining chambers. Aware of the heat that is already banking against the library door, the Scarecrow takes up a chair and applies it to the widow. He orders the girl to climb up and out.

She clambers onto the sill and feels a shard of glass lance her knee. "Where's Fred?" she says. "Where are Toto and Fred?"

"I'm going back to look. But you need to get out."

She stares at him, ashen. "Don't look for too long." But he has already drawn back. Lucy drops to the verge and drags in great gusts of night air. The air makes her cough and there is fresh blood on her shin and one shoulder is aching from where Fortnum-Hyde knocked her down. But she remains on the grass, gazing up at the glow of the window, waiting to see who will crawl out of it next.

The fire is torrential. It rages unchecked and the whole house is in danger. Truman-Jones is lost amid the holocaust. He reaches for a door but the handle is molten so that it solders itself to the pad of his hand. The pain is terrific but there is no detaching himself. With dogged persistence, he keeps pulling the door open and closed in an effort to be free and this turns the door into a bellows, fanning the flames that lick about its edges. Each time it swings open it fans a fresh blast against him and now Truman-Jones is alight as well. He sinks to his knees and places his chin on his chest. But he is still welded to the handle. He shoves the door open and then pulls it shut.

Clarissa is safe, she has reached the loggia. She smoothes down her green dress, drags a chair to the table and sits for a spell until her nerves have resettled. From this vantage she can observe the exodus of the remaining survivors through the rear door of the house. Out comes the under-butler, Colvin, at the head of a caterpillar of housemaids. Sweetpea Long has emerged unscathed, while Mrs Cleaver hastens by her chair as though embarked on some important errand. Her features are set in a preoccupied frown. Her heavy-browed gaze is fixed on some unspecified point up ahead. Clarissa will later be told that Mrs Cleaver has died. The smoke and the exertion have put too great a strain on her heart. At the moment she hurries past the small table, the housekeeper is leaving the garden in search of a secluded spot to lie down. A lifetime of service has prepared her for this. She would baulk at the indignity of expiring in public, where her skirt might ride up and her mistress might see her.

Presently Clarissa feels that she can risk a cigarette. She summons one of the footmen, her eyes still scanning the garden. Several familiar faces remain conspicuous by their absence. "I don't see Jules anywhere," she complains.

York Conway leaves off his coughing to afford her a theatrical shrug.

"Oh dear," sighs Clarissa. "Poor old Grantwood House."

It is 1882. It is the Peloponnese. Whitewashed homes stand against the scarp and the mountain goats congregate by the wall. The cobbled lane slaloms through the village before the land drops away to show him the blue sky. The church bells begin clanging in discordant glee, as though they have somehow been party to this heavenly unveiling. The vista is so perfect that he is coaxed out of the shade and onto the terrace to peer out at Delphi. Lord Hertford is buried so deep in his dream that he responds joyfully when light streams into the room and the great golden figure closes to claim him. "Raine," he exclaims. "You put me in mind of the sun god Apollo."

The butler arrives at the foot of the bed and proceeds to mount the coverlet on all fours. His hair and collar are aflame; his forehead cracks and drips fluid. Raine crawls up the bed and embraces Lord Hertford through the blankets while the fire pours in to kiss and suck at his heels. It consumes the goose-feather mattress and the canopy overhead. It makes no distinction between the servant and his master. It takes ahold of each man and sends them both off together.

Lucy stays on the verge for ten minutes or more. She stares up at the window and shouts, "Scarecrow! Toto! Fred!" She stands there until the window turns bright and the panes separate from the frame and the heat becomes such that she is forced to back-pedal. And once she starts to retreat she is powerless to stop and now she has turned on her heels and is running on the lawn. The noise of destruction is deafening: it sounds like woodland being flattened. Looking up, she sees that the upper floors are alight, which means that it's all over and that nothing can be saved. The inferno is determined to eat Grantwood House whole.

Even out here, the smoke is intense and she staggers in and out of its drift. She is running on soft grass and then she is running on gravel, which means she must have reached the side drive that leads around to the yard. She presses on, thinking to return to the cottage, but then out of the mist gleams a pair of round headlamps and an instant later Coach's old Maudslay appears on the track. The lorry has the gait of a wounded animal. It looks as though it is dying; it can barely manage the slope.

She scampers to one side and lets the lorry draw level. She cries out to Coach but it's the Scarecrow at the wheel. "Lucy," he says and is immediately overcome by a fit of choking.

She throws a glance at the back. "Where are Toto and Fred?"

The Scarecrow pulls open the door and staggers onto the drive. She thinks he is about to fall down and reaches out to steady him. He has spent too long in the house and inhaled too much smoke. And over his shoulder she sees that the night has turned brighter. The fire has found its way into the abandoned west wing.

When the coughing subsides he is able to speak. He gasps, "I hope she got out. Think she did. Don't know about him. Couldn't find either."

She shakes her head, bites down on her lip.

"We need to go. But I can't drive the lorry. Can't work the gears, hold the wheel. Not at the same time. My arm," he says. "Help me. Get us away."

She wants to tell him no chance. She wants to ask him, "Go where?" She wants to point out that she can't drive and only took the wheel a few times on those evenings in the woods. Instead she just nods. In that moment – with the ugly smoke swirling and the horrible house all ablaze – the Scarecrow's request strikes her as the most sensible thing that has been uttered in months. Get out, get out, the entire world is collapsing. Afterwards they can look back and gauge the extent of the damage.

He removes himself to the passenger side. She draws in

acrid air and throws the truck into gear and they lurch forward in spastic fits and starts, the masked one-armed man and his orphaned teenage chauffeur. Once on the main drive, she wrestles the stick and allows the vehicle to go faster. They plough past smoky figures who have fled through the main door and some of these step up, attempting to flag the truck down. She thinks that one of these figures is Rupert Fortnum-Hyde but he is there and gone in a flash; the Maudslay is gathering speed.

"He got out all right then. Fortnum-Hyde."

The Scarecrow snorts and coughs. "Of course he got out. He was practically the first out the door."

Beyond the truck's tailgate, Grantwood House is aflame. Its windows have smelted. Smoke rises from its roof. Orange cinders blow out across the lawn and one of these has set light to a sheep. The animal stands amid its neighbours, its fleece a guttering torch, until its legs buckle and it rolls onto its side. The westerly cedar tree appears to have gone up as well. The other will follow; how can it resist? By this point the blaze is so bright that it can be seen from the village. The schoolmaster, up late, has alerted the fire station at Hertford. Farmhands are busy filling buckets from the spigot. Yet these rescuers will arrive a full half-hour too late. When the timbers combust, the upper stories collapse. Chimney breasts concertina; the roof pours into the cellar. And this is how one of the great seats of England passes into dust. In years to come the guests who once stayed there will remember it as a golden place and lament that nowhere else they've visited has ever quite measured up. And while this was not quite the legacy Lord Hertford intended, he may not have been altogether displeased.

Out of the inferno bounces Coach's old Maudslay; the fire at its back, the cold ground up ahead. Lucy intends to stop when she reaches the Palladian lodge but the engine is roaring and the thought of wresting it to a halt is somehow more unnerving than allowing the reins to go slack. So they run past the lodge and turn onto the macadam where the hedgerows are as high as one man standing on the shoulders of another. And yet even this far afield they have not quite propelled themselves clear of Grantwood House's orbit, because a few hundred yards out they pass the Long Boys. As the truck bears down, the musicians turn and gawp in astonishment. They have been walking so long in this dark, empty land that they have begun to doubt they would ever see another living soul.

She sees George Washington stick out a hand. "Lulu! It's Lulu!"

"Don't stop," the Scarecrow tells her.

"Should I?"

"No," he says, and with some relief she reapplies her foot to the pedal and they mingle for a moment with the men on the road – two on one side, two on the other – before the towering hedgerows carry them round, up and out. The ground is ascending. The antique engine takes on a faint note of strain.

Near the crest of the hill the bushes drop back and the land opens out. They have emerged from the valley. She can feel the wind slap the truck and see thin clouds in motion across the expanse of night sky. In a corner of the windscreen, the horizon glows a dull, damp orange. The sight makes her heart jump; she thinks it's the first light of dawn.

"No," says the Scarecrow. "That's still Grantwood House."

But eventually even this sullen smudge is lost beneath the horizon and they ride on through the darkness, past primitive

342

tithe cottages and waterlogged fallow fields. The road up here is mercifully straight and they meet no oncoming vehicles. Lucy discovers that, so long as she keeps the wheel aligned and maintains a steady pressure with her toes, the act of driving is really no more upsetting than anything else. She supposes the concentration it requires counts as a blessing as well. It helps set her mind apart from the events of the night.

The Scarecrow leans forward, peering at the signs for unfamiliar towns. He coughs for a spell and then composes himself.

"When we reach a main road there should be directions to London. This little lane can't go on forever."

She shakes her head. "If we see directions to London I'm turning the other way."

"Lucy," he says. "It's time you were home."

"What home? I don't have a home." The realisation hits her like a splash of cold water. She accepts that it was the Maudslay that first took her away from the Griffin and therefore it's only right and proper that it should one day take her back. But she has travelled too far and is a different person these days. She is not about to steer Coach's truck through the morning traffic on Ermine Street. She recoils at the thought of walking into the pub in Clarissa's party dress, with dried blood on her shins and smoke in her hair, to tell them she's sorry she's been gone and then pick up where she left off. In a day or two she might feel differently. For now she is determined to point the truck away from the city and headlong into England. She plans to bear down on the pedal until the fuel tank runs dry.

The Scarecrow coughs and clears his throat, clearly in the grip of some dilemma of his own. Presently he says, "I have a

343

home. Or rather I did have a home."

"Ha," she says. "You told me you didn't."

He nods. "It might still be there, but it's more than a hundred miles away. It's right across country, far out to the west." He says, "Lucy, a favour. Can you drive me back home?"

Hertford market officially opens at eight, but Harry Sullivan has learned that if he is not there by seven, Pete Lang will have sloped in and set up at his stall. Lang always insists that he assumed it was spare, which is pure hogwash and adds insult to injury. If a man wants to steal another man's stall, he should at least be upfront about it. He ought to brazen it out and say, "I like this stall better and now I got first dibs." Don't make out it's the other fellow's fault for showing up at the correct hour. Don't make him say sorry for his lateness when he wasn't late at all.

Any road, he's been through this palaver before and accepts that the best course of action is to be there by seven, before some of the traders have even dragged themselves out of bed, and that way he can sit on his fold-out chair and give Pete Lang a wave when he scurries in. Anyone seeing that wave would put it down as a jovial salute; a merry greeting from one mate to another. Only Pete Lang knows what it really means. It means, "Hello, you old thief, look who's late today." It says, "Here I am on my stall. Now put that in your pipe and smoke it, you bastard."

The upshot is that he is out of the house before the birds have begun chirping, his fruit and veg stacked in the back of his van. The cabbages, he judges, are turning soft at the crowns; it's been a rough year for cabbage, but these things can't be helped. If a customer wants cabbage, his are no worse than the rest.

Halfway to market he passes a girl on the road. She is sat on the wall, a picture frame of all things propped against her bare knees. When the girl spots the van, she waves for it to stop. Sullivan is not in the habit of giving lifts, but a chap would need a hard heart to ignore a child in distress. There is something amiss with a world that sends a little girl out on her tod in the middle of nowhere before the sun has come up, where she might get knocked over or catch her death of cold.

He asks where she needs dropping and she asks where he's going. When he tells her Hertford, she replies that that'll do just as well. He has the feeling that she's not from these parts. But instead of increasing his concern for her safety, the notion makes him uneasy. All at once he's not convinced that he likes the mysterious creature he has let into his cab. Her dress is torn and her face is smudged and she stinks of smoke; it comes off her in waves. She brings a wildness with her, some tremor of mischief that strikes him as distasteful. It's a wicked world that sends children out alone in the night. But sometimes it is the children that are wicked and this is why they're abroad.

Their breath fogs. The picture frame grinds distractingly against his knee as he drives. She asks, "Is Hartwood full of rich people then?"

"Hertford," he corrects. "Have you been living in a box all your life?"

"Is it full of rich people?"

"There's rich and there's poor. Same as any town, innit?"

Brightly, the girl goes on to inform him that she is out on a mission. She wants to find some rich people who might buy a painting. She says it's an extremely nice painting and she would rather not have to sell it. But her poor mother is sick and the money-lender needs paying. She gnaws her lip and says, "Falconio."

"What's Falconio?"

"The money-lender. No, Falconio. Please, Falconio." And for some unaccountable reason this sends her off into cackles.

Yes, Harry Sullivan thinks, the girl is not right. Where on earth has she sprung from – this raggedy sprite with the sailor's laugh and the threadbare tale about an invalid mum? He would like to wind down the window and disperse the smell, but the nights have turned cold and the fields frosted over. Most of all he would like to push open the door and invite the girl to hop down.

"How old are you anyway?"

"Thirty-two," she says promptly. "How old are you?"

"Now then, miss. I don't hold with cheek."

They continue in silence until they reach the outskirts of town. Street lights sweep the cab but when the girl angles the frame to show him the painting, he can't make out head nor tail of the thing. He flicks a harried glance and sees a chaotic pattern on the oblong canvas. It is enough to tell him that the girl and her painting appear to be well matched. Each is as off-puttingly bestial as the other.

"Very good, I'm sure. And did you paint it yourself?"

"Course I didn't paint it. It's a very famous picture. It's worth at least fifty pounds."

"Right you are, miss."

"It's painted by a man called Pick-Arsehole."

He says, "Now what did I say? I don't hold with cheek and I draw the line at blue language."

"Honestly, no joke, that's his name. Pick-Arsehole."

"Don't keep saying it," Sullivan splutters.

"Pick-Arsehole," she says – and this time he can't help but giggle too. The whole thing is too ridiculous. He could never have predicted his morning would end up like this.

He crosses the Lea; he can see the malting house now. He explains that he is going to market and he can drop her off there. If she wants to hang about for a bit, then that's her look out. Who knows? She might even offload her picture on some short-sighted fool with more money than sense. Good luck to the girl. She can bag herself a free stall.

He says, "Tell you what, I know just the one. You can set yourself up at Peter Lang's stall." And she joins in with his merriment and lets fly with her loud, filthy cackle. She cries, "Oh, oh, Falconio!" and the van turns onto the cobblestone square and dips behind the rows of covered stands and it carries Winifred out of this story and off into another. The October morning is cold. She will find a way to keep warm.

THE SEA

29

T HEY RIDE INTO the west and it takes them all day. For the first leg of the journey they stick to the back roads, crawling behind farm carts and sliding in and out of quiet hamlets where the residents glance grudgingly up from their business. The going is hard; they keep losing their way. Faded, mud-spattered signs only point the direction to the next village and then the one beyond that, because nobody who uses these roads appears to travel more than five miles at a time. This makes Lucy feel as though they are crossing invisible borders, through a system of small, self-contained kingdoms that may very well extend all the way to the sea.

In fleeing the house she's become a fugitive. She mourns her lost earnings, left in the drawer at her bedroom in the cottage. Without those she has nothing. By rights her party tunic still belongs to Clarissa, while its kangaroo pouch contains the amulet that Elms killed his best friend to obtain. To make matters worse, she is sat behind the wheel of a stolen truck, fleeing the scene of a crime with a man who has been listed as dead. She can barely conceive of how many laws she is breaking. Past a certain number, she supposes it ceases to matter.

The windscreen vibrates; the cab is open at the sides. The low winter sun sends bars of shadow across the truck. When the Scarecrow notices the girl shivering, he removes his topcoat so that she can wear it. He searches the glove compartment and finds a briar pipe, a packet of tobacco and a folded envelope of petty cash. And here at last the fates are smiling on them. Either Coach was planning a major purchase or the groundsman liked to have emergency funds with him. The envelope contains banknotes and coins totalling just shy of six pounds. The Scarecrow says that this is more than enough. It will take them where they are going and allow them to travel in style.

Stolen money, she thinks. Stolen lorry. If they encounter a policeman, he will put them in irons.

She says, "I almost wish we were going to the sea. I've only been once before and I loved it."

"I once read that all human life began at the sea," the Scarecrow says. "When our ancestors crawled out of the sea, they carried a portion of it with them, because it turns out our bodies are largely made up of sea water. What are tears if not drops of sea water?"

"Is that where we're going, then?"

"No. We're going to the west."

He has a book in the pocket of his coat because he never likes to go anywhere without one. This is one she has heard of: *Adventures of Huckleberry Finn*. He reads aloud to her for about half-an-hour, after which the jolting motion of the truck becomes too much for his eyes and he has to give up.

"Not to worry," she says, although she had been enjoying the story.

Shortly before noon they alight on a wide thoroughfare where the Maudslay can run. The town of Reading is somewhere to the east and the city of Oxford far away to the north, but both might just as easily not exist, so completely are they concealed by these yellow wooded hills. The road is empty of traffic, but it has a history of violence. At intervals they pass the remains of foxes, squirrels and badgers. The animals have been flattened so completely that they stick to the surface like a series of cave paintings.

In the sodden forecourt of a lonely petrol station, a young man in shirtsleeves and high-waisted trousers saunters from his hut to top up the tank. He says, "I got some fresh eggs, if you're in the market."

The Scarecrow climbs from the cab to stretch his legs. He says, "I'll bet we're your first customers of the day."

"Then I win and you lose. I had a fellow drop by not an hour ago."

The Scarecrow smiles. "What desolate country this is."

"It's filling up," the young man replies, and for a moment Lucy assumes he is referring to the tank. "Every week, every day, a few more motors on the road. This time next year we'll probably have our first traffic queue."

"I'll take your word for it."

The man removes the pump and re-fastens the cap. "Sir, excuse me for asking, but was you hurt in the war?"

"I was," he says. "I was shot down in a plane."

The young man nods. "Sorry to hear it. I would shake your hand, sir, except mine's so mucky."

"That's all right," says the Scarecrow. "Consider us shook."

When the trees fall away, the sky is enormous. The road forks on open ground and they run past the edge of Stonehenge, which is smaller and more compact than Lucy had imagined, all but dwarfed by the plain and the clouds and the noise of the truck. After men crawled out of the sea they learned to worship the sun. The Scarecrow explains that these stones were raised by druids, thousands of years ago, but that no one knows exactly how they did it, or what purpose they served. He jokes that one day people might look at St Paul's cathedral and wonder why that was built too.

She says, "Maybe he was a druid. Mr Elms."

The Scarecrow, though, is unconvinced. He says Arthur Elms did not know what he was and that this was the problem, it might be why he was doomed. "The man had a gift but he could not name it or control it. If he'd been stronger – I mean mentally stronger – he might have managed better."

"Magic," says Lucy and then, taking one hand from the wheel, she retrieves the contaminated amulet from her kangaroo pouch. She shows it to the Scarecrow, explains how she came by it. More than anything, she wants to throw it overboard, onto the grass verge or into the road, except that he tells her not to be hasty. She might be able to sell it; the cash could come in handy. Sometimes, very rarely, good things come out of bad things.

Lucy shakes her head. "Is that even true?"

"Probably not." He flashes a grin. "It's just a thing people say."

The land out here is flat, given over to farms. At intervals, however, they pass an isolated home, set hard against the road. She devises a game where she marks each house with a score out of ten, mentally deciding which one she would live in. Most of the houses are upright, red-brick affairs; they stick out like sore thumbs. But she eventually sees one that she likes – a cottage half-hidden by greenery, wrapped in the landscape. Its walls have been rounded as if by a butter knife. A single chimney pot sits dead-centre on the roof. It is a dwelling that would rather not be spotted from the road and she decides it's all the more inviting for that. Lucy points it out to the

Scarecrow in the few seconds before the hedges crowd in and conceal it for good.

He cranes his neck. "You once said you wanted to live in a marquee on the beach."

"Ha," she says. "I've changed my mind."

After the Scarecrow saved Lucy and made her leap from the window, he had turned back into the din and the blaze of Grantwood's interior. He unbuttoned his shirt and clasped the cotton to his mouth. But the smoke meant that he could neither see nor breathe freely, while the heat was so fierce it stirred unquiet memories of his descent in the plane. Somewhere in the depths he heard Julius Boswell calling for Clarissa. He prodded the shoulder of a servant who had fallen, but the man was out cold; the fumes had stopped up his lungs.

He retraced his steps, forcing his way down the burning corridor that led to the drawing room. Halfway there, he had found Toto's wheelchair, lying on its side. He attempted to go further, searching for a body, but the gusts beat him back and his shoe leather wilted. So he stood alone in the smoke, whipped by the backdraught, the last of the four.

The Scarecrow recounts all this to Lucy on their long drive to the west. He talks of the fire, and of other things, too. He tells her about Audrey and Michael, his infant son, and his job at the printworks and of the rotary press that everyone called the Dreadnought. He describes the plane crash that burned him and his stumbling walk to the church and the mermen in the lake and how he had wanted to join them, even though they were soldiers and not really mermen at all. And he says that in a sense that was just what he did, insofar as he has spent the past five years in limbo, all the while thinking he could never go home. He says that he sees things differently now; he feels a weight has been lifted. He has been selfish and proud, but this is all in the past and he is returning from abroad. The prospect excites him, although it is frightening too. He laughs at himself and says, "Perhaps it's true what they say. There is no place like home."

"Bram," Lucy says and this makes him laugh all the more.

"Your real name is Bram. That's what I should call you."

He says, "Good God. I haven't been called that in years."

They are in the woods of west Wiltshire when the Maudslay overheats. The Scarecrow flips up the bonnet and refills the engine from a jug and when he crosses back to the cabin he sees that Lucy is fighting back tears. His talk of home and family has pierced the girl's armour and shaken the last of the Grantwood enchantment. She misses her brother; she has not seen him for so long. She promised to visit and she swore she'd send money and she must now face the fact that she has broken her word. She has been sitting here thinking how stupid and greedy the Scarecrow has been when it turns out that she has behaved just as badly as him.

He says, "I don't know about that. Maybe we both lost our way. Don't be too hard on yourself. It can all be set right." He adds that when they reach a post office she can send Tom some money. Whatever's left over will pay for her train ticket home. He does not want her making the return drive on her own and besides, he suspects that the truck is on its last legs.

"Poor old Maudslay," the girl says. "We used to all sit back there in the summer. Me and Fred and Edith and John."

"I reckon they're probably in better shape than the truck. At least they survived, they got out alive. Even Fred survived, I think."

"Fred," says the girl and now the tears are too much. If

she keeps crying like this she will flood the foot well with salt water.

This journey has been endless. She has been driving forever and her left leg has stiffened and swollen where she stabbed it on the glass. They squandered so many hours on the winding holloways beyond Grantwood House that it is mid-afternoon when they arrive at the town. Here she leaves the Scarecrow for a time to post a pound note to Tom at the Griffin. She prints the address on Coach's dirty envelope and on the reverse flap she writes, "From Lucy xxx". No doubt the money will be intercepted before it reaches the boy, but that can't be helped, and she is belatedly fulfilling her part of the bargain. Hopefully he will see her name and her kisses and be pleased by the news that she is alive and thinking of him.

The town, such as it is, strikes her as dilapidated and sad. The commercial parade operates on a subsistence ration. It is the sort of place where, were you to enter a shop or a tea room and ask whether it's open, the proprietor would grimace and shrug and say, "Can be, if you like" as opposed to replying with a straight yes or no. There would be a layer of dust on the shelves. The cakes would be stale and the tea would be stewed, and even the busiest weekday would have the texture of a Sunday. She thinks the town is as bad as Edmonton in its way, although the Scarecrow counts this as his home and therefore she decides it can't be as grim as all that. He was brought up on these streets and operated the Dreadnought in the printworks nearby. Tomorrow they will drive the three miles out to his village, but for now they should rest. They could both benefit from a bath; they still stink from the fire. They could both use some sleep; they are half-sick with exhaustion.

The George Inn, like the Griffin, has six guest rooms upstairs. She would be willing to bet it has six vacancies too. When they push open the door, the noise frightens a marmalade cat, which tears through the lobby like a flash of late sunlight. The girl at reception glances up and then screams.

"Excuse me, miss, I mean no harm. I'm wearing a mask because my face is burnt."

The receptionist flushes. Opening the leather-bound ledger with a furious motion, she says, "It wasn't that, sir. It was just the silly cat scared me."

They book themselves into a twin room at the front. Net-curtained windows look out at the high street. Two single beds stand against the far wall. The Scarecrow approvingly flicks the switch by the door. "Electric lights," he says. "Civilisation again."

Lucy draws a bath and sits in the stainless steel tub. Soaping her leg reopens the wound so that the water takes on a pinkish tinge. By now she has travelled to a point beyond tiredness. She feels rather as she did when she sniffed the white powder and she can still sense the lorry's vibration in her joints. She marvels at the fact she was able to drive the old Maudslay. Tomorrow, she supposes, she will have to do so once more.

Her thoughts fly back across the previous twenty-four hours. They rewind from the town to the stones to the dead animals plastered like wet leaves on the road. The passage of time is funny; it can run so fast or so slow. This time yesterday the Tin Man was alive and Grantwood House was untouched. It had dominated the valley for hundreds and hundreds of years and now all at once it is gone, vanished in a fat puff of smoke. And half the people inside – well, they are surely gone too.

Emerging from the bathroom, she sees the sun has gone down and that dinner is served. The Scarecrow has persuaded the kitchen to send up a simple meal of bread, cheese, ham and pickle, together with two bottles of beer and a jug of tap water. They eat at the small table, gazing at the street. Come six o'clock, the place has already shut down. It is as if the two shapes at the glass are the only living souls in the world. The Scarecrow claims that this was a half-decent town once and could well be again, if the economy picks up. He is excited about tomorrow morning and the drive out to the village. He can't wait to see Audrey; he has so much to explain. He says that he loved her, still loves her, and that this means there is hope.

The girl rejects beer and drinks the water instead. Hesitantly, she says, "You know you can take your mask off if you like. It might be more comfortable and I'm sure I won't mind."

"You asked me about the mask once before. Was that the same night that we saw the boy scouts?"

"Maybe," she says. "It might have been."

"I seem to remember we played football as well. Can that be right? And didn't we all eat from a bucket of ice cream?"

"Yes," Lucy says. "It wasn't always horrid, the forest."

"The Kindred of the Kibbo Kift."

"Bram," says the girl. "Stop hiding. Don't be silly."

And yet when he reaches around to unfasten the buckle, she finds she can't stand the tension and has to shut her eyes. She sits at the table with her face tightly scrunched until he calls her name and she looks up to confront the ruined man

359

she might have loved if a hundred things in her life had been different, or if he had taken more care that the damage he carried had not spilled over the sides and come to damage her, too.

She has decided in advance what to say to this man. "Good gracious," she will tell him. "It's not as bad as all that." But she has been through too much; she is sick of shadows and lies. She gulps a breath, shakes her head and takes in the spread of burn tissue and his blank, blunted features. She says, "Bram, bloody hell, what a terrible thing to have happened." And this makes him smile and tip his bottle in salute and so afterwards she will think that perhaps, after all, it was not such a bad thing to say.

Finally, here's the village. It is cosy and wholesome; it makes amends for the town. The church-tower clock chimes the hour of ten and a shaggy shire horse helps itself to a drink from the trough. A wooden bench on the green faces a row of brick cottages. The girl is bundled in a gentleman's topcoat. Her tan-masked companion sits silently at her side. He has not spoken a word since he climbed out of the truck.

Along comes an old woman. She's on her way to the shop. On spotting the man on the bench, she performs a violent double-take. Then she regains her composure and bids the visitors a good day. Lucy politely bids her a good day in return, but the Scarecrow says nothing. He is staring at the cottages.

At five past the hour a slender boy passes by, carrying a sheaf of papers on a wooden clipboard. Lucy judges him to be around eight or nine. The wind lifts and swirls. It tears the outermost sheet from the clipboard and sends it low along the ground until it arrives at the bench, where the Scarecrow stoops to pick it up. She believes that if he paid more attention he might have retrieved the thing sooner. But he is moving stiffly and his gaze is on the boy as opposed to the page at his feet.

"Here," calls the child. "Can I have it back please?"

The Scarecrow's fingers grope along the ground. When he at last finds the page, he briefly brings it up comically high, as though to cover his face, before lowering it again. So far as Lucy can tell, the page contains a pencil drawing of houses crowded about a steep cobbled street.

In a rusted voice, he says, "It looks like the view from Tucker's Lane."

By this point, however, the boy has turned wary. He looks from the Scarecrow to Lucy and back to the Scarecrow again. His dark hair is too long. His fringe hangs over his eyes.

"Why are you wearing a mask?" he demands.

Lucy waits a beat and then answers the question herself. "He was injured in the war. His face was burnt."

The boy takes this in. "My dad was killed in the war."

"Yes," Lucy says. "Mine was as well."

Now, finally, the Scarecrow leans out from the bench to return the paper. He says, "It's very good. The roofs."

"Thanks."

"I'm afraid I've left a thumbprint in the corner." The cold has made him shiver. Lucy can feel the motion through the rickety bench.

Following his gaze, she sees that a woman has appeared at the gate to the end cottage. The woman is tall and red-haired; still young, just about. She regards the figures on the green with something approaching alarm. "Mick," she calls – but it is the Scarecrow who jerks his hand up in a greeting.

The boy has pulled the clipboard to his chest. "I have to go," he says. "Goodbye."

The Scarecrow says, "Is that where you live?"

"Yes," says the boy. "I have to go now."

The woman calls his name again.

"Brothers? Sisters?"

He shakes his head impatiently. "Just me, mum and dad."

"Dad," echoes the Scarecrow.

"My new dad," he concedes. "He teaches me football as well."

Another croak. "Which do you like best? The football or the drawing?"

"I don't know," he says. "Both."

When the child turns to leave, the Scarecrow clears his throat. He calls, "You keep on practicing. You're going to be good."

The boy accepts this compliment with a complacent shrug; he does not need to be reassured of his talent. He swaggers away across the green. It is not easy to swagger when you're clutching papers to your chest and the wind has picked up, but his valiant attempt is very nearly convincing. He joins his mother on the step and she pulls the door closed at their backs.

The Scarecrow shivers. Lucy begins to feel guilty about accepting his coat. And yet even here, so close to the moment of their parting, aspects of the man continue to confuse her. Because when at last he decides to stand up from the bench, he appears restored to full strength; warm as fresh toast and positively cheerful again.

"Lucy," he says, as though surprised by her presence. "I'm

362

such a fool. This village isn't right. I've brought us to the wrong one."

"I don't get it. Did you forget where you lived?"

The Scarecrow is laughing. "Apparently. It's been that long."

So they drive out of the village and the trees pile up on either side of the lane. She can see dark clots of mistletoe in their bare upper boughs, but she is careful not to gawp at the scenery because she is finding the driving a good deal harder today. The lane is too narrow for Coach's old lorry. Each time she encounters an incoming motor, she braces herself for the scrape of metal on metal and only relaxes her grip on the wheel when the danger has passed.

Up ahead they find another settlement, more bucolic than the last – and beyond that another, rustic and forlorn. She enquires whether the Scarecrow's village is this one, or whether it's that one, but he tells her it's not and that she should simply keep going.

At length, as though making conversation, he says, "That poor woman at the house didn't know me at all."

"Did you recognise her then? The boy's mum?"

He snorts. "I think she might have been frightened of me."

The further she drives, the more concerned she becomes. By now they have travelled some distance from the town when he assured her that he lived only about three miles outside. It occurs to her that they must therefore not be driving towards his home but away from it.

"Scarecrow," she says. "Bram. Where do you think we are going?"

He says, "Christ, I don't know. This way's good enough."

"Yes, all right," Lucy says. "But where are you sending me now?"

The Scarecrow draws a breath and rearranges himself on the seat. He turns his head to the side so as to watch the trees streaming by. "Didn't you tell me you wanted to visit the sea?" he says, "Well then, that sounds all right. Why don't we do that?"

30

IN THE SUMMER of 1904 he had taken his bike from the shed and cycled ten miles south to Brackenbury Chase. Once there he stashed the machine behind a hedge and proceeded through the woods on foot. He had his tent in a kit bag, along with some water and food. He reckoned that if he rationed wisely, he could last three days out of doors.

The boy knew nothing of Brackenbury Chase beyond what he had heard – and even this was surely wrong because the Chase gave rise to tall tales and rumours. It was said that it extended for mile after mile. That it was a hideout for brigands; that wolves and bears were still at large in its dark interior. He did not believe in the wolves or the bears, but he was at pains to tread quietly in case he alerted a brigand.

While he didn't make it through to the far side of the Chase, he ventured far enough to believe that it was true that these woods remained largely unnoticed and that whoever came in was, in all likelihood, not wanting to be found. The northern fringe had crawled out to reclaim a series of abandoned stone houses, covering their roofs with damp moss and filling their gardens with nettles. Then a half-mile in, he found kicked-over campfires, wooden palettes and a number of makeshift canvas shelters. The shelters looked as though they might have stood there for some time and conceivably they had been abandoned too. But lying in his tent on the second night, he had heard from a distance the raised lusty voices of uncouth men and had prayed that the voices would not come any closer. Then, for a few shameful hours, he had shed his scepticism and accepted that even the most lurid stories he had heard were true after all: the Chase was a wilderness of bandits and bears. And what would he discover if he pressed on through the woods? A destitute army of cannibals, or some crumbling jungle temple where monkeys swung from the vines? At that stage of his young life, the Chase was the richest, wildest land he had encountered. Wherever she goes in the future, and whatever odd things she experiences there, the girl will find herself measuring them all against Epping Forest. He feels the same way about Brackenbury Chase.

Cribbs Farm sits deserted. The house is boarded and the nameplate has rusted. But it seems that some neighbouring landowner persists in maintaining a stake in these premises, because there are caterpillar tracks in the yard and bales of fresh hay stacked in the iron-roofed barn. It feels like the last outpost of English civilisation, with nothing at its back but the endless, rolling Chase, thick with ivy and nettles, tilting towards winter.

They have lunched at a country pub, the Horse and Harrow, and bought bread and cheese for the onward journey, assuming that the Scarecrow has an onward journey in mind. Lucy rather doubts that he does. They have both come so far only to tumble at the last hurdle with their destination in sight.

The cottage, she thinks. The boy with his sketches. The woman at the gate. "Bram," she says. But he will not meet her eye.

The Maudslay ticks and creaks as the engine cools. By now Coach will have noted its absence, although the missing lorry may well count for little when set against the loss of everything else. Tomorrow, perhaps, police will stop them on the road. That might be for the best. It would at least provide a resolution.

Until then, here they are – on the edge of the woods at dejected Cribbs Farm. The Scarecrow explains that he camped around here once before when he was not many years younger than she is today, and she replies that she likes it, partly because she has an urge to be kind and partly because it is not entirely untrue. She adds, "It's certainly peaceful. It makes a nice change from the house."

"If we're feeling the cold I can build us a bonfire."

"Bloody hell, please don't." She has had her fill of fires.

"Fair enough, I don't blame you. We can keep warm in the barn."

So they climb through the hay and hunker down like livestock. And the Scarecrow is right: the straw provides enough insulation that Lucy's teeth stop chattering. She winds the topcoat tightly about her torso and legs. If they have to spend the night here she might be passably comfortable. After that she supposes they will return to the world. One thing about civilisation, it keeps people warm.

From this vantage, high up in the barn, they can look out past the farmhouse and the lane at the fallow fields of the west, all of them apparently given over to crows. She recalls that there is an ominous name for a group of crows, like a murder or a slaughter, and she wonders why this is so – what the birds have done in the past to deserve such a name. A murder, a slaughter, a killing of crows. A butchery of starlings. A massacre of hens.

"Do you think there might be rats in this barn?"

"It's very possible. Every farm in the land has its share of vermin."

"Ugh," she says. "Rats."

"I keep forgetting, you're a city girl."

"But I do like the countryside. I like the space and the quiet."

And yet it transpires that even this far afield they are not completely alone. Shortly before dusk her ears pick up the whine of a motor and she spies a sunlit shape in the sky that cannot be a bird.

"Look," she exclaims, her senses suddenly stirred. "Look over there. What an incredible thing."

The aeroplane wanders in the sky – a mile away, maybe more. The Scarecrow judges it to be a two-seater biplane and guesses there must be a small airfield nearby. He says he has half a mind to investigate. Who needs Coach's old truck when there's a biplane to hand? They could ambush the pilot and hijack his machine. That way they could complete this curious journey in style.

"Right then, let's do it. Steal the aeroplane and fly south."

"I'd love to," he replies. "More than that, Lucy, I think we must." And sitting amid the straw of the barn, he explains to the girl exactly how it would be. The luckless pilot caught napping; the plane bouncing away up the runway before he quite realises it's gone. Lieutenant Bram Connors of 70 Squadron at the controls and Lucy Marsh of north London tucked in right behind. The propellers rotating and the rudders engaged and then one bump, two bumps, and the craft leaves the ground.

"And then that's it," she says. "It's just us and the sky."

She has always imagined herself being weightless, like a

368

goose feather borne aloft by warm currents but the Scarecrow explains that that is not it at all. The plane is fashioned from plywood and the engine is ferocious and the petrol stink terrific. You feel every straining yard of ascent in the pit of your stomach and through your solar-plexus and the experience, if anything, is all the more exciting for that. They rise up from the fields, turning laboriously, like a pack-mule tackling the hairpin bends of a mountain path, and below she can make out the patchwork of farmland, the thatched roof of a house and the loose silver coil of a river she had not even noticed before. The starboard wing points at Brackenbury Chase, but the woods slide inconsequentially by, after which they ride out over a gentle kingdom of meadows and church towers and rolled cricket lawns. At this lofty altitude the wind is altogether more fierce. It makes the plane pitch and yaw, so that she clutches the chassis and braces her knees. The propellers have blurred to a tranquil haze. They resemble millponds, blissfully unmoved by the tumult all around.

The plane comes streaming across Dorset as the October day crawls off to the west and it is already full dark by the time they find a place to land on the coast. The sea, the sea! The girl catches a glimpse of its sweep during their spiralling descent. She can smell ripe, salty ocean even over the fumes.

Now down they come, with a bang and a bounce. The noise of the engine is such that people run gawping from their homes. Several frenzied children pursue the plane as it taxies. And when she clambers down she discovers that her knees have unhinged and her legs gone to jelly and she might have collapsed had the Scarecrow not grabbed her. He cries, "Lucy, we're here. The very lip of the world." And peering over his shoulder she watches the blades of the propeller separate and revolve and finally come to a halt, which means that their journey together is over and that they can now part as friends.

She says, "Do you even think you could do it, though? Pilot an aeroplane with one arm?"

The Scarecrow grins and shakes his head.

She sighs. "It probably wouldn't do any good if you could. I mean, it wouldn't make up for all the rest of it, would it?"

"No," says the Scarecrow. "Not by a long chalk."

The sun has gone down. The temperature drops. Seeking added shelter, they reorder the bales into a fortification as high as her shoulder. The Scarecrow unbuckles his mask and lays it on one side. From this angle, he might almost pass for unblemished. He could walk out on the road and nobody would notice anything different about him unless they stepped close and looked hard. Something rustles the straw far away in the corner. She hopes it's the wind. She has a horror of rats.

She draws the book from his pocket so that he can read aloud for a spell. But the light has dwindled so much, he can't even find the page they were on. This reminds him of a joke. "Outside of a dog, a book is a man's best friend. Inside of a dog, it's too dark to read."

"That's quite good. Did you make it up?"

"Not me, I'm afraid. It's an old music-hall thing." He closes the book and sets about dividing the remains of the bread and cheese.

Beyond the barn's exposed rear flank, Brackenbury Chase registers as a thick black band. The Scarecrow never did discover how far the woodland extended. Most likely he never ventured more than a mile inside because he grew too scared to continue and was too young, back then, to know that the world contains worse dangers than a few lonely men that have set themselves apart from their neighbours. He says he was told that this particular forest is vast and untracked and that its trails fade away or circle back on themselves and that even the most experienced orienteer can be lost within minutes. But Lucy has her doubts. She wonders if such places exist in England anymore; there can't be a patch of earth that has not had someone's boot put upon it. She has heard that the population has dipped but is now rebounding again. Every day that goes by, thousands of fresh babies are born. It's not the woods that are endless, it's this arrival of babies. They keep exploding out into the light, squawking and hungry and casting about for a spare spot of ground where they can plant their pink feet.

She remembers what the man at the petrol station had said. She says, "If you come back in ten years there'll probably be a town over there."

"You might be right. Come back when you're grown and tell me how much it has changed."

She nods.

He says, "Imagine that, Lucy, 1933. Or come back later still and bring your family with you. Come back in 1953. You'll be a middle-aged woman."

"Will I?" Would she? The prospect is exhausting. "Why yes," she says, yawning. "I suppose I will."

He has propped his elbow on the bale. He is peering out at the black line of trees. Presently he laughs, mostly to himself. He says, "This is the strangest sensation. I feel as if I've just woken up. So thanks for that, Lucy. I think it's been mostly your doing."

"That's all right," she murmurs and a few heartbeats later sleep comes to collect her, and the sleep carries with it a disconcerting dream of Grantwood. She fancies she navigates the stone steps from the Italian sunken garden and picks her way through the corridors until she reaches the drawing room with its blazing orange hearth. At first she believes that the chamber is deserted and yet, on lifting each of the velvet wall hangings in turn, she discovers that each one is concealing an occupant of the house. Behind the folds, against the wall, stand Arthur Elms and Sweetpea Long, Rupert Fortnum-Hyde and Clarissa. Their faces give no sign that they have just been disturbed. They gaze at her and through her. They stand still as waxworks, or those queer plaster gods. "Found you!" she cries. "Monster hunt!" But when she releases her grip the folds drop back into place. The figures are hidden from view once again, if they ever existed at all.

In the half-light of dawn, with the topcoat wrapped around her and the Scarecrow's mask in her hand, she climbs down from the bales and proceeds out into the yard. Her leg is pulsing and sore, the cut is inflamed, and so she circles the farmhouse several times until she is satisfied that the muscle has loosened. Mist rises from the field and she exhales in a cloud. Her very movement is thunder; her shoes scrape and scuff. But there is nobody else up. Even the crows are at rest.

Heavens, it's cold. She needs to find better clothes. She tries to remember whether they consumed the last of the bread the evening before and decides that most likely they did after all. She is chilled and hungry. She's put herself in a right sorry state.

She crosses the field, shoes squelching now, and emerges from the mist on the outer edge of the Chase. Wind plays in the trees' bony upper boughs. The forest floor thuds to a percussion of dead branches. Fifty yards in she makes herself stop and draw breath. She calls his name again and again. "Bram! Bram! Bram!" If it is true what he heard, this woodland rolls out for mile upon mile.

Back at the yard, the mist is already thinning. But Jesus Christ, it is still so bloody cold. She tugs open the door and the feel of the seat against her calves makes her start and then shudder. On dropping the mask into the glove compartment, she gathers the money to count. They have not spent a great deal; there is a little shy of three pounds remaining. A few miles out she might find a cafe to buy breakfast and maybe a shop that stocks winter clothes.

The engine needs cranking, she truly hopes it will start. Her breath fogs the cab and salt tears blur her eyes. She says, "Well hello, old Maudslay. It's only you and me now."

31

TAP, TAP, TAP.

She doesn't hear the door at first. Or rather, she hears it quite well but elects to pay the knocking no mind. The frame has a tendency to rattle whenever a vehicle goes by and she is vaguely aware that one has been at large; some unfamiliar-sounding lorry on the front lane by the green. On top of that, the Simons' dog is in a state of uproar again. The creature has got itself tangled in its chain. Its bark has taken on a distinctly hysterical note.

Tap, tap, tap. This time she hears it – and in the hearing supposes that she was half-right all along. Because whoever is at the door must be related to the lorry. It stands to reason that an unfamiliar vehicle will signal the approach of a stranger; she knows the sounds of the other engines that wander through the village, as reliable as clockwork mice. The curate's Austin coughs like a consumptive. Oliver Smith's Ford sings a quavering song of unoiled springs, while John Cooper's lorry arrives as a festive sack of nuts and bolts; Santa's iron sledge. You can detect its approach from half a mile away.

Who travels the roads that connect these westerly villages? Locals, in the main, because this is a closed and intimate country. The roads link the villages in much the same way as a corridor and a staircase will link the chambers of a house, and the inhabitants wave and tip their hats as they pass. When they encounter a stranger they are understandably surprised.

For all that, she is aware the land has turned more frantic and troubled. The news tells of uprisings and unemployment and migrant labour on the move and this surely accounts for the increase in foreign visitors. If work dries up and people are moved on, it follows that those people will venture further afield. If she were in their shoes, she would do the same thing. And so she tries to receive these strangers with kindness even though she has no work to offer and not a great deal to spare. They are only passing through, after all. The road leads them in and it carries them out again.

Also, she admits that the strangers are fascinating. She has grown so used to living in the same small village amid the same old faces that the sound of an accent (a Gloucestershire burr, northern country vowels) is oddly exciting. She wonders at the origins of these people and what has brought them so far and what they hope to find in this place that they could not find in their own. Most arrive at the door with a show of politeness that is no doubt genuine but nonetheless feels worn thin from overuse. But she has met some who have struck her as either angry or sly – and still others who seem broken and defeated. She doesn't think much to the long-term prospects of this last group – and yet it is to these people whom she tends to give most generously so they must, at that, be onto something.

The most outlandish of all are the spiritualists. Most likely they can be counted as the most desperate as well. Sometimes they refer to themselves as seers, or mystics, or mediums. They claim to possess supernatural powers. They boast that they can commune with the dead, like the one who called on Margaret, who then – infuriatingly – batted the fellow on to her. She had prepared a ham sandwich and poured him some tea and, mainly by dint of her airy disinterest, was able to squire him to the door before he could begin his routine.

Tap, tap, goes the door. The neighbour's dog redoubles its yelping. The woman replaces her sewing and removes her spectacles.

Last April a travelling troupe called the Family Fantastic played for one night in the village hall. The father and son performed conjuring tricks while the elderly mother provided accompaniment on the upright piano, except that the tricks all went wrong and the father and son eventually came to blows. An awkward, slapstick fist-fight that she had initially assumed must be part of the act until she saw that the old man's nose had been bloodied and the son began weeping and several spectators (Jim among them) had to intervene. At this point she had wondered whether the Family Fantastic was really a family at all, and yet apparently they were, because Jim had eventually been able to escort them backstage and there the younger man was inconsolable and kept saying, "Father, I'm sorry."

What a thing, what an evening, the Family Fantastic. And so, yes, she has witnessed her fair share of ragamuffins and chancers over the past however-many months, but perhaps none has been quite so abject as the specimen who taps at her door this Monday mid-morning. "I'm a spiritualist," the creature declares.

Audrey looks her up and down and laughs. "How nice," she says drily. "We haven't had one of you in these parts for a least a week now."

Tall as a reed and as pale as a lily. A gentleman's topcoat pulled over a filthy party dress. Mud-spattered nylons torn up the shin and then a wound like a mouth below the right knee. The girl is not much more than a child, perhaps sixteen, at a push. But she has the wary, semi-feral air of a vagrant who has spent too long out of doors.

Audrey Winter shakes her head and resists the urge to shut the door. She says, "Come on, then. The least I can do is put something on that leg."

In the low cottage kitchen she has the girl remove her nylons. She applies a dab of soap to the flannel and rearranges the chairs so that they face one another. The wound is infected, that's immediately clear. But the surrounding veins appear normal, which means that the blood is not poisoned. When Audrey leans in to apply the flannel, her forehead connects with something small and hard and she notes this pitiful creature is wearing a scarab pendant, horned and unsightly, strung on a chain about her dirty neck.

She says, "And what's your name, little spiritualist?"

"Lucy."

"No," says Audrey. "That'll never do. We ought to call you something like Zenobia, or the Great Miss Ingenious. No one's going to take counsel from a seer called Lucy." She gestures at the pendant. "Can you get that thing out of the way for me, please?"

"The amulet," says the girl. "The amulet allows me to speak with the dead." But she makes this boast with a misery so acute that it's almost comical. It is as though the girl realises what a cheap lie she is having to tell, and is mortified by the charade.

Audrey nods. "Ah, I see, an amulet, well that does explain it. But try to get it away from my face while I look at your leg."

The dog keeps on barking. The girl sits rigidly on the chair. She gives off a damp farmyard smell with an undertow of smoke. She does not thank Audrey for attending to her leg. It seems it is all she can do to acknowledge her presence.

When the wound bleeds afresh, Audrey dabs it dry with a towel. She splashes on disinfectant and hunts in the cupboard for gauze. She knows she has gauze somewhere; Jim cut his hand on the chisel not three weeks before. She shuffles items on the shelf before she locates it near the back.

She says, "I suppose you're probably hungry as well," and then instantly regrets it because there is something about this child that she does not care for; something blank and unwholesome. It would have been better to have simply slammed the door when she still had the chance.

The girl sounds like a cockney. She is coarse and unschooled. She says she has travelled a great distance with a message from her husband and Audrey can't help herself; the information makes her laugh. She replies that her husband left for work not quite two hours ago. She can't imagine his message can't wait until he comes home for his tea.

"Not that husband, miss. Your other husband."

"Of course, silly me." But when she stoops to bandage the leg of this urchin, the woman is aware she is pulling the strapping too tight, as though the gauze is a ligature and the leg the girl's throat. Anything to choke that nonsense talk of dead husbands. She pays a stranger a kindness and this is how she is thanked, with a slippery scam, with this casual cruelty. Begging would be better. There's an honesty to begging.

"He said that he loved you," the girl goes on. "He said he always loved you. And I thought you should know."

Audrey clenches her jaw. Her fingers work at the bandage. "Did Margaret send you?"

The girl shakes her head.

"Well, I think she did." Because it now occurs that she has seen this foul creature before, fairly recently, although she cannot pin down the exact circumstance. Most likely she has been working the neighbourhood and finally landed on Margaret, who told her all about Bram. She resolves to confront Margaret about this as soon as she's able.

"And you charge money for this? For the muck and drivel you spout."

But the question seems to stump the visitor. She makes no reply.

"There," says Audrey. "All done." She sticks a piece of adhesive to hold the bandage in place and takes a final look at this pitiful child, this poor little bitch, this horrible thing.

She says, "Lucy. Zenobia. Whatever you're called."

"Lucy."

"Lucy, fair enough. Excuse me for saying you're not cut out for this trade. You're no good at it and you look an absolute fright. Honestly child, find some new line of work."

For a moment she thinks that her words have hit home. The girl gets up from the chair and flexes her leg as though preparing to leave. But no, hard luck, it is not to be. Staring hard at the ground, the girl begins to speak very quickly, flatly, like a mediocre student reading aloud from a book.

She says, "Your husband was Bram Connors and he was shot down in the war. His plane crashed and he was burned and he lost an arm because it got caught up in some wire. But he didn't die in the crash because he walked a good way after that. He walked a long way until he came to a farm and there was a lake at the farm that was full of dead men. He looked into the water at all the dead men and he thought, 'Maybe this is the right place. I shall climb into the water and then I can rest'."

"All right. Stop this."

"His name was Bram Connors and he said he always loved you."

"All right, good to hear. Out you go now."

She says, "On the day after your wedding you both went out along the quarry train track. There was a drunk old man on the track. You both saved his life."

"Lucy," she begins – and is then brought up short. And strangely, what jumps through her mind is the memory of her accident with her friend Jean's electric fire. Of all the things to think of in that instant: Jean's electric fire, her pride and joy, which had been purchased as a Christmas present by her jolly solicitor husband. The contraption plugged into a wall socket at Jean's grand house in the town. Its metal tubing threw off gusts of dry heat. But the appliance was faulty; it did not always work. And then, when Audrey had stooped to tighten the connection with a screwdriver, some spark leapt from the point where the tubing met the frame. The current had thrown her across the room. She landed on her back with her faculties scrambled. How curious that she would remember that moment right now.

"Lucy."

Finally the girl risks a glance up from the floor. It is a nervous, appraising glance, but there is something else below the surface – something knotted and wounded and oddly furious. She says, "Sir Lancelot Coombs, I think that was it. The Scarecrow gave him a coat, maybe a coat like this one, but the man didn't know because he was drunk. Sir Lancelot Coombs, that's what you both called him. He had been cheated out of his rightful inheritance. Something about a racehorse, I can't really remember. You both saved his life but the man never knew. Only the two of you knew."

380

Outside in the yard, that endless barking. Listen for too long and it sends a person insane.

Audrey clears a frog from her throat. "What scarecrow? There wasn't a scarecrow."

"Bram, I mean. I didn't mean to say scarecrow."

"But still," Audrey says. "You couldn't know about that."

The girl shoots her another of those knotted, scalding looks.

On and on the barking goes. It will never stop. Audrey attempts a smile and says, "You know, I'm really going to have to go and attend to that dog". She puts a hand on the chair-back to steady herself, turns as if to make good her escape and then abruptly wheels back to where the girl is still standing.

"And you think that this helps me? Is this a proper way to behave?" Her voice lifts but still sounds oddly distant to her ears. She believes that if the dog barks one more time, she may simply start screaming.

Except that now, unaccountably, it is the girl who is struggling to order her thoughts. She pauses and gulps and stares down at the floor. In that awful flat voice, she says, "I don't know. I don't care. I'm not saying he was a good man. Don't think I'm here to say that. I would never say that. Because he wasn't a good man. He did a lot of bad things, like the Mench and all that, and he really hurt people. But I don't think he hurt you, I think he loved you. Or maybe he did hurt you, but really not very much." Another pause, a further gulp. "Probably the worst thing that he did was not coming home when he should."

Audrey laughs raggedly. "I imagine that was somewhat beyond his control."

"Yes, maybe. Maybe it was. But I still think that he probably could have tried a bit harder."

"Lucy," she says. "Whoever you are. How could you know about the coat and the man?"

"He told me," she says. "And he told me he loved you and that he was sorry. It's just he wasn't able to come and tell you himself."

There is so much, she thinks, that is wrong with the world. It is wrong to come upsetting people, rattling skeletons, raking over old coals. But it is also wrong to keep an animal chained up all day long. It is cruel and thoughtless; it should not be allowed. If a dog isn't wanted, it should be allowed to go free and fend for itself. And if the Simons won't do it, then someone else should.

Wondering whether she might be about to be sick, Audrey declares that she is stepping outside. She says that she will be gone for no more than a minute and that when she gets back she will check her purse for some money. No doubt the girl will want paying and she is welcome to whatever is there, although it may well not be much, she can't think what's in there. Without waiting for a reply, without even looking at the creature sitting on the chair in her kitchen, Audrey takes the side door and clambers over the low wall, past the chicken wire and into the enclosure where the dog – a spindly mongrel, mostly Border collie – has got itself hopelessly wound in its length of chain. She supposes it might bite, it must be out of its wits, but the animal welcomes her arrival with a flurry of hoarse, panting yelps; she supposes that it must recognise her. Audrey pats its quivering flank and then startles herself by planting a dry-mouthed kiss on its head.

"You're all right," she says. "You're all right, don't worry."

It takes no time to unwind the chain and unclip the collar. After that she kicks away the chicken wire and unceremoniously hauls the dog over the back wall by the stream. "Go on," she says. "Get." And when the dog appears to hesitate she slaps lightly at its rear-end, as though urging on a horse, and it lopes off through the blackberry bushes and weeds without so much as a backward glance. "Don't come back," she calls, although she suspects that it will, if only because the foul yard is its home and it will have grown used to its chain, and even a foul home is better than no home at all. But she is still glad that she freed it and she no longer feels sick. And now, sitting on her haunches beside the sluggish village stream, she hears the sound of a motor lurching into life, something wheezing and unhealthy preparing to depart.

She rubs her dirty hands on her dress and mutters, "Go on then," because this is surely for the best and she was dreading the prospect of completing the exchange. She thinks the girl will almost certainly have made off with her purse and if so she reckons this will be a small price to pay. But when she arrives back at the kitchen the purse is just where she left it – on the oak table, beside her sewing and spectacles. The money is in it, which means that the girl left with nothing. And all at once she feels so tired she could drop.

What became of the woman after the current jumped from the electric fire and ran up her arm? It seemed to her that she remained on the floor for a spell. Her body was fizzing and her thoughts were dislodged – and yet these effects did not last very long. After that she got up off the carpet and apologised to Jean. She said she hoped the amazing contraption was not broken for good.

Still, sometimes she worries what became of the current. That electrical voltage, precisely where had that gone? She knows it was released; she felt the uproar in her limbs. But if it had travelled elsewhere, wouldn't she have been aware of that too? Jean's ornate coffee table would have jumped on its hind legs. The reddish Afghan rug would have turned up at the corners. Yet they had seen nothing, felt nothing, and this has led her to wonder. Is the fierce blaze of that moment inside her even now? Maybe it is, because where else could it be? Sometimes she fancies that she can feel it bouncing in her innards, with no hope of escape. And perhaps even this is not so untoward.

Look around; it's happening all over. People carry the storms of the things they once did, the people they once were. They come ambling through the village with their systems ablaze. They contain fireworks, sunbursts, holocausts. Peer closely and you might see orange cinders jumping in their eyes, like those tin grenadiers they lined up at the country fair, except that no one notices or cares because they are in the same state themselves. It's as much as they can do to keep moving their feet and tipping their hats.

Intending to put away the clothes she has mended, Audrey climbs upstairs and stretches full-length on the bed. She believes she may close her eyes and take a deep breath or two – and this is the last thing she knows for more than three hours. She sleeps through the heavy jingle of John Cooper's lorry and the noisy return of the Simons' dog and is only awakened when Michael, having shrugged off his satchel and left his shoes in the hall, steals into the room and lays his hand on her cheek.

32

ABOVE THE COASTAL town of Lymington is a high, soft shoulder of open ground. It is a place of small windswept ponies, robust gorse bushes and the sort of buoyant, mossy grass that trampolines underfoot. In springtime the bushes bring forth bright yellow flowers that perfume the bare land all around. The gorse smells, pleasingly, of macaroons.

Here and there, away from the trails, unwanted items have been left out to rust. It's not uncommon for ramblers to stumble across a corroded bedstead or legless ironing board, a buckled bicycle frame or the hull of an industrial mangle. If there exists an afterlife for mankind's metal servants it can be located up here on the heath, amid the bouncing turf and the sprays of gorse.

Between two twisted bushes stands an abandoned lorry. You wouldn't know it was there until you were hard up against it. Its tires are flat, the windscreen has been shattered and its driver-side door is rusted shut. The engine is intact and might conceivably be salvaged, assuming someone possessed the wherewithal and energy to drive out to retrieve it.

In the months since it was first discovered, the lorry has become a plaything of the children who live on either side of this heath. It has doubled as a pirate galleon and a Sopwith Camel. It spent a week as an Antarctic base camp and has latterly served as the cave of a fearsome grizzly bear. The intrepid hunters approach the lair on their bellies, taking great care not to alert the beast. Then they rise up from the grass in a riot of noise and furiously set about the truck with their sticks.

Time flies like an arrow and accelerates as we age. But in infancy, on the heath, its movement is more leisurely. The passage of a week can feel like a month, while a month might as well be an eternity. And already some of these children have forgotten their first sight of the Maudslay one chill autumn morning when it had looked for all the world as though it were merely passing through. They had loitered beside it, casting anxiously all around until one brave youth had taken it upon himself to pull open the door. Inside on the seat he found a tan leather mask and a horned pendant on a chain. The mask would later be confiscated by the history master at school and now resides inside a locked desk in the staffroom. Nobody can recall what became of the pendant. It slipped from a pocket or was trodden on and broken. Either way, it has gone and few remember it now.

Two miles south, the land shelves away. The traveller steps off the plateau and is spilled through a swatch of pink-flushed farmland to the town; he can smell the salt and hear the gulls. Whitewashed cottages crowd the cobbled streets and triangular pennants snap on the overhead lines. The shops sell croquet sets and tennis balls. There is a queue to get at the ice-cream stall.

Now here at last is the quay itself where the fishing boats scrape against wooden jetties and the children load crabs into buckets of seawater. The crabs clamber listlessly over and across one another. They appear in no particular hurry to escape.

The public house on the quay is called the Hope and Anchor. It contains a taproom and restaurant and a number of well-appointed guest chambers which look out on green water. Business is brisk and the pub employs three full-time barmaids whose duties extend to waiting on tables and preparing the beds. Two of the barmaids are local; the third previously worked at a public house up in London. They all share a room in the one-storey staff annex, although the London girl has explained that she will be moving out soon. She has been setting money aside and plans to rent a small flat of her own. Each week she writes to her brother back home. She says that once she has a flat, he can come out and join her.

Dear Tom, the girl writes. Please come out in the summer, that's only three months away. I am going to send you the money to buy a single rail ticket. You won't need a return because you will be staying with me. The seaside is lovely. There are seagulls and ducks. I am saving up money, more and more every week. Waitressing is the best because I often get given tips, but being a housemaid is not so bad either because some of the guests leave tips there as well and one day I walked in and found a five-shilling note on the bedside table. So please come out when it's summer and we will live by the sea.

On days off, mindful of the importance of not spending her wages, the girl makes a habit of talking long walks up the shore. Once away from the inn, the concrete quay points across the Solent and through a thicket of masts to where she can see open water. The Isle of Wight ferry departs from here every day and beyond that is France and the warm folds of Europe, a whole world of foreignness upon the horizon.

She packs sandwiches for her lunch and a book to read while she eats and then walks up the coast until her legs start to tire. Ahead is a small shingled bay where she likes to break her journey. When the tide is high, the little beach is submerged, but when it goes out she can take off her shoes and walk upon it barefoot. Nobody else is around. Few people venture this far and this suits the girl, who enjoys her own company.

On each of these visits at low tide, the retreating sea exposes a man's canvas kit bag. The bag, it seems, has made itself a home in the shingle. It has been stiffened by salt water; its creases and strap turned as rigid as driftwood. Time and again the tide drags in and drags out. But it leaves the bag fixed securely in place, so that the girl has grown used to its presence until she walks up one April morning and discovers it gone. Some loosening of the shingle, some overnight swell of cold water has carried it quietly, invisibly away to the depths. The girl smoothes her dress and sits down and stares out at the sea. She finds herself reassured by the tide's ebb and flow. She decides that they very nearly make sense, all of the choices it makes. The things it elects to leave be, the things it comes in to collect.

ALSO AVAILABLE FROM SALT

ELIZABETH BAINES
Too Many Magpies (978-1-84471-721-7)
The Birth Machine (978-1-907773-02-0)

LESLEY GLAISTER
Little Egypt (978-1-907773-72-3)

ALISON MOORE
The Lighthouse (978-1-907773-17-4)
The Pre-War House and Other Stories (978-1-907773-50-1)
He Wants (978-1-907773-81-5)
Death and the Seaside (978-1-78463-069-0)

ALICE THOMPSON
Justine (978-1-78463-031-7)
The Falconer (978-1-78463-009-6)
The Existential Detective (978-1-78463-011-9)
Burnt Island (978-1-907773-48-8)
The Book Collector (978-1-78463-043-0)

NEW FICTION FROM SALT

RON BUTLIN
Billionaires' Banquet (978-1-78463-100-0)

NEIL CAMPBELL
Sky Hooks (978-1-78463-037-9)

SUE GEE
Trio (978-1-78463-061-4)

CHRISTINA JAMES
Rooted in Dishonour (978-1-78463-089-8)

V.H. LESLIE
Bodies of Water (978-1-78463-071-3)

WYL MENMUIR
The Many (978-1-78463-048-5)

ALISON MOORE
Death and the Seaside (978-1-78463-069-0)

ANNA STOTHARD
The Museum of Cathy (978-1-78463-082-9)

STEPHANIE VICTOIRE
The Other World, It Whispers (978-1-78463-085-0)

Finally thanks, above all, to my beloved wife Sarah, who basically held my hand throughout the entire undertaking. Perfect reader, best editor, life collaborator. We walked though these woods together and came out the other side.

Acknowledgements

WRITING IS SUCH an inherently lonesome trudge that one comes to treasure the people who point the way forward or lend a hand when you fall. Thanks, in the first instance, to Victoria Hobbs and Sam Edenborough, Eloise Millar, Sam Jordison and Max Porter, who offered valuable input and guidance as to where the manuscript might be placed, as and when I got around to completing the thing.

I know nothing about jazz but my dad is an expert. So thanks to Michael Brooks for his advice on the composition of the Long Boys and the songs they might play. Any inaccuracies are mine and not his.

I wrote large portions of this book upstairs at the National Theatre on London's South Bank; sat at a small table with a fabulous view of the Thames. The staff were unfailingly courteous and discreet. Nobody asked what on earth I was doing. No one was obviously bemused by my presence. This is a public space to be cherished. The people who work there are to be cherished too.

Like Lucy Marsh, this book was an orphan. Unlike her, it was lucky enough to find a loving and nurturing home. My thanks to Jen and Chris and the team at Salt for their generosity, passionate support and astute, graceful editing. This book is better because of them. It could not have been raised by a finer family.

RECENT FICTION FROM SALT

KERRY HADLEY-PRYCE
The Black Country (978-1-78463-034-8)

CHRISTINA JAMES
The Crossing (978-1-78463-041-6)

IAN PARKINSON
The Beginning of the End (978-1-78463-026-3)

CHRISTOPHER PRENDERGAST
Septembers (978-1-907773-78-5)

MATTHEW PRITCHARD
Broken Arrow (978-1-78463-040-9)

JONATHAN TAYLOR
Melissa (978-1-78463-035-5)

GUY WARE
The Fat of Fed Beasts (978-1-78463-024-9)

This book has been typeset by
SALT PUBLISHING LIMITED
using Neacademia, a font designed by Sergei Egorov
for the Rosetta Type Foundry in the Czech Republic.
It is manufactured using Creamy 70gsm, a Forest
Stewardship Council™ certified paper from Stora Enso's
Anjala Mill in Finland. It was printed and bound by
Clays Limited in Bungay, Suffolk, Great Britain.

LONDON
GREAT BRITAIN
MMXVII